Praise for
THE SIXTH FLEET novels
by David E. Meadows

"An absorbing, compelling look at America's future place in the world. It's visionary and scary."

—Joe Buff, author of *Deep Sound Channel*, *Thunder in the Deep*, and *Crushed Depth*

"If you enjoy a well-told tale of action and adventure, you will love David Meadows's series, *The Sixth Fleet*. Not only does the author know his subject but [his] fiction could readily become fact. These books should be read by every senator and congressman in our government so that the scenarios therein do not become history."

—John Tegler, syndicated talk show host of *Capital Conversation*

"Meadows will have you turning pages and thinking new thoughts." —Newt Gingrich

"Meadows takes us right to the bridge, in the cockpit, and into the thick of battle. Meadows is a military adventure writer who's been there, done it all, and knows the territory. This is as real as it gets." —Robert Gandt

"Meadows delivers one heck of a fast-paced, roller-coaster ride with this exhilarating military thriller."

—*Midwest Book Review*

Berkley titles by David E. Meadows

FINAL RUN

DARK PACIFIC
DARK PACIFIC: PACIFIC THREAT
DARK PACIFIC: FINAL FATHOM

JOINT TASK FORCE: LIBERIA
JOINT TASK FORCE: AMERICA
JOINT TASK FORCE: FRANCE
JOINT TASK FORCE: AFRICA

THE SIXTH FLEET
THE SIXTH FLEET: SEA WOLF
THE SIXTH FLEET: TOMCAT
THE SIXTH FLEET: COBRA

FINAL RUN

DAVID E. MEADOWS

BERKLEY BOOKS, NEW YORK

THE BERKLEY PUBLISHING GROUP
Published by the Penguin Group
Penguin Group (USA) Inc.
375 Hudson Street, New York, New York 10014, USA
Penguin Group (Canada), 90 Eglinton Avenue East, Suite 700, Toronto, Ontario M4P 2Y3, Canada
(a division of Pearson Penguin Canada Inc.)
Penguin Books Ltd., 80 Strand, London WC2R 0RL, England
Penguin Group Ireland, 25 St. Stephen's Green, Dublin 2, Ireland (a division of Penguin Books Ltd.)
Penguin Group (Australia), 250 Camberwell Road, Camberwell, Victoria 3124, Australia
(a division of Pearson Australia Group Pty. Ltd.)
Penguin Books India Pvt. Ltd., 11 Community Centre, Panchsheel Park, New Delhi—110 017, India
Penguin Group (NZ), 67 Apollo Drive, Rosedale, North Shore 0632, New Zealand
(a division of Pearson New Zealand Ltd.)
Penguin Books (South Africa) (Pty.) Ltd., 24 Sturdee Avenue, Rosebank, Johannesburg 2196,
South Africa

Penguin Books Ltd., Registered Offices: 80 Strand, London WC2R 0RL, England

FINAL RUN

A Berkley Book / published by arrangement with the author

PRINTING HISTORY
Berkley edition / May 2008

Interior text design by Kristin del Rosario.

For information, address: The Berkley Publishing Group,
a division of Penguin Group (USA) Inc.,
375 Hudson Street, New York, New York 10014.

ISBN: 978-0-425-22117-4

BERKLEY®
Berkley Books are published by The Berkley Publishing Group,
a division of Penguin Group (USA) Inc.,
375 Hudson Street, New York, New York 10014.

PRINTED IN THE UNITED STATES OF AMERICA

10 9 8 7 6 5 4 3 2 1

Foreword

This story is about 1956, a year of transition for the U.S. Navy. It was a year when the Soviet Union was pursuing the age-old dream of an oceangoing Navy capable of operating across the globe. It was a year when World War II veterans of the United States still existed on active duty, patrolling the sea lanes against the Soviet dream, and reliving the combat missions of the war in the thin fabric of peacetime between the Soviet Union and the Western nations.

America had launched the first nuclear-powered submarine, *Nautilus,* on January 17, 1955. *Nautilus*, SSN 571, can be seen at the Submarine Force Museum, on the Thames River in Groton, Connecticut.

With the exception of the *Nautilus,* diesel submarines made up the world's Navies in 1956. Junior officers of World War II were now commanders and captains. Commanders and captains of that Great Patriotic War—as the Soviets called it—wore the broad gold stripes of admirals.

The Soviet Union was thought to be chasing the same dream of a submarine whose submerged limitations were only of a human and mechanical nature. Rear Admiral Hyman Rickover had taken over the U.S. Navy program to build the nuclear submarine and within two years had convinced the Navy it was time to shelve the diesels and bring into naval warfare a nuclear-powered submarine force that would change the nature of modern warfare.

The *Nautilus* started the underseas arms race of two nuclear Navies that would become one of the three arms of the mutual assured destruction doctrine (MADD) that kept the Cold War from going hot. Its veterans still held positions of leadership within the Soviet Navy, and its entire submarine force was diesel. Pursuit of atomic-powered submarines for the Soviet Navy was a point of national honor as well as national survival.

Two submarine captains; two different Navies; similar patriotic love of country; and a challenge for America to keep its nuclear edge, and a chase by the Soviets to meet or surpass every naval technology of the West. And throughout this race to be the global supreme naval power were the spooks-spies-cryptologists-intelligence gurus of both nations, doing their best to report with certainty what the other was doing.

This story starts eleven years and a few months after World War II ended in Europe on May 7, 1945. The conflict had changed the geopolitical landscape of the world. Winston Churchill at Westminster College in Fulton, Missouri, on March 5, 1946, warned the world, *"From Stettin in the Baltic to Trieste in the Adriatic an iron curtain has descended across the Continent."*

The United States led the West. The Soviet Union was the common enemy. The world was catapulted into the Cold War.

This book is a fictionalized account of the first subsurface mission in search of an assessment of where the Soviets were in developing a nuclear-powered submarine force. It is told through the eyes and emotions of the characters involved. From this point until the Soviet Union dissolved itself, the subsurface war between these great nations will only be known as history marches forward and classified documents become available. To take a page from Las Vegas, "what goes on beneath the sea stays beneath the sea." It will be decades before the world truly knows the war that occurred beneath the oceantops during the Cold War.

Some literary flexibility is taken in the story. For example, throughout the book, Greenwich Mean Time is used for both Navies, though the Soviet Union always used Moscow time for its fleet. Trying to coordinate two different time zones was too confusing for the writer to keep track. The Western world refers to World War II as World War II. The Soviet Union referred to this conflict as the Great Patriotic War. Naval ranks for the most part are the same in both the U.S. Navy and the Soviet Navy. Why? Because the history of both our Navies is tied to the two hundred years of British naval power, and it was from that influence that many of the traditions of both were derived. I have tried to use the Russian names for Navy ranks and ships with the exception of the *Whale*, which is the name given the *K-2* project of the Soviet Union. I used knots for speed for both Navies, but tried to keep to the metric system for the Soviet Navy and the English measurements for ours.

There is one thing I would like the reader to take away from this book other than enjoying the story: it is that regardless of the Navy, sailors who man their nation's fleets are cut from the same jib. They love the sea. They love the work. And they love their country. Another thing to remember is that this is an action-adventure novel and is not based on true events.

Cheers,
David E. Meadows

ONE

Wednesday, November 14, 1956

"DIVE! Dive!" Commander Chad Shipley shouted. He stood aside on the bridge. The familiar "oogle-oogle" of the horn filled the air and the interior of the submarine. The noise of the horn drowned out the sound of shoes hitting the deck as the men rushed to clear the topside of the *Squallfish*. Belowdecks, Shipley knew sailors and officers were rushing to their diving stations.

Shipley was bumped twice as the men topside scurried through the small hatch leading to the conning room below. He glanced up, holding his binoculars close to his chest. Shipley stood aside as the topside watches jumped through the hatch. They grabbed the steps inside as their bodies propelled through, boondockers riding the outside rails much like firemen down their brass pole. Shipley flinched, expecting to hear the sound of breaking bones, if they missed the conning tower and hiccupped another deck to the control room.

"You now, COB!"

"Aye, sir." Chief of the boat, Torpedoman Senior Chief Cory "Wad" Boohan, answered with a salute. The older man turned and slid smoothly through the small hatch, bending his left shoulder slightly to get his broad shoulders through the hatch.

Shipley clicked his stopwatch as Boohan's head disappeared.

Shipley did a quick check of the watch positions to make sure everyone but he was below, then he stepped to the hatch. The cries of seagulls flying overhead drew his attention for a second. He looked southeast, where clouds marked the beginning of landfall. The slight smell of fish whiffed through the air coming from the Scottish fish factories that dotted the coastline of the Western Isles just out of sight over the horizon.

Water washed over the bow, quickly covering the forward part of the submarine. He looked aft. Water was inching its way across the aft deck. The aft portion of a submarine in a normal dive would disappear within seconds of the forward half. Looking forward again, Shipley took notice of where during World War II a deck gun would have been. The loss of the deck gun meant a smoother, quieter ride. The modern submarine in the new Cold War would never fight a gun battle, they said. It would either sink the opponent with a torpedo or escape. No one mentioned the third alternative.

Shipley did not enjoy being the last man down—never had—but he was the skipper, and the men and the boat were his responsibility. Every submarine on which he had served had seen the "old man" the last to leave the bridge. It set an example of what was expected of a good submarine commander. It also ensured that the skipper was sure no one was left topside when he gave the order to dive.

He turned quickly, stepped into the hatch, and a couple of seconds later stood aside in the conning tower as a sailor rushed up the ladder to check the watertight integrity of the hatch Shipley had closed behind him. Everything about a submarine depended on keeping the water out and the air in. A successful submarine cruise was an equal number of surfacing to the number of submerges.

"Report!"

"Vents opened!" Boohan shouted.

"Inboard and outboard main exhaust valves closed."

"Switch to battery?" Shipley asked.

"Still on snorkel, sir. You want us to switch?"

"Not yet."

"Bow planes rigged out, Captain," Boohan reported.

"Christmas Tree?" Shipley asked, referring to the board where a series of red and green lights told the watch if a value or hatch was secured or opened.

"Control room," Lieutenant Commander Arneau Benjamin, Shipley's executive officer, called into the intercom between the conning tower where they stood and the control room below. "Christmas Tree?"

"One red; else all green, sir," came the reply.

Shipley recognized the voice in the control room as Lieutenant Weaver, his operations officer. Good; he had the top men on his boat in the right locations.

"All secure, Captain, with exception of snorkel," Arneau Benjamin said.

On board a warship, regardless of the commanding officer's rank, the skipper was referred to as "Captain." Chad Shipley's silver commander oak leaves still had the shine on them, but he was still the *Squallfish*'s skipper: the captain.

"Very well, XO. Make your depth sixty feet. Then level off so we can check the radar, the periscopes, and the snorkel."

"Recommend snorkel first, Skipper," Benjamin offered. "We're still on diesels at this time."

"Very well, XO. Make it so."

Shipley's eyebrows furrowed as they always did when he was giving serious thought to a problem. He and his former XO, Daigus Blackfurn—whose name was a mouthful, so everyone called him "Mouthful"—had a great relationship. Mouthful knew what he wanted before he even asked.

This was Shipley's second patrol with the new and untested lieutenant commander. The man was Jewish. Shipley bit his upper lip. He mentally shrugged. It mattered naught to him, he told himself. Old man Kahn, who owned the corner store in the neighborhood where he grew up, had been Jewish. Shipley thought of the few times the old man had given gumballs to him and the others after a game of sandlot baseball in the vacant field across from the store. The man would sit on his chair on the front porch of the store and watch them. He was their audience. Shipley wondered if Kahn was still alive. He had been gray, bent, and old way back then.

Would he and Arneau meld the way he and Mouthful had? Another strike? No, the only strike against the new XO so far was that Benjamin had come from the skimming Navy—the surface warships. Worse yet, the man had been a destroyerman—a killer of submarines. A skimmer who switches to bubblehead was viewed as shaky material in the wardrooms of the subsurface

Navy. No one volunteers for submarines after a tour on a surface ship. They were too used to the fresh, open air of the sea. What would he do if Benjamin started screaming and trying to open the hatches while they were underwater?

Shipley recalled a young sailor during a West Pacific mission losing it during a long period of depth charges. Someone took one of the shaft wrenches and clanged him upside the head, knocking him out.

So he inherited an officer who had switched to submarines less than a year ago. An officer BUPERS had ordered into an XO billet on board his submarine—an officer who was a skimmer. BUPERS was the Navy acronym for Bureau of Naval Personnel, on a hill alongside Arlington National Cemetery overlooking the Pentagon.

Shipley reached up and wrapped his hand around a two-inch water pipe running along the bulkhead of the conning tower. He wriggled his fingers. This was his ship, and BUPERS had given it to him. *"God praise BUPERS,"* he said in a prayer parody.

"Sorry, Skipper; did you say something?"

"No, XO; just thinking out loud. Depth?"

"Forty-three feet. Trim her?"

"Trim her."

Every officer, chief, and sailor in the Navy depended on the paper pushers at BUPERS to decide who went where and when. Why they had to assign a skimmer to be the XO on his submarine was beyond his comprehension.

"Coming up on sixty feet, sir."

"Very well, XO," Shipley responded. As long as his new XO kept asking before executing, they might understand each other. Friday before they sailed, the man had refused to socialize with the wardroom at the Holy Loch Officers Club. Any man who refused to have a drink or two so the skipper could judge the cut of his jib had something to hide, in his opinion. What did Arneau Benjamin have to hide? Everyone had something to hide.

"Sixty feet," the helmsman said.

"Trim sixty," Benjamin said.

"Watch the snorkel," Shipley cautioned.

The two men controlling the planes worked to level the boat. The planes control positions were aft of the helmsman along the port bulkhead. Shipley tightened his grip for a moment on the pipe.

"Final trim," Boohan reported.

Shipley relaxed his grip on the pipe. His feet remained level, and he felt neither a tilt to the right nor the left. Good trim, he thought.

"Good call, COB," he said to Boohan.

"Sixty feet, Skipper," Arneau said.

"Snorkel?"

Arneau glanced at the gauges. "Snorkel raised and functioning, sir."

"Check with Lieutenant Bleecker and see what Greaser has to say," he corrected.

Arneau pressed the button on the intercom and called the engine room.

"CHENG here," the steady voice of the mustang chief engineer responded. A mustang was a Navy officer who had risen through the ranks from enlisted to a commissioned officer. It was hard to do, and few enlisted ever managed to break the intrinsic barrier between the enlisted ranks and the hard Annapolis door leading to the wardroom.

"Report status."

"Snorkel running. Main induction vents closed as the Christmas Tree must have shown, or we'd be treading water by now. Engines one through three connected to the motors. Engine four diverted to keeping the charge topped within forward and aft battery compartments."

With his free hand, Shipley jerked the microphone from its cradle. "Lieutenant Bleecker, Captain here. Everything look okay to you?"

"Aye, Skipper. All four diesels up and running. What a damn fine bunch of Fairchilds, sir. Three on propulsion. Fourth topping off the charge in the batteries, as I reported."

Shipley gave a weak grin at hearing the voice of the mustang lieutenant, Danny "Greaser" Bleecker—his chief engineer—the *Squallfish*'s CHENG. In his mind he saw an older man with sometimes a shaven face; yellow, smoke-stained teeth; and a grease-stained T-shirt pressing the talk button on the intercom box. Fact was, even though Bleecker looked older, both of them were World War II veterans, and Shipley was a year older. Without doubt, a long, grease-stained rag was hanging from Bleecker's back pocket.

Greaser Bleecker never saw a khaki shirt he liked. It took a direct order from Shipley to get the CHENG in a khaki uniform shirt, and then it had to be for a command appearance such as an award ceremony. Otherwise, Greaser Bleecker and his black gang lived, ate, and slept in and around those diesel engines. No one slept near the batteries.

The grease- and sweat-stained T-shirt was the uniform of the heat-racked world of the black gang. Bleecker would be lightly scratching the front of the T-shirt, alternating between scratching and pulling the front away for a moment to free it.

Arneau edged around the periscope tube to check the helmsman, the planesmen, and to read the ballast gauges.

Shipley shrugged. The black gang could look any way they wanted as long as they were belowdecks. They could go naked if they wanted. He didn't care as long as he had power when he needed it. He'd wander down later when he did his walk-through. Management through walking was a key leadership trait learned from his first submarine captain, Commander Mark Anastos. He shook his head. The idea of naked snipes and, even worse, Greaser Bleecker, was too much even for him.

"Snorkel working well, Skipper, as far as I can see," Bleecker said. "We should be able to give you up to twenty knots while on snorkel submerged—more if we had all four Fairchilds connected to the motors. No casualties at this time," the mustang continued, the word "casualties" referring to the engine room equipment. "These are fine Fairchild engines we have, sir. Did I tell you that, Captain? Did I recommend, sir, you send a letter to the yard thanking them for the refit? I may even light a candle to the Fairchild Corporation."

"Yes, you did, CHENG, and thanks for the report. As I said, you write the letters and I'll sign them," Shipley replied, envisioning the sly smile of the CHENG scratching the stubble on his chin. "Status of the batteries?"

"They're nearly fully charged, sir. You can have sixteen hours submerged at four knots or any variation thereof. Last time down we drained them a little, but we weren't down that long. If you don't mind me asking, Skipper, are you planning to do a few more dunks today or are we staying down for a while?"

"Haven't decided yet, Lieutenant Bleecker, but you'll be the first to know."

"Aye, sir."

"Very well, CHENG." Bleecker loved his engines like most men loved their mistresses. And if Shipley didn't cut him off,

Greaser Bleecker would provide a running monologue on the status of everything within the chief engineer's domain, like a new father showing off photographs of his first child.

Most wardrooms on the warships of the U.S. Navy were filled with regular Navy officers. Annapolis graduates had the choke hold on the senior ranks of the Navy—ring knockers, as those less fortunate to attend the legendary school of Navy heroes called them. On the other hand, the Academy failed to teach how to keep diesel engines and batteries operating to full capacity. It was a skill learned with the book closed and hands fiddling with the gear. Bleecker could fix a diesel in his sleep—with one hand. Unlike the other submarines in the squadron, Shipley kept the mustang, despite less than tactful suggestions that he accept a "real" officer. He knew a good thing when he had it.

The most recent attempt to replace Bleecker had been last week, when Shipley had diverted an attempt by the Submarine Group Commander, Commodore Jeff "Sink 'em" Lightly, to replace Bleecker. Commodore Lightly was a full four-strike Navy captain who, like Shipley, wore the submarine warfare device—the symbol of a successful war patrol. You had little choice but to respect a man who had sunk ships and survived depth charges. Those assigned as the Submarine Group Commander were given the honorific title of "Commodore," much like his as "Captain" of the *Squallfish*.

"You know, Chad," Lightly had said, as if he had just thought of the idea, "Lieutenant Bleecker is only a limited-duty officer. LDOs are supposed to provide their technical expertise, not be put in position of authority." When Shipley had opened his mouth to interrupt, the commodore had raised his hand and waved him quiet. "I know, I know; it's your submarine, and if you want to keep him, I'll understand, but I have several other junior submarine officers who need their turn in a division officer slot—an engineer slot. Your LDO is taking up one of those slots now. I can move a lieutenant over—an Academy grad. You can keep Bleecker. Bleecker can be the man's assistant division officer. Teach him what he needs to know. He'll understand. He's former enlisted. They're raised to understand."

Shipley also knew Commodore Lightly could just as well order the transfer to occur without Shipley having any recourse. After all, he was the commodore for the eight submarines at Holy Loch. He was responsible for their war-fighting readiness, and exercising his command prerogatives, Lightly could have done it for the "good of Group readiness." Shipley also knew that if anything went wrong on board the *Squallfish* because of such a unilateral command decision, Lightly would bear some of the responsibility. Lucky for *Squallfish*, Lightly was nearing retirement and was a World War II veteran. The commodore may want to put a "real" officer on board as the *Squallfish*'s chief engineer, but Lightly also knew the importance of the responsibilities of the commanding officer. The commodore had a reputation for sidestepping actions that shifted responsibilities onto his own shoulders when he could leave them on others'.

"Periscope up," Shipley ordered, squatting so when the eyepiece rose, he could rise with his eyes already against the periscope as it ascended. He flipped the handholds out as they came up. Through the handles he felt the tremor of the hydraulics raising the scope. The hum of motors raising it mixed with the low-level noise of the conning tower. Smooth. That's what he wanted. He leaned forward, his eyes against the eyepiece. Water filled the scope for a moment before it broke surface, the smear quickly draining away as the periscope continued upward.

When he wanted the periscope, the last thing he needed was cranky motors generating noise in the water, or the periscope failing to rise all the way. Sixty feet was maximum depth for the snorkel, radar, and periscope to work. Surfaced, the periscope doubled sometimes as a surface watch. Having a skimmer emerge without detection over the horizon was a black mark on the watch.

"Christ, I love this ole boat," he said.

"Won't be long before these diesels have to give way to the nukes," Arneau said.

"Bite your tongue, XO. Nukes are a fad."

Shipley heard the light laughter in the conning tower. The XO was right. If he were lucky, he'd finish his career before the Navy decommissioned the last diesel. He didn't know if he wanted to be confined to a boat that never had to surface. What would you do all day?

He spun the search periscope, making a 360-degree search of the sea. Off to the southeast, the cloudbank was visible covering the Western Isles of Scotland. They'd reach the Iceland–U.K. gap tomorrow. Once outside the protected waters of the United Kingdom, then began the growing games among the U.S. Navy, the

Royal Navy, and the Soviet forces looking for each other's submarines. Today, the hunted; tomorrow, the hunter. Which one depended on the event. He preferred being the hunter.

"Down periscope." Shipley stepped back. He never rode the periscope down. No value in watching the scope sink beneath the waves. Always value in the few seconds a quick look provided on the way up.

The light noise of the hydraulics kept everyone quiet as the scope descended. Shipley thought of the USS *Gar* (SS-206) and his sixteenth combat mission in January 1945. A few months before that final mission of the war—a mission never recorded.

He recalled his first wartime mission as vividly as he recalled the sixteenth and final one. He had barely checked in when the submarine arrived at Pearl Harbor before, in the early-morning hours of the next day, *Gar* had eased out of Pearl. It had returned to the Pacific Theater. They had penetrated Tokyo Harbor to launch several buoys configured to look like fishing buoys, but with sensitive acoustic sensors that transmitted the noise inside the harbor. Once outside the harbor and several miles out to sea near deep water, the skipper had invited the new Ensign Shipley to look through the periscope. When he spun the scope, the bow of a destroyer filled his view.

"How did we do, Skipper?" Arneau asked, interrupting Shipley's thoughts.

Shipley drew back from the periscope and looked at the XO for a couple of seconds as his thoughts returned to the present. His face scrunched, he nodded crisply, and he replied, "It took twenty seconds to clear the bridge; fifty seconds for all secure; and nearly a minute and a half for us to reach final trim." He looked at his watch. "Raising the scope is optional time. I don't count it in getting this boat below the water, out of sight, and out of harm's way. We can do it faster. Goal is eleven seconds to clear the bridge; forty-five seconds for water to cover the bridge; and no more than sixty seconds for the ship to be completely out of sight." Shipley paused. "We're improving, but we still need to improve."

"The crew and I are getting better, sir. Maybe we should do another one now while everyone is at their stations?"

Shipley shook his head. "Let's not," he said with a sigh. "We've done five dunks since we got under way early this morning. Let's give the crew a rest. Set normal steaming for the time being. We might do a nighttime dunk or two later."

"Aye, aye, sir."

"Aye" was the Navy term for "yes." Two of them back to back meant acknowledging and understanding the order.

Shipley glanced around the conning tower. Twenty-one years since World War II ended. Only three members of the crew remembered what it was like to be depth-charged. There was he; Bleecker; and the colored cook Crocky. An important sailor, he had been cajoled-enticed-bribed even to come aboard the *Squallfish.* A good cook made all the difference in crew morale.

Shipley shifted himself to his familiar place inside the conning tower. He leaned against the starboard bulkhead, allowing his memories to go back to his first submarine. There were still members of the *Gar* on active duty. His first skipper, Commander Mark Anastos, had died of a heart attack years ago. The XO on the *Gar* was a two-star admiral on the Chief of Naval Operations staff. He kept in contact with the others and tried to make the annual reunion, but active duty seldom complemented reunions.

"XO, you have the conn. Check with the CHENG and when ready, secure the snorkel and take her down to two hundred feet; continue on current heading and reduce speed to six knots. Stand clear of the sea lanes. Once trimmed, set the normal underway watch. Call me if you have any questions or concerns. If you aren't sure about something, call me anyway."

"Aye, sir."

Shipley turned from the conning tower and started down the ladder. "I'll be in my cabin for bit, XO. Once the underway watch is set, grab the OPSO, and you two join me in the wardroom mess. Time to open that package those two communications technicians delivered from CINCNELM." Curiosity is a strange creature. He had been wanting to open the couriered package since he had signed for it an hour before they cast off lines and got under way. What did Admiral Wright, Commander, U.S. Naval Forces, Eastern Atlantic and Mediterranean, sitting at his desk in London, England, want them to do? He had no doubt it was something dangerous and something covert. Couriered packages were not used for cake and cookies.

Shipley disappeared down the ladder leading to the control room below the conning tower. Communications technician was a new rating in the Navy. These technicians wore a lightning bolt crisscrossed over a feather. "Lightning-fast chicken pluckers" someone called them.

No one really knew what they did, but he suspected it had to do with the Ultra program from World War II. He took a deep breath as he stepped into the control room beneath the conning tower. His mission was to patrol the Iceland–U.K. gap to search for Soviet warships that sometimes ventured this far out.

"Captain, how we doing, sir?" Chief Topnotch asked.

"We're doing fine, Chief. How's the torpedo rooms look?"

"Sir, my men are ready fore and aft. Just say the word."

"Good, Chief." Not many full-blooded Cherokee Native Americans in the Navy that he knew of. Topnotch looked like the stereotyped television Indian with his broad chest, short legs, and dark hair. He could imagine the man in a loincloth, riding bareback.

Shipley spoke a few words of encouragement to the sailors at the Christmas Tree as he left the control room through the forward hatch, heading toward officers' country. His experience during World War II had dealt with last-minute changes to missions, and most times couriers delivered them. Whatever it was had better not last longer than sixty days. He had outfitted for that duration only.

"YOU better be careful, boy. You got too much anger trying to leap out and git yoreself killed."

Washington dropped the pans into the open drawer. The clang of the shiny aluminum pans hitting the others filled the small galley kitchen.

"Why you do that, boy?" Crocky said, jumping at the noise. The career Navy mess cook put his hands on his hips and stared at the young sailor. "You don't be careful and I might rip that head of yore's off and stuff it up yore ass like a Greek water fountain."

Washington squatted and started shuffling the pots and pans around so the drawer would shut. "Petty Officer Crocky, you tell me to be careful?" Washington asked, the noise of the heavy metal cooking items nearly drowning out his words. "He a cracker bastard is what he is. Why I got to be careful? He the one better be careful." Washington stood up.

Crocky stretched his foot out and shoved the drawer shut. "Boy, if you ain't careful, you gonna get whacked. Lots more of them'ums then us'ums."

"Whacked? I'm gonna get whacked?" Washington jammed his thumb into his chest. "I ain't gonna get whacked."

"Stop that shit. Bring me the salt from the cupboard and stop yore daydreaming, boy."

"He's the one gonna get whacked."

"On board the boat, you be the one who get whacked, if you git out of line. You already seen the ole man once; he don't like to see sailors twice."

"Whacked," Washington muttered, reaching up to pull the huge container of salt from the top counter. His T-shirt drooped at the arms, revealing a heavy stock of underarm hair. "All he gotta do is leave me alone and I'll leave him alone. I ain't the one who started this shit, Crocky."

Washington lifted the huge container of salt over the inch-high metal bar mounted across the front of the shelves to keep stuff from sliding onto the deck when the submarine rolled. He walked along the serving counter, between it and the long iron frying surface to where Crocky, the *Squallfish* head mess cook, stirred water in a huge pot.

"This what you want?" Washington looked toward the door leading into the small, twenty-man mess hall.

"Fightin' ain't got no place on board a submarine. The ole man will have you both carried off in cuffs and slammed into the brig. If you think Potts is bad, you ain't seen nuthin' until you seen the southern boys they—"

Washington twisted and did a full turn. "But why do we put up with this shit?" He leaned forward. "You know, Crocky, you ought to join the NAACP." He reached for his wallet.

"Don't drop that salt, Wash." Crocky straightened, continuing to stir the heating water with one hand while pulling a white wash-cloth from his rear pocket and wiping the sweat from his face. Crocky looked at the young sailor. Washington and he were the only mess cooks in the Supply Department. The two Filipinos, Santos and Marcos, were more a two-man cleaning crew than cooks.

Crocky had seen angrier and better-built young men than Washington try to change inherited racism. Most were civilians now. He jammed the washcloth back in his pocket, ignoring the beads of sweat that dropped into the water.

"Washington," he whispered, "you join any damn thing you want. I'll keep my joining to myself. We got one job on the *Squall-fish*: that's feed the crew. Ain't no job on board the boat for fightin' them. I know you don't want to hear it, but most of them white boys are all right. There's always a bad apple in the bunch just like there are bad apples in ours." He pointed at Washington. "You keep yore temper, ya hear? You know there are worse things than takin' the man's arrogant comments. I don't want you thrown off the boat and into the Holy Loch brig—no, siree, I don't want that."

"Why?" Washington asked, his eyebrows furrowing.

Crocky looked down at the water. "Why? You don't think I want to have to do all this myself, do you?"

Washington grinned. "Here I was beginning to think of you like my father."

"I thought you said your father ran away when you was a kid."

"He did; the bastard."

They laughed. "You know, boy, you gotta mouth on you that gonna git you killed one day."

"I won't reach Kingdom alone. Old Saint Peter is goin' to want to know why I brought a parade with me."

Crocky laughed, but he stopped stirring and looked at the young man. He had heard that tone many times in his sixteen years. He heard it in '40 when he joined, sixteen years ago. He heard it through World War II, but a lot less than after the war. "When you're fightin' for yore life, there ain't no color barrier."

"You're right there."

"Right where? What you talking 'bout, boy?"

"You said, 'When you're fightin' for yore life, there ain't no color barrier.' "

"Sometimes, Washington, us veterans of the war think out loud. It don't mean it has anything whatsoever to have to do with you."

"You keep yore blade where it belongs—outta sight." He stirred some more. "There, I think it's about the right temperature." He looked at Washington, seeing both fear and anger in the eyes. How many times over his life in the Navy had he seen the same emotions? There was a time when they were his emotions. "I'll see what I can do about Potts. Every boat has a Potts. Most times, they disappear quick. Potts been on board long enough that his rep for bad liberty and beating up people should be known to the bosses."

"The COB ain't gonna do anythin'." Washington stood there cradling the salt container. "I'm the only one who can make sure he stops."

"Who said I was gonna talk to Boohan? I didn't say I was gonna talk to the chief of the boat; that's what you said, so don't go tellin' people ole Crocky is runnin' his mouth to the COB."

"Well, who else you gonna tell? We don't have a chaplain on board, and if we did, he'd be white."

"Washington, don't be an asshole. The world is tough enough without another asshole in it. Let Potts and his assholes have their world and we'll have ours." He pointed to the huge bowl of peeled potatoes on the nearby shelf. "Hand me that salt and slide those taters over here. This water is quickenin' to boil, so we gonna shave these potatoes and surprise the crew."

"Why? They never had potatoes before?" Washington asked with a laugh.

Crocky shook his head. "Don't give up yore day job, boy. A stand-up you ain't."

Washington passed the salt to Crocky. Bending down, he gripped the handle on one side of the huge polished bowl filled above the brim with peeled potatoes. Grunting, he slid it across the few feet of deck so it was a few inches from the boiling water.

"Yeah, how you gonna handle someone like Potts if a few pounds of potatoes make you grunt?"

"In Philly, we fight to win."

"You never win in a fight in the Navy. All it does it starts a new one, and when everyone's head comes up for a breath, you discover yores is in the brig."

"Okay, Crocky. I can handle it. Don't mean I like it, but let's see what your friend the COB can do."

"That's better," Crocky said, nodding. "Wait a minute! I ain't gonna talk to Boohan, so you can just quit that. I have my one way of takin' care of things." He pointed to the drawers near the shelf area. "Now go grab us a couple of knives. Don't get sharp ones. With your razor humor and quick wit—"

"Whackin' wit."

"A good whackin' is what ya git if you screw with the white boys. The skipper is a good man, but even good men can be forced to do things they don't wanna do because of good order and discipline. Don't think bein' in the right makes one innocent in the Navy. All it does is make you sit alongside the guilty ones in the brig."

"If he calls me a n—"

Crocky held up his hand. "President Truman has taken care of that. Leave this to me." He didn't mention that he had already talked with Lieutenant Bleecker. Only three of them on the boat who were World War II veterans, and he was one of them. Crocky lifted the salt, unscrewed the lid, and grabbed a handful of salt. He dumped the salt unceremoniously into the slow-boiling water. Two more handfuls followed. "There; that should be enough."

Washington squatted and lifted the knife. He ran his finger along the blade. "These knives are pretty good for government issue."

"And they gonna stay that way." Crocky screwed the lid back onto the salt container and set it down on a nearby carving table.

Washington stopped and looked up. "Well, I ain't gonna take much more, Crocky. This Potts needs to learn some respect. I'm gonna teach him."

"What you gonna do, Petty Officer Third Class Steward's Mate Washington, is keep yore lips shut and yore hands beside yore sides."

"Like this?" Washington said, standing up and slapping both arms rigid alongside.

"Without the fists."

Washington relaxed. "But my fists is what I'm gonna need."

"All you need to learn is patience. Patience is how we get things done in the Navy. We don't gotta knock down every fence in our way. Some of those fences we climb over; some we walk around; some even we can repaint and make them ours before those who put them up discover they were even there." He lifted the giant metal spoon from the boiling water and knocked it twice on the side of the pot.

"But we can't knock down everything that stands in our way. Hand me that knife." Taking the knife from Washington, Crocky grabbed a potato and with several quick slices sent potato pieces into the water. "Otherwise we'll be just like that potato: one moment whole and happy, the next all cut up and in boiling water besides."

Washington grabbed a potato and started slicing. "You think that potato was happy before it had its skin peeled off?"

"What you mean, boy? 'Skin peeled off.' Potatoes don't feel anythin'. You just be careful, and—believe me, I know how hard it is—keep yore anger bottled up."

"You might be right."

"I know I'm right. I been in this man's Navy for over sixteen years. I fought every day of the war and look at me: I'm a first class petty officer. Ain't many colored can say they made first class. Why? Who knows? I might retire as a chief." A handful of sliced potatoes followed his words into the pot. "But I'm one who done it." He waved his knife around the galley, pointing over the counter to the six bolted-down tables on the other side. "This is my kingdom, and I'm tellin' you, this kingdom is much better than the cotton mill in Georgia I left to go off to war."

Washington pulled a chair over and sat down.

"What you doin'?"

"I'm sittin' down."

Crocky reached over and slapped him upside the ear. "Yore momma teach you any manners? Have some respect for your elders. Go get *me* a chair."

Washington walked around the edge of the counter to where the chairs were pushed under the tables and grabbed one. Behind him, the nemesis he had talked about moments before walked into the mess. Accompanying the huge man from Ohio was the smaller Fromley. Fromley was the audience Potts took everywhere with him.

"Well, well, looks as if the new nigra has found his niche in life," Potts said.

Washington jumped.

Potts laughed, grabbing a coffee cup from the rack. "Yeah, I'd be nervous if I was you, boy. Never can tell when something might happen on a boat. You been greased yet?"

Crocky walked out into the dining area. "Do you want somethin', Potts, or you just come in here to dirty my mess hall?"

Potts's nose wrinkled in disgust. "I wasn't talkin' to you, Crocky."

Crocky waved the knife at him. "I said, Petty Officer Potts, 'Do you want somethin'?' "

"I came for a cup of coffee."

"Then, I suggest, Petty Officer Potts, that you go get your own coffee cup and come back. Too many of my cups have disappeared to those who want to use the mess's instead of their own."

Potts slammed the half-full cup down on the metal rungs beneath the huge coffeepot. Coffee spilled over the edge, draining into the reservoir beneath the rungs. "I always bring them back. You know that."

"Come on, Tom, let's go," Fromley said from behind the man, grabbing the shirtsleeve of the dungaree shirt.

Potts jerked away.

"Potts, I don't know shit except whenever you come in here

you bring a world of hate and hurt with you. You want to use one of my mess cups? Then you bring the other twenty-six I'm missing from those who always bring them back. You don't mind roundin' up my coffee cups, do you?"

Potts's face turned red, and his lower lip twitched.

Crocky nearly smiled, but a smile might cause the huge snipe to rip both him and Washington into shaven pieces of black potato. He knew the only thing keeping the Ohioan from mouthing off was that Crocky was one of the few on board who had been through the war. Crocky's word would carry more weight with the skipper than from someone who had never survived depth charges and long, fearful days running from the enemy.

"You mighty uppity."

Washington stepped alongside Crocky. Crocky reached out and with a quick, tight grip grabbed the lean sailor by the arm.

"*I'm mighty uppity, Petty Officer First Class Crocky*, is what you meant to say, ain't it. Potts, I don't want to see you in my mess again until your leading petty officer come sees me. You understand?"

Potts turned and headed toward the door. "Your day is coming, you know."

"Oh, I know that, Potts, and when that day comes you gonna be one surprised petty officer to see how it looks."

Potts disappeared into the passageway.

Crocky dropped his grip.

Washington turned and grinned. "You want me to be calm?" He placed spread fingers on his chest. "You want me to be calm and you stand there waving a blade at him threatening to slice that bigot and you want me to be calm?" His breathing came rapidly, Washington's ribs easily discernible through the thin cloth of the white T-shirt. "Oh, man, Petty Officer Crocky, you are one calm mother. Did you see the scaredness on his face?" Washington's lower lip pushed up against the upper; he put both hands on his hips; and he stared at the door where Potts had just left. "Wait until next time, cracker. I'm going to *whup yore ass*."

Crocky relaxed, a deep sigh escaping. "No you ain't, because there ain't gonna be no next time for you. You hear me?"

Washington nodded, a deep grin still covering his face.

"Man, you gonna get yoreself killed is what you gonna do."

"I saw what you did, Petty Officer Crocky, and you didn't even raise a hand."

"What I do and what you do is two different things. I been around the Navy a few years. You ain't even reached twenty yet and you talkin' trash about what you gonna do to that white trash. He'd break both of us like a small limb, laugh while he doin' it, and take wallet photos for his grandchildren." Crocky turned and walked back into the galley. "Now you gonna stand there musin' 'bout things, or you gonna bring me my chair like you supposed to?"

"I got it, mastah; I got it." Washington made several exaggerated bows as he walked across the galley.

"It ain't him you gotta worry about with the blade, you keep talking trash actin' like nigra. I'll be the one whackin' ya."

"OKAY, you f'ing black gangers!" Lieutenant Greaser Bleecker shouted from his chair, blocking the end forward hatch of the forward engine room. He was leaning back, the metal straight-back chair precariously balanced on its back two feet. "We ain't down here for our health. We heading down to two hundred feet. What does that tell you?" He pointed at the young, overweight sailor near the fuel lines. "You—Otto—shit-can that doughnut and tell me what going to two hundred feet means."

The sailor jammed the remainder of the stale pastry into his mouth, rapidly chewing it and trying to swallow at the same time.

"Someone bring me a gun," Bleecker said, shaking his head. "Shit-can means throw away, Shithead, not eat the damn thing." Bleecker leaned forward, bringing the chair with him onto all four legs. He stood, took a couple of steps, and lightly slapped the sailor on the back of the head. "Otto, we could be dead by the time you finish that thing."

"Ah, Lieutenant," Seaman Otto Lang garbled out through a full mouth. Bits of doughnut splattered the nearby leading petty officer.

"Shit, Otto," Petty Officer First Class Gledhill snarled, wiping the crumbs from his T-shirt. "Now look what you done."

"Sorry, LPO," Otto sputtered, more crumbs flying.

"Well, we won't have to go to the mess hall to eat," Potts said from behind the two men.

Half the engine room sailors laughed—everyone but Bleecker, Gledhill, and Otto, who was trying to finish his doughnut.

"Damn, Otto, we'd be dead, but you'd have a full stomach," Bleecker said with a shake of the head.

He turned to Adam Gledhill, his leading petty officer. "Gledhill, we got the snorkel up, so let's practice switching to battery before the old man decides to do it for real. Okay?"

"Aye, sir," Gledhill replied.

Bleecker looked at the group as Gledhill went through the checklist with the electrician mates, making sure the gauges read correctly, the engines were percolating fine, and everyone understood their job. On a surface ship, make a mistake in the engine room and everything came to all stop. You floated while you fixed the cause. On a submarine, you might be able to float, but you floated deep under the surface of the ocean. And if you didn't fix the casualty in time, you could find yourself floating forever beneath the surface of the ocean, ships passing overhead never knowing the coffin beneath their hulls. Bleecker waited patiently near the hatch leading forward, a hatch he kept dogged shut most times.

"Potts, you gonna stand there staring at the thing, or you gonna tell me what you're supposed to do?" Gledhill asked.

Bleecker's eyes narrowed. The engine room was too small for private conversations. He saw Potts turn to say something to Gledhill, but Otto Lang excused himself, unknowingly stepping between another confrontation between his LPO and Bleecker's problem child. All members of the black gang had the potential to be problem children. He had been one until his first chief took him on liberty in Hong Kong, told him he was on the path to spending the rest of his life in the brig, or he could straighten up and become a real sailor. Then the chief had proceeded to beat the shit out of him, leaving him lying in an alley near the Lotus Blossom.

He had barely made it to the boat before it sailed. The chief never mentioned the "counseling session" in Hong Kong, and Bleecker made sure he never received another one. He wondered whatever happened to the chief.

He stood alone near the dogged hatch. Gledhill had his hands on his hips, talking with Potts. Otto Lang—the sailors teased the Dutch German from Pennsylvania, but in the six months since he joined, the teasing had churned into where Otto Lang was more mascot than outcast. Amazing how human nature resolves a lot of conflicts without much intervention. He had been on the verge of asking for Lang to be replaced—more for the sailor than the crew—but things had changed. With the exception of Potts and the bully's sycophant Fromley.

Potts and Fromley stood alongside the fuel controls.

The intercom blared.

"Engine room here, CHENG speaking."

"We're taking her down. Switch to battery power," came the voice of the XO.

"Roger."

"Gledhill, make sure the snorkel is secured." Before the leading petty officer could answer, Bleecker glared at Potts. "Potts, you and Fromley get your asses up to the forward battery compartment where you're supposed to be and check those batteries once we switch over. Morgan and Garcia, don't stand there staring at the overhead. Get your asses to the aft battery compartment and keep an eye on it for a while. I'll be along as soon as the diesels are secured." Without waiting for an answer, Bleecker pushed the sweat-matted hair off his forehead as he grabbed the microphone from the cradle. "Conn, engineering; we are switching to battery at this time, securing snorkel." He hung it up when the new XO acknowledged the report. Garcia was the last of the four sailors to leave the engine room, securing the watertight hatch behind him.

Bleecker opened the hatch and stuck his head into the aft battery compartment. Morgan stood near the logbook, and Garcia had already started reading the charges on the battery cells. Forward of the aft battery compartment was the pump room. "Morgan, stick your head inside the pump room and give me a quick check."

Morgan spun the wheel and opened the hatch. The sailor stuck his head through the hatch, looked around the smaller compartment, and then drew back inside the battery compartment. "Everything looks okay to me, Lieutenant Bleecker."

"Thanks," he said, shutting the hatch and securing it again. Give him a diesel engine any day over batteries. Salt water hit the batteries, and the next thing you knew the whole submarine was a floating graveyard of dead and dying sailors as sulfuric acid air filled it. Nope, maybe this nuclear thing the Navy was playing with was all right, but he didn't want to be below the waterline when they discovered they needed a diesel. He had seen the photographs of Hiroshima. He loved these engines.

"You think these nuclear submarines are going to replace diesels?"

Bleecker put his hands behind his neck, looked at Gledhill, and leaned back. He hated people who could read his thoughts. "Ain't a snowball's chance, Gledhill. Diesels are forever. This nuclear shit ain't any good except for blowing up Japs and scaring the Ruskies." He lowered his arms and leaned forward. Every sailor in the engine room looked toward him. "Besides, those nuclear submarines they building put too much noise in the water. What you think is going to happen when we finally have to fight them God-hating, Commie pinkos?"

After a few seconds Otto asked from the far end of the engine room, "What, CHENG?"

Bleecker put his hand to his ear, his eyes widening. "Otto, is that you?"

"Yes, sir."

"Damn, sounds like you finished your doughnut."

"Ah, Lieutenant—"

He heard the slight hit of a slap and knew Gledhill had tapped Otto Lang on the back of the neck. He smiled. "They going to be able to find us without even rousting the crew to general quarters, we're going to be generating so much noise. Then you never-been-to-war sailors are going to find out how much fun depth-charging is."

He felt the silence and the slight tinge of fear. Better they know what to expect than find out all of a sudden.

"We are going to have Russian tin cans all over our ass, dropping depth charges, and scooping the bodies of you kids up with straining nets, trying to put the body parts back together."

"I read in the *Sun*—"

"Page three, girl," Andersen said from the port side of the number two engine.

"Ain't so," Otto whined.

"Hope you ain't doing anything you ain't supposed to in the rack above me," Electrician Mate Max Brown said as he stepped through the hatch from the aft engine room. "Everything's okay with engines three and four, Lieutenant. Both shut down."

"We've switched power to the electric motor from diesel to battery, boss," Gledhill said from behind Brown.

"Okay, leave Lang alone," Bleecker said. "I don't care how you bunch of grease-stained snipes spend your off time, but I do care when you're in the engine room. Gledhill, get control of your crew."

"You heard the lieutenant." Gledhill made a downward motion with his hand. "You guys leave Otto alone. Every one of you is turning those Navy sheets into fantasy palaces. We're going to be out for at least sixty days, and you don't want to be rolling over and hearing the sheets break."

Bleecker shouted over the engine room noise and the varied actions ongoing. "The rest of you, grab the 3-M checklists and let's plan our preventive maintenance schedule for the voyage. Petty Officer Andersen, you're the 3-M coordinator, so have you done any preliminary work schedule like I would expect someone with that duty to do?"

Andersen grinned, reaching up to wipe back a lock of blond hair that had matted to his steep forehead. "Yes, sir, Lieutenant. I have. I did it before we set sail."

Bleecker grinned. "Andersen, you never cease to amaze me. Grab it and let's go over it. Meanwhile, the rest of you grab some rags, go over these sweet Fairchilds, and clean up any oil, grease, or anything you see spoiling the virginity of my engines."

After several minutes of going over the preventive maintenance schedule for the week, glancing at the monthly, and scrubbing for the umpteenth time the actions done the previous week, Bleecker blessed Andersen's plan. "Good job. Just make sure it gets done."

"Aye, Lieutenant."

Bleecker stood, his T-shirt bulged across the chest where years of heavy work in the engine room had built sinewy muscles that seemed to ripple along the chest and down the arms. "I'm going to the forward battery compartment. Gledhill, check on Morgan and Garcia periodically while you're overseeing the engine rooms."

"Aye, boss."

BLEECKER ducked as he walked along the narrow passageway in the pump room. Being six-one on board a World War II–vintage diesel submarine made it cramped, but after twenty-two years of Navy submarine service, he had grown used to it. Submarines were not for the claustrophobic. The soft sound of the oil sump and the cycle of the bilge pump complemented the oily smell of the room. He knew the air was breathable, but being breathable did not mean being odorless. Bilge water was where excess waste, excess oils, and excess anything fluid eventually congregated. It was the twenty-four/seven job of the bilge pump to keep the stuff pumped off the submarine. The pumps were secured when they were at battle stations or avoiding antisubmarine forces, but until those moments, the continuous mechanical actions of the pumps worked to keep the submarine afloat.

Bleecker opened the hatch at the forward end of the pump room. The smell of ozone mixed with the ever-present tinge of sulfur burned his nostrils—a slight burn that served as a warning of what could happen to the air inside a submarine if salt water covered the batteries.

When Bleecker entered the forward battery compartment, he caught the exchange of glances between Potts and Fromley. Bleecker grabbed the bar of the watertight hatch and secured it. "Fromley, you go to the mess hall and see if Petty Officer Crocky has some fresh pastries." Bleecker watched the sailor as Fromley closed the hatch.

Fromley looked as if he had been abandoned like some waif of a dog cast aside by a reluctant master. Fromley had the human features of a weasel-thin face pockmarked from teenage acne, and a protruding chin nearly as long as the sailor's too-thin nose. *It must have scared the shit out of Fromley's dad when he first saw his son*, Bleecker thought. "Jesus Christ! It's alive!"

"What's alive, Lieutenant?"

"Nothing, Potts; just thinking out loud."

"I can't see in this red light," Potts complained after a couple of steps.

"Shut up. When you finish the checks in the battery compartment, the sub is going to be on red lights, so I expect it to stay on red lights. You've been in the Navy long enough to know your eyes will adjust." Bleecker reminded himself to make sure Gledhill kept the engine rooms in red lights also.

"I thought we were going to do some more dunks, Lieutenant."

When Bleecker failed to answer the question, a nervous Potts asked, "You want me to secure the hatch, Lieutenant?"

Bleecker acknowledged the question. His eyes rapidly took in the battery room. Batteries were his bane. There was a multitude of things that could sink a submarine, and most of them were on board. Depth charges were the least effective method of sinking them. All it would take is salt water to turn this compartment into a huge gas generator like those the Nazis used in the concentration camps. He had seen the photographs. While he worried about the idea, he also believed that if it ever happened where salt water covered the batteries, they'd be long dead before the sulfuric acid burned through the linings of their lungs. They'd hit the bottom of the dark Atlantic long before the poison air reached them.

Bleecker pointed to the meters along the bulkhead. "We'll need to read the batteries, Potts. Grab the logbook. I'll read off the battery and the charge reading."

"That's what Fromley and I were just fixing to do, Lieutenant."

"Well, you weren't doing it when I came in."

"But we were fixing to," Potts said, opening a small cabinet. Several green logbooks lay on top of each other, each one lighter than the one below it. Those books represented every battery check since *Squallfish* was commissioned in 1943.

When Potts turned around, he found himself staring into the eyes of Bleecker.

"I heard, Potts, you been fucking around with the steward mates."

Potts leaned back, away from the angry face of Bleecker.

"Let me tell you something, Petty Officer Potts: Crocky has been around this man's Navy longer than you been alive. He tells me you been giving a bunch of white man–colored man shit to the new cook. He further tells me you been giving him some lip."

"Look, Lieutenant—" Potts said, trying to explain.

"Don't 'look' me, Potts. I've seen troublemakers like you and Fromley before. The Navy has a lot of experience in taking care of shitbirds like you two." Bleecker backed away, but took satisfaction that Potts remained braced against the cabinet. "You got potential, sailor, but you won't have it if you keep screwing with Crocky. He'll have your nuts for his mantel if you piss him off enough."

"But Lieutenant, I didn't mean to upset them."

Bleecker crossed his arms, thick, sinewy muscles rippling along the forearms, while thick biceps bulged the ragged sleeves of the T-shirt. "Don't lie to me. Yes, you did mean to piss them off. You went out of your way to insult them. Crocky is more a man than you are, and I don't want you to forget it." He reached out and poked Potts hard a couple of times in the chest. "This is what we call in the Navy a counseling session, Potts."

"Counseling?"

"Counseling." Bleecker backhanded him, knocking Potts's head into the cabinet, breaking the skin slightly above the ear. He crossed his arms across his chest. "I think you want to apologize to Crocky."

Potts held his ear. "Apologize? Apologize to a bunch of—"

He never saw the second slap coming. The right side of Potts's head bounced off the metal cabinet.

"That wasn't a question, Petty Officer Potts. I don't care about the new steward, but Crocky does, and what Crocky cares about, I care about," he said, accenting each work with a thumb in his chest. "You get my drift, Potts, or do we have to continue this counseling?"

Potts reached up and ran his hand along the right side of his head. Bleecker saw the swelling growing alongside the upper hairline. Sometimes a sailor needed a kick in the butt to straighten him out. Sometimes, like the chief did for him, it sinks in quickly, and you regain a sense of direction.

"I understand, Lieutenant."

Bleecker reached out and grabbed Potts by the throat. He put just enough pressure to ensure the sailor knew there was a lot more pressure where that came from. With his huge thumb, Bleecker raised the man's chin. "Here is what you are going to do: within the next couple of days you are going to find an opportunity to apologize to Petty Officer First Class Crocky so he can forget about killing you." Bleecker saw with distant amusement the shocked look on Potts's face. "Yeah, I said 'killing you.' You think a veteran of depth charges and the war is going to let some asshole whippersnapper like you piss on his parade? He isn't." He let go of Potts's neck. "We understand each other, Potts?"

"Yes, sir, Lieutenant," Potts mumbled, rubbing his throat.

"Good." Bleecker turned away for a moment, then spun around from the waist. "You know, Potts, if you get your act together and quit trying to be the big man on campus you were in some hick high school, you might make a good engineer. Right now, you're working your way to the morgue or to the brig. Either one is going to disappoint your parents."

"Yes, sir, Lieutenant."

"Now, pick up that logbook before it gets damaged. Let's get to work on checking the batteries before Fromley comes back. We won't speak of our counseling session, now, will we?"

Potts bent down and hurriedly picked up the logbook. "No, sir, Lieutenant."

For about five minutes Bleecker did the readings. He enjoyed doing them periodically because it renewed his belief that if you take care of the little things, the big things will take care of themselves. Bleecker traced the lines from the battery cells to the meters that checked their status to the lines exiting the compartment heading toward the diesels.

When the submarine reached a depth where the snorkel could no longer provide air for diesels to operate, these battery cells powered the boat. Battery power was nowhere as fast as diesel. The more speed demanded from the batteries, the less time a submarine could stay submerged. So when submerged and on battery power, submarines tended to transit at four to six knots, reserving battery power for when they may need it. In an emergency situation, if you had sufficient battery power, a submarine could hit twelve knots for a short burst of escape speed. But that burst also could cost a submarine any edge for error.

When Fromley returned with a couple of hot pastries, Bleecker took both of them and left the compartment, expecting the two sailors to finish the status readings.

"ARNEAU, slide in here. Alec, you slide around on the other side of me," Shipley said, motioning the young operations officer to the left. Near his coffee cup on the table lay the brown double-wrapped package. He could have opened it sooner, but these things were always bad news. He smiled, wondering what the others would think if he raised the envelope and held it against his forehead like some mystic and then announced he foresaw "bad news." Shock would cover their faces, for it would be out of character.

The three officers filled the front half of the wardroom. Here the officers ate, tried to relax, and was where wardroom meetings were held. The wardroom mess was big enough for eight officers at a time, in comparison to the crew's mess one deck below.

The crew's mess was a marvel of operation. Crocky and his team of two Filipinos and the sailor Washington worked 'round the clock to keep the food flowing. Food was the morale builder of the submarine force. If you had a good cook like Crocky, then the crew was happy—for the most part. Bad cook meant bad morale and short tempers. The Navy ought to do a study on it, for in the crew's mess, in shifts of twenty-four, sailors wedged themselves together for the three daily meals. Assholes and elbows, as they said, bumping into each other, shoveling the grub for a quick savory taste, then back to the duties of the boat until the next meal.

On board surface ships, the captain's cabin was big enough for meetings, but on the older diesel submarines such as *Squallfish*—only one of her class—the captain's cabin was more a private closet. He had the only one-rack stateroom on board the World War II diesel submarine, and it measured less than four feet across and about seven feet long. Every inch of it filled with a rack for sleeping, a small desk barely shoulder-width, and a cabinet for cramming his uniform items away. No wonder submariners looked as if they slept in their clothes. He had hung a mirror on the inside of the cabinet door. Beside the mirror, taped to the bulkhead, were photographs of his wife, June, and two children: Dale, who had just turned eight, and his daughter, Marilyn, who was learning to walk.

"Will do, Skipper. Coffee?" Arneau asked, waving an empty cup at Shipley and turning his head toward Lieutenant Alexander "Alec" Weaver.

Alec Weaver, the operations officer—OPSO, as they called him aboard the *Squallfish*—waited patiently, blocking the door leading from the passageway into the wardroom. The walking space between the serving line where the coffeepot constantly recycled whatever remained from the fresh morning brew and the three small booths where the officers sat for their meals was only wide enough for one person at a time.

Shipley pushed his cup out. "Thanks, XO."

Arneau hoisted his cup at Weaver.

"No thanks, XO." Weaver shook his head, reached up, and pushed his glasses off the end of his nose. "Already had two cups today."

"What's a sailor without a cup of java?" Arneau asked, reaching down to pick up Shipley's cup. "Come on," he cajoled, pushing his body against the coffee urn. "You can get by."

Weaver eased by the XO, placing his hands lightly on the man's shoulder as he pushed by the officer. Then he easily slid his lanky frame onto the small padded bench. His hip touched Shipley's.

Shipley bounced the unopened brown package a couple of times on the top of the table. He noticed Weaver watching the action.

Arneau set the filled cup in front of the skipper and slid into the left side of Shipley. Submarines were not warships for those who needed privacy or had an aversion to physical contact. Every inch of space held something. Human comforts were the last consideration in the design. Nothing was done aboard the *Squallfish* without bumping, touching, rubbing against each other. If you didn't get along with your fellow submariners, you didn't last long in the submarine service. There was no room for incompatibility.

He had seen it in World War II. Lots of sailors and officers thought submarines where were they wanted to serve. Submarines were the first warships to carry the war to the enemy. Many officers and sailors barely made it through their first mission before they found themselves hoisting their seabags onto their shoulder and lumbering down the docks toward the destroyers.

"I'm surprised you haven't opened it, Skipper," Arneau said, raising his cup to his lips.

"Thought I'd wait until all three of us could be here." He tossed the envelope onto the table. "I want you two to understand how unusual this is and why I've put off opening it." He glanced at both of them.

"I would have ripped it right open before I left the dock," Arneau said.

Shipley nodded. "I can understand the urge, but the letter that accompanied the orders said not until we were under way, but no later than seventy-two hours after we sailed."

"I only meant—"

Shipley shook his head. "I know what you mean, XO," he said in an understanding voice. He had been there, done that, and was now doing it again. Mysteries at sea were as dangerous as couriered letters and packages.

"Orders?" Weaver asked. "You think this is redirecting our mission?"

Shipley laughed. "I don't think it's an early Christmas card from CINCNELM." He bounced the package one more time. "Gentlemen, I've received only two of these in my career. That was in World War II. This is the third one."

"Then they are altering our mission," Weaver said emphatically. "Hope it doesn't mean we'll be out past our maximum sixty days."

Shipley looked at his young operations officer. *How old is Lieutenant Weaver?* he thought. *Twenty-five? Twenty-six? Most likely.* He twisted his head to look at Arneau Benjamin. "XO, what do you think?"

"I think we ought to open it and find out what kind of mess our beloved Commander-in-Chief of the Eastern Atlantic and Mediterranean is throwing us," Weaver said.

Shipley put his hand over the package. Weaver wanted to grab it and rip it open, he could tell. The tension was too much, but in a perverse way, Shipley was enjoying this.

"Sounds like it might be a more exciting mission than patrolling the Iceland–U.K. gap," the XO added.

"Always a mission somewhere," Shipley answered. "A submarine mission never fails to include a primary and a secondary course of action." He turned the package over and began pulling off the tape that some enterprising security officer had used to double-seal it. "The big question will be if the commodore and his staff are aware of it. During World War II, the two times I received something such as this, it was the commander of the sub Group who delivered them, and he delivered them personally." He rolled the tape into a sticky ball and placed it on the table.

Weaver reached over and pulled the trash toward him, cupping it in his hand.

Then, with his thumb and finger, Shipley worked the brown flap away from the envelope.

Arneau let a deep sigh escape, drawing a look from Shipley. "Nervous, XO?"

"Not like it was Christmas."

"Didn't know you practiced Christmas."

"If it involves gifts, candy, and food, no good Jew would ever turn down the holiday just for something as benign as religious differences."

Shipley and Weaver smiled.

"Unfortunately," Shipley said as his effort reached the end of the flap, "deliveries such as this are less than joyous occasions."

"What were the other two times you received things like this, Skipper?" Weaver asked.

Shipley looked at the operations officer. Weaver leaned toward him, his eyes fixed on the thick brown envelope.

"One was during the Battle of Luzon after MacArthur had gone ashore. The submarine was detached from protecting the resupply effort of our troops ashore to search for Japanese transports evacuating troops from the Philippines. The second one was the dangerous one. It sent us into Tokyo Bay, where we set a few buoys the boys from OP-20G had designed. Don't really know what the buoys did, but they did break the Japanese code—"

"Ultra? Wasn't it called Ultra?"

Shipley shook his head. "Ultra was the operation that broke

the Germans' Enigma code. Not sure if we had a code name or operations name for our efforts in breaking Japan's naval code. We just did it."

The flap came open, and Shipley stuck his hand inside. "What I do know is that if it had not been for the cryptologic efforts of the on-the-roof gang of World War II, we might still be fighting."

"I heard we won the Battle of Midway because of their success," Weaver added.

"Yep. You're right there. I think there's a lot more we don't know, but eventually—maybe during our lifetime—we'll find out about it," Shipley added. He pulled out a sealed white letter envelope. "Someday we may know the whole story."

"Box within a box," Arneau added. "Like those Russian dolls I saw one time."

This time Shipley wasted little effort. He ripped opened the end of the envelope and pulled the folded papers out. He unfolded the papers, smoothing them out on the table. Arneau and Weaver leaned forward for a better view, the blue logo of CINCNELM easily discernible across the top.

Shipley picked it up and quickly read the cover letter before handing it to his XO.

"Jesus Christ!" Arneau said. "He can't be serious, can he? I don't know if we have the garb on board to go that far north."

Shipley forced a smile as he nodded. "Ours is not to reason why . . ."

". . . But ours is to do or die," Weaver finished with a heavy sigh, reaching across the table for the cover letter.

The XO pulled the letter back. "Just a moment. I haven't finished."

Shipley unfolded the attachment. He rubbed the pages apart—three pages; this seemed awfully lean for such a mission. He scanned the pages quickly. Looking up once, he saw Weaver reading the cover letter. Cover letters were nothing more than a synopsis of what the orders contained, but this cover letter was stamped in bright red "TOP SECRET," with a compartmented code word he did not recognize in smaller print after the word SECRET.

Shipley leaned back and took a sip of his coffee. Then he read the orders again, each and every word, interpreting the nuances of the sentences and the "between the lines" meanings of the orders. He took his time, trying to grasp the impact to the *Squallfish.* This was different from those of more than a decade ago.

They were not at war right now, and he did not want history to show him at the helm of starting the next one.

His mind quickly organized the mission without him even aware he was doing it—a natural habit of a leader forged in combat during the roughest of times when nearly a third of submariners never returned from their mission.

When he finished the first page, he passed it along to the XO. What would he need to meet this change of orders? Did he have the resources on board? Admiral Wright would not think kindly if Shipley pulled into port somewhere because he had failed to fully outfit the boat. Submarine skippers were expected to have their boat fitted out properly, fuel topped off, and ready to meet any contingency within their primary and secondary warfare areas. He handed the second page to Arneau, who then passed the cover letter to Weaver.

Weaver's eyes quickly scanned the letter. "Skipper, is this real?" Weaver asked, pushing his glasses back, off the end of his nose. "This could be dangerous."

Arneau laughed. "Dangerous? Can't imagine why you would say that."

Shipley nodded, his lips tight. He alone knew how dangerous this was, and they had yet to read this last page. "The orders are real, Alec. We are going into the mouth of the bear."

"You'd think they would have made this decision with a little more forethought in the planning," Arneau offered. "Running down to the dock as we're getting under way"—he made an underhand throwing motion—"and tossing a change of orders at us isn't what I would have expected."

Shipley lowered the last sheet. "What did you expect?" he asked without rancor.

Arneau shrugged. "I would have expected them to have briefed us with sufficient time so we could ensure we had the right things on board for a mission in the Arctic waters"—he lifted page two—"not just hand us this to read while we're two hundred feet below the surface."

"Is this the way they did it in World War II, Skipper?" Weaver asked.

Shipley shook his head. "No. During the war we had several hours' notice when our mission changed. But sometimes we received change of orders during routine comms cycles." He looked at the two men. If something happened to him, these two would shoulder the responsibility of bringing *Squallfish* and the men who rode her back to Holy Loch. "In answer to your question: they thought about it. This isn't something that was hatched overnight. They brought this down to us while we were casting off lines and getting under way for one reason: to ensure no leak ashore and to give no observers any indication that we were doing anything other than the normal Iceland–U.K. gap patrol assigned."

"Still dangerous," Arneau said.

"If we didn't like danger, then we wouldn't be submariners, XO."

"Aye, sir."

Even as Shipley said that, he continued to weigh what these orders meant to his boat. They had little to do with either the primary mission of the *Squallfish* to search out and destroy enemy forces, or its secondary mission of antisubmarine warfare. They would do it. Of that, there never was a question. Unfortunately, there were a multitude of questions on what could happen if he screwed this up.

And so the three top officers of the *Squallfish* sat quietly in the wardroom, reading and rereading the orders. After a time, Shipley pulled his small green Navy-issued notebook from his shirt pocket and began to write notes, discussing things with his XO and OPSO that they needed to do. The coffee in his cup grew cold over time, and when other officers stuck their heads into the wardroom and saw the three meeting, they quickly withdrew.

"CROCKY!" Bleecker roared when he stuck his head into the mess.

The heavyset steward's mate first class turned to face the mustang who blocked his mess. He wiped his hands on his apron. "Well, as I live and breathe, you are still alive, Lieutenant. Lost a little weight, I see."

Bleecker smiled as he stepped inside the mess. "Petty Officer Crocky, I haven't lost a pound since we first met, and you keep saying that as if any moment I'm going to cave in on myself from lack of food. We get enough in the black gang."

Crocky laughed. "My, oh, my, Lieutenant; why you engineers want to call yourself the black gang and not a black face among you is beyond me."

Bleecker laughed. "It reminds us of . . ."

". . . Of how dirty those spaces are. You ought to start eating in the wardroom, where I can at least give you some clean food."

"Food without the taint of oil and the smell of diesel fuel ain't really food for a good engineer."

"Then you must be one spectacular engineer, Lieutenant."

Bleecker noticed the young colored sailor squatting near the shelves in back, searching for something. "Thought I'd swing by and let you know that they're going to tell you to get your food out of the torpedo tubes."

"Why?" Crocky kept wiping his hands. It was normal aboard submarines to use the torpedo tubes to store some of the fresh foods such as fruit until the skipper needed the tubes. "I thought we were on a nice, normal, leisurely rump along the gap. What the ole man thinking of doin' now?"

They both smiled. "Old man?" Bleecker asked. "I think he's about half your age, old man."

"Maybe; he's definitely half yours."

"He's a year older."

"Then you musta led a spectacular life in the Philippines."

"No photographs; no proof."

The sailor to the rear stood up with a huge tin can in his hands. "I found it, Petty Officer Crocky."

"That's good, Washington. Put it on the counter and see if you can open it without ripping off a finger." He looked back at Bleecker. "Wouldn't want more meat in the pot than the recipe calls for." He lowered his voice. "Got any idea what we are doing? Rumor has it the skipper, XO, and Weaver were holed up in the wardroom all morning with the couriered mail."

Bleecker's forehead wrinkled, drawing his face as his lips pursed upward. He reached up and scratched the bald spot on the top of his head. "What mail?"

Crocky told Bleecker about the unusual event when they sailed and how Shipley tucked the slender package into the back of his pants along his spine.

"Shit, Crocky, you got more information than I do. Why don't you do what you usually do and find out?"

Crocky feigned innocence. "What you mean?"

"Take them some coffee and pastries, then read over their shoulders."

"I'd never do that, Lieutenant; wherever did you get such an idea?" Then they both laughed.

"Besides, they never tell us engineers anything until they need power or we're about to sink."

"You let me know if it's the latter."

Bleecker turned to leave.

"Thanks, Lieutenant."

"What for?"

"The early heads-up. I'll need a working party to help move the stuff."

"Yeah, right, Crocky. If you can find a working party, you let me know."

When Bleecker reached the door, he turned. "By the way, Crocky . . ."

Crocky raised his eyebrows.

"I've taken care of our problem. Let me know if my counseling fails to take. As we both know, not every lesson takes the first time."

A wide grin spread across the steward mate first class's face. "I owe you."

"I've lost count of who owes who the most. See you later." Bleecker disappeared down the passageway.

Crocky figured the mustang was heading aft, to engineering country. Bleecker and he had been aboard the *Tang* under Richard O'Kane for a couple of missions before the two of them had been detailed to different submarines. Nothing bonded like war. Seeing Bleecker here was a sign of respect. Everyone knew Bleecker seldom ventured from his assigned work compartments unless it was to check maintenance on the values and pipes that pumped water, air, and fuel around the *Squallfish*. The man had his forward and after engine rooms plus the two battery compartments, and a pump room. It was Bleecker's empire to run. Without him the submarine would never move.

"You can have yore dark and oily spaces," Crocky said to himself. He took a deep breath, enjoying the aroma of biscuits cooking. Crocky sure didn't need to use the excuse of shifting the food from the torpedo tubes to the mess to find out what was going on. He'd know by nightfall, he told himself, wiping his hands on his apron.

The chief of the boat had already told Crocky he needed to shift his supplies out of the tubes. Nope; the only reason Bleecker had swung by was to let him know that he had taken care of Potts. The problem was that people such as Potts never truly changed their colors. They only buried them deeper, until they found an opportunity when no one was looking. He let out a deep sigh. At least his boy Washington would have some peace for a while.

"You say something, Petty Officer Crocky?"

"No, I didn't, and if I did, you'd be the first to know." He looked around the mess. "Now, where did Santos and Marcos disappear to?"

"Santos said he had to go to the head. Marcos went also."

Crocky shook his head. "That Santos gotta learn how to operate the shitters before he blows himself out the hull."

"Yeah, I know."

Crocky laughed. "It only took you one time to learn how, didn't it."

Washington scowled. "Ain't funny, you know, standing there covered in your own—"

Crocky waved his hand and chuckled. "Enough said." He turned back to his cooking. "When Marcos and De La Santos return, you take them to the forward torpedo room and start moving the food out of the tubes. Skipper wants us to store it here."

Washington looked both ways. "Where we going to store it? Don't have room for what we got now."

"Shut yore whining, boy. There is always room to store something. We just gotta be judicious. Now, check those biscuits. I want the crew to have something hot and special."

"Judicious?"

"No, hot and special."

SHIPLEY climbed into the control room. He glanced up at the opening in the deck leaning into the conning tower.

"Evening, Skipper," Lieutenant Junior Grade Van Ness said. "We are steering course zero three zero, depth one-fifty, sir. Sonar has two surface contacts. Revolutions indicate merchant ships."

Shipley waited a couple of seconds. "And?"

Van Ness's eyes widened. "Contact one is on a course of two four zero, speed ten knots, range forty-five hundred yards. Contact two is heading toward Iceland on present course of zero one zero, speed ten knots, range six thousand yards."

"Opening or closing?"

"Both are opening."

Shipley detected a slight tremor in the young officer's voice.

Better a tremor while you're learning than a full-scale panic when it's too late.

"Very well, Officer of the Deck."

Van Ness grinned.

Did the officers of today have to look so young, or was he reaching the age where the term "old salt" applied to him now?

Van Ness was his navigator and administrative officer. This was Van Ness's second cruise with Shipley. Both Van Ness and his XO had arrived on the same day. He wondered for a moment if he was as nervous as Van Ness when he was a junior officer. He grinned his tight-lipped grin with a raised right lip. Yep. He probably was.

"Clifford, may I talk with you a moment?"

"Yes, sir, Skipper."

Finding where two people could have a private conversation on board a submarine was nigh impossible. In the conning tower, the sailors and the chief of the watch moved forward, giving the two officers as much privacy as a crowded conning tower would permit. Shipley never expected his words to remain private; nothing remained private in the confines of a submarine, and few secrets failed to make their rounds quicker than a shark in a feeding frenzy.

He could tell Van Ness thought he was about to get his butt chewed. He recalled the same beliefs at similar times during his first few years in the Navy.

"You're doing a good job," Shipley said quietly. "I need you to do some things."

Van Ness's face became a mask of concentration as Shipley spent the next few minutes telling the navigator to work with Weaver to map out the navigation necessary to reach the edge of their mission area. He also cautioned the officer to keep this as closely held as he could for the time being. There was always a chance that CINCNELM would change his mind and orders back to patrolling the Iceland–U.K. gap. He mentally crossed his fingers, but his experience with flag officers who made up their minds was that they had more important things to think about than changing them.

"Captain," a voice said from the opening in the deck.

Shipley turned. It was Petty Officer Baron, the radioman who worked for Lieutenant Junior Grade Olsson, the communications officer. Seeing Baron as the radioman crawled into the conning tower made him realize that Olsson seemed to be avoiding him.

He didn't think of himself as a harsh leader or captain, but maybe Van Ness and Olsson did. He would sit with them one night at dinner and see if he could get them to relax.

"What you got, Baron?"

"Captain, received this a few minutes ago from Naval Intelligence in London," he said, handing Shipley a brown guard mail envelope with signature blocks along the edges of it. "Mister Olsson asked that I find you and deliver it immediately."

"Thanks," Shipley replied as he took the envelope and initialed the cover sheet on the clipboard.

"Thank you, sir," the radioman said, turning, and hurrying to the hatch leading down. "Excuse me, sir," Baron said, standing aside as Arneau climbed into the conning tower.

Shipley unfolded the message from inside the envelope and read it. He looked up and motioned to Arneau. "Read this, XO. Looks as if we are going to pick up some riders."

TWO

Wednesday, November 14, 1956

ANTON Zegouniov stood in front of the mirror, fighting his tie. Why did Igor's tie always look so straight, smooth, and his always as if a pair of pigeons had scratched the cloth into a knot? A pair of slim hands emerged from under his arms, smooth arms following with familiar breasts pressing against his back. He dropped his hands to his sides.

His wife giggled. "You look like what your officers and sailors call you behind your back."

He smiled. "You mean 'Bear.' "

Her hands reached up to the unfinished knot.

He turned and leaned forward, his eyes squinting slightly. "I don't think I look like a bear," he said, straightening.

"Anton, you worry too much about your appearance. You are not Igor Kuvashin—hot, dashing—"

"You think he is hot and dashing?" he said, feeling the heat rise into his cheeks.

Elena Zegouniova laughed. "He does have a destroyer." She laughed and slapped him lightly on the chest. "You are too jealous. Don't you think we women know what he is after?"

He straightened. "He hasn't . . ." He left the question unfinished.

"Igor has been the consummate gentleman with me. Why wouldn't he be? Because I am Madame Elena Zegouniova, wife of the new captain first rank, commanding officer of the ship *Whale*."

"Woman," he said with a laugh, "it is a submarine. A boat, not a ship. And yes, it is called *Whale*, but its real name is *Prototype 10 of Project 627*, or *K-2*, as most refer to it."

"Wow," she responded, her hands pushing the knot up against his neck.

"Don't strangle me."

Elena responded, "Today I am going to stand around with the other officers' wives—one of whom is an admiral's wife—and tell them you are the commanding officer of *Prototype 10 of . . . of . . . of* whatever? I can't even remember it now." She pulled her hands away.

He heard the pout in her voice, felt the way her lips pursed when she grew slightly agitated at his seriousness. She was right. He was too serious, but in today's Soviet Navy, being too light-hearted drew too much attention, and he had yet to sit down with his political commissar to discuss the party direction for his new command.

"And yes, you do remind people of a bear. Look at the chin; look at the hair."

He looked at his reflection in the mirror. "There is nothing wrong with my hair."

She laughed, her hand covering her mouth for a moment.

Anton smiled. Seventeen years of marriage, and he loved her more each day. Her eyes bubbled with radiance when she was happy. Of course, he had yet to convince her that her duties did not extend to promoting his career. He had given up. Elena was the consummate military wife, considering whose wife was more important than another and which wife she must always be nice to because "that wife" had a husband who could jeopardize Anton's career.

He nodded once. "You are right. I am a captain first rank in the world's most powerful Navy." Then he thought of the American Navy.

"Your hair is everywhere. Why don't you cut it shorter, like Admiral—"

"Admiral Katshora? You must be kidding, woman. His hair is everywhere, and the last time he had short hair was when he was born."

"So the hero of the Great Patriotic War has long, gray hair. Yours is shaggy and projects like wings from the sides when you forget to cut it. Wives notice these things, and we discuss."

"Then next time I will ask his wife for advice on what to do with my hair."

She turned him around and jerked the tie tighter. "See! That's what a wife is for." She leaned forward until her chin touched his chest.

"You nearly choked me."

"And if you say anything to his wife, I will, my bear."

He grabbed her in a hug, bussing her face with a series of kisses as she giggled. "That is what a wife is for."

She pushed away playfully. "You are such a bear, Anton." She reached over to the nearby vanity and pulled the Navy hat off it. She ran her hands lightly over the embroidered gold on the edge of the visor. "This feels so nice, my love," she said, smiling up at him. "The children and I are so proud of you. Your own ship—"

"Boat," he corrected. "Ships go above the water, and by now—"

She covered her mouth as she laughed, her dark black hair shaking with her amusement.

"Ah, Dorogojj," he said, slapping her on the butt. "After this many years of being married to a submariner, you know what we call them."

"But now you are a captain first rank. Now you have your own boat," she said with a slight twinkle in her eye as she emphasized "boat," puffing the word out. "I intend to ensure that every wife at today's luncheon knows what my husband is and how he was picked by the party from the ranks to head this *Whale*."

"And what would this accomplish?"

"This will make them envious and they will be forced to be nice to the new wife within their midst." She clapped once. "Isn't this fun?"

Anton leaned down and kissed her. "Sounds very dangerous to me. What if you upset a wife of someone senior to me?"

"Then she will go home and tell her husband, who will dismiss her as a gossiping old bag, but he will know your name. And he will know that you have a wife worth watching."

"I think you and I will enjoy Siberia."

Her smile disappeared. "That is not something to joke about, Anton. Too many—"

He put his finger to his lips.

She stopped talking and looked around their bedroom. Then, as if the topic had never surfaced, she continued, "You are destined to be an admiral. Right? Don't they pick men for this type of job—a most secret job—because they have great plans for him?"

He turned back to the mirror and adjusted the cap so the visor was square with the nose. The key to a sharp uniform was having the pants zipper, the belt buckle, the shirt line, and the cap aligned together. It made for a sharper image. Of course, his tie knot was perfect now, thanks to his ambitious wife, but the shirt still looked wrinkled. It mattered little how much effort Elena put into the laundry; as soon as it was put onto his body, the effort fell apart. His broad shoulders pulled the press from the ironed fabric.

"You must never discuss my job or refer to it as a secret job, Elena. What I do, I do for the good of our nation; for the party," he scolded lightly. Then he leaned down to her ear. "Others will talk and they will think you know more than you should. Then they would want to talk with us as they talked with Maks and Gennadiy."

She stepped back slightly. He ignored the fright he gave her. But fright was better than being visited by the Committee for State Security—the KGB. Fright was better than discovering too late. He had no idea whatever happened to Maks and Gennadiy. Rumor had it they were in Siberia, but rumors were whispered in such a manner that they were not to be considered true, even if so. He took a deep breath. Luckily for him, he thought, Elena and Gennadiy had little contact—both considered their husbands competitors for promotion.

"But let's not worry about them. That was long ago, and I am sure whatever happened, they deserved it. The state does not make mistakes."

She smiled and stepped back toward him. "The state has made the right choice with your promotion, Bear. They know a loyal member of the party when they see him." She shivered.

They smiled at the farce they played even in the privacy of their home—a Navy home near a secret Navy base on the other side of Kola Bay from Severmorsk where the larger Northern Fleet Headquarters was located.

"You are cold," he said.

"We are now north of the Arctic Circle. It is hard not to be cold," she said, her lips pursing.

He laughed. "Ah, Elena; you do act as if you are such a weak, innocent Soviet woman. I pity anyone who crosses you."

She smiled. "And I hope you never forget it." She leaned forward and hugged him. Stepping back, her hands stroked the shoulder boards. "My captain first rank," she said with a sigh. "I cannot tell you how hard I worked for this promotion."

"Oh," he exclaimed. "And I suppose you think I had little to do with it."

She stepped back.

There was that twinkle in her eye. He loved the twinkle. He loved the slender neck that after this many years and through the war with the Nazis never grew a line or a mark. Men's eyes turned when her narrow waist swung that gorgeous butt when she walked. He sighed.

"What are you thinking, my husband?"

"I am thinking the cold weather will require you to hide your body beneath layers and layers of wool and cotton to keep it from freezing so hard you would be unable to walk. With so many layers you would waddle instead of walk."

The smile left her face, and her blue eyes widened. "What a horrid thing to say. Stop thinking like that. Let's change the subject. When will you make admiral?" she asked, wrapping her arms around him. "I do so want you to make admiral."

"I just made captain first rank, Dorogojj. The party will determine if I can serve it at a higher, or even lower rank."

"Never a lower rank. You are so loyal. We have sacrificed so much for the party and for the Soviet Union. They will recognize your dedication and professional zeal—"

He interrupted, "You talk like . . ." He couldn't think of a good word to finish the sentence.

"See," she said, "even you know you will be an admiral one day."

"Why? So you can show up those wives who rub your nose in the success of their husbands?" he asked with a chuckle.

"Of course," she answered petulantly. "Wives enjoy the ranks of their husbands as much as their husbands do. Now that you are a captain first rank, I can sit in the front row."

He frowned. "Let's hope no one hears my beautiful wife talking about class status." He bent down, his eyes flickering from side to side as if searching for something. "Someone might hear."

Her smile disappeared. "I told you—don't joke about that," she said.

He nodded, his smile disappearing also. "You are right. It is a bad joke." Then in a louder voice, Anton added, "Whatever is good for the party is what I will do. Our people sacrificed so much in the war, and now we must sacrifice for the good of our people."

She turned, her nightgown whirling seductively as she walked away. She looked back over her shoulder. "What time do you have to be on the boat?"

He looked at the small Soviet-manufactured clock on the side table of the bed. It showed four o'clock.

"Did you wind the clock last night?"

"Yes, I wound the clock. It only works for a few hours, so I find myself spending all day winding the clock. Nothing works—"

He looked at his wristwatch and interrupted, "It's ten to seven."

As if hearing him, a car horn beeped from the road in front of the house. "My driver is here." He grabbed the heavy wool bridge coat off the chair and slid the coat on quickly.

"Why doesn't he come to the door and knock? Shouldn't a captain first rank deserve a knock instead of a beep?"

He smiled. "We are all equal in the Soviet Union."

"I don't want an equal husband in the Navy; I want to be an admiral's wife. Make him wait."

"He might drive off without me."

"He would never!" she said with a trace of shock. "Never drive away and leave a captain first rank stranded at home."

He walked toward the door. "Come here and kiss me away, Dorogojj." Most likely the driver was KGB, but his wife knew this as well as he did. Those most likely to disappear into the background of life as drivers, sweepers, trash collectors; all of them could be members of the Committee for State Security. The fact never bothered him, for there were people within the Soviet Union who would die to destroy the socialist life being developed for all. If you were innocent, then you had nothing to worry about. As his father always told him, you can never make an omelet without breaking a few eggs.

She walked to him; her eyes locked with his, and then she stood on tiptoes when he bent down to buss him on the cheek. "I would kiss you on the lips, but this close to the door, they would freeze together."

"Then I would have a hell of a time explaining to the admiral why I have my wife attached to my lips this morning."

She stepped back and put her hands on her hips. "You didn't tell me you were going to see the admiral this morning."

"There are many things in the Navy we don't tell our wives because they ask too many questions and sometimes they talk too much."

He grabbed her and kissed her on the lips. "There! We were lucky this time. We did not freeze together."

ANTON took in the Kola Bay morning as the driver weaved around potholes, a near-constantly blowing of the horn at everything and everybody as he sped along the narrow road leading toward the other end of the sealed base. The car took a sharp right turn in the road, nearly throwing Anton into the middle of the backseat. The turn brought the ribbons of dense smoke rising from the hidden dark, gray factories of the city of Murmansk into view. Sludge from the mining operations ran into Kola Bay, on the eastern side of the city. Murmansk was around the far bend to his right; Kola Bay separated the man-made city from the research and development facility where he was to work.

He wondered for a moment what weapons he would be testing on the *K-2* project. Elena would be shocked to discover that he had no idea what he was to be doing, much less the name number of his boat.

"The smoke of the workers," the driver said with a nod from beneath his woolen black hat.

"Yes," Anton answered. "They are being very productive." The man was obviously not a sailor. He had expected a Navy person to be his driver. As he studied the man's face, the driver reached up and scratched his rough-shaven cheek. Fingers stuck through missing fingers of a glove, probably cut away to make driving easy but keep the hand warm at the same time. The fingers were clean and gave an impression of being soft—not the fingers of a man used to hard work.

"You know, comrade, that Murmansk is the largest inhabited city north of the Arctic Circle."

Anton acknowledged the comment. Murmansk was new by Soviet standards. The party created it in 1927 along the ice-free Kola Bay. The unfrozen body of water ran northeast nearly fifty-five kilometers to the Barents Sea. Murmansk was the manufacturing, mining, and fishing industry might of the North. The smoke poured from the stacks of hundreds of plants sitting side by side near the shores, disrupting the clear Arctic morning that settled over the perpetually frozen city. Kola Bay, at one time, must have been a natural paradise, disrupted only by the occasional hunter, sparse fishermen, and the cries of wolves. He would have loved to have seen it.

"The party has done so much for this region. Until Murmansk, there was only Severomorsk and the Northern Fleet. Now we have industry; people have food; and all thanks to the foresight of the party."

"Comrade, you are so right," Anton added. "Are you from Murmansk?"

"*Da*, comrade. But I was born in Leningrad. My parents moved here before the Great Patriotic War. They helped to raise the city from the frozen soil and tundra to what it is today."

"Then you should be proud."

"I am proud my parents and family have been permitted to be part of this great success."

Anton looked out the window, feeling the eyes of the driver on him. The KGB must be hurting for eyes, he thought, to have someone so obvious on their payroll.

The bay sped past as the ZIM bumped along the half-paved road. They paralleled the shore, only yards away. The water lapped against the rocks pushed by the sea against the coast, rocks that looked as if a giant hand had casually tossed them along the edges of the inland sea. The Northern Fleet had located to Kola Bay because it never froze over. The warmer fresh waters of the rivers running into it brought heat to the Arctic waters shoved south into the bay. Even during the coldest of Arctic days, the Kola waters remained ice-free. Ships could steam into the bay to conduct exercises, check repairs, and train their crews. Submarines could submerge and practice their own tactics. Antisubmarine warfare was an art that could be practiced within Kola Bay and out of range of the prying eyes of the United States.

"Have you visited Murmansk, comrade?"

"Yes," Anton replied. He opened his mouth to say more, then decided against it. His wife had enjoyed the visit, but he knew the avenues of Murmansk paled against what she had in Moscow.

How long until Elena decided she did not like the social life here and started to complain about the missed beauty of Moscow? Every social event worried him about her butterfly antics from person to person; her transparent ambition for his career—all dangerous professions if you offended the wrong person. On the plus side, the men gravitated toward her. She had a way with her eyes that promised much. His eyes widened. He didn't think she had . . . He shook his head. Elena would never go that far.

Elena had enjoyed Murmansk, but he wondered if she enjoyed it because the people deferred to her as she shopped in the sparse government shops, or if she really enjoyed the adventure offered by the Arctic. He smiled. "Adventure" was a new term for Elena. Her idea of adventure was sneaking Western sheets onto the bed. The smile left. No doubt the KGB knew of her shopping adventures and it would matter if he should ever fall out of favor, which was easy to do in Chairman Khrushchev's government, where no one really knew whether they were in favor or not until they disappeared or were promoted. He smiled again. He had been promoted, ergo, he was in favor.

The waters of Kola Bay simmered a dark blue in the rising sun. Around the bay, steep mountain terrain rose sharply, much like the fjords of Norway, where he had spent time in a Soviet submarine during the war with Germany. Where he ate packaged food stamped "USA." Of course, no one would mention the arms, food, and other war supplies provided by the West. He saw Western war surplus often, with the source of the articles painted over with the "CCCP" of the Soviet Union. A national farce done for the good of the nation and the party. Anton saw nothing wrong with this propaganda. What was good for the people was good for the Soviet Union, and it was up to those such as himself and other members of the party to ensure a sense of unity across this great land. He felt pride over the size of the Soviet Union. It was the largest nation in the world, stretching through thirteen time zones, from the Pacific Ocean to halfway into Europe. No other nation had the resources of the Soviet Union or the patriotic tenacity of its people. They would overcome, and they would be the example of what this world called Earth could become.

"You smile, comrade?"

"Yes, I do. I was thinking of how happy I am to be allowed to have this opportunity to support our party and our country."

The driver laughed. "I go to bed at night and rise in the morning thinking the same thing."

"What is your name, driver?"

The man shrugged. Then, almost hesitantly, he replied, "My name is Viktor Popov, not that it matters."

"You are Navy?"

Popov shrugged again. "I used to be, during the war, comrade, I was in the Baltic Fleet, but after the war I returned to Murmansk and met this young woman who enticed me with a twist of my arm into the civilian way of life. Now I drive a limousine for senior officers such as yourself or for party officials who visit here."

The car twisted around the next bend, bringing the ZIM nearer a protruding lip of the bay. Then the car picked up speed as it headed north, the right wheels riding the edge of the road that separated Anton from the cold waters below.

"So, are you assigned to me permanently?"

Popov shrugged, an audible sigh reaching Anton's ears. "Of course, comrade. I am assigned to you until you ask for someone else. Then they will reassign me to another car and another person. This is what makes our country so great: everyone is equal, but they have little choice of their driver."

Maybe he wasn't KGB, thought Anton, ignoring the last comment.

Ahead of them, the silhouette of Severomorsk rose like a dark stain across the bay. While Murmansk was the largest inhabited city within the Arctic Circle, there at Severomorsk was where he wished his boat were moored among the cruisers, destroyers, and auxiliary ships that made up a massive, oceangoing capability. A fleet that could sortie out when the Barents Sea permitted, meet anything the Americans might throw at them, and win.

"We are nearly there, Captain," the driver said.

Anton was surprised. Until then, the driver had only referred to him as "comrade."

His stomach rose as the ZIM topped a slight rise and then seemed to fall as it bounced down a steep portion of the road. Shoreline filled the front windshield as the car swept along, speed increasing, and no sign that the driver intended to use the brakes to slow down.

"We'll have problems making it up this tonight, Captain. The mud will be frozen ice. The roads are terrible on automobiles," the driver offered.

Anton fell against the right door as the driver jerked the car to the left, avoiding another pothole, and decorating the maneuver with severe words best never uttered in mixed company. To curse was admirable in the Navy, but to curse with poetry was a compliment to the originator. He had even applauded the chief engineer of his last boat for skill and art in cursing that could reduce the recipient to wordless appreciation.

They bounced as the ZIM hit the bottom of the hill and leveled out. Ahead of them a wire fence appeared. Razor wire curled along the top, giving Anton the impression of a prison instead of a base. He wondered where the razor wire came from. Along the fence every fifty or so meters a small guard box rose. Some stood straight, but most tilted to the right or the left.

As if reading Anton's mind, the driver spoke. "It's the permafrost. Permafrost is never permanent, and it melts just enough to cause the shacks to tilt to the right or to the left."

The driver turned and looked at Anton, never taking his hands off the wheel and never slowing down. It seemed to Anton that the ZIM put on a few more kilometers in speed.

"The fence surrounds the facility, Captain," the driver offered before turning his attention back to the front. "Where the fence rises, many of the shacks have already fallen back against the fence. I heard a few months back that one soldier was in a shack when it decided to come downhill, rolling through the fence, where it came to rest near one of the outbuildings, trapping the young man for hours."

"Seems to be a great challenge."

"Not as great as for that soldier. He was found guilty of deserting his post."

Anton ignored the comment. To acknowledge something wrong meant risking . . .

"Of course, how can one desert his post when he took his post with him?" The driver laughed at his own humor.

"I am sure the incident was investigated fairly."

"Of course, Captain," the driver said, his laugh stopping instantly. Then he added, "You will need your papers, Captain."

Minutes later they were through the rigorous papers check and easing to a stop in front of the main facility.

"You are here, Captain," the driver said, glancing at Anton through the rearview mirror.

He had seen buildings such as this one. It was a massive covered dock, with the front part of the building jutting into a manmade channel leading into the waters of the bay.

He opened the door and stepped out.

The driver rolled his window down. "What time should I pick you up, comrade?"

Anton's eyes traveled the massive building. Within that building was the *K-2*. But the Navy called the submarine *Whale*. It must be there where he would find his command.

"Captain?"

"Oh, sorry. I'm not sure when I will be finished today."

"I will be here at seventeen hundred hours in the event you are ready by then, Captain. If not, I will track you down for an update."

"Thanks. That will be fine."

"Comrade, if we are here past nineteen hundred hours we will be here all night, for the hill will be a sheet of ice." Without waiting for Anton to reply, the driver rolled up the window and drove off.

He turned his back. A splatter of cold mud from the left rear tire hit his bridge coat. He glanced down and swept it away with his hand, leaving a smidgen of Arctic along the base of his hand and a smudge of brown against the black wool of the coat.

He took in the surroundings. Bleak and gray seemed to be a proper description for everything. Murmansk was bleak and gray. Severomorsk was bleak and gray. The sky, the land, the hills were bleak and gray. The only thing not bleak and gray was the freezing blue water of Kola Bay. It was a crystal clear body of water, with the exception of the mining sludge flowing into the bay east of Murmansk.

He looked along the building, finally spotting an entrance. A set of double doors the same color as the facility blended into the building off to his right. There had been no one to meet him. His face scrunched in slight apprehension.

Admiral Baikov, the head of the Soviet Navy classified R&D section, had told him how important his new job was when the elderly war veteran had promoted him to captain first rank. Anton climbed the wooden steps leading up to the building edge and then went along the narrow walkway toward the doors. If he were so important, then why would they not at least meet him? Admiral Katshora had seemed impressed at the social function the other day. Anton had no idea.

A couple of approaching sailors saluted and stepped into the mud to allow him to pass. Elena was right: being a captain first rank did have its privileges in a nation without privileges.

He reached the door, pulled on the handle, and was surprised to see it opened effortlessly. For a secret facility, entry seemed too easy. The noise of typewriters and several conversations filled the air, coming from open doors along the hallway ahead of him. He pulled the door shut.

From the end of the hallway, a chief petty officer looked up from his morning *Pravda*. The chief frowned, folded the newspaper, and walked toward him. Almost too lean, thought Anton as he watched the sailor walk toward him. The man looked down for a moment, and Anton noticed a couple of bare spots on top of the man's head in the middle of the short-cropped haircut.

"Comrade, do you have papers?"

Anton smiled. Elena would be furious at the lack of deference to the shoulder boards of a captain first rank. She would never understand that communism only confirmed to chiefs that they were equal to any officer. Without speaking, he reached inside his wool bridge coat and pulled out his national identity card along with his orders, handing them to the chief.

The chief glanced at them for a few seconds, a couple of grunts escaping. After a few more seconds of turning the card one way, then the other, almost as if the man were unable to read, the older sailor grinned, revealing a row of missing teeth along the left side. Deep yellow stains on the remaining ones revealed long years of cigarette use. He handed the papers back to Anton.

"My apologies, Captain. Here, at the Soviet Navy's premier research and development facility—unlike across the bay—we take security seriously." He shrugged. "Besides, we were told to expect you tomorrow."

"Tomorrow?"

"Tomorrow." He shrugged again. "Anyway, comrade, welcome aboard." The chief stood straight, looking up a few inches until their eyes met. "I am Chief Petty Officer Ekomov, the lead electrician technician in the engineering department of the *Whale*."

"So, they do call it the *Whale*?"

Ekomov shrugged, his lower lip sticking out. Holding his hand up and wiggling it, he said, "I call it the *Whale*; the crew calls it the Whale." Then he jerked his thumb over his shoulders. "But the scientists and those who refuse to see their handiwork at sea prefer the term '*K-2* prototype'—Ekomov waved his skinny arm in the air—"something or other." Looking away, he smiled. "Who knows what these landlubbers think when they fuck around with our boats?"

He could like this man, Anton thought, if the political officer liked him.

"Been here long, Chief?"

"Too long, sir."

"And the crew?"

"We have replacements almost monthly."

"Monthly? Seems excessive."

Ekomov turned and started back toward his chair. "Best you talk to Doctor Zotkin. He has his own opinion as to why so many of us get sick." He picked up his newspaper, opened it, and put his feet on the table.

"Doctor Vasiliy Zotkin?"

Ekomov lowered the paper. He nodded several times, his lips pushed out, raising his sparse mustache against his nose. "Not many Zotkins around here, Captain. You will grow to love Doctor Zotkin, as we all do," Ekomov replied with a hint of sarcasm. He raised his newspaper again, covering his face.

Anton nodded as he stuffed the papers back into the pocket of his bridge coat and followed. "Chief, would you take me to Admiral Katshora's office so I may check in," Anton ordered. If the chief was part of his crew, it was time to establish who was the captain and who was the chief.

Ekomov dropped the paper. He leaned across the table, his hands clasped on top of the *Pravda*. Several mustache hairs fell out, coming to rest on the chief's chin. Ekomov scratched the side of his face for a moment, his forehead wrinkling. "Comrade, I'd like to take you to his office, but the admiral's office is at Headquarters in Severomorsk"—he pointed back toward the entrance—"across the bay. He is seldom here. He is to be here tomorrow to meet you."

"Well, then take me to my boat."

Ekomov nodded. "I can do that, sir, but Doctor Zotkin would be angry at me—with you"—he pointed up—"with God." He shrugged. "He is always angry with someone about something. The good thing is he never remembers about what."

Anton's forehead wrinkled. In today's Navy, the man was destined for reeducation in Siberia, and then he realized Siberia would be little different from the weather here around Kola Bay.

Ekomov put both hands on the side of the desk, then looked at

Anton. "First you have to be cleared by Doctor Zotkin. The good doctor does not like anyone going aboard the *Whale* without his personal approval." Ekomov shook his head. "No, sir; without his approval, you may be shot before you even take command."

Ekomov pointed toward the door to the left. "Doctor Zotkin's office is down that hallway, third door on the left." Ekomov raised his feet again, plunked them on top of the desk, and then crossed them at the ankles. The newspaper once again covered the electrician's face.

At least the man had shined shoes. Morale was always a problem with a new skipper. If the chief was an example of the level of morale he faced, then his work was going to be a challenge. Without speaking, Anton opened the wooden door. Behind him, Ekomov peeked from around the newspaper for several seconds before once again burying his head into the *Pravda*.

Anton stepped into the hallway; behind him he heard the chief mumbling complaints about something he was reading.

At the third door, he reached for the knob, but before he could open it, the door was jerked open. Before Anton could move, the man exiting bumped into him, knocking both of them backward.

"Who are you?" the man shouted, stepping back a couple of feet and brushing imaginary dust from his white smock.

Anton snapped to attention. "Sir, I am Captain Anton Zegouniov, reporting for duty."

A tight smile crossed the man's face. A stock of white hair cascaded along the sides, covering the top of the ears. "Captain, you are a day early. Did you not get the word?"

"What word, sir?"

"The word that you were to report tomorrow. Tomorrow—when Admiral Katshora would be here. Tomorrow is when we scheduled our indoctrination and project status brief."

"Sir, may I assume you are Doctor Vasiliy Zotkin?"

The man's eyes widened and the smile disappeared. "Assume? Of course you may assume I am Doctor Vasiliy Zotkin, because I am Doctor Vasiliy Zotkin." He stepped forward. "Now if you will excuse me, I have a place that I need to be."

Anton stepped aside, watching Zotkin march off down the long hallway. The unshielded single bulbs barely provided enough light to chase away the shadows of the interior.

Zotkin turned. "Well, are you going to stand there, Captain, or are you going to come with me? I can't leave you here to your own devices. You sailors are too curious for your own good." His hand motioned rapidly for Anton to hurry.

Anton walked quickly to catch up with the scientist. He found himself nearly running as the two men silently walked along the hallway. Such a long one, he thought.

"If you are wondering about the length of the hallway, it is because on that side of the wall—or bulkhead, if you insist like that grouch of a chief you have on your boat or ship or whatever you want to call it—is your submarine."

Anton looked at the bulkhead as they continued walking.

"May God save us," Zotkin said. "You can't see it, you know. We haven't invented transparent walls in the Soviet Union." A moment later Zotkin muttered, "Yet."

"Will I get to see it?"

"See the *K-2*?"

Anton nodded, glancing over at the scientist.

Zotkin's eyes widened and his lips pursed, as if trying to comprehend what Anton had asked. Several steps later, Zotkin waved him away and kept walking. Finally the hallway turned a ninety-degree angle to the right, and the men started down it. Halfway down, two of the bulbs were burned out, forcing the men to walk in darkness for nearly fifty meters.

"In answer to your question, Captain, no. I don't think you will get to see your boat today. Then again, maybe you will. It's not on the schedule, and my schedule is full today. Having you along is only going to make my schedule harder to keep. I don't see any time available today for me to show you the boat."

They reached the far end, turned right, and started down a hallway parallel to the long one they first entered.

"I am qualified in submarines, Doctor Zotkin. I am sure I will be all right finding my way around it."

The man stopped so abruptly, Anton took two more steps before he stopped also.

"Listen to me, young man: no one goes aboard the *K-2* until I have personally cleared him." Zotkin started walking again.

"Doctor, I am afraid I don't understand."

"You don't understand anything, Captain. It is not your fault, but the work we do here is for the good of the Soviet Union and the party. It is a step toward building the most powerful Navy in the world—to show the world what people working together for a more morally superior purpose can achieve."

"But—"

"Did you know that Chairman Khrushchev himself gave me leadership of this project?"

Before Anton could answer, Zotkin continued, "But, of course, you would not. You sailors are the best the party has to offer, but you have little concept of what we in the party do for our country and our people."

Zotkin stopped, his forehead wrinkling. He looked ahead, glanced back the way they came, looked ahead again, then glared at Anton. "Captain, I only have so many hours in the day, and you are slowing me up." He pointed back down the hallway. "We were supposed to go up those stairs back there."

What stairs? Anton thought. He didn't recall seeing any stairs during their forced march through the hallways encircling what he believed to be a covered dock for the submarine.

Zotkin made a throat noise, then started back along the way they had come, his pace quickening. Anton was nearly running with the shorter man. Sweat was forming beneath the heavy bridge coat.

Suddenly Zotkin cut across the bow, snatched open a door, and disappeared through it. Anton hurried after the man, catching a glimpse of the white smock, as Zotkin seemed to flow up the zigzags of stairs. Anton passed one door, then a second on the ascent. He heard the scientist's feet pitter-pattering on the steps as Zotkin hurried for whatever appointment the doctor was headed to. Several more doors passed and then suddenly Anton was at the top. Zotkin was gone. Anton tried to recall when he last heard the man climbing—the sound of boots on metal—but his own breathing was rapid from the exertion.

Anton stood for a moment. He lifted his hat from his head, pulled a handkerchief from his pocket, and wiped the sweat away. Maybe this mad doctor intended to lose him in the maze of the covered dock. He doubted Zotkin even knew he was missing. There were moments in their minutes together when Anton felt the doctor had forgotten he was walking alongside him as they made a mad dash around the dock.

The door burst open. Zotkin stuck his head inside the stairwell. "Are you coming or not, Captain?" Then the door shut.

Anton tucked the hat under his arm and hurried after the man, the door slamming behind him.

Zotkin was to his right and walking quickly away.

As Anton hurried to catch up, Zotkin spoke, his voice loud so Anton could hear him. "You will start your education at this meeting, Captain Zegouniov. This is the morning status report. If you have questions, don't ask them. We don't have time. Tomorrow is when I have time for you, but today I can only keep you with me so you don't get into trouble."

He was a captain first rank. Captains first rank don't get into trouble.

THREE

Thursday, November 15, 1956

"COMRADE Captain Zegouniov, welcome to the ice hole of the world," Admiral Katshora said, his raspy voice filling the office. The admiral extended his hand as he walked briskly across his office to greet Anton. "I am so glad you are here, Anton." Katshora gripped Anton's hand with both of his. "And how is that lovely wife of yours? Has she reached cabin fever yet? She was a pleasure to talk to the other day, and I am sure you both are finding Murmansk a far cry from the activities in Moscow."

"We are still unpacking—"

The admiral looked across the room at the sailor standing near the coffee bar. "Miskin! Bring us our coffees!"

Anton nodded slightly and blushed at the exuberance of the commander, Northern Fleet Submarine Force. Admirals he had known were less enthusiastic over a captain first rank, much less a war hero of Katshora's renown. He was more impressed than the admiral could ever be. He was standing here in the presence of the man who led the sinking of the German troop transport *Wilhelm Gustloff* in the Baltic. Everyone in the Soviet Union knew the ship was evacuating their trapped soldiers from East Prussia. Now, with the war over and the West demonizing the Soviet Union, they say the *Gustloff* was carrying civilians and that the nine thousand who died were mostly children. The West said anything to make the Soviet Union look heartless.

Katshora dropped the handshake and stepped back. "Yes, yes. You are truly lucky your household goods have arrived," he mumbled as he turned away. "Anton, I think you are going to find this new job of yours a challenge, but when you finish, you will have leapfrogged the Soviet submarine force ahead of most of our adversaries."

Everything Anton had heard of the gentleman appeared true. His great stock of gray hair seemed as much in disarray as Doctor Zotkin's, though the admiral stood ramrod straight, not leaning into the wind, as Zotkin always appeared.

Zotkin moved as if perpetually lost, tacking at a fast pace from one side of the passageway to the other, as if seeking assurance he had missed no exits. Yesterday the good doctor had bumped into Anton so many times that eventually Anton walked a couple of steps behind him to give the man room for his maneuvering.

Katshora turned around and surprised Anton by gripping his hand again. He held Anton's hand with both of his. Katshora was a couple of inches taller than Anton. Katshora's eyes narrowed as they locked with Anton's. "You are going to do well, Anton. I know it. I can tell by looking a person in his eyes whether he has the right cut for any job where he is assigned. Matters little if it is bringing us coffee as Miskin, or looking into the eyes of someone personally chosen by Admiral Gorshkov to lead the submarine force into the future."

Katshora dropped his hand. "There," he said with a smile. "I have embarrassed you. Even that red flowing up through your face tells me that you are a humble sailor at heart and unused to the flattery that I find comes more often as you ascend the ladder of rank. You know, of course, that as you go up the ladder of rank, the more your butt is exposed," Katshora said as he moved away to the larger chair sitting at the end of the coffee table. He motioned for Anton to sit down.

"This is more a greeting from me to welcome you aboard than to give you any instructions or orders for how you are to carry them out. That you were specially chosen for this important project and approved by Admiral Gorshkov himself for it is sufficient to convince me and the others within the force that you are more than capable for executing it."

"Thank you, Admiral," Anton replied. The back shirttail of the admiral's white dress shirt was half in his pants; the right side hung partially out. The admiral's belt had missed the loop at the very back of the dark trousers. But then, the admiral was a massive man, and it might be impossible for his hands to reach the loop. That realization meant the admiral seldom if ever went out on his submarines.

"Here, sit down, Captain." Katshora pointed to a couch. The admiral turned, facing Anton, looked down, and put both hands on the arms of the cushioned chair. He then eased himself onto the cushions, dropping the last couple of inches. He grinned at Anton. "Old bones make for shaky moments when one reaches the twilight years of being a sailor, don't you think, Captain?" He then motioned downward and laughed. "Sit, sit."

Anton sat down.

"Of course you don't. Look at you—young, new epaulets on your coat, and a young wife to keep you warm at night." Katshora leaned forward. "Don't ever pass up an opportunity to enjoy life, Captain—or you wake up one morning and discover it has passed you by."

Katshora looked past Anton, who turned in the direction of the admiral's gaze. He was looking at the sailor named Miskin, who was taking his time preparing their coffee, but then this was the Soviet Union, where everyone was equal; some, such as Katshora, were just more equal than others. Miskin turned toward them.

"Admiral Gorshkov is a great choice by Chairman Khrushchev, don't you think?" Admiral Katshora asked with a sharp nod, bringing Anton's attention back to them.

Anton turned to find Katshora staring at him. The thick, gray, bushy eyebrows of the veteran submariner of the Great Patriotic War projected over the deep-set brown eyes of the commander of the Northern Fleet Submarine Force.

"Sir, I am honored to have been selected and hope that I meet the expectations of Admiral Gorshkov and of you."

Katshora laughed, the booming guffaw filling the office space. "Ah, Captain, everyone hopes they meet the expectations of the party and of their leaders. I don't think anyone goes out their front door in the morning hoping they fail them."

Anton felt the blush that had been fading, returning. What he really wanted to know was what had happened to the officer he was replacing. He nearly asked, but then thought it might be misunderstood.

Katshora made a downward motion with his hand as his laugh abruptly stopped. "My apologies, Captain. Sometimes I see the irony and the humor in what we do." He waved his hand in a circular motion. "Here, in the Arctic, one must find their fun where they can." Then in a serious tone he continued, "There is no doubt in my mind nor in that of Admiral Gorshkov over what you will accomplish here. We—the Soviet Union; your bosses"—Katshora laughed—"and the Soviet Navy know you will succeed."

"Thank you for your confidence, Admiral," Anton said, glad his voice did not shake.

"I met with Admiral Gorshkov when this project began. When we were able to have the rubles earmarked for this project, he assured they would not be redistributed when he relieved Admiral Kuznetsov."

Gorshkov was still new to the Office of Commander of the Soviet Navy. His was the recent appointment by Chairman Khrushchev to replace Admiral Kuznetsov, who had led the Soviet Navy through the Great Patriotic War.

"Admiral Kuznetsov was a great man."

"*Is*," Katshora corrected. "Admiral Kuznetsov *is* a great man."

"I meant—"

"Not to worry, Captain Zegouniov. Someday when you leave the Navy, even if you continue to come to the officers' club, you will become past tense. They will say, 'Captain First Rank Zegouniov was a great captain. He led the Soviet Navy into the twentieth century,' and you will be sitting there hearing them talk of you in the past tense."

"Yes, sir."

"But you are right. Admiral Kuznetsov may never receive the praise he richly deserves as the father of our modern Navy. But with Admiral Gorshkov continuing in the same direction, I have no doubt we will reach and pass the Americans, who have used the Great Patriotic War to put their imprint in every sea across the globe." Katshora waved his hand in a circle. "Yes, we will."

Anton agreed.

Katshora looked at Anton, his eyebrows arching into a "V." "You know I served with Admiral Kuznetsov?"

"No, sir, I did not."

It had been Kuznetsov who had convinced the Kremlin that the Navy was more than a coastal force. It was Admiral Kuznetsov whose vision of a Navy with global dominance had tapped the ambition of the party leaders. It had been Kuznetsov who had paved the way for the cruisers and submarines continuing to come out of the Soviet yards every year.

Anton's thoughts turned to the fact that Kuznetsov was an example of how success does not ensure job security. Success never fails to raise the ire of those around you when they see you as a threat to their own power, or their envy grows so strong that they are willing to sacrifice anything to stop you.

Kuznetsov's power, prestige, and dominance of the military had caused the admiral to oppose the party when Khrushchev denounced Stalin earlier this year. Failing to fall in line with the party risked a one-way trip to Siberia. But Kuznetsov was so powerful he was able to retire with full military honors. Of course, no one really knew where he retired to, so it may have been Siberia.

Anton realized Katshora had quit speaking. "Admiral Gorshkov is a great thinker and intellectual," Anton replied quickly. He hoped the answer fit whatever the admiral had said.

Katshora nodded, his head turning at the approaching sailor. "My apologies if I am boring you, Captain."

"No, sir," Anton protested. Daydreaming when an admiral was talking to you was not a good way to start his tour of duty.

Katshora smiled, a twinkle in his eye as if relishing Anton's discomfort.

"Here. Finally Miskin has brought us our coffees."

Espresso was the shot in the arm that started the day for every citizen of the Soviet Union—at least those who could afford it or had access to it.

There were burdens to bear for every citizen as the Soviet Union recovered from the Great Patriotic War. Sacrifices from the war continued as the face of the enemy changed to the growing threat of the Americans and their lackey British ally. Someday, Anton thought, the world will be a better place where everyone shared Earth's bounty; where no one kept the stranglehold on the wealth that capitalism brought with it.

"You are right, Anton. Admiral Gorshkov is the right man for this time of our Navy. He is a great thinker and intellectual. He is the type of leader who will have the tenacity of leadership needed in this epic moment of our Navy. Someone who can build upon the war-fighting expertise and spirit Kuznetsov gave our Navy"—lifting his hand, he put his fingers and thumb together and moved it to the palm of the other, as if lifting something—"and move it from the remnants of the Great Patriotic War into the modern frigates, destroyers, cruisers, and submarines that are filling our ports today."

Miskin handed a small cup of espresso to Katshora, and then turned to Anton, who lifted his from the tray.

Katshora lifted his espresso and cradled it in his hands. The cup shook slightly. "I am so honored to play a small part in this resurgence of our motherland."

"Miskin, that will be all," the admiral said.

Anton lifted his cup, but then saw that Katshora was resting his on the arm of the chair, so Anton held his between his hands, enjoying the heat against his cold palms.

"Admiral Kuznetsov did a lot for our country and our party while he was admiral of the fleet, but in every destiny there is a time for change. Serving with Nikolai Kuznetsov was an honor."

Anton shook his head. "Yes, sir."

"Nikolai and I fought together in the Great Patriotic War, and we worked together in our younger junior officer days." Katshora looked at his cup as he spoke. "Nikolai Kuznetsov is a hero of the Soviet Union. You know his story?"

Then, without waiting for Anton to speak, Katshora grunted. "Of course you do. Every officer in the Soviet Navy, every comrade of our great nation knows the story of Admiral of the Fleet of the Soviet Union Nikolai Kuznetsov. The story of how he fell in with a bunch of sailors marching along the countryside during the revolution. How he never returned home. How he earned his command of the sea in the Black Sea Flotilla." Katshora's voice seemed to quaver for a moment. The admiral lifted his cup and drained the thick, hot espresso.

Anton followed suit, lifting the cup and throwing the espresso into his mouth, splashing across his tongue. The aroma of the strong drink lifted along the back of his throat as the sharp smell filled his nostrils and the strong taste assaulted his tongue. He wondered if it were the great sensations of aroma and taste rather than the trip of the espresso to his stomach that made the morning ceremony.

"Admiral Sergei Gorshkov is a thinker—methodical, looking to the future, preparing us for world leadership on the seas," Katshora said, tapping his finger against his head. "Kuznetsov pointed us on the way. He lined up the Kremlin and the party to build a great Navy, and now the chairman in his wisdom has given the intellectual challenge of building the world's greatest Navy to Gorshkov—our greatest Navy thinker. Do you agree?"

Whenever anyone asked Anton to agree, he weighed the agreement with a thought of Siberia in the background. Too many friends and comrades of the sea disappeared from agreeing to words uttered socially. He lifted the cup again and pretended to drink for a moment.

"Thank you for the drink, Admiral."

"So?"

"Admiral, Chairman Khrushchev is the greatest leader of our times. I don't presume to understand his thinking. Admiral Kuznetsov is a hero of the Soviet Union. Admiral Gorshkov will take our Navy on to bigger and better things." He stopped, and when Katshora did not immediately reply, Anton added, "As you are, Admiral Katshora."

Katshora laughed. "Don't worry, Anton," he said.

The admiral called him by his first name. It was unusual. Most prefaced the ranks with "Comrade" to show their party loyalty.

Personal friendships were always suspect. Seldom in his career had others in the Navy referred to another officer by his first name unless they were very close friends or at a social event. Rank was everything.

"Anton; you don't mind me calling you Anton, do you?"

"No, sir." *But why would you want to?* he asked himself.

"Good. I don't want to stand on ceremony too much. You have been given a most important job, one that will catapult the submarine force of the Soviet Union to the same level as the United States and its closest ally, Great Britain, which the Americans are helping. It is a job that is dangerous—let no one tell you differently—but it is a job that Admiral Gorshkov and I believe only you can do. Do you know what the job is, Anton?"

Katshora placed the cup on the small coffee table in front of them and then leaned back, his hands clasped together, his elbows resting on the arms of the chair. A thin smile crossed the crevices of the wrinkled face. "Do you?"

Anton opened his mouth to answer.

The admiral's voice hardened. "You are to be the 'first broadside' of the new Soviet submarine force. A broadside called atomic power. You are going to command the first atomic-powered submarine of the Soviet Navy." Katshora shrugged. "Granted, it is a prototype, but prototypes are always the first broadside." He looked at Anton. "So it is my honor that I am to be the admiral of the man who will command the *Whale*."

Anton's mind was in a whirl as he took in what Katshora was telling him. In the back of his mind was the question as to what had happened to the commanding officer before him. Chief Ekomov had talked about the *Whale* as if they had been out to sea trials before now. Ergo, there had to have been another skipper. Anton met Katshora's gaze and wondered if could ask without . . .

"First broadside; that will be in your record, and I would not be surprised, Comrade Captain, if you are destined for higher honors when we finish the sea trials and atomic power becomes the staple power of the submarine force."

The term "first broadside" grew out of a comment in 1934 by Admiral Sverdlov. Sverdlov was another hero of the Great Patriotic War. He had been a gunnery officer in the early years of the Soviet Navy. He had been a proponent of major ships taking the battle for supremacy of the seas onto the seas.

During a proof of concept in the Black Sea, he had led a gunnery exercise—the first of its kind in the new Soviet Union—that scored perfect hits on a towed target even after the target had rolled into a fogbank that had risen unexpectedly. Everyone wanted to delay the exercise, but Sverdlov had raised his hand for silence and said, "When we fight at sea or take the battle to the coast, we will never have control of the elements. Continue the exercise."

Afterward, when the cruiser *Chervona Ukraina* approached the target being towed by the cruiser *Krasny Kavkaz,* Admiral Sverdlov had stood stoically as his staff celebrated the discovery of the target having been hit several times. When the celebrations had calmed a little, Sverdlov had turned and announced to everyone that what they had witnessed was the "first broadside" by the Soviet Navy.

In the years leading up to the Great Patriotic War with Germany five years later, the Soviet Navy had increased its profound ability to deliver broadsides. Every new innovation within the Navy as it grew under Chairman Stalin was announced as the "first broadside." Here Katshora was telling him he was to deliver another "first broadside" for the Soviet Navy. He took a deep breath as he felt the pride of being chosen, bringing a deeper chill in the Arctic cold within the office.

Katshora grinned. "Anton, you are listening?"

"Sorry, Comrade Admiral," Anton answered quickly, bringing his thoughts back to the room. "I was thinking of how honored I am."

"If your thoughts wander while I am speaking, then I must assume I am boring you." Katshora laughed when Anton blushed. "You must relax, Captain. I am on your side and have been where you are now. You will do well." The admiral let out a deep sigh and put both hands on his knees. "I think you were wondering why you were chosen, and was there a skipper before you, and if there was, then what in the hell happened to him? All good questions, but we don't have the time this morning to cover all of them. As for your predecessor, he did not live up to expectations. He viewed atomic power as something to be afraid of instead of harnessed." Katshora nodded. "I was right in my assumption that you had little idea what the *K-2* prototype really involved. This raised the question as to what happened to the *K-1* prototype. Another topic for conversation between us later. Meanwhile, what I have shared with you is between two sailors. I don't like my Navy officers to have less information than the civilians they must work with. I know you understand, but hopefully you understand better now. No?"

Anton nodded. "I am so honored to have been chosen," Anton said, his voice shaking slightly.

"Yes, you are honored. I am honored to sit here with the captain first rank who is going to catapult our Navy into the fight for leadership on the seas with America," Katshora replied, the words sounding like a rote he had said many times. "You know, I wish I could see the face of the American Chief of Naval Operations, Admiral Fechteler, when he discovers that you—we—have an atomic-powered submarine." Katshora's booming laugh filled the office once again, bringing on a deep, wet bout of coughing.

Anton's eyes widened. Then he leaned forward, about to stand.

Katshora waved him down. The coughing stopped. "My apologies. This Arctic weather is not good for old men." Katshora leaned back, taking a couple of deep breaths. "You have met Doctor Zotkin, I believe?"

Anton acknowledged he had and told of spending yesterday trying to keep up with him.

Katshora nodded. "You will be working with him on this project. He is the leader of it, and you are to do whatever he asks."

It was as he thought after spending half a day trying to keep up with Doctor Zotkin. His impression of the doctor was one of him being disorganized and lost; he had been unable to get the good doctor to talk to him about the *Whale*.

Katshora laughed. "He won't tell you anything," Katshora said, slapping his knee. "Zotkin is a scientist. Scientists, by their very nature, are paranoid about everyone and everything around them. When they are on the verge of being recognized for their achievements, then it becomes even worse. I think Zotkin sees himself as the father of the atomic Navy." He waved it away. "Let him have that mantle if it achieves what we need in our Navy. Until then, I think he views everyone as a threat." Katshora looked at Anton. "Everyone as a threat," the admiral repeated, his eyebrows rising.

"Thank you, sir. I believe I understand."

Katshora leaned forward. "You didn't really know what your mission was to be until this very moment, did you?" He punctuated each word with his finger poking into the soft arm of the chair. Then he leaned back, motioning Anton away. "You don't have to answer. It is best we keep those things that others have no need to know away from them. I'd be surprised if your crew knows anything more than that they are testing a new propulsion system. So today, when Doctor Zotkin is briefing you, pretend to be surprised. Pat him on the back about atomic energy. You'll have a friend for life—unless he thinks you lack deference for his contribution." A couple of seconds passed. "Then be careful, Comrade Captain."

Katshora's warning meant Zotkin had his own chain of command where the scientist could influence events. It also meant that Katshora's command of the *K-2* project was more limited than what Anton had thought.

"I won't be going with you for your briefings today, Anton. I have assigned Miskin to be your steward today, to make sure you do not get lost. If you need to talk with me, you can trust Miskin to get word to me." Katshora waved his hand around his office. "I have informed Doctor Zotkin that you have use of my office here. Treat it as your own."

"Sir, I would hate to use your office. You will need it on your visits."

Katshora shook his head. "I seldom come to this side of the bay. Too cold for these old bones. I have told Doctor Zotkin that I would need you to come to my headquarters after each period at sea or at least periodically to brief me on Navy-related issues. He's probably not too happy about it, but he understands that we Navy types are real pains in the ass when we want to be."

Katshora stood.

Anton quickly stood also.

The admiral reached out and gripped Anton's hands.

Anton gripped back, drawing a smile from the old admiral. " 'First broadside,' Comrade?"

" 'First broadside,' Comrade Admiral."

Katshora dropped the handshake. "I think I am going to enjoy working with you, Comrade Anton." Katshora picked up his coat and thick Arctic cap off the stanchion. "As I said, the office is yours. Miskin is yours, and he will ensure that you stick to your schedule."

"Thank you, Comrade Admiral, for your insight and frank discussions."

Katshora finished putting on his bridge coat and hat. The door opened, and Miskin entered. "Ah, Miskin, I am leaving." He nodded at Anton. "Take care of our good captain."

"Yes, sir," the slim sailor answered. "As I would you, Admiral."

Katshora laughed and looked at Anton. "I don't know if that is a good thing or not."

Katshora headed toward the door, Miskin stepping aside to let the admiral leave. At the last instant, Katshora turned. "And tell the lovely Elena I asked about her. We will be having a dining-in for my officers and senior captains in a couple of weeks. I hope to see both of you at it." Then he left.

Miskin shut the door behind him and then turned to Anton. "Sir, you have a briefing with Doctor Zotkin at ten A.M. I will return fifteen minutes prior to escort you there, unless there is anything else?"

Anton shook his head. "No, Seaman Miskin. I will see you in about an hour."

Anton waited until the door shut before sitting back down on the couch. So this was to be his first broadside for the party and for the Soviet Union. A first broadside that would change the course of the Soviet Navy, and he was to deliver it. Maybe Elena was right. Maybe he was destined for the stars of an admiral. He shook the idea away.

AT precisely fifteen to ten, the door to the office opened. Anton had used the time to inspect the office and see what was available. The sparse selection of books, such as *The Party of Lenin*, were the same in Katshora's office as they were on board the ships.

"This way, Comrade Captain," Miskin said, pointing down a side passageway.

Within minutes Anton was sitting in the front row of the morning briefing by Doctor Zotkin. Anton acted surprised when the doctor told him of atomic power. Zotkin was pleased with his reaction.

IT was after one o'clock when the meeting ended, with sandwiches brought in for a working lunch. When Anton left the meeting, Miskin met him in the hallway.

"Sir, if you will follow me, I will take you to your boat."

A feeling of elation filled him. Finally he was going to see the submarine Zotkin kept referring to as the *K-2* project. He wondered why a seaman was the person taking him as he followed Miskin.

Finally, Anton thought. *I'm going to see the* Whale. How many other commanding officers had been kept away from even seeing their boat for an hour, much less nearly two days? On a Navy base run by a real naval officer and not by mad scientists, the second thing—right after the handshake with the Group commander—would have been seeing the boat. Only someone who had been a commanding officer of a submarine could understood the initial thrill of a commanding officer when he first sees his boat.

Regardless of what Zotkin said, not every submarine was the same. Some had great reputations for carrying the fight to the enemy, such as the *S-13*, which had sunk the *Wilhelm Gustloff*. Admiral Katshora led that sinking. Because of the *S-13* and Katshora's submarine, the Navy had stopped the German Army from evacuating over 8,000 troops from their entrapment by the Soviet Army.

To the victor goes history, and the Soviet Union had been more a victor than the other Allies, Anton thought as he followed Miskin. It had borne the wrath and the might of the German juggernaut while the other allies built their Armies and Navies.

"We are here, Comrade Captain." Miskin grabbed the wheel sealing the watertight door and gave it a couple of spins.

A hatch leads to the sea, was Anton's belief. Sometimes it took more than two, but if you kept opening them, eventually the waters appeared. On board a submarine, everyone knew where every hatch led. On a surface ship, it was no mean thing to open a hatch just to see what was on the other side. If you didn't know what was on the other side of a hatch on a submarine, you should not be a submariner.

The hatch flew back suddenly, breaking Miskin's grip and bouncing lightly off the bulkhead of the passageway before stopping a few inches from it. A stiff breeze of Arctic wind whipped through the hatch, hitting Anton in the face. The cold air took his breath away for a moment as it filled his lungs. He unconsciously raised his hand and quickly slipped the large top button of the bridge coat through the hole, sealing out the cold.

"It is so warm inside the floating dock, Comrade Captain, that the temperature seems colder than it is." Miskin nodded, tightening the neck strap on the foul-weather coat he wore.

Anton ducked to avoid hitting the metal arch above the hatchway. He stopped a few steps on the other side. In the dim light of the artificial night created by the huge hangar covering the floating dock, it took a few seconds for his vision to adjust.

Miskin struggled against the wind for a few seconds as he shut the hatch, quickly spinning the wheel to seal it. "Captain, this is the *K-2*. The boat they call the *Whale*."

He nodded without looking at the sailor. So, he would call her the *Whale*. Before and during World War II nearly every nation called their boats by a letter-numeral indicator, but during the war the Allies began naming theirs. The Soviet Union still used the letter-numeral designation, but when party officials refused or forgot to name a boat, crews named them.

For Doctor Zotkin and his assistants, he knew his boat would always be the *K-2* project. Submarines without names are like men without balls—a eunuch; useless.

"Did you say something, Captain?"

"No, Comrade Miskin; I was thinking of how much I enjoy

serving our nation, our party. And how honored I am to have been chosen for this mission." He smiled. Over the years, he had gotten this self-written cliché down to a pat answer. An answer that covered nearly any circumstance.

"Doctor Zotkin and his scientists call the *Whale* the *K-2*, but then you already know that, Captain. We sailors call her the *Whale*."

"There is room for both names, Miskin."

"That is what Admiral Katshora says also, sir."

For the public and for the enemy, letters and numbers were good operational security, but for a crew who disappeared into a warship that could become their coffin, a name created a sense of comfort. He did not understand how, but he knew it to be so.

Letters and numbers were inhumane to submariners. You would never call your wife "K-2" or "S-3." Submariners were fiercely loyal to their boat. They lived, ate, slept, and shit together. The boat was their family, and family deserves a name. *Whale* was a great name for a new boat. Why could he not have seen it yesterday?

"Because you were a day early" is what Zotkin had told him.

He could have been here hours ago except for the good doctor's love of his voice.

The briefing had taken longer than any self-respecting Navy officer should have to suffer. If you can't tell your story in thirty minutes, then you don't know your story. Thirty minutes is all a submariner needs to know the mission; receive orders; and ask any last-minute questions as he scrambles from wherever and whoever was delivering the stuff.

The mission part of the brief took only minutes: prove that the Soviet submarine *K-2* was a fully functional submarine capable of using atomic power. He smiled at the epiphany of the moment when he realized that Zotkin and his assistants lowered their voices almost reverently whenever they used the word "atomic."

"Yes, sir; it is a magnificent sight," Miskin said upon noticing Anton's smile.

Anton's smile broadened. "Yes, it is, Comrade Seaman. Shall we go aboard it?"

Miskin stood at attention. "Sir, this is as far as I go. It is your boat. The admiral would not understand if I went aboard with you."

Anton's eyebrows furrowed. "Why is that?" He turned and looked at Miskin.

"I am his steward, sir, and while he has assigned me to you, my duty station is not aboard the boat. He frowns—"

" 'Frowns'?"

Miskin's lips pushed together as his eyebrows lifted for a moment. Then Anton realized that Miskin was frightened over the idea of going into a submarine. There were many unable to bring themselves to go through the narrow hatches that led inside. There had been some during the war who discovered their mental incompatibility with the rigors of submarine life, but eventually went on to serve the party and the motherland heroically on board surface ships.

Anton bit his lower lip. No reason to tear through Miskin's obvious lie.

" 'Frowns' is probably a gentler word than what our war hero does when he is upset with my performance."

Normally Anton would have burrowed deeper into the explanation. Sometimes discretion is better than knowledge. He nodded and turned back to the *Whale*, grasping his hands behind his back as he waited for his vision to acclimate to the lower light.

"With your permission?"

Anton nodded, not turning when he felt the air rush by him as Miskin opened the hatch and left the main part of the floating dock.

Anton walked slowly toward the bow of the submarine, stopping at the edge of the pier across from the boat's bridge. The *Whale* was dark black, as all submarines were. There were no white letters showing her as the *K-2*, and he did not expect to see the name "*Whale*" embossed on her, either. Anton unclasped his hands to pull the bridge coat away for a moment to let some of his body heat escape.

That was where he would stand when the boat was surfaced, he told himself as he stared at the bridge. Never is a captain's responsibility more evident than when he is standing on the bridge of his boat.

Here he would navigate the boat through the "sea and anchor" detail as the *Whale* arrived at and departed from a port. Here his sailors would scramble up the huge tower as lookouts, and from here he would be the last to scramble down the unseen hatch in the deck leading to the conning tower below.

His eyes traveled up the conning tower to where masts rose several meters above the bridge. He mentally tallied the masts as his eyes stopped on each one, basking in the joy of exercising his knowledge. On top of each mast were unique fixtures that told him the purpose of each. The large and small lenses on two identified them as the periscopes, one for navigation and one for firing; another mast had the small radar—the hydraulics would open it for use once surfaced or at periscope depth; then the one least expected to see based on Zotkin's brief was the snorkel. Snorkels were like long pipes penetrating the surface of the sea so air could feed the diesel engines when the submarine was submerged. It also allowed the air for the crew to be replenished. The only time the snorkel was used was when the threat of the enemy was nonexistent.

The Americans were everywhere, so he doubted he would use it outside of the Soviet Union's national waters. Then he saw an unusual shaft, at the same height as the others, but forward, and separated from the radar and snorkel by the periscopes. Anton concentrated for a few seconds before he surmised that this must be the new electronic warfare system Zotkin had mentioned. He knew that EW was something the Americans, the British, the Germans, and even the Japanese had during the war. The Allies refused to share this technology even when the Soviet Army was fighting—he nearly thought *retreat*, but the Soviet Army never retreats; it only fights in a different direction.

Anton looked around, ensuring he was still alone. *Why am I alone?* he asked himself. A new commanding officer, and no one to greet him? Do they think so little of themselves and those who lead them that even his XO was unavailable?

He looked back at the EW mast. He wondered if the scientists had worked the bugs out of the EW gear like they had for radar. If so, he would have two pieces of equipment that most times failed to work. Most submarine commanders seldom used the radar—only when failure to use it might cast aspersions on their respect for Soviet engineering and science.

The EW system was passive, so there should be no danger of them being detected if they used it. But you never knew what engineers would do. He had never met an engineer who had ever completed a project; not because the project was failing, but because they always saw a "much-more-better" way to improve on improvements. He and his fellow submariners joked that as soon as an engineer achieved success, they should be tackled, tied up, and dragged ashore, never to return to the boat.

His footsteps echoed as he continued his walk, heading toward the bow of the boat. Other footsteps joined his, and he heard them approaching. He thought about turning around and waiting, but decided to let them be the ones to announce their presence. After all, this was his boat, and he was the commanding officer.

FOUR

Saturday, November 17, 1956

ANTON leaned over the side of the bridge, watching the *Whale* ease from the confines of the concealed dock. The morning light reflected off the clear waters of Kola Bay, and the tight breeze of the past two days had disappeared. He blew his breath out, watching the cold clouds that produced. Even in the protected areas of the covered dock, the Arctic made sure you knew it was there.

"Cast off number six," he said.

"Cast off number six!" his executive officer and the diving officer for today's trip, Commander Georgiy Gesny, shouted. Anton grinned without looking over at the XO.

Gesny was a head shorter than Anton, had shocking black hair that fought any semblance of control, and a pudginess that belied the seriousness the Georgian gave to everything about the boat. Anton's smile disappeared. They would be a good team. The attention to detail for this project needed an officer such as Gesny.

Anton glanced toward the stern and watched the number six line fall off the bollard, the weight of the line pulling it off the pier and into the icy water.

Yesterday had been interesting. He had finished the day with a deeper appreciation of the honor the Navy had bestowed on him to command the Soviet Union's first atomic submarine.

In his wardroom, for the most part, were veteran submariners. Only one young officer was assigned. That officer was his *zampolit*—his political officer. Before the Great Patriotic War, the zampolit was assigned to military units to ensure the assimilation of former Czarist officers and men into the new military services. Then, a zampolit could override the commands of a commanding officer. But warfare quickly shoves aside extraneous people, restrictions, and organizations. Early in the war zampolits became victims of their purpose and quickly discovered the authority gone if it interfered with the orders of the commanding officer. But Anton knew that everything did, said, and heard on board the *Whale* by this Josef Tomich would be documented with the KGB. So alongside him and Gesny stood Tomich.

"Last line on board, Captain," Gesny said, each word punctuated distinctly and with vigor. An explosive breath punctuated the sentence. A thicker cloud of vapor came with the report than the ones coming out of Anton's mouth.

"Very well, XO. Make revolutions for two knots," Anton said.

Gesny leaned into the open hatch and shouted the command into the control room.

"Making revolutions for two knots!" the officer of the deck—the OOD—repeated.

Every command on board a ship that controlled speed, courses, and directions were repeated a minimum of twice; once by the person giving the order, and once by the person executing it. This ensured clarity of command and served to reduce risk to the ship and crew.

"Sir, making revolutions for two knots," Gesny relayed to Anton, though Anton could hear every word said. The bridge of a submarine was a confined area in comparison to the huge bridge of a destroyer or a cruiser. Here everyone stood shoulder to shoulder, though his XO would have to borrow a crate to stand shoulder to shoulder with him and Tomich.

"There is something funny, Captain?" Gesny asked, his voice serious.

"No, no, XO." He patted his chest through the heavy bridge coat. "I am enjoying the moment of actually getting under way again." He nodded. "In Moscow there is not much opportunity for enjoying the sea."

Gesny grunted and raised his binoculars.

Anton shifted his observation to the aft portion of the submarine. The last line was aboard and being rolled up. The boatswains would stow it away inside the tower until they returned.

Lieutenant Tomich stepped back a couple of steps to give Anton more room.

"Thanks," Anton said, cocking his head at the young man. "How old are you, Comrade Tomich?"

The young officer snapped to attention.

It is going to take some time to unwind this one, thought Anton.

"I am twenty-nine years old, Comrade Captain."

Anton gave the young officer a sharp nod. "You know I need you to tell me anything I may be unaware of on board the boat," he whispered to the zampolit. "Together we will make this a great success for the Soviet Union."

"For the party," Tomich said with a serious eagerness that surprised Anton.

"For the party," Anton replied in the same low voice. The young officer would have been sixteen or seventeen when the Great Patriotic War ended. "Did you see action during the war?" Many as young as fourteen wore the uniform in the dark days of the war when German troops pushed deep into the Soviet Union. Russia is like a great sponge that soaks up invaders by its vastness. Like Napoleon before Hitler, eventually the tide turned and the Red Army fought, killed, and pushed the invaders away, across the borders, and eventually across Germany. It was a great victory for the Communist nation.

Tomich looked embarrassed. "No sir; I was too young."

Anton nodded. Too young? Why was Tomich too young while so many Communist youth gave their lives for their country?

The *Whale* inched forward, moving away from the pier, and toward the channel leading out of the dock. Anton raised his binoculars as the XO lowered his. He scanned the area of the bay waiting for them at the end of the channel.

"Keep an eye on the port fender!" Gesny shouted to the forward "sea and anchor" detail.

Anton lowered his binoculars slightly to see what the XO was taking precautions against. He watched two of the sailors near the bow of the *Whale* take position near the edge where the boat would sail past the huge rubber fenders lining the docking area. Fenders served to keep a ship from damaging itself by hitting the hard concrete and metal of a pier.

Zotkin told him the boats and shipping lanes would be closed during the morning to allow him to maneuver the boat for the day. This was his "familiarization cruise," as the good doctor called it. It would be the only one because Zotkin needed the *K-2* tied up so he could prepare it for the at-sea trial in the near future.

"How long will we be out today, Comrade Captain?"

"As long as it takes, Lieutenant Tomich. This is to familiarize me with the boat; its capabilities; the energy of our new propulsion system. We have six weeks before we take it out on sea trials, so we want to be ready."

"We are excited over your arrival. The other captain . . ."

Anton recognized the pause of the young officer as an attempt to draw out what Anton knew. But he knew nothing other than one moment the former captain was the captain; and the next, he was gone. He wondered for a moment if this young man had anything to do with it. Most likely yes. Whenever someone disappeared suddenly in the Soviet Union, people such as Tomich were nearby. Youthful exuberance mixed with unfamiliar power made for tyrants in zealotry.

"What about the other captain?" Anton finally asked.

The young officer shrugged and joined Anton at the front of the conning tower, almost touching him, they were so close. The XO shifted over a couple of steps, opening up his distance from Anton and Tomich.

The young man was confident in his position on board. Who did he know? Anton's lower lip pushed up against his upper. This officer was too young to be a zampolit on such an important project without some high official approving it. Maybe his first name, Josef, was the key. He was young enough to have been named after Stalin, but Khrushchev had discredited Stalin earlier this year. Then why was this young man still in this position of authority where his youth, exuberance, and ambition could destroy the greatest opportunity for the Navy? No; someone had top cover for this young officer, and it would be in Anton's interest to keep the young man close. Keep Tomich happy. Tie the man's ambition to the success of this project.

Anton took a step to starboard and glanced back. The stern of the *Whale* was clearing the dock.

"Not much longer," he said.

"Yes, sir."

"Recommend course zero eight zero!" the navigator shouted from the conning tower.

"Sir! Recommend course zero eight zero!" Gesny said.

Anton lifted the brass covering of the voice tube, looking at Gesny. He leaned down and spoke into it. "Very well, come to course zero eight zero, speed two knots," Anton said. Why shout through the hatch when you had a voice tube at your service? Maybe the XO could explain why later.

The next twenty minutes moved the *Whale* from its hidden berth into Kola Bay. As far as Anton could see, not a single civilian ship was visible, not even the fishing vessels that had seemed to dot the never frozen waters of Kola Bay. North of them—he counted from left to right—four destroyers weaved back and forth.

They were there to ensure that no one interfered with him and to protect the *Whale*. He also knew they were there to sink the *Whale* if he tried to head away from the operational area assigned. They had never had a Soviet Navy ship or boat mutiny yet, and professional sailors never would.

He looked south. On the horizon the pall of industrial smoke filled the skies above Murmansk. He looked north across the bay and could make out the cold morning outline of Severomorsk. Severomorsk was better. Admiral Katshora's office was in this city, and it was here where the commander of the Northern Fleet's Submarine Force spent his days.

Severomorsk had little industry in comparison to Murmansk, but it was in this smaller city where the administrative headquarters of the Soviet Northern Fleet was located. He pitied the parts of the Northern Fleet located in the hard-to-breathe air of Murmansk.

Anton moved to the other side of the bridge, leaning over the stanchion to make sure everything was stowed from the sea-and-anchor detail.

Gesny lifted the brass cover of the voice tube. "Depth?" he asked into it.

Anton smiled when he saw the XO ask the question. *We will get along well*, he thought.

"Twenty-five meters."

"Still too shallow to dive," Gesny said to Anton.

"How far out do we have to go to reach suitable waters?"

"About two kilometers, Captain. Then the bottom drops off rapidly, but within two kilometers of the facility, I recommend staying surfaced."

Anton nodded. "I am going below, XO. You have the conn."

Gesny saluted, lifted the brass covering, and said, "This is the XO. I have the conn."

Below, in the conning tower, someone would make a notation in the logbook of the shift of maneuvering control from the skipper to the XO.

Anton turned to Tomich. "I think we can go below and practice some dives. What do you think?"

The young officer snapped to attention. "I agree, Comrade Captain."

Of course, if he failed to build a sense of partnership with this zampolit, he could always throw him overboard. He looked at the XO and was surprised at the hostile look he caught on Gesny's face as the man's narrowed eyes watched the zampolit scurry down the hatch. He bit his lip, wondering if it was because Tomich went below before him, or if there was something else, something he should know. In the Navy, there was always something else to know.

"XO, let me know when we reach diving depths. I am going below to the conning tower and prepare to dive."

Gesny look up at Anton. "It is your decision, Comrade Captain. We can do it here, but the shallow waters risk us hitting the bottom. Or we can go farther into the bay."

"Call me when you think we can risk a dive."

"Aye, sir."

FIFTEEN minutes later, as Anton stood behind the planesmen listening to Chief Ship Starshina Mamadov, the chief of the boat, describe the gauges and levers surrounding the conning tower, Gesny's voice came through the intercom.

"Captain, depth is two hundred meters, sir. I recommend we dive."

Mamadov was a squat, stockily built man who had a voice that would rival a tenor in the disestablished Soviet Opera. Anton and Elena had been privileged to attend the last opera in 1946, after which the state ceased to fund it.

"What do you think, COB? Think it is time to see what the *Whale* can do?"

"Yes, sir. A submarine is not a submarine when it is above the waterline."

Anton turned to the officer of the watch. "Lieutenant Nizovtsev, I am going topside. Prepare to dive."

Gesny moved aside as Anton climbed onto the bridge. "Well, XO, why don't you do the honors."

"Sir?"

"Dive the boat."

"Dive! Dive!" shouted Gesny. Then the XO reached beneath the stanchion and hit the Klaxon horn. Across the still air of Kola Bay rode the "oogle" noise of the submarine alarm, warning everyone on board that the *Whale* was submerging.

Anton stepped aside as the men aloft slid down the ladders and disappeared into the hatch leading to the control room. He glanced forward and saw the sea and anchor detail disappearing through the forward hatch; and before he turned aft, he already knew that those back there were doing the same.

In a minute, only he and Gesny stood on the deck of the conning tower. "XO, after you, if you please."

"Yes, sir, Captain," Gesny said. The man walked casually to the hatch and quickly disappeared belowdecks.

Anton took a quick look as water rushed over the bow. He glanced behind. The aft portion of the *Whale* disappeared beneath the sea. No one could understand the thrill of a submariner as he challenged the dangers of the sea by challenging it beneath the waves. You could never control the waters of the oceans, but with luck you could survive them.

He turned and stepped quickly down the ladder leading into the conning tower, reaching above him to seal the hatch. As he leaped onto the deck of the control room, Anton stepped aside. A young sailor raced up the ladder and double-checked the hatch. There was never room for a mistake on board a submarine.

For the next hour, he took the *Whale* through the depths of Kola Bay, enjoying the handling of the submarine. The speed impressed him. Unlike battery power, all Anton had to do was shout out a speed and the atomic power surged, leaped, soared to the command. Battery power rose slowly and dissipated quickly. Here was truly the future of the Soviet Submarine Force. Here was their ability to meet the Americans in the open ocean. Since Peter the Great, Russia—now the Soviet Union—had dreamed of an ocean-going fleet that met the expectations of a country that stretched across two continents and half the world.

Anton pursed his lips and blew out, seeing no clouds of vapor.

What he really liked was the heat atomic power gave to the boat. Diesel submarines were always freezing in the Arctic because battery power lacked the energy to do more than keep the temperatures livable but cold.

"It is great, isn't it, Comrade Captain?"

Anton looked over at Gesny, who stood near the planesmen. "It is, XO."

Gesny continued, "I know how you feel, sir. Like you, I am a veteran of the Great Patriotic War, and to feel such power in our boat while submerged gives such a thrill to know what our Navy can be doing."

Anton nodded with a smile. He found it amusing how someone who spoke so calmly and without emotion acted when he became thrilled. For him, he smiled and in the pit of the stomach a feeling such as one has on a circus ride bounced along with his emotions.

"How fast will she go while submerged, Comrade Diving Officer?" Anton asked, addressing Gesny with his watch position title.

"We have reached fifteen knots while submerged, and she could have gone faster."

Anton leaned back slightly to adjust for the maneuver of the *Whale*.

"Passing one hundred meters," the officer of the deck relayed.

"One hundred meters, aye," Gesny acknowledged.

"Trim the boat, XO."

"Trim one hundred meters," Gesny ordered, his voice toneless.

"One hundred meters, aye," the officer of the deck acknowledged.

Anton straightened as the *Whale* began to level off.

"As I said, Captain, we have reached fifteen knots while submerged. I know we could have gone much higher."

"Why didn't you?"

"Because we have these tests of our most reverend scientists who want to do everything in incremental efforts." Gesny shrugged. "I have suggested that we go until the boat starts to shake, but I believe they are concerned that we will shake apart if we go too fast."

"Maybe they are right."

"Maybe everyone is right in our Navy."

Lieutenant Tomich entered the control room. Gesny glanced at the zampolit and wordlessly stepped over to where the officer of the deck stood. Anton's eyebrows arched as he tried to recall the name of the OOD. Oh, yes, Nizovtsev, the navigator. It was unusual for a navigator to be doing this. Every ship in the Soviet Navy was assigned two navigators, and while the navigators were in those august jobs, all they did was navigate. They were the only officers exempt from the zampolit's political-party work.

"Comrade Captain, I have checked the crew's mess as you asked. I think it is a brilliant idea you have suggested for me to walk through the mess during the serving hours. You can hear so much, and it does, as you pointed out, allow me to have a better feel for the morale and political dedication of our crew."

"For such a young officer, Comrade Lieutenant, you are very astute. I think our crew and our officers can benefit from your insight." Anton saw the beam of pride in Tomich's face. There were ways to make the zampolit a valued member of the wardroom; driving him away was not one of them. As long as one remembered that in the end, the officer was still a zampolit.

"I think you are right, sir."

"Final trim!" came a shout from Mamadov, who was looking over the shoulders of the planesmen aligned along the port bulkhead and helmsman who manned the wheel near the forward end of the control room.

"Captain, we are depth one hundred meters, steering course zero four zero, speed ten knots," Nizovtsev calmly announced.

Anton turned to Gesny. "Let's bring her up a knot at a time until we reach fifteen knots, Comrade XO."

"Aye, Captain."

"Increase speed to eleven knots."

Anton barely felt the increase, but it was there. It penetrated the soles of his black shoes, the speed—the power. It was like a man with a new woman for the first time. Thrilling. Here was the future of the Soviet Navy. It was no wonder the American Navy enjoyed the command of the seas, but their time was coming, and he—Anton Zegouniov—would lead the way in the *Whale*.

"Did the captain feel that?" Gesny asked, his face expressionless.

"For us old battery-powered sailors, XO, it is indeed an amazing moment for me," he acknowledged.

"I have never been on a conventional submarine," Tomich added.

Anton's and Gesny's eyes met. Without a word or movement,

Anton knew he and Gesny were thinking the same thing about the young zampolit, who would act as an equal with them. Both were veterans of the war. Tomich had never known the fear, angst, or emotion of survival that a submariner veteran had experienced. Anton looked away. Since this was the only atomic-powered submarine in the Soviet Navy, Tomich's comment meant the zampolit was on his first submarine.

Anton bit his lower lip. This Tomich must have friends in high places, if the zampolit's first assignment on board a submarine was on the most sensitive and classified one in the Navy. There was that feeling of pride swelling in Anton again as he thought of the future he would help bring to his country. And, almost as an afterthought, the party.

THE sun was touching the edge of the hills behind the facility as Anton stood on the bridge, listening to Gesny conn the *Whale* toward the opening that marked the concealed dock. About thirty minutes until they were inside and another hour to ensure that his boat was securely tied. Then he could think about heading home to Elena. Wait until he told her of his first trip out on his boat. *His* boat!

Anton lifted his binoculars and swept them across the facility areas, looking at the varied buildings and guard posts that dotted the rough hillside and coastline that made up this secret facility. He surmised that the reason why the area had never been properly organized and cleaned up like a naval facility should be was that it helped in camouflaging the true purpose behind their work here. It was the only thing that made sense.

"What is the captain looking at?"

Anton lowered his glasses. Tomich stood alongside him. He had not heard the zampolit come up the ladder.

"This is the first time I've had to view our facility, Lieutenant. I am amazed at how farsighted our leaders are in taking what is easily the most important thing for our Navy—our future—and hiding it in plain sight."

"I thought the same thing," Tomich replied. "Our enemies are thinking we are pursuing an atomic-powered submarine in our Pacific Fleet headquarters at Vladivostok. They would never think of us doing it in the Northern Fleet."

"Or maybe they think we would be doing it with our Baltic

Fleet or Black Sea Fleet?" Anton asked. He knew Tomich was sharing classified information with him. Was Anton underestimating the zampolit? Was Tomich testing him? Would this information later become valuable to him, or would it be used against him? Regardless, the more information he knew, the better he could weave his career through the minefields of Soviet politics.

Tomich shook his head. "I don't think they ever considered Kaliningrad. The Baltic Fleet is trapped at the end of the Baltic and is too exposed for our enemies to exploit anything we might do there. As for the Black Sea Fleet"—Tomich laughed—"Chairman Khrushchev had known all along the evil of Stalin, and to put this project in the Ukraine where we have a bastion of traitors would be inconceivable."

Anton nodded. "You have a keen analytical mind, Lieutenant."

Tomich smiled. "Yes; once again the party has proven superior." He tapped his head. "While the Americans and their lackeys patrol off the Pacific Fleet headquarters, hoping to find our atomic power program, we have hidden it under their noses in the most inhospitable part of our country: the Arctic." He laughed and with an almost schoolboyish voice added, "Isn't it great?"

Anton nodded. The zampolit was smart. Anton had not considered why the Northern Fleet. He doubted he would ever have given the intellectual effort to have reasoned it as this young political officer had. Anton shivered slightly, as if the Arctic wind had whipped up his trouser leg.

"It is indeed great, Lieutenant Tomich. For you and for all of us who are embarked on what will be a historical event in our Navy's history."

"Captain!" Gesny shouted. "Recommend coming to course three two zero at this time."

"Very well!" he shouted. Gesny did not need to ask permission; he had the conn. He turned to his XO standing nearer the front of the bridge, but the man had his back to Anton.

"Captain, my apologies," Tomich said. "I am distracting you from your duties. We should talk later. I am sure you have many questions about my party-political plans for the crew. Tonight we are doing a 'Life of Lenin' project. You are welcome to join us."

"Could we have it when we dock, Lieutenant? I would be enthused to participate, and if we can do it prior to nightfall, then we can have those who must travel on their way in time to avoid the harsher time of the day."

"Yes, sir. I would be glad to do it," Tomich said, enthusiam running the words together. Then the zampolit added, as if the young man felt he had to say something else, "I am, like you, so proud of being asked to be part of this great adventure."

Anton acknowledged the young man's parting comment and then watched for a second as the zampolit scurried through the hatch, heading down the ladder to the conning tower. When he looked up, Gesny was staring at him. His XO nodded, raised his hand with a slight two-finger salute, and then returned to conning the boat toward the dock.

Anton raised his glasses and returned to viewing the facility. Along with seeing how the facility was laid out and how the construction lacked so much infrastructure, he listened to Gesny's orders.

With experience in the Navy came so much nautical knowledge tied up inside one's brain. As he listened, he visualized the changes the conning crew were doing, the shifting of the rudders, the seesaw noises of the electric motor as it changed its speed. It seemed transparent to him as he easily translated the courses and speed changes into a vivid mental chart of the *Whale* as it maneuvered. Most submariners had this innate ability of envisioning navigational movements without seeing them. It became ingrained the longer one stayed in the submarine force because navigation was always done in the dark confines of submerged operations. A captain who could not visualize his navigational picture with its myriad of contacts would never survive a battle at sea where most, if not all, of those contacts were trying to sink you.

He wondered if this Tomich would wet himself when he experienced his first depth charge. He saw movement to the right of the concealed dock and shifted his binoculars to the area. Wetting oneself did not mean the sailor would never survive a war at sea. Many he had known had gone through the terror of depth-charging, lying on the bottom, praying—though not out loud—to survive; and who then went on to become veteran submariners. He recalled his own terror.

He tweaked the focus on the binoculars. A couple of trucks were backing up to a loading platform along the back side of the dock. The current course of the *Whale* allowed him to see, but he would be able to watch for only a minute before their course and speed caused the opening to the dock to block the trucks from view. Probably delivering supplies.

He recognized the tall figure when he came into view. Doctor Zotkin walked ahead of several other white-gowned figures. *Members of Zotkin's staff*, Anton thought. The dock began to obscure the activity, but not before he saw men coming onto the loading platform carrying stretchers. He counted seven before the opening blocked his view. Three of them had blankets covering the faces. The others were uncovered.

"We are nearing the entrance, Comrade Captain," Gesny interrupted.

Anton dropped his binoculars and glanced forward. Gesny raised his binoculars slightly and let them drop. Gesny nodded and turned forward. Why was his number two warning him about the binoculars? Why could he not look around his surroundings? A good naval officer needed to know what the coastline looked like as much as he needed to know the depth, current, and wave action of the seas in which he sailed. But he was new to this project, and there was much to be curious about and much that could find him and Elena learning how to chop wood for heat in Siberia.

Gesny took a couple of steps back, his eyes never leaving the forward portion of the boat. "Captain, your operations officer, Lieutenant Lebedev, would like to discuss next week's planning board for training. Have you had an opportunity to speak with Lieutenant Lebedev yet, sir?"

"I met him yesterday. He seems to be a dedicated officer." Anton nodded. "I think it would be a good idea, Commander. But only for a few minutes, as it has been a long day and Lieutenant Tomich has some party-political work for us."

"I heard, sir," Gesny said drily.

"Then a few minutes for Lebedev, then all of us need to have some sleep before tomorrow's engine room drills."

Gesny nodded. "Aye, sir. And we can discuss the drills for tomorrow."

"XO," Anton said in a low voice, "I saw trucks alongside the dock, and it looked as if—"

"Come to course three one two!" Gesny shouted. "Captain, with your permission, I have to concentrate on getting the *Whale* into her berth. The current can be trecherous here. Also, the evening brings Arctic winds, and you never know just when they will appear, but when they do, they will hit the sail of the *Whale*. Without our attention the currents and the wind could push us into the rocks." Gesny pointed toward the beach running along the right side of the entrance. Huge rocks lined the coast, probably shoved there by ancient glaciers. Huge rocks also lined the channel leading to the facility, but there was little doubt they had been placed by human efforts.

Anton nodded, shocked over being interrupted. Maybe he was wrong about this Gesny. It was uncomfortable to have a subordinate interrupt him. So he watched quietly, acknowledging the slight course changes as Gesny aligned the prototype atomic submarine with the gaping mouth of the covered dock. Minutes passed before Anton grasped another alternative. Maybe Gesny was stopping him from asking his question about the trucks. There were things in the Soviet Union just as he supposed there were in America where some questions and curiosity were best left unasked and unsolved. It would explain the interruption. Anton promised himself to ask the question later, when the two were alone. Then again, even if Gesny seemed to be helping, it did not mean the man failed to have a hidden agenda. Survival was a hidden agenda when the party was involved, and everyone was fodder to be thrown between you and them.

ANTON stepped onto the dock, glancing back at the submarine. Because it was not considered a fully operational warship, minimal crew was on board, primarily for security and fire watch. The XO saluted from the bridge. As soon as he closed the hatch leading away from the dock and into the main facility, those who stayed behind waiting for him to leave would be scurrying for home. He smiled at the deference showed to the commanding officer, but he knew how junior officers thought. Sure, by now all on board knew this was his first command, but it was his sixth submarine, and he had served with some of the best the Soviet Union had to offer.

If anyone was unable to sleep, all they had to do was attend one of Tomich's party-political workshops. He was surprised his eyes were still open, even though it had been more than an hour ago.

Anton reached the end of the passageway, looked to his right, and turned left toward the exit leading away from the concealed dock and to home. He was near the last exit when voices drew his attention down the corridor. He looked at his watch: eight o'clock was not late for a Navy base. He grabbed the wheel to open the hatch when one of the voices rose to almost a shout and he heard, "We can't keep doing this, Doctor Zotkin! We have had five die in two weeks, and all because—"

"Shut up, Danzinger! You are alive because of me—"

"I am alive because of what I know and what I brought with me from Germany. You are alive because of the KGB."

Anton dropped his hand from the hatch and stepped into a nearby shadow. What were they talking about, and who was Danzinger? The voices lowered to where Anton could barely make out individual words, much less what they were talking about. He stepped to the hatch. Behind him he heard footsteps, turned, and saw Gesny approaching.

"Ah, Comrade Captain; I figured you would have been gone by now."

Anton spun the wheel. The squeeking of uncared-for hinges reverberated down the passageway. Movement at the far end of the passageway drew his attention. Doctor Zotkin stepped into the doorway of his office. He looked at Anton and Gesny before wordlessly stepping back inside and shutting the door.

"Somewhere a village is missing a mad doctor," Gesny said in a low voice.

The two officers stepped outside into the dark Arctic night. Freezing wind and the tingling of ice crystals pelting their cheeks greeted them.

"Glad it is a warm night," Gesny offered.

"Comrade XO," Anton said, "my thanks for your performance today. It is indeed a good first mate who makes the captain look good and hides the new captain's lack of familiarity."

Gesny nodded without smiling. "That is my job, Captain."

Anton's eyes narrowed, and he bit his lip for a moment, debating asking about what he had seen on their way back into port and what he had heard in the passageway before his executive officer had stopped him.

"It is late," Gesny said.

"Yes, it is," Anton said, the moment lost.

Gesny saluted and said, "Captain, with your permission, I have a family waiting for me. Tomorrow is a busy day as we start preparations for our sea trials."

Anton returned the salute and watched the stocky submariner amble toward a bus idling near the end of the short driveway. Looking around, Anton saw his car idling also, in the parking space reserved for him. A moment later he was opening the door and sliding into the warm air of the backseat.

"About time, Comrade Captain," Popov said, grabbing the gear stick and jerking the car into reverse. Without waiting for a reply, the driver slid out of the parking spot onto the road. "It is going to be a slow, long ride home. Did I not tell you that to leave after six meant we might have to stay overnight?"

"There will be days that carry into evening here, Comrade."

"I will give you the telephone number of my building. You call and tell my blushing virgin bride that her husband is not out drinking with his comrades nor spending the night with another blushing virgin."

Anton saw the man shake his head.

"In the Arctic, when winter arrives, no man is out after dark without malice in his heart or his brains below the belt."

FIVE

Wednesday, November 21, 1956

"CHECK the time again, XO!" Shipley shouted. "I don't like being surfaced during the daylight hours."

"Aye, sir," came the muffled reply from the control tower below.

Shipley looked at the voice tube in front of him on the bridge. He flipped the voice tube cover open once again. "Can you hear me?" he asked into it. No reply. He slapped it shut. Damn thing.

Shipley raised his binoculars and scanned the horizon. On the left side of the bridge, one of the signalmen swept the horizon for contacts. A second sailor, in foul-weather gear, leaned against the railing encircling the bridge, sweeping the sea with his binoculars. Both had binoculars and both scanned the sea and the air for contacts.

Shipley had ordered several short radar sweeps—no more than thirty seconds—without any joy in detecting the surface ship that was to rendezvous with them north of Iceland. He took a deep breath. God! What were they thinking? Here he was on the surface, which all submariners hated—and it was daylight, no less.

On the good side, the diesels were recharging the batteries. Even so, Shipley intended to surface later, when the sun set, and top them off again. Diesel-electric battery-powered submarines such as the *Squallfish* had to surface every three days or the air grew stale, headaches increased as carbon monoxide levels rose and the batteries grew low. The Navy said that in less than ten years the diesel boats would all be gone, replaced by the new nuclear-powered submarines. Build one nuke such as the *Nautilus* and the Navy thinks it's going to replace diesels! What are they thinking? This Rear Admiral Hyman Rickover will find himself retired early, was Shipley's bet. Though, they say, the *Nautilus* can stay submerged for days.

Regardless, that didn't stop the operational mind-set that the surface was not their friend, especially during daylight hours. But here he sat, like a dumb merchant target wallowing along at a bare four knots, waiting for a team. What team? Who are they? Why was he—the commanding officer—being kept in the dark? God, he hated spooks when they send them to sea. Keep them ashore and just send him their analyses, like they did in World War II.

He looked at his watch. Thirty minutes since the last sweep. As he looked up and grabbed his binoculars again, he felt the static electric charge as the radar operator belowdecks energized the radar sweep across the bridge. Less than thirty seconds later the sensation disappeared as the operator secured the energy. He lifted his watch cap and brushed his hair back down into place.

"Any joy?" he shouted through the hatch.

Several seconds passed before Arneau shouted back, "We have a closing surface contact bearing two eight zero range three zero nautical miles, Captain. We have another four contacts on separating course. Those four are in the navigation lanes."

"We have any electronic warfare hits on them?"

"Not on the one that is constant bearing, decreasing range. The other four show merchant ship radars. We've been watching them since we surfaced, sir."

"Very well." Surface contacts separating from them were okay. Chances of a contact sailing over the horizon being able to pick them up on radar were low. Surfaced submarines had a low profile, and many times waves protected them from radar hits. His orders were to pick up this spook team at this location. He bit his lower lip. He knew without thinking about it that Naval Intelligence was involved in this somehow. Anytime a warship was jerked around from its mission, it was because those intelligence dogs were barking at something.

He wondered if the team arriving would have another set of orders changing their mission objective. Patrolling the Iceland–U.K. gap was routine and boring, but they knew where and when the mission would end. Now he was heading into the Barents Sea, which was owned by the Soviet Navy, even if the world called it international; a Barents Sea that at this time of the year was freezing over. He doubted the Soviets were putting out more than coastal operations at this time of year.

A gust of cold Arctic wind whipped across the *Squallfish*, reminding Shipley that he was on the edge of the North Sea preparing to sail into some of the most treacherous waters of the world. Treacherous waters where a man overboard lived less than a minute in waters so cold they sapped the life from a person so fast he was long dead before he could have truly realized his situation.

"Contact continues to close, Skipper! Still no EW contact . . . Wait! We have a sweep from it, sir. It's an SPS-4 surface search radar according to the whirly operator," Arneau said, referring to the AN/WLR electronic warfare system on board as "whirly."

"Do we know which ship?"

"That's a negative; but it's definitely American."

The Navy did have a World War II destroyer escort stationed in Iceland, he recalled. The USS *John J. Stevens*—the name popped into his mind. The *Stevens* was a World War II destroyer converted into a radar picket ship as part of the Cold War defense against a Soviet attack. It had been deployed to Iceland a few months ago to serve as part of the early-warning network. Part of the defense of America involved converting thirty destroyer escorts into radar pickets. What a horrid job having to sail through weather that was seldom as calm as today.

"Sir! It's probably the *Stevens* out of Keflavik. Edsall class destroyer escort, Skipper!"

"Roger, XO; got it!"

"Here it is, Captain; 306 feet long!"

Shipley raised his binoculars as Arneau continued to rattle off the armaments, crew complement, and other specifics of the Edsall class DE. At times such as these, he wanted to lean over the hatch and say, "Thanks, but no thanks, XO," but if nothing else, the recital from *Jane's Fighting Ships* was good training for the others in the conning tower.

Christ! He hoped the bunch they were picking up weren't civilians. Civilians were a scurvy lot, as Chief of the Boat Boohan was fond of saying: when they're not complaining, they're in the way. Ought to have a civilian locker on board submarines so we could stash them away until we reach shore and can offload them. Christ! He hoped CINCNELM wasn't that cruel a bastard to send him a pack of civilians as they headed into the worst seas of the world. It wasn't that Shipley was against civilians; he even married one, as sailors are prone to do. But at sea, where space was limited and danger unlimited, having excess human cargo meant additional work for the crew. If they had a major emergency, civilians were more likely to be hurt. Granted, he told himself, they were nice enough on shore, but what in the hell do you do with them when you're at sea? They clutter the wardroom talking civilian shit and taking away the one spot on the boat where the officers have some semblance of privacy—*if they shut their eyes and no one spoke*.

Shipley shook his head. That bastard! I bet they're civilians.

"They've turned off their radar, Skipper."

Probably don't want us to sink them. The tin-can sailors are probably laughing their heads off over bringing civilians to him. "Very well, XO. Power ours up for a thirty-second sweep, then shut it down."

"Aye, aye, sir."

A few seconds later, the XO shouted up, "Captain, the contact has adjusted his course and is CBDR."

"Very well. Secure our radar." CBDR stood for constant bearing, decreasing range. A CBDR contact was destined to collide with you unless you or it changed course, speed, or both in sufficient time to change the event.

Whatever Admiral Wright had in mind for *Squallfish*, it seemed to Shipley, all he was supposed to do was provide transportation. He wondered where they were taking this team. Or, where the team was going to take them. Patrolling up and down the coast of the Soviet Union in the Barents should be safe, but you never knew what the Arctic was going to throw at you.

An hour later, the approaching ship topped the horizon. The

starboard-side signalman identified it as an American destroyer escort. Even Shipley could make out the dark gray color and hull numbers near the bow common to American warships.

SHIPLEY maintained course and speed as the *Stevens* maneuvered upwind, creating a lee to deflect the wind picking up from the north. The *Squallfish* sea and anchor detail parties were topside in foul-weather coats encumbered with their Mae West life vests.

The boatswain mate on board the *Stevens* stepped to the safety line with the shotgun contraption that fired the gunline. The sailor raised the gun, paused for a moment, and shouted, "All on deck, duck!"

Both forward and aft the sailors crouched, watching the boatswain mate on the *Stevens*. There was nothing to hide behind unless you were on the bridge.

The monkey fist on the end of the gunline was halfway across before the shotgun sound reached the *Squallfish*. The line crossed over the aft deck, splashing into the starboard-side waters. The *Squallfish* sailors pulled the line from the water. Then, hand over hand, they began pulling the line from the *Stevens* as sailors on board the DE played it out. Across the narrowing curtain of water separating the two warships, the larger phone and distance line—PD line, it was called—followed the gunline.

Shipley watched as the first of the distance flags started its transit across the narrow distance between the two ships, now traveling alongside each other at four knots. The *Stevens* took the wind on its starboard beam. Green, red, yellow, blue, and white flags decorated the distance between the submarine and the surface warship. Each flag represented 20 yards of separation. The second red flag emerged as the first green flag reached the *Squallfish*. About 120 yards of separation. *Never forget how far away a ship is from colliding with you*, Shipley thought.

Along with the distance flags trailed a sound-powered telephone line beneath them. When it reached the *Squallfish*, one of the sailors disconnected part of the phone line, raced over to the tower, climbed up it, and quickly handed the telephone to Shipley. He pressed the talk button and discovered the commanding officer of the *Stevens*, Commander Hewitt Stewart, on the other end.

Shipley looked over at the *Stevens*. The sailors were pulling in the distance line. The red flag was back aboard it with the green flag, marking 100 yards, seemingly inching back aboard the *Stevens*.

After the obligatory greetings and exchanges, Stewart informed Shipley he was transporting a young lieutenant and two photographer mates with him. During the conversation, Shipley leaned down to the hatch and ordered rudder shifts to keep the *Squallfish* and the *Stevens* at about 120 yards of separation.

As the two commanding officers talked, the *Stevens* lowered a motor whaleboat, and within minutes the team of three was aboard. The young lieutenant saluted Shipley before *Squallfish* sailors hustled them down the aft hatch. Movies from the *Stevens* followed, and his own movies went into the motor whaleboat. Ships at sea exchanged movies seen or movies hated whenever they chanced upon each other in the oceans or in foreign ports. Much to annoyance of the Navy film librarian—several of whom the Navy had had quit in frustration trying to keep track of the films.

Shipley lifted the telephone to his ear as the motor whaleboat started its trip back to the *Stevens*. A gust of wind nearly took his watch cap off his head, causing him to slap his hand up to hold it down. The earlier, taut distance line between the two vessels dipped suddenly. Sailors on board the *Stevens* were hurrying to pull the distance line in, but as Shipley watched, he saw the blue flag marking 80 yards pass over the transom of the warship, and the line was still dipping. The wind was pushing the *Stevens* toward the *Squallfish*.

"Captain," Shipley said, "thanks for the movies and the personnel. The wind is pushing you toward us. I'm going to cast off."

"Good sailing to you, sir," Stewart replied. "The *Stevens* will be on station near this location until you return. It's all in the packet sent over with Lieutenant Logan. You got him now. I wish you the best," he finished with a chuckle.

Shipley dropped the sound-powered phone over the edge of the bridge to the sailor below.

Ames lowered the telephone and shouted down to the boatswain mates on the deck of the *Stevens*. The *Stevens*'s sailors picked up the pace of hauling the line back aboard.

Shipley watched for a few seconds as the *Squallfish* chief directed the playing out of the line. The line lay in a loose coil on the deck. If they shoved all of it into the water at one time instead of waiting until it reached the bitter end, there was a risk of the line wrapping around the shaft and propeller.

A couple more minutes and they would be free and safe. The yellow flag marking 40 yards dipped and went into the water. A stronger gust of wind whipped across the bridge. The stern of the *Stevens* turned toward them. Stewart disappeared into the bridge. The wake of the *Stevens* showed that the destroyer escort's skipper was putting over a hard right rudder.

The smallest of the antisubmarine warships in the U.S. Navy looked awfully big as it closed the distance between them.

Too late to be concerned about the shaft and propeller. The submarine was in danger. He leaned over the tower stanchion, shouting, "Chief, shove the line into the water! Now! Get the men belowdecks!"

The coil of line hit the water. There was no more physical contact between the two ships and no danger to the sailors manning the line.

Squallfish sailors were hustling down the aft escape hatch. Shipley bent down to the hatch. "XO! Immediate left full rudder! All ahead ten knots!"

"Aye, sir; left full rudder, helmsman!" came Arneau's muffled command. "Increase speed ten knots!"

The *Stevens* was still bearing down on them. Shipley shouted through the hatch, his eyes on the destroyer escort, "XO, all head full!"

His view was blocked by dark gray of the *Stevens*. The yellow flag was being pulled aboard the *Stevens*. On board the warship towering above them the sides were manned by sailors watching the two ships fight to avoid collision. The bow of the World War II DE edged to starboard, but the World War II steam engines of the warship responded slower than the diesels of the *Squallfish*.

The boatswain mates on board the *Stevens* pulled the last of the line on board, the bitter end banging against its side as it cleared the water. Water dripped from the black telephone receiver.

The diesels kicked in as the submarine raced to full speed. The *Squallfish* tilted to port as it pushed away from the destroyer. The stern of the *Stevens* whipped toward the stern of the *Squallfish*. Shipley braced for the collision, gripping the stanchion with one hand as the other reached for the collision alarm. His finger was on the red button, but at the last instant the vintage destroyer's propellers churned the water, throwing up a huge wave that washed across the aft end of the submarine. The wave caught two of his sailors, throwing them to the deck and pushing them toward the smooth side of the submarine. He watched, unable to do anything, as the two fought for handholds on the metal deck of the submarine.

The chief leaped toward them. As the chief hit the deck prong, another sailor grabbed his legs, sticking his boondockers into the narrow ridges between the wooden planking of the deck. The chief managed to grab both sailors by the arms as they slid toward the icy North Sea.

The stern of the *Stevens* opened the distance between them. When Shipley looked back, the two sailors were being hustled belowdecks. Their faces looked blue from the drenching. He knew that once below, in the relative warmth of the submarine, they'd quickly recover. Knowing they were entitled to medicinal brandy would also help them recover.

"Sir!" the signalman above him shouted. "*Stevens* asks, 'Is all well?' How should I reply?"

"Tell him that everything is fine and that we will rendezvous with him when we return."

He watched for a moment as the sailor used a handheld signal device with blinkers over the front of a battery-powered light. The destroyer was about half a mile from them now and continuing to open. Lights flashed back, and while he could read Morse code, it was a science best left to those whose ratings required it, such as radiomen, signalmen, and communications technicians. He pulled his stopwatch from his trouser pocket, then took several deep breaths as he watched the chief in charge of the underway replenishment detail check the topside and head toward the aft hatch. Forward, everyone had already disappeared belowdecks, and the forward hatch was secure. He glanced aft. The aft hatch was flush with the deck.

"Okay, XO, let's dive the boat." He looked up and shouted, "Clear the deck! Dive! Dive!" He hit the button on top of the watch.

The signalman bumped him slightly as the sailor slid past and down the hatch. Shipley waited for a second, making sure topside was clear, and then shouted the order to dive once again.

He slid down the ladder to the conning tower, the repeating "oogle" of the horn giving satisfaction that they were leaving daylight behind and returning to the bosom of the depths. He looked up as the sailor double-checked the hatch, ensuring that he—the skipper—had done his job properly.

"Make depth sixty feet," Shipley ordered. He looked at the stopwatch.

"Christmas Tree?" he asked.

From the control room one deck lower, he heard Weaver report, "Main induction valves still open!"

"Switch to battery power," Shipley ordered. "Close main induction valves."

Almost immediately, a new report came from the control room below them. "All green!"

The vibration of the diesel engines stopped, bringing almost silence to the boat.

Across the conning tower, Boohan worked the levers, opening the vents of the ballast tanks.

"Planes out," Boohan reported.

"Planes out" should have been reported as soon as he closed the hatch, Shipley thought.

The sound of water rushing into the tanks filled the void surrounding them. The deck tilted as the submarine continued down, but then began almost immediately to ease on the angle.

"Passing fifty feet," Arneau reported.

The planesmen spun their wheels in unison, keeping the boat on course while leveling the *Squallfish*.

"Depth sixty-five feet," Arneau reported.

Shipley looked at the planesmen. Boohan stepped over to them and whispered something in their ears. The two sailors turned the wheels a little farther, bringing the boat level.

"Seventy feet."

Boohan pushed two levers closed, hit a blast of compressed air, and the *Squallfish* rose a few feet.

"I make our depth six zero feet," Arneau said.

"Final trim," Boohan reported.

Shipley looked at his stopwatch. Every eye was on him in the conning tower. He smiled. "Considering that this was a real surprise test for submerging, it wasn't too bad." He put the stopwatch into the pocket of his foul-weather jacket.

"Up periscope."

"Wait, Skipper," Senior Chief Boohan said. "You gotta tell us the time," he pleaded.

Shipley smiled. "Eighteen seconds to clear the decks. That's two seconds better. Forty seconds for Christmas Tree green. Periscope depth and final trim not as good. It was one minute fifty-five. That's five seconds longer than our last dunk. But I am very happy with the emergency-dive sequence. Once we're below the waterline, a second or two is less important than it is when we're surfaced."

Boohan slapped the backs of the heads of the two planesmen. "Okay, you did good."

"Steady up on course zero three zero."

"Aye, sir. Helmsman, left ten degrees rudder, steady on course zero three zero. Planesman, maintain depth sixty feet," Arneau ordered.

"Coming left, ten degrees rudder, to course zero three zero, sir," the helmsman said.

"Keep us at periscope depth for a while, XO. Run up the scope and take a look-see so we can make sure the *Stevens* decided to turn back and finish the job. Where are our guests?"

Arneau nodded aft. "The chief of the boat—"

"Aye, sir!" Senior Chief Boohan shouted from his navigation position near the planesmen.

"COB, where are the visitors?"

"Norton is supposed to take them down to forward berthing. We have several sailors who don't have hot-bunk partners yet."

"Very well, COB," Arneau replied before turning back to Shipley. "The officer is waiting for you in the wardroom, Skipper."

Shipley nodded. "Thanks, XO. When you are ready, secure the special bridge watch and set the regular underway watch. Then join me in the wardroom. We'll talk with one of our visitors and do the night orders while we are there."

"Aye, sir. That was close. Whew!" Arneau shook his head. "We only missed by inches."

"Close is okay; inches are okay." Shipley let go of the pipe he was holding. "I'm going to the wardroom to talk with the young lieutenant who has disrupted our mission and caused us to have to surface during the day."

Arneau grinned. Bright white teeth lit up his tan skin. "Probably some surface skimmer who knows no better, Skipper."

"He looked sunburned to me, Skipper," Senior Chief Boohan added. Submariners were renowned for pale skin and a propensity for burning easily when they did hit the beach.

"Skipper off the bridge!" the junior officer of the deck

shouted as Shipley disappeared down the hatch to the control room, heading forward toward officers' country and the wardroom mess.

SHIPLEY ducked and stepped into the wardroom mess. The officer was sitting at the first table. The man jumped up, barely missing the pipes running across the overhead.

"Be careful," Shipley said grimacing, his eyes glancing up at the pipes. "You'll knock yourself out if you're not careful while you're aboard."

The officer raised his head to look and bumped his forehead on one of the pipes, causing him to crouch quickly.

"Or raise some bumps on your head," Shipley finished, his voice trailing off. "You okay?" He stepped to the coffee urn and poured himself a cup. When he turned, the officer was still standing. He looked him over. He had to be more than six feet tall.

Anyone over six feet in a diesel submarine ran the risk of doing themselves a head injury. There was no spare room for spreading out in a submarine. Everyone molded their life around crowded conditions, low overheads, and short bunks.

"How tall are you?" Shipley asked.

"Six-foot-one, sir."

"You're going to have to be careful while you're on board, Lieutenant. You have any experience on board a submarine?"

The officer shook his head. "First trip."

Shipley nodded and turned back to his coffee. The man's feet were going to hang over the edge of the rack. Seemed squared away, but then lieutenants are supposed to be. The officer had the notorious Navy regulation haircut. Tapered brown hair down to within a couple of inches of the shoulder line; sideburns even with the ears. Shipley turned back to the table as he quietly stirred powdered milk into his coffee.

He watched quietly for a moment. The officer was leaning slightly to the right as his eyes tracked the overhead piping. Then the man reached up and ran his hand over the small bump growing on his forehead. He then looked at his fingers.

"It's not bleeding. If that's the worst that happens, you'll survive this mission. I'm Commander Chad Shipley, the commanding officer of this boat that had to surface during daylight to pick you and your men up, Lieutenant. We're not much on protocol aboard the *Squallfish*. We don't have the room or the time to do it. So sit down before you hurt yourself again."

Shipley slid in on the other side of the man.

"I'm Lieutenant Jeffrey Logan, sir." Logan awkwardly extended a hand, which Shipley shook.

Firm handshake, Shipley thought. "You have anything for me, Lieutenant?"

Logan reached on the seat beside him and lifted a familiar brown guard mail envelope taped up inside wax paper. "Sir, this is from my boss via CINCNELM and the Director of Naval Intelligence. It directs—"

Shipley held up his hand. "Don't tell me, Lieutenant Logan. Let me read it; then you can explain it." He looked at Logan. The man had an expression that reminded Shipley of a dog when it did something wrong. He smiled. "It helps me put into context for our follow-on discussion." He looked at Logan's cup. "You ought to have another cup after that trip from the *Stevens*. The North Atlantic can be a rough customer."

As Logan slid out of the seat he asked, "How are the sailors who fell into the drink, sir?"

Shipley smiled. "Luckily they didn't fall into the sea. We managed to grab them before that happened, but they were soaked. From here, I'll head over to sick bay and see what the doc says. But they'll be all right."

"I overheard one of the sailors say they had fallen overboard and . . ."

". . . Were near death when we finally got them back onboard?" Shipley finished.

"Yes, sir; something like that."

"Scuttlebutt is all it is, Lieutenant. Sailors and Southerners are some of the best storytellers our nation has, and I think we have a submarine full of them." Shipley ripped the wax paper off, laying the crinkled trash on top of the table. Then he unwound the string to open the guard mail envelope. "Top Secret," he said, glancing up at Logan as he pulled the inner envelope out.

"Yes, sir. With your permission, Commander, I would like to use the safe in your radio shack to store the classified material."

"You have other classified stuff with you?"

"Not much, sir, but the two sailors I have with me may have some."

"'May have some'?"

"Well, sir, we were put together pretty quickly because of the importance of this mission."

"I understand from Captain Stewart that the two sailors are photographer mates?"

Logan shook his head. "No, sir. They are both communications technicians."

Shipley looked up, his eyes narrowing. "Why do I have CTs on board my boat?"

Logan set his cup on the table. "I'm an intelligence officer—"

"I know that," Shipley interrupted. "I'm used to intelligence officers, but I know what CTs do and have done. I know about OP-20G."

"World War II?"

"Yes, World War II. CTs are the descendants of Joe Roquefort and his band of code breakers in Hawaii. We have never taken them on board submarines, so why now?"

"They aren't code breakers, sir. They are both trained in detecting atomic particles and being able to determine their level of radioactivity." Logan nodded at the paper in Shipley's hand. "I think it is explained in the letter, sir. The two enlisted are a Naval Intelligence team trained to analyze the radioactivity and associate it with the photographic evidence. It helps our analysts determine source and capability."

"Okay, I don't understand what you're trying to tell me, so sip your coffee while I read, Lieutenant." Before he opened the papers, Shipley raised his head. "How can you analyze the air if I don't surface?"

"Main induction valves, sir."

"Using main induction valves means we'd have to be on the surface. The Soviets aren't as dumb as London and the Pentagon would like them to be. They're paranoid and destructive with anything that comes within what they perceive to be their home waters and territories."

Logan took a deep breath.

Shipley chuckled. "Guess you're used to asshole submariners who have a lot of questions?"

Logan smiled. "No, sir. Usually they're surface ship skippers. About the safe in radio, sir?"

"What about it, Lieutenant?"

"Once we finish gathering our intelligence information, the photographs and the air samples will become classified. Both will have to be stored in an approved facility until we return to port."

Shipley laid the orders facedown on the table. "I see. Well, Lieutenant Logan, I have yet to read this, and I'm not sure I'm going to like what I read when I finish. When I was talking with the commanding officer of the *Stevens*, he indicated we were going to rendezvous with him on our return trip. At that rendezvous you and your men are disembarking. I am presuming that once we return to Holy Loch, there will be no proof the *Squallfish* ever went on this mission."

Logan reached up and gingerly touched the bump on his head. Then he clasped his hands together on the table.

"You're not nervous, are you?"

Logan straightened. "No, sir; I don't think I am," he answered, his eyes looking around the wardroom mess.

"So answer me: when you get off the *Squallfish* after we rendezvous with the *Stevens*, where will you go?"

"I'm not really sure, sir," he answered, shaking his head. "All I know is that you are to take—"

Shipley held up his hand, palm out. "Don't tell me. Let me read these." He lifted the paper and started reading it. "Top Secret" in red-stamped ink kept drawing his attention to the top and bottom of the page. Top-secret documents were things the submarine service was used to, but not seeing them carried around in a guard mail envelope by a fresh-faced lieutenant in the North Atlantic. Where was the briefcase with the lock on it that was supposed to be used to transport top-secret material?

Shipley took a deep breath and a quick drink of the coffee. The tannic acid of old coffee crossed his mouth as he swallowed. If it were morning, he'd have Crocky up here making it himself. But it was late in the afternoon, and on board the *Squallfish*, only one fresh pot a day was the norm.

He continued reading the orders until he reached the last paragraph, and when he read it, he looked up sharply at Logan. "Are they kidding?"

Logan shook his head. "No, sir. The Director of Naval Intelligence has coordinated this with—"

Shipley laid the paper facedown on the table and cocked his head at Logan. "Don't tell me; I know you're an intelligence officer, Lieutenant?"

Logan blushed. "Yes, sir; but I've got lots of sea time."

"But not on board a submarine?"

Logan licked his lips. "No, sir, but I'm a fast learner."

"It'll take more than a fast learner to discover every danger on a submarine." He lifted the paper again and reread the last paragraph. "Lieutenant, I hope this is worth the risk to the lives of the crew and to the *Squallfish*. This is the most dangerous and dumbest mission I have ever heard of, and I can understand why they waited until we got under way to tell me about it and that your Admiral Frost wants us to do it."

"Sir, if we could move to the radio shack, where we can talk freely—"

"You mean talk classified shit, Lieutenant Logan?"

"Yes, sir," he said with a quick nod. Logan looked around the wardroom. "This is pretty open."

"This is as open as it gets on these old boats, so get used to it."

"Sir?"

"Lieutenant, this is my classified briefing room as well as our wardroom mess. So speak up. Everyone on the *Squallfish*, including our engineers, is cleared up to top secret, so you aren't going to spill the beans on anything we are doing. Even if you did, it wouldn't make one hell of a difference, because word on a submarine is quicker than the speed of light. What is said in the forward torpedo room is known by the aft torpedo room before you or I could walk from the bow to the stern on this boat." Shipley slapped the paper in his hand. "So tell me, young man, how you expect us to do this without getting ourselves blown to smithereens?"

Logan took a deep breath and began telling Shipley what he knew about the mission: about how Admiral Frost, the Director of Naval Intelligence, wanted proof positive of what the Soviets were doing; and that he and his team were assigned to bring back that evidence.

The spooks had brought with them special equipment to secure the camera to the search periscope, and the special environmental collector to one of the main induction valves. Shipley did not bother asking how they intended to take a photograph of another submarine. Just because the submarine was Soviet did not mean its skipper subscribed to any premise other than that a submarine mission could only be accomplished by staying submerged.

An hour later, Shipley stood. "Lieutenant, I know we are going to talk again, but I need to see to the boat. You can use the safe in the radio room. It's not big, but the COMMO, Lieutenant J. G. George Olsson, will help you. I'll have him track you down. We should be on station in ten days. That should give you time to get acclimated to the boat."

Logan stood as Shipley started to leave. At the entrance to the mess, Shipley turned around. "Lieutenant Logan, this is your first time on board a submarine, you said?"

"Yes, sir, but—"

"Before you try to flush one of our toilets, you have someone show you how. We don't have the luxury of daily showers out here, and I don't want me or the crew having to smell you until your shower day." Without waiting for a reply, Shipley turned and headed aft, toward sick bay.

Behind him, Logan asked, "Shower day?"

POTTS squatted near the third battery in the row. "Zero six one, charged; operating." Then he moved to the next one, reciting the number on top and repeating the words "charged" and "operating." Whenever the *Squallfish* submerged, he and Fromley, two of the six electrician mates on board, checked the batteries. Two other sailors were in the aft battery compartment doing the same thing. Without batteries, once the *Squallfish* reached a depth below fifty feet and the diesels kicked off, the boat would have no power. Batteries were also very temperamental, as his asshole lieutenant Greaser Bleecker enjoyed saying. Temperamental, hell! *If salt water soaks them, they short out, and the next thing you'd know we'd be breathing deadly chlorine gas. Thankfully, not for long.*

Of course, any sailor knew that if salt water was soaking the batteries, you were already near death, like those sailors in 1939 aboard the USS *Squalus*.

Across the compartment, Fromley leaned over a small shelf with a logbook propped open against the bulkhead. The stubby pencil needed a sharpened point. He licked the point before each entry as he scribed into the venerable logbook every word Potts uttered about the batteries.

"I ain't going to take that shit from anyone," Potts complained as he moved along to the next battery. "Who the hell does he think he is to threaten me like that? This ain't the coal-firing Navy of the thirties."

Fromley lifted his pencil. Should he write down those words? He didn't want to, but the Navy said everything should be in a log. Potts spoke up with another battery report, resolving the dilemma.

"Battery zero six four, charged and operating." Potts straightened. "If he thinks he's got me bullied out, he's full of shit. You know me, Froms; I ain't nobody's queer." He poked himself in the chest as he moved to the next battery.

The whistle on the sound-powered circuit drew their attention.

"There he is now, checking up on us two. I don't think he trusts us."

"You want me to answer him?"

"Well, somebody has to answer him. You want me to do everything?"

"No," Fromley replied nervously. "I just wanted—"

"Answer the damn thing before Bleecker comes busting through the door and I have to coldcock him."

Fromley lifted the microphone. "Fromley here."

"Fromley! You're supposed to say 'forward battery compartment,' " Petty Officer Gledhill corrected.

"Yes, sir, Petty Officer—"

"And quit calling me 'sir'; my parents are married."

"I think I'm going to be sick," Potts said as he squatted by the battery. "Tell him we're doing the battery check and are about halfway finished."

Fromley passed the word along, then hung up the microphone. "He said we're too slow."

"I heard him, asshole. He can just wait until we're done. If we do it too fast, then we get 'you can't have checked everything you're supposed to.' If we do it too slow, then we get 'you're too slow, hurry up.' There's no pleasing them."

"Kind of like Goldilocks, ain't it?" Fromley asked, chuckling. "Goldilocks. Funny."

"No, it ain't like Goldilocks and it ain't funny, From; why in the hell do I put up with you?"

For the next few minutes, Potts moved along the batteries, checking them closely and reporting them accurately. He never noticed the glisten in Fromley's eyes caused by his harsh remarks.

He had grown used to being told how shitty he was while growing up, and he did everything he could to live down to those expectations as a sailor.

It would take nearly thirty minutes to check the condition of each of the batteries, then another half hour to go through the final checks of the battery compartment. Potts looked up at the large round Navy clock someone had mounted on the bulkhead. "What time did we submerge?"

Fromley flipped the logbook back a page. "I have seventeen forty-seven on my logbook."

The clock read 1830 hours. "We're running behind."

"That's what the leading petty officer said."

"I don't give a shit what he says, and you don't, either. The point is I know we are running behind."

"Maybe if you—"

"It isn't me, Froms; you're writing too slow."

"How can I write too slow?"

Potts stood and walked over to the taller but thinner sailor. He slapped Fromley upside the back of the head and laughed. "Because I said you are."

Fromley smiled. "I'll try to write faster."

Potts walked to the other side of the compartment and started down that row of batteries. "I'll try to talk faster."

As Potts moved down the row, hurrying to finish before Gledhill called again, he tried to speak faster, casting a look each time at Fromley, wondering if the man was catching everything he said. He'd better, or he'd beat the shit out of him.

The *Squallfish* had two compartments filled with battery cells. The forward compartment was sandwiched between the forward torpedo room and the pump room. The pump room was directly beneath the control room.

The aft battery compartment was immediately forward of the forward engine room, which was immediately forward of the aft engine room. The forward and aft engine room nomenclatures gave a wrong impression to nonsubmariners, who upon hearing the description believed a submarine had one engine room in the forward portion of the boat and a second in the aft section. The two engine rooms on the *Squallfish* were aligned together, with the forward engine room containing two of the "beloved" Fairchild diesels directly forward of the aft engine room, with its two Fairchilds.

The engineer could head aft from the forward engine room to step through the next hatch into the aft engine room.

Potts looked at the clock. It read 1847. An hour since they submerged. That was too long. "We should have finished half an hour ago. You been writing down the times I been giving you for the battery checks?"

"Yeah." Fromley stood back, his head cocked downward, looking at the logbook. "I got each one timed correctly."

Potts walked over and jerked the logbook from him. "Well, you got the times wrong. Let me correct them for you."

Fromley watched as Potts erased the time entries and added new ones. He knew it wasn't right, but this was Potts—the only friend he had. They were shipmates.

SIX

Sunday, November 25, 1956

THE cramped room for today's briefing convinced Anton there was something about Arctic life that mandated smaller being better. He pulled one of the many straight-back wooden chairs out and tossed his notebook onto the long conference table.

"Captain?"

Anton turned and accepted the offered small glass filled with espresso from the steward. He nodded at the sailor, whose eyes never lifted to meet his. "Thanks," he said.

The sailor gave a quick nod without raising his eyes or acknowledging Anton's gratuity. What is going on here? On board his ship he would have the chief of the boat at his stateroom in an instant, demanding to know why he had not been recognized with a formal reply. Instead he placed the espresso on the table and sat down. This facility was not the Navy in many ways, and that steward probably had less sea time than most fishermen's daughters.

Dr. Zotkin walked into the briefing room. "Walk" was the wrong word, Anton corrected. The perceived rudeness by the sailor was forgotten with Zotkin's arrival. "Flew" or "raced" or "quick-stepped" would be better ways to describe how the head of the facility moved from one location to another. He smiled.

Marx. That was who Zotkin reminded him of. Not Karl, but Groucho—without the mustache. Zotkin walked with his upper body ahead of his legs.

"Ah, Captain Zegouniov, you are happy this morning, no?" a gentleman in a white smock, sitting across from him, asked.

"Yes, thank you," Anton replied with a nod, wondering about the accent.

Anton had been surprised the morning after his first day to discover stiffness in his legs with trying to keep up with the energetic Zotkin. Even now, though everyone insisted he was early, he knew he arrived on the right day at the right time. Eleven days spent in the facility around this Soviet scientist genius, and Anton knew little of the man.

"Captain Zegouniov!" Zotkin shouted. The man's hair flew in different directions, as if static electricity pulled every which way. The scientist started clapping. The other scientists clapped with energy.

Anton felt his face turning red. He glanced at his XO, Gesny, and saw him join the applause. Their eyes met, and Anton thought he detected a slight mirth in the eyes of the expressionless face he was growing used to seeing near his side every morning at quarters. Morning muster was new to the crew of the *Whale*, but it was not new to the Navy.

Zotkin stopped clapping, and the applause immediately died out. "Gentlemen, I have decided that it is time for the *K-2* to test the atomic engine outside of Kola Bay. In eight days, Captain Zegouniov will take the *K-2* from here—from our facility, from our hidden cove where we have hidden our great leap from the Americans. I know I have said it so many times it goes without saying, but we few, we few proud scientists working under the guidance of the party have developed atomic power for the Soviet Navy." Zotkin leaned forward, his voice going lower, and said conspiratorially, "And we have kept it secret from the Americans and their Western 'friends' by hiding it in this hidden facility." Zotkin laughed.

Continuing, he added, "Atomic power designed, engineered, implemented, and operated by some of the best minds in the Soviet Union."

Polite applause rose from those around the table. Anton joined. So finally he would be able to test the atomic engine in a real ocean, though at this time of the year the first ice was already creeping south toward the shores of the Barents Sea. There was a thrill of the moment. He understood why Zotkin was so passionate, why the scientist's face seemed to radiate with joy.

"Captain Zegouniov, allow me to introduce Doctor Nikolai Forov." A heavyset bear of a man stood up near the end of the table across from him. A brown beard speckled with gray hid the contours of the man's face. The doctor nodded at Anton, his face breaking into a huge grin.

"Doctor Forov is your new medical surgeon. As everyone knows, the *K-2* has been without a real doctor for some time due to many, many reasons, but now I am happy to announce that in time for the trials, the Kremlin has answered our request."

"Welcome aboard, Doctor Forov," Anton said.

"Thank you," Forov acknowledged as he sat down.

More importantly to Anton, he would have an opportunity to take the *Whale* into the open ocean. A submarine dockside was like the boat's name; it was a *Whale* trapped inside the bay. Or as Elena was fond of saying about those who made her uncomfortable, "She's sweating like a whore in church—impatient for the chance to get back to business." He smiled even as he shut his eyes for a second, recognizing the insolence of the comparison.

"See, even our taciturn Captain Zegouniov has honored us with a smile," Zotkin announced, his voice filling the room. Laughter erupted for a few seconds, with several applauding.

"And what were you thinking, our good captain?"

Anton was caught off guard. *Taciturn?* He was not! Discretion was an art best learned by observation or fear—or maybe a mix of both. "I am thrilled over the idea of us finally taking the *Wha—K-2*—into the open ocean. It is in the ocean where submarines should be, submerged, taking the fight to the enemy. I know I speak for Commander Gesny when I say we are honored to be the two who will test a technological breakthrough that will catapult the Soviet Navy submarine force to par with the Americans. I think if Admiral Katshora was here, he would say the same."

"Yes, he might," Zotkin added, his voice even.

Zotkin sat down at the end of the conference table. "Today we will discuss the goals of the sea trials we expect Captain Zegouniov to accomplish while the *K-2* is at sea." Zotkin opened his mouth to say something but stopped. The scientist made a sweep of his right arm toward Anton and added, "And, of course, we have Captain Zegouniov and Commander Gesny here to provide us with their thoughts and recommendations."

Zotkin continued, never once asking anyone for their thoughts as he went over the history of the program. Anton had heard the spiel several times in the past month. Zotkin was determined that no one forget his leadership in pushing the Soviet Navy into the atomic age. Anton doubted there was a verb in the Russian language that Zotkin could not conjugate in the first person. He tuned out the history of the program as Zotkin spoke. After nearly two weeks, Anton already knew the spiel by heart.

Zotkin continued on how he had led a small group of Communist scientists to the shores of the facility. Anton had discovered that Zotkin had been selected by Stalin himself. Zotkin covered each part of the *K-2* project. The *K-2* was a former diesel submarine of the Great Patriotic War. Zotkin led the scientists onto the beach where they had engineered the atomic technology; designed the atomic plant; and tested it ashore before dropping it into the aft portion of the *K-2*. Nervously, they had tested it again and again. They had integrated it into the legacy parts of the boat. And when they finished, atomic power turned the shaft with more power than ever before believed. Today, Soviet scientists in the Pacific Fleet were working on new technology to turn foul air into clean air. With atomic power and the ability to clean carbon dioxide from the air, it would only be mechanical limitations and human frailties that limited the time a submarine could stay submerged. The Soviet atomic engine Zotkin had fathered was foolproof. It could run forever. Nothing could stop his atomic engine.

As he spoke, a young man and woman wearing white laboratory coats wheeled in a portable blackboard. A sheet covered the front of it.

Anton blinked a couple of times. The squeaking of the wheels on the stand had shoved away the drowsiness the monotone had sneaked upon him. He shifted in his seat, forcing himself to pay attention to Zotkin.

"Additionally," Zotkin continued, "I have already started work on identifying what we want to find out, such as how far down the submarine can go and the engine still work, and how much speed we can generate while beneath the ocean surface." He smiled, his bushy eyebrows rising, causing his eyes to widen. "The only thing that limits the speed that atomic power can bring is mechanical limitations. This is our opportunity to establish a baseline. Determine how fast we can go with the mechanical limitations of an aged submarine. From our lessons learned here, we can make future changes to our submarines that will increase speed and durability." The scientist stopped, smiling, his eyes wide, looking around the table. The smile slowly disappeared when silence greeted his comment. "So, no one has anything to say?"

Anton looked around the table; no one answered. He cleared his throat. "Doctor Zotkin, we should also capture the cavitation we create while going through the speed changes." He looked around the table. Only Gesny and he were sailors. "Cavitation, as everyone knows, is what the propeller does as it moves the submarine through the water. The faster a submarine goes, the more cavitation it creates. That wave motion creates noise in the water, and antisubmarine forces are always looking for noise in the water to locate their prey."

Zotkin cleared his throat, a slight red creeping up the head of the facility's neck. "You are right, Captain Zegouniov. I was asking what everyone thought of the idea of taking what we learn and incorporating it into future submarine designs. Don't you think that is a great idea for the next step in bringing atomic power into the Soviet Navy?"

"Of course," Anton said, with a slight nod to the left, "it is something I think all of us would have expected. What I wanted to do was add to your already comprehensive ideas on what we are going to test when we go to sea. I know the more we can provide to the Navy, the more we can expect their support."

Zotkin looked down for a moment before raising his head. The red along the man's neck was gone. "Captain Zegouniov is correct. He has offered us another element—another metric for determining the effectiveness of atomic power against mechanical limitations against operational considerations." He pointed at a young scientist sitting on the right side of the table near the top position. "Marc, write down a new category. Title it 'Operational Considerations.' " Zotkin looked at Anton. "Good of you to enlighten us, Captain Zegouniov."

Anton nodded. He glanced at Gesny, who was looking down at the table. Zotkin was less than happy over his contribution, but atomic power was useless unless submarine warfare was taken into consideration. Every submariner who had fought in the Great Patriotic War knew that speed was not the essence of winning an underwater fight. Stealth was the essence. Sneak up on an unsuspecting enemy and put a torpedo or two into him, then sneak away before the antisubmarine forces found you and sank you. Atomic power could be the element of stealth that would enhance submarine warfare. No more battery limitations to submerged operations. If a submarine could stay submerged for days, it could eventually lose the dogs chasing the fox.

The man who had spoken to him earlier cleared his throat, catching the attention of the table. Anton appraised the man.

He wore the white smock of Zotkin's scientists. The man had to be about fifty or sixty. Heavyset, a stomach from fine food and drink. A mixed mustache of gray and red trimmed too close to the lip on the left side interrupted the features of the red-flushed face.

Zotkin stopped his talking and looked at the man. "Doctor Danzinger, you have something to say?"

"Yes, I do, Doctor Zotkin. Your plan of testing the depths, the speed, and the power of atomic power will work until the hull collapses. I have told you that. The first test must be limited. It must take the submarine through its tested limitations, not beyond. Then we bring the *K-2* back to the facility and see what, if any, damages are present. We need three to five at-sea tests, not just one." Danzinger raised a hand and made circling motions above his head. "Before we rush off to declare victory. I am concerned we risk the future if we do."

Anton had seen this polar bear of a man several times since his orientation voyage into the bay. Each time while Zotkin engaged Anton in conversation this scientist would disappear, casually, as if headed to another meeting or going home; but whatever the reason, the man never stayed when Anton appeared. This was the first time he had heard the man say more than a word or two, but it was enough that Anton detected a slight accent in the Russian the man spoke.

Zotkin's eyes narrowed. "I agree, Doctor Danzinger. But we have to ensure we understand every capability and every fault our submariners will face in using atomic power." Zotkin walked to the blackboard and wiped his hands on his laboratory coat. "Don't you agree?"

Behind the anger in Zotkin's voice, Anton detected a slight trace of nervousness. His eyes trailed back to Danzinger, who had picked up the pencil in front of him and was now drumming it on the table.

"I agree we need to test the combination of a submarine with atomic power," Danzinger finally acknowledged. "We also need to discuss the dangers—"

"I have told you," Zotkin interrupted, "that there were no dangers. We have tested everything we know, and we are satisfied with the safety of the program."

Anton watched the interplay between the two men. Why did this man make Zotkin both angry and nervous? What dangers were they talking about?

"We don't know what we don't know." Danzinger looked at Anton. "Captain, how many trips on the *Whale* have you made?"

Anton straightened. Getting in the middle of what was appearing to be an internal scientific disagreement was something he would prefer to avoid. "Every day I have been aboard the *Wh—K-2* prototype, Doctor Danzinger."

"And every day you have inspected the submarine from bow to stern?"

"Doctor Danzinger!" Zotkin interrupted. "Can we discuss this later, after we cover the purpose of today's briefing?"

Danzinger looked at Zotkin, then glanced back at Anton. "Captain, my apologies. Like Doctor Zotkin, I want this sea trial to be a great success for the glory of the Soviet Union and the expansion of its Navy," Danzinger said, as if repeating a rote phrase learned during his time in the Soviet Union.

Zotkin grunted, then turned back to the board. "Let's continue with the purpose of today's meeting." He flipped over the covering sheet.

Anton turned away from Danzinger, not answering the scientist's question, and read the board. Nothing new there. He had taken submarines out to sea for routine trials, and he saw nothing new for a Navy leader. Zotkin started reading what was on the board to the assembled members, making Anton wonder why people did that. Why read something aloud that everyone could read themselves?

". . . Getting under way at this time. The Northern Fleet will provide escorting warships to ensure privacy in the operational area. They will be in the area four days before the *K-2* sails." Zotkin tapped the board with his ruler. "It is a glorious day for us. Our first sea trial with the *K-2*."

"What if it sinks?" Danzinger asked.

Zotkin stopped talking.

What was wrong with this Danzinger? Submariners, regardless of which Navy they served, were a superstitious lot at heart. Danzinger had cast a pall over the *Whale*. "It won't sink," Anton said. "It is my boat, and with officers such as Commander Gesny, who have such experience on the *K-2*, the worst that could happen is that we shut down the atomic engine, blow ballasts, and surface."

"But that's not going to happen," Zotkin protested. "The sea trial is well planned. The tests on the engine have been flawless. We are not going to sink. We are not going to have to turn off the atomic engine, blow ballasts, and surface. Everything is going to go well!" Zotkin said, his voice nearly shrill in opposition to both Danzinger and Anton's comments.

" 'Flawless'?" Danzinger asked, his graying eyebrows arching.

" 'Flawless,' " Zotkin said, wiping his hands on his smock. He dropped his ruler but did not bend down to pick it up. He stared at Danzinger. "Very flawless, as you know, Doctor." His words were short and harsh.

Why was this Danzinger deliberately antagonizing Zotkin? And him also? Anton kept quiet, though he wanted to object to anyone discussing the idea of the *Whale* sinking. He was glad that only he and Gesny were here from the boat.

After a few awkward seconds, Danzinger sighed and said, "My apologies, Doctor Zotkin. You are right. We have had typical Soviet flawless tests. What in the world am I thinking?"

The accent and the name came together in his mind. Doctor Danzinger was German.

Anton had heard of how the Americans and the British had taken German scientists in the dead of the night after the war, spirited them secretly to their countries, where today they worked on their rocket programs. Maybe his government had done the same thing—only they took the atomic program scientists. Maybe being a German scientist was good—or maybe it was a bad thing to be at the end of the war? He had heard rumors. He had tried during his career to discount rumors. Rumors have a way for those repeating them to wake up one morning and discover the pleasures of chopping frozen trees in Siberia.

"Captain Zegouniov?"

Anton looked at Zotkin. "My apologies, Doctor Zotkin; I was thinking of the upcoming sea trials."

"And so am I. My question was, do you see anything on this

board that is out of the ordinary, or do you have any additional recommendations for the sea trials?"

Anton cleared his throat. "If I may, Doctor Zotkin." Anton stood and glanced around the table, deliberately ignoring eye contact with Danzinger. "I would like to thank everyone involved who have worked so hard and done so much to bring us to where we are today. Atomic power will cease to be the sole property of the American Navy, and when we finish our sea trials"—he looked at Doctor Zotkin—"for we know many sea trials are needed to furrow out any issues, problems, or criticalities of a new technology. Commander Gesny and I are dedicated to this project; we are dedicated to the Soviet Navy; and we are dedicated to the Soviet Union, and we recognize the honor of serving with the scientists who have worked so hard to bring us atomic power. You should be proud of your accomplishments for the party and the state."

"To the glory of the Soviet Union!" everyone shouted.

He glanced at Danzinger, who even raised his empty espresso cup.

"This one sea trial may be all we need," Doctor Zotkin continued to protest. The clapping started to subside, and when no one acknowledged his statement, Zotkin added, "Maybe we won't need more than one."

Anton added, "You may be right, Doctor Zotkin. It would be a great achievement to have only one sea trial. I know how you feel. I have always thought when testing new technology that I would like to do it once and then be finished. But as we have discovered with radar, high-speed modifications, sophisticated silencing techniques, sensitive sonic technology, and electronic warfare detection systems there are unforeseen events in integrating new technologies and techniques.

"Thanks to you, atomic power will move us along with the other technological advancements to a day in the not too distant future when we will sail ahead of the Western forces. But in sea trials you don't know what you don't know." As soon as he echoed Danzinger's earlier words, Anton wished he could have withdrawn them.

Red began to creep along Zotkin's throat. The repeat of Danzinger's earlier warning had not gone unnoticed by Zotkin.

"But I would like to add that never have I seen such a well-run, well-organized, and well-thought-out technological marvel." He nodded at Zotkin. "And I, for one, attribute that to the leadership of Doctor Zotkin."

Zotkin gave a sharp nod. Polite applause followed the words. The red seemed to disappear again. Anton glanced at Gesny, who dropped his eyes for a moment before looking toward the front of the room at Zotkin.

Zotkin looked at his watch. "We have thirty minutes before my next meeting." He bent and picked up his ruler. "The *K-2* will leave the facility before daylight eight days from now. It will be escorted on the surface by the destroyer *Razyarenny*."

Razyarenny? Anton nodded. *Razyarenny* was a Soviet destroyer launched in 1941 and that fought in the Pacific Theater before it shifted to the Northern Fleet. It was not one of the modern prototypes he had expected, but it was a proven Soviet warship.

"While the *Razyarenny* is your escort, Captain Anton, you are to stay close alongside her and are not to submerge until you reach the Barents. We don't want to chance an inadvertent collision with the fishing fleet or having the *K-2* hit the shallows along the bay."

What an insult. The idea that he and Gesny would be unable to avoid fishing trawlers and shallows was ludicrous. Both of them were submarine veterans of the Great Patriotic War! He took a deep breath. He had already upset Zotkin once; no need to do it again.

"Once in the Barents, the commander of the Northern Fleet Submarine Force, Admiral Katshora, will assume command of the test. I will be with the admiral as his scientific adviser." Zotkin nodded with a grin. "Together we will watch the *K-2* submerge. Captain Zegouniov, there are to be other destroyers engaged in this sea trial. They are there to track the *K-2* while it is submerged. We know why, don't we?"

Anton nodded, because if he tried to leave the sea trial area, the destroyers would sink him.

Zotkin continued, "Because they will be gathering data on your maneuvers to help us further identify the glorious advantage atomic power will bring to the Soviet Navy and to the Soviet Union."

As Anton brought his gaze back to the table, he saw Danzinger's eyes roll skyward. The man's face was a bright red, Anton noticed, just before the scientist rolled to the left and collapsed on the floor. Neither scientist on the sides of Danzinger moved to help; they just looked down, as if it were something they had seen before.

"For love of Siberia," Zotkin said with a grimace. The scientist tossed his ruler toward the table, but it hit the edge and bounced onto the floor. One of the scientists at the head of the table leaned down and picked it up. Zotkin walked to the door. "You two, come take Doctor Danzinger to his quarters."

The young man and woman who earlier had helped with the blackboard hurried to where the German scientist had collapsed. No one spoke as they helped the scientist to his feet. As they neared the door, Zotkin spoke: "Search his quarters and remove any drink you find."

When the door shut, Zotkin continued as if nothing had happened. "Captain Zegouniov, you will be submerged for five days." Zotkin held up his hand with his fingers spread. "Five days! Can you believe it? We are going to take a submarine to sea and submerge her for five days." He picked up his ruler. "The Americans have proven they can do it for more than thirty days. When their USS *Nautilus* set sail using atomic power, it was only two years ago. Before the age of the Soviet Union, we would never have caught up with the Americans. Now we are only two years behind them, and we will surpass them in atomic power technology."

"Thirty days?" another scientist asked from the far end of the table. "I think, Doctor Zotkin, we are able to surpass that."

Doctor Zotkin picked up the ruler, pointed it at the young man, and smiled. "You are so right, Doctor Minsky." Zotkin looked around the table. "If the Americans can do thirty days under the surface of the ocean, then we can do twice that."

Anton took a deep breath. Staying underwater for more than three days exhausted the batteries and burned up the air of the crew. If atomic power permitted unlimited time beneath the sea, it did not mean the air would last that long. He immediately saw that the critical element for sustained underwater time was not the atomic power or the food—they could carry and ration enough food for sixty days—but it would be the air. Five days? The technology to remove the bad air was in the Northern Fleet.

Plus, things break on board a submarine, and while no one would say it aloud, things broke more often on those things built within the Soviet Union.

"All we have to do is figure out how to reclaim the oxygen

from the carbon dioxide that breathing produces," Zotkin continued, the blackboard forgotten.

Oh, just a little thing, Anton thought. He noticed that Gesny was writing down the list from the blackboard. *Good*, he thought. They'd need to scrutinize it closely in the next four days to develop their navigational plan. Regardless of how good the destroyers were, the *Whale* was his boat and his responsibility. No matter what orders were given or directives issued, eventually responsibility for everything that was done on board a warship came back to the commanding officer, and he was the commanding officer.

An hour later, thirty minutes longer than Zotkin had scheduled, the meeting ended. The past hour had been spent on available technology to reclaim oxygen from carbon dioxide. Even diesels had chemicals in each compartment that worked sufficiently to give them an extra day submerged, but if battery power was the limiting system, then the chemicals made little difference.

THE briefing was much too long. Anyone knowing his subject should be able to explain anything in thirty minutes. Otherwise they lost their audience; especially admirals and generals, whose aged bladders dictated the length of a meeting. As the meeting droned, Anton had begun to think of other things, such as the sticky ballast valve on the water line running across the overhead of the control room. Then there was his lack of confidence in the crew to be able to perform a number of critical exercises that every submarine crew should be able to do.

He had had two familiarization cruises since he arrived. Both of them back to back; one on Saturday, the seventeenth, and the second on Sunday, the eighteenth of November. Not sufficient to take the *Whale* out to sea for intense operations, but enough to do the basics. The first was nothing more than to show him how the boat handled on the surface and while submerged. Even that event was insufficient to him.

Real submarine crews could spend weeks at sea going through exercises from damage control to fire to flood to blowing emergency ballasts and never achieve the crew cohesiveness to fight the boat. He was commander of a submarine where he was denied access to the engine room. Regardless, the Navy would never allow that to take away his responsibility for it.

His executive officer, Gesny, furnished him the logs showing the crew training. One thing for sure, the young zampolit had been doing his party-political training. Each crew member was either a dyed-in-the-wool, pure-blooded Communist, or a raving lunatic by now. Anton believed in communism. He believed in the party. It had brought a feudal, mid-eighteenth-century family rule into the twentieth century. And just in time, too. Pulling Russia—the Soviet Union—out of World War I gave the homeland time to build on the principle that every man was created equal and that work by all constituted work by all.

The Great Patriotic War against Hitler, as terrible as it was, melded the diverse people of the Soviet Union into a country of one. The war built patriotism between everyone. It solidified the bond of communism across a nation that encompassed thirteen time zones. It was moments such as these when Anton felt the pride of patriotism sweeping through his body. These young men who served their nation today have no appreciation for the sacrifice the average Soviet citizen gave for his or her nation during that war.

The hero city of Stalingrad; the flight from Moscow; the rout of the Germans in the Ukraine. No, they would never know the depression of sacrifice and the thrill of victory that the Great Patriotic War brought to the Soviet Union.

Now Anton stood on the precipice of another historical event that would continue the voyage of his nation in the twentieth century: atomic power. Atomic power developed by Soviet scientists in Soviet laboratories. He shook his head once. If this was true, then what was the German scientist doing here? Was he a Communist sympathizer who had defected? Or as he questioned himself earlier, could this Danzinger be a prisoner from the Great Patriotic War with Germany?

He turned the next corner, continuing his thoughts about his nation, about what it would mean to have an atomic-powered submarine force, and occasionally thinking about Danzinger, who had to be helped out of the conference room, apparently drunk.

Several minutes later, he glanced at his watch and realized that fifteen minutes had passed. Anton stopped, raising his head to realize that somewhere along the way he had managed once again to lose his way in the myriad of passageways, floors, and laboratories that surrounded the covered dock that hid the

Whale from the prying overhead eyes of the United States.

He stopped, debating whether to try to retrace his steps, when he heard voices ahead of him. Where was he? The lights were dimmer in this portion of the facility. Anton's nose twitched at an unfamiliar odor that seemed to lie beneath the cold air he was breathing. In his thoughts, the faint odor had gone unnoticed, but for submariners every breath of air when submerged meant a moment longer of living. Every submariner recognized when the air grew stale and carbon dioxide increased. Every submariner could tell by the smell of the air from the bow to the stern which compartment he was in.

This odor had a tinge of a hospital smell. Maybe he was near more laboratories. If so, he'd find some of the scientists there, and they could point him in the right direction.

As he approached the bend in the passageway, the noise of wheels squeaking as they turned across a rough floor reminded him of the shopping carts in the state-run shop Pretroyska. The noise of the wheels masked the voices he was hearing.

Anton continued toward the sound of activity. Someone there would direct him toward an exit that would take him back to the *Whale*. He looked at his watch again. Zotkin was to meet him there in an hour for his first tour of the engine room. No captain should be barred from any area within his boat, but then the *K-2* was not just any boat, it was the *Whale*. Then he realized that for all his pride in being the captain of this historic submarine, the true captain was Doctor Zotkin. The couple of times he had ordered Anatole Tumanov, the lieutenant commander who was the chief engineer of the *Whale*, to do something that involved the engine room, the naval officer told him that it had to be cleared through Zotkin. He thought of throwing Tumanov off his boat, but Zotkin had somewhat pacified Anton's ire with the explanation of the dangers of atomic power. Anton did not like it, but for the good of the Soviet Navy, he accepted it.

Anton turned the corner, finding himself in the shadow of the faint light ahead. Instinct more than caution caused him to stop and watch. An Arctic breeze whipped down the passageway, causing him to button the top of his foul-weather jacket.

Crossing the passageway from right to left, men in white smocks pulled and pushed stretchers from an unseen compartment on the right toward daylight on the left. Had he discovered the loading platform he had observed two weeks ago during his familiarization cruise? Some internal warning told him to keep his presence quiet.

In the Soviet Union, lack of curiosity was a virtue that could save your life. Anton watched, not moving, not wanting to draw attention to his presence. Of the five stretchers he watched pass, three of the occupants had sheets drawn across their faces. The occupants of the other two had their faces uncovered. The person on the last stretcher seemed to be staring right at him, and their eyes locked. The man's hand fell off the gurney, revealing deep swatches of dark, purple skin. Something fell off the hand onto the floor.

Around the bend at the end of the passageway, the noise of the wheels stopped, unmasking the voices. Anton was able to catch some of the words.

"Do they leave tonight?"

"I don't think so," a different, older-sounding voice replied. "I think Doctor Zotkin wants to examine them later, and according to his schedule he is going to be on the *K-2* most of the afternoon. They'll have to wait until tomorrow."

"How about these two?"

Anton could envision a shrug as the older man answered. "Give them some water. And if they regain consciousness and want some food, give them some. Otherwise, place the stretchers near the drains in the event they void any body fluids."

A third voice spoke. "Doctor Zotkin wants test tubes filled with anything coming out of their bodies. He also wants blood work done before they leave."

"Yes, Comrade Doctor," the older man answered. "But they are not going to leave until Doctor Zotkin says they can leave."

"Hey! Get that hand back onto the gurney!" someone shouted from the left.

The two men with the gurney stepped away. "Not me," one of them said. "I have no gloves!" he shouted in reply.

Scuffling noises came from the left and a burly man appeared, wrapped in a heavy parka for the Arctic weather outside.

He reached out roughly, and with a gloved hand lifted the sick man's arm back onto the gurney, tossing it as if it were no more than a chunk of wood. The arm was now exposed on top of the sheet.

The burly man stepped back. "Damn," he said, lifting his foot.

"Look what you assholes have done. He is shedding on the floor." He shook his finger at one of the helpers. "When we finish loading this bunch, get them over to the clinic before these two freeze. Then you'd better get this mess cleaned up before Doctor Zotkin sees it. You understand?"

"Yes, comrade, I understand," the helper replied, his voice shaking.

"You'd better unless you want to join them." The burly man turned and left the area, returning inside to the warmth of the facility.

The parting threat hung in the air, and Anton wondered more about what was going on. The man on the gurney had looked familiar. Had he seen him earlier since he had been here? Anton grimaced, realizing that the condition of the face was similar to that of the arm and hand, the skin seemingly peeling away, as if baked in some oven.

A hand touched Anton's shoulder, causing him to jump. He turned. Gesny stood there. His XO put his finger to his lips and then motioned Anton to follow him. The two Navy officers stepped back into the corridor. Without a word, he followed his executive officer down the passageway, and with two quick turns and a set of ladders leading upward, the two men quickly left the area behind.

Near a watertight door that Anton knew led to the covered dock, Gesny stopped. He looked over his shoulder and placed his finger to his lips. "Captain, you must forget what you saw," he warned.

"Why?" Anton asked, forgetting for a moment to hide his curiosity.

Gesny shrugged. "It is only a recommendation, comrade. The last captain grew too involved in the misfortunes associated with this great opportunity for our nation. He has since been transferred." Gesny tossed his head to the side and sighed. "We can imagine where he has been transferred, but we never discuss it."

In a low voice, Anton continued, "Who were the men on the gurneys? I saw two of them but did not recognize them."

Gesny seemed to be weighing whether to answer Anton, then replied, "They were former engineers of the *K-2*—the *Whale*."

"What is wrong with them?"

"Radiation poisoning," Gesny answered with a shrug. "It is one of the reasons why they keep you and me away from the engineering room. It is one thing to lose men who have little to live for or who have only their lives to contribute to the Soviet Union, but for us, we are capable of much more," Gesny replied quietly.

Anton could tell that Gesny truly believed this. One man's life was more valuable than another's? This was not the communism he was trained to accept, but he could understand the reasoning behind it. There are many underlying currents within government of which he had become aware and chose to ignore. Maybe this was one of them.

"But the chief engineer—Lieutenant Commander Tumanov? He has been with the project since the start, and he seems all right."

"You won't find Tumanov in the engine room except when he has no choice. He has seen what comes out of it."

Gesny's words would have both of them cutting frozen wood in Siberia. He half expected strong arms to pin him against the bulkhead from the blasphemy uttered. Several tense seconds passed between them. Anton glanced behind him.

"There is no one there, Comrade Captain."

"How do you know that this 'radiation poisoning' is the cause of their demise? Could it be influenza caused by the extreme conditions of the Arctic?"

Gesny shrugged again. "Influenza doesn't cause your skin to fall off."

Before Anton could ask another question, Gesny shrugged again. His XO was a man of many shrugs. He looked past Anton. "We should go, Comrade Captain. I strongly recommend that you forget what you saw. Many die when science moves forward. Even the Americans test their drugs on their people, who also die."

Without waiting for a reply, Gesny stepped to the watertight door. "Remember Madame Curie and her discovery of X-rays?" He asked between grunts as he opened the watertight door.

"Yes."

"She died of lung cancer because of it. We may expect more deaths, but in the end, their sacrifice will be good for the Soviet Union. Without their sacrifice, we may find ourselves in another Great Patriotic War against our Allies from the last one."

"Many have marched toward Moscow in history."

Gesny waited for Anton to step through before shutting the hatch and securing it. "That is true, but Mother Winter won't always be our ally from history. A true atomic power on a par with

America would ensure that the avenues of Moscow remain free."

The *Whale* stood in front of them. Where they had emerged had put the two senior officers of the submarine near the starboard aft side of the boat. Several sailors moved across the deck of the submarine, taking care of some housekeeping chores such as scouring away new rust. A submarine was only as effective as its ability to move silently through the waters; otherwise the immense antisubmarine resources of the Soviet Union's enemies would quickly detect them. While scientists at the facility worked quickly on developing atomic power for the submarines, another group of scientists, at the Black Sea headquarters, were working on something called anechoic coating. Once Soviet submarines were covered with this special coating, it would reduce drag beneath the waves. The noise signature of the submarine cutting through the water would be near zero. Anton smiled. So much technology, and all of it so near. Wave after wave of new things hastening the Soviet Union into achieving the age-old goal of Russia to be a formidable sea power. Gesny was right: forgetting what he saw was best for the Soviet Union. It was also best for him and Elena.

"She is so beautiful," Gesny offered.

"Is this your first tour as XO?"

"Yes, Comrade Captain. But you are the second commanding officer, so I don't know what that says about my abilities as an XO."

"What happened to my predecessor?"

Gesny looked around. Voices echoed in the cavern of the covered dock. He shrugged. "One day he was here; the next he was gone. Doctor Zotkin said the captain had had a nervous breakdown."

"But you said—"

Gesny looked at him; then, in as quiet a voice as possible in the echo-laden open of the covered pier, he said, "As I said, the captain was curious. He wanted to know what was going on aboard his boat."

"As I do."

Gesny nodded. "The captain did not have your connections to the Kremlin. He was Ukrainian."

"I am Ukrainian," Anton said.

Gesny looked perplexed. "Umm; I don't think Doctor Zotkin knows."

"I think he does. It is in my records, and my records were forwarded to the commander of the Northern Fleet Submarine Force—directly to Admiral Katshora."

"I think the admiral is the only one who has the necessary"—Gesny seemed to searching for the right word—"credentials to disagree with Doctor Zotkin." Before Anton could say anything, Gesny added quickly, "Not everything, but some."

"Such as?"

Gesny shrugged. "Hard to say, Comrade Captain. Short-stature XOs of the rank of commander are seldom privy to the thoughts and confidences of their seniors." He looked up at Anton and nodded. "Not even yours."

Anton stopped and turned to Gesny. "Why are you sharing this information with me?"

"Maybe it is because I am your XO, Captain, and as your XO my loyalty—not counting my extreme loyalty to the Soviet Union and the party—is to you." Gesny glanced to his left for a moment, then turned back to Anton, his voice still low. "I do not want to see this crew go through a third skipper. Our project—the future of the Soviet Navy—is too important for crew morale to suffer more than it already has."

"I need to visit the engine room, and I need to talk with the chief engineer more than short nods and hellos in the passageways of the facilities. I know that Doctor Zotkin views the *Whale* as an extension of his laboratories, but it is a Soviet warship under the command of Admiral Katshora."

Gesny turned forward, extending his hand toward the gangway. "Maybe we should continue on board the *Whale*, sir. Doctor Zotkin is due soon to discuss the test trials further. Maybe you can ask him about the shielding to the atomic reactor."

Anton turned, and the two men continued their walk along the starboard side of the submarine.

"And if we are lucky, maybe he won't tell us again the history of how he convinced the party that he could bring atomic power to the Navy."

The gangplank ahead of them lacked the normal canvas sides with the submarine number and name on it. It was a clean, steel walkway leading from the pier to the deck of the *Whale*, highlighted by the faint Arctic daylight at the huge opening leading into the exit channel.

"Lead, right? We are using lead?"

Gesny nodded. "Lead is the element known to stop radiation. But from what I know, it is the thickness of the lead in proportion to the radiation that protects us. The lead being used is from the factories in Ust-Kamenogorsk."

Anton's eyebrows furrowed in question.

"Ust-Kamenogorsk is a city in Kazakhstan. It is a center of heavy metal industries, of which lead is one." Gesny continued, poking himself in the chest, "I believe there is a problem with impurities within the lead shielding that is allowing too much radiation to escape."

"And what does Doctor Zotkin say about that?"

Gesny shrugged. "He disagrees, and he is the chief scientist."

"Can we modify the air purifiers to circulate the radiation off the boat?"

"We have tried. We are trying now. Since the reactor has come online, we have had two air purifier failures in the engineering spaces. Both times radiation built up. So you are right, Captain; air purifiers and circulation help a little in keeping the radiation down; but what we discovered is it also raises the exposure throughout the boat."

Anton pointed ahead of them, not at any specific thing, but to the casual observer it would appear that the two senior officers on the *Whale* were speaking about something on the boat. "That would not be good if we were submerged for a long period."

"It was not nice when we were on the surface. Even now, the atomic engine continues to run. It runs forever. Never has to be shut down. Never cries for rest. Just keeps running—churning and churning. We could submerge outside the dock and disappear beneath the waves, with only mechanical failures and human needs being the reasons for surfacing, as Doctor Zotkin pointed out."

The two men stopped. Anton looked over Gesny's shoulder at the deck of the *Whale*. Several sailors were about a hundred feet away, working on the deck of the boat. One was repairing some of the rusty deck, while another shouted instructions, as if the seaman doing the work needed additional leadership to complete the job.

"It is indeed a glorious example of Soviet science," Anton said.

"Even if it were not Soviet science alone that did the discovery, even if they had access to American science or German engineering, we need it for our survival. Our nation needs this power or the Soviet Union will never be the global sea power needed for its survival and defense."

They both turned at the sound of the hatch opening behind them. A young officer in the dress uniform of a lieutenant shut the hatch and headed toward them. He saluted as he arrived.

"Captain Zegouniov?"

"Yes."

"Admiral Katshora sends his regards, sir," the lieutenant said, handing a white envelope to Anton.

Anton looked at the name tag on the man's right chest. "Lieutenant Serigy," he said, holding the envelope up. "And this?"

"I am sorry, sir. The admiral did not say. He handed that to me early this morning and told me to bring it to you. I would have been earlier, but it took a couple of hours to arrange a boat to bring me across the bay." The lieutenant had his hands behind his back in a formal parade-rest position.

Anton nearly grinned. How did Katshora manage to get himself saddled with a skimmer? The surface Navy was so prim and proper. Try taking a submarine to sea with more than a hundred men crammed into a two-hundred-foot boat, sharing racks, no showers, open toilets that fail continually, and see how prim and proper you'd be after a month. You come back with fifty happy couples, goes the joke.

Anton nodded at the lieutenant. "Give the admiral my respects, Lieutenant Serigy. Anything else?"

"No, sir." The man snapped to attention and saluted the two men.

Anton and Gesny stared for a moment. "Oh," Anton exclaimed before raising his hand and returning the salute.

The two submariners watched the young aide leave the dock area, and once the hatch was secured behind the officer, Gesny turned to Anton.

"Well, Captain, that was refreshing."

Anton chuckled. "It is a good reminder of the caliber of those riding the monotony of the surface while we fly beneath the waves."

"That gives me great confidence," Gesny replied without breaking a smile.

The concussion hit both men simultaneously, knocking them to the deck. The sound of an explosion immediately followed.

Anton started to get up but was hit by something that slammed him back into the metal deck and bounced away. Anton looked left. The sailor who had been shouting directions to the seamen moments ago had landed on him. The sailor lay in an awkward pile several feet away.

Anton pushed himself up. "You okay?" he asked Gesny as he stood also.

"I think so."

Both men looked toward the aft portion of the submarine, saw smoke coming from it, and took off at a run toward the gangway.

The general-quarters alarm began to "oogle" as the two officers ran across the gangplank. Smoke poured from the air exchange valve near the engine room.

Anton grabbed Gesny at the base of the conning tower. "You get on board and take charge. I'm going aft."

Gesny grabbed him before he could let go. "That smoke is radioactive."

"I don't care! We have sailors down there. We'll worry about ourselves later. Get everyone out who isn't part of the damage control party!" He jerked Gesny's hands away. "Now go!" Anton raced toward the rear of the submarine. He did not see Gesny hesitate for a few seconds, watching him, before the XO scrambled up the ladder to the bridge area.

Chiefs and sailors scurried out of the aft hatch. One of the chiefs grabbed two of the sailors. Anton heard the chief shouting orders for deploying the hoses, starting the deflooding pumps, and approved.

Anton hurried to the main induction valves, useless to the *Whale*, since it no longer had diesel engines. Someone had opened them. Smoke poured from the two far port and starboard ones. The chief who had taken charge rushed up alongside him.

"Captain! We have men trapped!"

ANTON leaned against the bulkhead, looking at the *Whale*. The smoke from the aft air exchange had stopped, but the smell filled the trapped enclosure of the covered dock. The usual debris from a firefight—hose, foam, several exhausted sailors, and an odd ax on the pier—dotted the aft portion of the *Whale*.

"Captain, some water, sir?"

One of the sailors, his face soot-smeared, held out a glass in a hand likewise befouled from the fire. It was the man's foul-weather jacket that caught his attention. Fire had burned away fabric. Water from the firefight had already frozen across the shoulders of the foul-weather garment.

He took the glass, paying closer attention to the sailor's bare hands. "Thank you. Now, you go see the doctor."

"He is too busy right now, sir. Besides," the sailor added, holding up his hands and twisting them in the air. It was then Anton realized that beneath the soot, the hands had been blistered in the fire. "The air is cool on them. They can wait."

"They look bad."

"Yes, sir; and they feel bad, but they are not as bad as they look. And I am much better than the two the doctor is treating."

Gesny walked up. The sailor saluted Anton and turned toward the long table set up alongside the rear wall of the dock.

"Well?" Anton asked. He lifted the glass and drank deeply, the water icy cold as it went down. He shivered slightly.

"Reflash watch is set in the aft torpedo room. We were able to keep the damage to that area."

"I don't think we lost anyone," Anton said, straightening and looking around the port side of the dock where most of the sailors were congregating. "Do you have the final muster, XO?"

"Three crewmen have some third-degree burns. Two of them are serious enough that once the medical team is done here, they will be transported to the hospital. We have a few crewmen with some minor burns; most of them are out here with you. Doctor Zotkin told me that medical teams from Northern Fleet headquarters are on the way over, on board one of the warships."

"That's good of him to be concerned," Anton added.

Gesny grunted. "His only concern is whether the fire is going to delay the test." He jerked his thumb over his shoulder at the *Whale*. "Doctor Zotkin and his team are in the engineering room now. They are assessing damage, if any. I don't think they'll be done anytime soon, and when they are done, he'll come out here and tell you he sees no reason for not going forward with the at-sea trials next Monday."

"The fire was restricted to the aft torpedo room. Depending on the damage to the hull integrity, the valves, the pipes, the tubes, we might be able to do it," Anton said with a measure of cynicism.

"Aye, Comrade Captain; he knows that. He could care less about the torpedo room. If the aft and fore ends of the boat fell off, he'd be concerned about the engine room only."

Anton nodded. "We will do our own assessment when the temperature has cooled." He set the empty glass on one of the steel beams running along the dock wall. "I want to know what caused it."

Gesny shrugged. "Don't know. We won't be able to get in there for several more hours until it cools down. We are lucky there were no torpedoes on board. The third at-sea test scheduled involves a torpedo exercise along with multiple depth maneuvering."

"We do have torpedoes in the forward torpedo room, XO."

Gesny held up four fingers. "Only four, and two of them are exercise torpedoes." He crossed his arms. "Have no idea why they would give us two live torpedoes along with the exercise torpedoes. Probably a supply foul-up, where they either did not have the time to remove them or the means to transport them away, so the easy solution was to leave them on board."

"Do you think we should insist they be taken off? After all, we are a test platform and won't return to full fleet duties until Zotkin is satisfied with his atomic reactor."

Gesny looked down at his feet for a moment; then his eyes locked with Anton's. "I would just leave them, Captain, is my recommendation. If the crew misunderstands why we are removing torpedoes from the forward torpedo room, no telling what will go through their minds."

Anton nodded. "I want to know what caused the fire, and I want to make sure we don't have a similar incident in the forward torpedo room." He put his hands on his hips.

Over Gesny's shoulder, Lieutenant Gavril Lebedev, his operations officer, approached. "Excuse me, Comrade Captain—XO." He handed Anton a foul-weather jacket. "For you, Captain. It is growing colder."

Anton looked at his watch. Nearly four hours since they had returned to the dock. It seemed longer. Fires were a sailor's bane. A fire could burn a ship to the waterline and sink her in minutes. Most fires brought flooding with them, but water could be pumped out of a compartment and you still had a compartment. Everything else became secondary when you were fighting a fire at sea. Control the fire and you save the ship.

He took the jacket and slipped it on. "Lieutenant Lebedev, when the fire started, there appeared to be no organized damage control party."

Lebedev's thin eyebrows narrowed. "Comrade Captain, I beg to differ, sir; with all due respect."

Anton continued in a calm voice. "What I saw was a chief putting together an ad hoc fire team when the explosion happened. He was shoving men here and yonder as they worked loose a hose from deck storage. I had to help them."

"Sir, while they were doing that abovedecks, I was with the damage control party belowdecks working our way around engineering to the aft torpedo rooms. The sailor who gave you the glass of water was from that damage control party."

Anton looked at Gesny.

"It is true, Comrade Captain. You were topside for most of the firefight. I moved aft with Gavril and his team. I watched them move the engineers away from their stations. It was he and his men who braved the aft torpedo room to control the fire." After a pause, Gesny added, "And it was his men who rescued the two sailors trapped on the other side of the watertight hatch—the two sailors who are heading to the hospital."

"Why were they trapped?"

Gesny took a deep breath and glanced at Lebedev. "We are not permitted to allow free passage between the aft torpedo room through the engineering spaces."

"I know that," Anton said. "It is too dangerous, but the aft escape hatch is directly above the torpedo room. They could have climbed out there."

"Unfortunately, the fire blocked that way."

"There is also the side passageway along the port side that circumvents the engineering spaces."

Gesny agreed, "That was as close as they got before smoke overtook them. Otherwise they could have used the aft escape hatch once our sailors started using it for fighting the fire."

Anton grunted. "Okay." He looked at his OPSO. "How long did it take you to get the team together and at the scene of the fire? The topside makeshift fire team was pouring water into the fire within a minute of it starting."

Lebedev straightened, his head raised. He stood at attention. "Comrade Captain, my men and I were there as soon as we could get there. I do not have an accurate time, but it was minutes, not hours."

So Lebedev was angry about his questions. That was too bad. A captain's job was not to make friends or be easy on the crew. It was to turn a bunch of sailors and officers into a crew. A crew that could respond to any emergency as a team does—*smoothly*—with each person understanding his role and responsibility regardless of the casualties involved. He was not convinced that this crew was ready for any emergency, much less what most would consider a medium event of a fire pierside.

"XO, let's go find Doctor Zotkin."

"He's in engineering," Gesny said.

"Then we are going to engineering." Anton stepped away from the wall and headed toward the gangway.

Gesny ran a couple of steps to catch up with him. "Captain, if I may, sir; I think you may have been too harsh with Lieutenant Lebedev. He is a good officer—"

"Survival of the *Whale* depends on more than good officers, Commander. It depends on how well the crew is trained. You fight like you train. I will want to cover the training plans for the *Whale* tomorrow."

"Yes, sir."

They walked in silence to the gangway.

"Sir, Doctor Zotkin will not be happy if you enter engineering without his permission."

"Then he will be unhappy, XO. The *Whale*—or the *K-2* project, as Doctor Zotkin calls it—is *my* boat. The boat and the crew are *my* responsibility, and even though it is viewed as an extension of the facility only here to test atomic power, the Navy is still the Navy."

Gesny did not reply. Seconds later the two men were climbing down the ladder through the conning tower, down one more level to the control room. Then, ducking through the aft hatch, the two men continued aft, pausing once to scurry down a short half ladder through crew quarters. This would have been one of the battery compartments on board the *Whale* when it was a diesel submarine. At the hatch leading into the engineering spaces, an unfamiliar white-cloaked scientist stood outside it.

The scientist held up his hand. "I am sorry, Comrade Captain, but Doctor Zotkin and his assistants are inspecting the power plant. I cannot let you enter."

Anton leaned close to the man's ear. "Comrade, I am going to enter." As he continued to speak, Anton moved his head a few inches from the scientist's head, as if inspecting every inch of it. "If you don't step out of my way, there is an ambulance taking two of my burned sailors to the hospital. You may have time to join them." He did not see the half smile break the usual passive countenance of Gesny's face.

The young scientist stepped away, his face registering his shock. "Sir, he will have me removed if I let you go in."

Gesny stepped forward and slapped the man lightly on the cheek. "There. You can tell him you were physically overwhelmed by the captain and his XO."

The scientist moved to one side. Gesny grabbed the lever and swung it up and to the right. Anton reached forward and pushed the hatch open. He should have been allowed in the engine room long before he had to take matters into his own hands.

"You have to delay."

"There is nothing wrong. We won't—"

It looks as if we have entered in the middle of a scientific argument, Anton thought.

Stepping inside, he was amazed at the pristine condition of the spaces. No stale odor of old oil or fuel fumes filling the space. The bulkheads had been painted white—that would have to go once atomic power was dispersed into the fleet—and ahead of them stood three white-smocked civilians.

The center civilian was Doctor Zotkin, who turned and glared at them. The other two leaned down, blocking his view of what they were looking at.

"Captain Zegouniov, I was going to send for you shortly," Zotkin said unconvincingly.

The two men behind Zotkin seemed to be arguing, words garbled by the intensity and low voices.

Zotkin turned. "We'll discuss this later."

The two men stood and turned.

One of the men was the German, Doctor Danzinger. The last thing he saw of the German this morning, Danzinger was being carried out of the meeting. He seemed sober now.

Anton stopped a few steps from Zotkin. Behind him, Gesny turned and glanced at the young scientist who had followed them through the hatch. The XO leaned over to the young man and whispered something. Immediately the man turned and rushed back, out the hatch.

"What did you say to my man?" Zotkin asked.

It appeared that he and Gesny's presence had disturbed the head of the facility. Or did they disrupt the heated conversation between Danzinger and Zotkin? Anton wondered how hard it would be to have a discussion between just him and Danzinger, out of sight of Zotkin.

Gesny shrugged. "I reminded him that you had ordered him to guard the hatch."

"He did not do well," Zotkin replied.

"He had little choice," Anton said. "How is the engine?"

"The atomic reactor is fine as far as I can tell," Zotkin answered, turning back to the small hatch hidden behind them. "Come here, Captain, and look. See what you and your men will bring to the glory of the Soviet Union."

Danzinger grunted, drawing a warning glance from Zotkin. Anton deliberately ignored it.

Anton bumped through Danzinger and the other man, whom he also recalled being at the meeting this morning. The meeting seemed so long ago—it could have been weeks instead of hours, since time had elongated with the fire.

Zotkin stopped at a small hatch with a large porthole in its center. "Look."

Anton bent down to peer through the porthole. Another, smaller compartment of comparable pristine condition was visible on the other side. Zotkin bent down, looking into the compartment with Anton, their cheeks nearly touching.

"Amazing, isn't it?"

"This is the reactor?" Anton asked.

Zotkin reached down and twisted his lapel, looking at what appeared to be some sort of litmus patch. Anton's curiosity was focused on the compartment on the other side.

"So this is—" Anton started to repeat.

"Yes, yes," Zotkin replied with enthusiasm. "It is the atomic reactor. See the glow around the edges of the top?"

Anton nodded.

A broad smile stretched across Zotkin's face. "The reactor was never disturbed by the fire. It is a great tribute to my—to Soviet science. It never stopped running." Zotkin straightened. "This is good news." His lips pursed, and he shook his head. Then he raised his hand and twisted it in the air. "Feel that? That's the ventilation system designed to circulate the air within the engineering spaces, filtering out impurities." A curt smile spread across Zotkin's face. "I see nothing to stop us from conducting the test on time, Comrade Captain. That is the good news I tell you. I know it is something that would have worried you as it has me."

Anton straightened. "I am glad, Comrade Doctor, that the atomic engine is okay, but—"

"Reactor, Captain Zegouniov, not engine. What we have here is a reactor."

Anton stopped, frustrated at the imperious manner of the doctor. Civilians never seemed to see past the skin of the onion. Zotkin might be the smartest scientist in the Soviet Union, but he was not a sailor. Zotkin might be the father of the atomic reactor on board the *Whale*, but Anton was the master of the boat. Zotkin probably had less sea time than those who sailed the ferry between Severomorsk and the facility. Anton took a deep breath, holding it for a second.

"I am glad, Comrade Doctor, that the atomic reactor is okay. Fortunately for us, and everyone else, the fire was just aft of the atomic reactor. It was in the torpedo room."

"See! I told you so." Zotkin looked at Danzinger, then back to Anton.

Ignoring Zotkin's comment, Anton continued, "We won't know the condition of the aft torpedo room for hours; may even be days. We first must wait until it cools. Then we can put men in there to start cleaning it up, checking everything, and discovering what caused the fire."

"We can always seal it until after the test," Zotkin offered.

"It would be a poor test if we submerged and discovered the aft torpedo room flooding, pulling the *Whale* to the bottom," Anton said. Did not these mad scientists understand the rules of submerging or what the ocean could do with a single, small defect in the watertight integrity of a submarine hull?

"He is right," Danzinger said from behind the two, his heavy accent and deep voice easily filling the compartment. "We will have to delay the test until we are sure the damage will either permit it, or is repaired."

Zotkin whirled. "I told you we would discuss the test later."

Danzinger fanned the air in disgust. "You are not listening, Doctor Zotkin," he said, accenting the lead scientist's name as if it were a curse word.

"Doctor Danzinger, you are not that valuable to me," Zotkin warned. "We need to do this test, on time."

Danzinger opened his mouth to say something but thought better of it, and instead looked down. "Yes, Herr Doktor."

"And don't call me that!"

Danzinger said nothing.

"We will have our first assessment by morning," Anton said, turning his attention back to Zotkin. He nodded to Gesny. "The XO is already working on a team to start the inspection."

Gesny's eyebrows rose at this first-heard order.

"Once we are done, we will provide a verbal report to you, Doctor Zotkin."

Zotkin turned to the white-cloaked individual standing alongside Danzinger. "Ivan, tell the Navy engineers they can return to their stations."

He turned back to Anton. "Captain, the primary purpose—no, the *only* purpose—for you and your sailors is to prove atomic power as the way ahead for our submarine force. If we are unable to succeed, then there is little need for any of us to continue this work."

Most threats were veiled and sometimes missed. Not this one. "I understand, Doctor Zotkin. Like you, I intend to ensure that the test is a success. For me to do my job, it is necessary for me to ensure that the *K-2* is capable of performing like a submarine is supposed to perform. I know that in the Kremlin there are many people watching the progress here. I am sure they had rather see us delay for a few days than risk losing everything."

Zotkin looked at Anton for several seconds before his face seemed to relax and a smile broke across the coarse features of it. The gray hair stuck out in many directions, as if static electricity drew it.

"*K-2* is the right name for the submarine, Captain," he said, reaching forward to grab Anton by the shoulder and playfully tug it a couple of times. "I have no idea where the crew came up with this name '*Whale*.'" Zotkin raised his hands and made quotation marks in the air. "I will wait for your report in the morning. We both want the same thing, Captain, and together we will deliver a great achievement for the party and the Soviet Union."

Anton's arm was bumped as Ivan reached out and touched Zotkin. "The patch," Ivan said in a soft voice, almost inaudible against the background of a steady hum from inside the sealed reactor room.

Zotkin flipped up his lapel, looked at the litmus patch, and grunted as he dropped the lapel back into place.

The steady hum continued, and riding on top of, through, and sometimes below the hum was the oscillating noise of the compartment electronics. He imagined that the sailors and the engineering officer cramped into this area would grow used to it, as he already had.

Zotkin nodded. "We must leave, Captain, so your engineers can return to their posts. I look forward to your report first thing tonight."

"Tomorrow morning."

"Okay; first thing in the morning. Six o'clock."

Anton nodded. "By zero six hundred we should be able to provide a verbal debriefing on what we know."

Zotkin stood. "Doctor Danzinger, would you do me the honor of accompanying Doctor Moskum and me back to the laboratory so we may further discuss how this incident may affect our timetable?" Both the young scientist and Danzinger acknowledged Zotkin's orders. Moskum and Danzinger walked through the hatch, leaving the engineering compartment.

When Anton and Gesny stayed put, Zotkin glared at Anton. "Well, Captain, I will follow you out."

"I would like to check the aft bulkhead of the compartment from this side to ensure that there has been no damage."

"That is good, Captain Zegouniov," Zotkin replied, glancing over his shoulder at the aft bulkhead. "It looks good to me." He reached up and touched Anton on the shoulder, the pressure trying to turn him toward the forward hatch. "Why don't we let my people work with your chief engineer, Lieutenant Commander Tumanov, and have them provide you with a full report? I think it would be best."

Anton turned toward the front hatch and took a couple of steps until Zotkin's hand dropped. Then Anton turned. "Doctor Zotkin, this isn't an atomic reactor or power issue. This is a hull integrity issue, sir. If the hull is damaged between the aft torpedo room and the atomic engineering spaces, then the risk of flooding to the torpedo room is risk of flooding to these spaces. It won't take long."

"I really must insist, Captain, that you do your inspection from the other side."

"I don't understand, Doctor Zotkin. Is it you do not trust me?"

"I never said that, Captain. It is just that with atomic power we must be careful of radiation. Tumanov and my assistants know how to work with radiation. They have been doing it for months. I would not want your death on my hands."

Anton glanced at Gesny, who put his finger to his mouth.

"Very well, Doctor Zotkin; if you would have Lieutenant Commander Tumanov report to Commander Gesny, then we can tell him what information we need."

"Information on what?" Zotkin asked sharply.

"Information on the hull. That is all I need."

Zotkin laughed. "Of course. I will see that this happens." Zotkin waved his hand toward the hatch. "I think we have been here long enough. After you, comrades."

Minutes later, Anton and Gesny stood on the pier, watching Zotkin leave through the rear door of the covered dock.

"That was fun," Gesny muttered.

"Doesn't want us alone in the reactor areas," Anton observed.

Gesny shrugged. "Personally, I don't want to be in the reactor area alone or with a crowd or at any time, Captain Zegouniov." Gesny reached down and grabbed the crotch of his pants. "If you want more children in the future, you should not spend a lot of time down there."

What in the hell was Gesny talking about? There was lead on the hull between the reactor and engineering spaces; he saw it. Touched it while he was in there. He wondered if the aft bulkhead also had lead on it. After several seconds and a questioning look on his face, he asked Gesny what he meant.

Gesny leaned close to Anton. "Comrade Captain, who do you think you saw being transported out by ambulances a couple of weeks ago and earlier today?"

Anton shook his head.

"Most of them were former engineers who have radiation sickness."

"Are you sure?"

Gesny shrugged. "Who really knows what this atomic power is capable of? All we know is that we have had many of our original engineers replaced since this project started nearly a year ago."

"Maybe it is the weather?"

Gesny shrugged again. "And, maybe they met my mother-in-law in a dark ally? All I know is that this many sailors do not come down with pneumonia or flu or chest colds or a myriad of other illnesses so severe each has to be replaced." He snapped his fingers. "Here one day, gone the next."

"How long has Tumanov been on the project?"

"He has been with it since it began. He is a favorite of Doctor Zotkin."

"He hasn't come down sick, has he?"

Gesny shrugged again. "No, but you did not see him in the engineering spaces either, did you? He doesn't go in there unless he has to, and then he comes out as soon as possible." A despairing look met Anton when he glanced down at his short, stocky XO. "Did you hear the young doctor called Ivan say something to Zotkin about the patch?"

Anton nodded.

"He was referring to some sort of radiation litmus, or something they wear, that I think tells them when they've been exposed to radiation, or how long they've been exposed to radiation."

"Why don't we have those patches, if this radiation is so dangerous it kills?" Anton asked. Gesny looked uncomfortable. "If what you say is true, Commander Gesny, then everyone on our crew should be wearing them."

Gesny lifted his hat and ran his hands through his hair. "The last captain asked Zotkin the same question."

"And the answer?"

"Not sure. The captain was gone the next day. One moment here, and the next, gone." He looked up at Anton. Then in barely a whisper he added, "Almost a mantra of the Soviet Union, don't you think? 'One moment here, and the next gone.' Somewhere in the West, someone is probably writing a song with those words in it."

Anton straightened. Gesny could be KGB. "I think you forget yourself, XO. We are sailors of the Soviet Union, and our allegiance is to our country and to the party."

Gesny straightened, his face again impassive. "My apologies, Comrade Captain. I meant it as a joke."

"Jokes can be dangerous."

"Let's hope our country never reaches the point where humor is overridden by political correctness."

Anton tightened even more. Was Gesny testing his patriotism? He wanted to know more, and Gesny had the information. At the same time, he did not make captain first rank by joking about the Soviet Union or expressing reservations about what he was doing. Orders were orders, and as a Soviet military member, his loyalty had never been questioned. He had no intention of it being questioned here, especially since he was leading a historical moment in Soviet Navy history. He had already identified the dangers to him, to Elena, and to his career. The fire was another danger.

Though Elena was convinced, he doubted he would ever make admiral. But even those with no chance never intentionally burn the bridges of opportunity. He could see . . . Anton stopped. Where was his mind going?

At the back of the hangar, a commotion broke out as one of the firefighters collapsed onto the hard deck before anyone could catch him. Gesny took a step away from Anton.

Anton looked at the profile of Gesny. Gesny was a career sailor, the same as he. Even with the crisis of the torpedo room fire, he saw where Gesny had used a damp cloth to remove the soot from the bridge coat. The man's shoes looked as if they had just been shined. No KGB agent would understand the desire of a submariner to always look his best when ashore. Submerged was another world that few brought topside with them.

Gesny turned. "Exhaustion."

"I know how they feel."

"We need to get them back on board or send them to their quarters." He turned and faced Anton. "Captain, Doctor Zotkin said to keep the men here, but even here, the Arctic wind casts some of its strength. We'll be dealing with frostbite and exposure if we don't get them out of this cold." Gesny pulled a glove off, wet a finger, and raised it. Ice appeared almost instantly, lightly encasing the finger. He showed it to Anton before shaking off the ice and putting the glove back on. He slapped his hands together. "With your permission, Captain?"

Anton took a glove off, raised his hand, and felt the small breeze circulating the freezing air. *One knot of wind lowers the temperature another two to three degrees*, he thought, as he slipped the glove back on.

Doctor Zotkin cared nothing for the Navy. He was dangerous, but he was the Soviet Union's hope for an atomic Navy. If his XO continued to express opinions that could hurt the morale of the crew or affected the chance of the test being a success—well, a captain must make a lot of unpopular decisions for the good of the boat.

"If the captain would excuse me, sir, I believe I have offended you with my poor choices of words moments ago. I need to start organizing a working party to start our assessment in the aft torpedo room. May I send the men either to their quarters ashore or bring them back aboard the *Whale*?"

Anton nodded, declining to answer the question about moving the men. "You have not offended me, XO. I appreciate your candor. I hope that you and I finish this project together here and do not find ourselves in a colder area together where more than a finger can freeze and fall off."

Gesny agreed. "I understand, sir."

"Go ahead and send those you don't need to their quarters inside the facility. Send the others below. Any who must remain outside are to be relieved every thirty minutes."

Gesny saluted and walked away, heading toward a group of officers and chiefs near the makeshift canteen.

Anton looked at the *Whale*. It was a fine boat. It was his first command. Many thought Admiral Gorshkov had handpicked him because of his Kremlin connections. Zotkin probably thought the same thing with Anton's comment on the Kremlin. It was half true, but some explanations are best left unsaid. It looked as if both he and Zotkin kept veiled secrets.

SEVEN

Wednesday, November 28, 1956

SHIPLEY shoved back the curtain to the wardroom. Lieutenant Logan sat nearest the entrance. Beside him Lieutenant Commander Arneau Benjamin sat beside him, both their cups about half empty. At the second table were his OPSO and his communications officer, Alex Weaver and George Olsson.

Intelligence Officer Logan stood as Shipley stepped into the wardroom. Olsson did the same, but then Olsson had been in the Navy only three years since graduating from the University of Minnesota. Olsson wasn't a ring-knocking Naval Academy graduate like Benjamin, Weaver, and Shipley.

"Don't get up," Shipley said sharply, ignoring the raised eyebrows exchanged between Arneau and Weaver, who remained seated. Shipley stepped to the coffee urn.

"Skipper, you want my seat?" Olsson asked, the vapor of cold air coming from his mouth.

"No, George," he answered, shoving the heavy Navy mug beneath the spout and filling it.

"Gentlemen," Shipley said after taking a sip. He leaned back against the coffee table, careful not to bump the spigot. More than one officer had had hot coffee travel down his shirt. "I think after five days on board, all of you have had a chance to meet

Lieutenant Jeff Logan." He saw the nods. Shipley took another sip, followed by a deep breath.

"I'd be careful of Crocky's coffee this late in the afternoon, Skipper," Arneau said, grinning.

"We could save it for removing paint topside," Weaver added.

"Yah, in Minnesota we would use it to melt the ice for fishing," Olsson added, his deep Swedish accent rolling the sentence to an end as if it were a question.

"What does that mean, George?" Weaver said, leaning over and slapping the young officer lightly upside the back of the head.

"I meant it—"

"Okay, can it," Shipley said. "We're here to discuss the mission. Where's the navigator?"

"Van Ness said he had to swing by his office and pull different charts than the one he had."

"Why didn't he . . ." Shipley started to ask, but stopped. "XO," he pleaded.

"Yes, sir. I understand."

Van Ness stuck his head inside the wardroom. "Sorry, Skipper, I'm here." He stepped into the small space, two charts rolled beneath his arm. Quickly he unrolled one of them on the nearest table, Olsson and Logan holding the top down so it would stay unrolled. Then Van Ness unrolled the second and laid it down on top of the first.

"Are these what we need?" Shipley asked, his voice tight.

"Aye, Captain," Van Ness answered without turning around.

"Cliff, why don't you move to the right a little so you aren't blocking the skipper's view?" Arneau asked, reaching over and touching the navigator on his side.

Van Ness turned and looked at Shipley. "Sorry, sir," he said as he scooted over a couple of steps.

Shipley stepped to the chart. It was a large-scale chart that showed the northeastern coastline of Norway, the small coastline of Finland that touched the Barents Sea, and then the next several hundred miles of the Soviet Union's coastline. "Where are we?" he asked.

Van Ness scratched his head once, then reached forward and put his finger off the northwestern coast of Norway. "About here, Skipper. We are approximately one hundred nautical miles on a bearing of one three zero from where the borders of Norway and Finland merge."

"How long until we reach our OP area?"

"At current speed of six knots, about seven more days."

Logan raised his hand.

"Speak up, Lieutenant. This isn't a classroom."

"Sir, when I boarded, we estimated ten days to reach the mouth of Kola Bay. If we are adding another two days to our transit, then we run the risk of missing the event we have been sent to watch. Is there any way we can reach the mouth of Kola Bay sooner? We need to be there within five days, as originally estimated. Otherwise we . . ." Logan stopped.

" 'We' what?" Shipley asked. "Finish what you were saying."

"We are two days off schedule, Captain," Logan finished.

"Lieutenant Logan, there are things about a diesel submarine it seems the intelligence community doesn't understand," Arneau interjected.

The right side of Shipley's tight lips rose slightly as he straightened from the chart. "The XO is right, Lieutenant," he added. "Unfortunately, when we are submerged, unlike the new nuclear-powered *Nautilus*, we are on battery power, and battery power limits our speed. Unless we want to take a chance on having to snorkel or surface."

"That is a great idea, sir. If we use the snorkel or do the transit on the surface—"

Weaver whistled. "Wow! What do they feed you Intell officers ashore, Jeff? Razor blades for breakfast? The snorkel leaves a wake behind it that would expose *Squallfish* to the first airborne reconnaissance mission that flies by. Surfaced, they will even have an easier time of spotting us."

Logan leaned forward, his eyes sweeping the officers in the wardroom, gazing upward at Shipley as the last one. "Sir, I understand the risks of us being detected if we snorkel, switch to diesels, and increase our speed, but could we do it at night and make up the time?"

Shipley looked at Van Ness. "Okay, Cliff, if we travel six knots while submerged like we are doing, and come up to sixteen knots if we stay surfaced during the night hours—"

"And here in the Arctic, the nights are longer," Logan added.

"Don't interrupt the skipper," Arneau said.

"Sorry, sir."

"Plus, if we have to surface, Skipper, that means you and the XO will have to go port and starboard in manning the bridge. It's colder than a witch's—" Weaver added.

"You could be in the rotation," Arneau offered.

Shipley looked at the OPSO and the XO, then directed his question at Van Ness. "When would we arrive off Kola Bay?"

"We could do it in five days," Van Ness immediately answered. "I need to work out the navigational picture to give you a more exact answer."

"Sir, we still run the risk of being detected the longer we are on the surface."

"Tell me, Lieutenant Logan, are you willing to risk your life and the lives of every person on board the *Squallfish* to meet an arbitrary date-time?"

Logan sat back, nodding slightly. "Yes, sir."

"Then I guess we'll—"

Logan raised his hand slightly, and then brought it down. "Captain, there is more to our mission than waiting at the mouth of Kola Bay."

Shipley's eyes narrowed. "More that you haven't told me?"

Logan shrugged. "Well, we won't know until tonight's comms, but when I left, they expected the Soviet Union's sea trials to start in five days. Unless something unexpected happens, if we continue submerged at this speed, we'll arrive on station in the middle of a Soviet Navy force assigned to provide protection to the test we are suppose to observe, collect data on, and report about."

"Which means we need to go deep, stay silent, and to hell with the arbitrary time on station," Weaver said, slapping his hand on the table. The OPSO eased out of his seat at the table.

"When were you going to share this with us?" Shipley asked.

"I was told to wait until we arrived on station and they had more information."

"Who are 'they'?" Arneau asked.

"Admiral Frost, Director of Naval Intelligence. And I understand it was a point of discussion between him and Admiral Burke."

Arleigh Burke, Chief of Naval Operations—World War II hero and a fellow Academy grad.

"I thought this was between your Admiral Frost and the

commander, eastern Atlantic and Mediterranean—CINCNELM; Admiral Wright. The tasker you brought me was signed by Admiral Frost, but the cover letter to the papers delivered pierside at Holy Loch was signed by Admiral Wright. So who is behind this mission, Lieutenant?" Shipley asked.

Logan swallowed. "Sir, the CNO himself has approved this operation. Admiral Frost and Admiral Wright are the officers in tactical charge."

Shipley shook his head. "Lieutenant, you have a lot to learn about working with the submarine force." Shipley leaned down and in a whisper all could hear added, "Is there anything else you have failed to tell me? Do you know which Soviet warships will be operating in our OPAREA when we arrive?"

Logan nodded. "I have a good idea, Skipper. We know which ships have successfully passed their most recent refresher training and are destined to deploy to the Mediterranean early next year."

"The Soviets have never deployed the Northern Fleet to the Mediterranean," Arneau said.

"That is correct, Captain. It has always been elements of the Black Sea flotilla," Logan added. "But the Soviets intend to show the world that theirs is an oceangoing Navy, one that can deploy ships from any fleet to anywhere in the world."

Shipley waved his hand. "Back to the question: do you know which class of ships will be out there when we arrive?"

"Just what I said, Captain; I have an idea based on the warships assigned to the Soviet Northern Fleet. Most likely they're going to use their destroyers. They can track their own submarines."

"Soviet submarines are going to be out there?" Shipley asked curtly. "Soviet submarines, and you didn't think this was important enough to mention? I can understand the purpose of your mission, but during the war, submarines were the best antisubmarine force the Japanese and we had. We submarines fought each other nearly as much as we tried to avoid destroyers."

"I think there will be only one submarine out there, and if our intelligence is right, that submarine is what they will be tracking."

Shipley bit his lip. "Then take your good ideas and work with the OPSO here so we can know what we are going to be facing when we arrive," Shipley replied.

"It can't be a good thing when the word 'Fleet' is part of the opposition force," Weaver said.

"And, about our speed, Captain?" Logan asked.

Shipley turned to Weaver, who now stood alongside him. "Looks to me, OPSO, that we will have to increase our speed to get on station. I want to be there before the Soviet Northern Fleet arrives on station."

"Sir, if the Northern Fleet puts to sea, there is a good chance we are going to be detected. It is a great risk," Arneau offered.

This was like World War II missions, Shipley realized, astounded to realize he was looking forward to the operation. The thrill of pitting his lone craft against the forces of the second most powerful Navy in the world. He could understand their trepidations about going into harm's way, but when they came out he would have a seasoned wardroom. It was doubtful the Navy would award them a combat pin because of security reasons, but he would still have a wardroom ready to go anywhere.

The sooner they got on station the better the odds of him controlling events rather than having events control him.

"I appreciate everyone's arguments for and against how we maneuver to arrive on station," Shipley said.

He straightened, looked at the officers, and then tapped the chart on the table. "During World War II we did what was called 'end arounds.' We would detect an enemy formation miles ahead of us or speeding past us, knowing we couldn't catch them as long as we were submerged and on battery power. Battery power lets you bore a hole in the ocean, but it's a long, slow hole when you're hitting six knots. So when night fell, we'd surface and speed ahead, leapfrogging to where we thought they would have to pass. Then we'd submerge and wait for them to come to us." He scratched his chin. "I can't think of a time when a submerged sub during the war ever caught up with a target sailing away from it. Unless when they were zigzagging, they zigzagged right into your lap."

No one said anything. He wondered if his reminiscing went over their heads, or if they were thinking, *How in the hell did I get this crazy man as my captain?*

Shipley looked at Logan. "We'll increase our submerged speed a couple of knots, to eight during the day. That will depend on battery power. I don't want to find us with no spare power to make a submerged evasive run. We'll surface at night to make up time." He paused, "But we are not going to do more than that to make up time. The lives and welfare of the boat and the crew come first. Do we understand?"

"Yes, sir."

"Cliff," Shipley continued, pointing at Van Ness, "you work with Alec and Lieutenant Logan to work out a dead-reckoning approach to put us in the Soviet Navy OPAREA off the mouth of Kola Bay no later than three days from now. See if we can do it in two days."

"Sir, two days is going to be nigh impossible. Three is chancy."

"Ya," Olsson said. Every head turned toward the broad-chested Swede, who waved his hands in front of him and shook his head.

"Then show me, Cliff." He turned to the XO. "Arneau, would you see me in my stateroom?"

"Aye, sir."

Shipley stepped out of the wardroom and headed to his small stateroom. He understood the feeling of euphoria. When the war ended abruptly in 1945, many captains found themselves disappointed. Maybe that was the word here: disappointed. This mission might be the closest he ever came again to reliving the anxiety and emotions of combat he experienced in World War II. No one would voice the word "thrill," but it was there. For a brief second, he nearly loved Logan. Then he shivered over the idea of his boat being used as a reconnaissance vehicle.

A couple of sailors turned sideways, their backs to the bulkhead of the passageway as Shipley passed.

"Morning, Skipper," they both said.

Shipley acknowledged their greeting and continued onward. He should not feel thrilled. The routine patrol of the Iceland–U.K. gap was forgotten. The adrenaline wasn't racing through his body yet, but he recalled the fear of the depth charging north of Luzon and the thrill of life when they managed to evade and escape the Japanese destroyers. Then, within an hour of that event, the submarine had merged into the center of a Japanese task force, firing fore and aft torpedoes, with the expectation of escaping during the carnage. They had been wrong. A Japanese destroyer had detected them again, and for two days the Imperial Fleet had chased them, dropping depth charges, until either the destroyers had run out of them or thought they had sunk the submarine. Either way, they finally escaped. Life never seems sweeter than when you escape death. Even the topside air smelled better.

He had been three days in Pearl before he finally sobered up. This was World War II again—a lone submarine against an entire fleet—the fear of forces above him and the thrill of life afterward.

He—Bleecker—Crocky—probably the only ones on board who could know what his emotions told him. Fellow veterans of depth charges; the joy of surviving; and the hard alcoholic hazes ashore after a mission. No one knew the inane emotions combat created unless they lived through it.

Going into the middle of the Soviet Fleet and unable to fire on the targets! If the Soviets were half as good as the Japanese, the *Squallfish* was going to have to be very careful, or this time he wouldn't escape. Shipley was discovering the excitement within him for the mission, but it did not cloud the thoughts of holding his wife and kids when he returned to Holy Loch.

He reached the hatch leading to officers' country, the part of this boat above the forward battery quarters. Officers had the luxury of their own racks, but Shipley was the only one with his own stateroom.

Within this narrow part of the *Squallfish*, officers could have some modicum of personal privacy and to relax, if such terms were truly understood on board a submarine. And this was where they slept.

The officers' head was at the forward end of officers' country, in the forward torpedo room just past the administrative nook where the boat's yeoman worked.

Shipley pulled his curtains apart and stepped inside his stateroom. He pulled the drawer out from his desk and lifted the small tattered notebook from it. Sitting down on the edge of his rack, he opened the notebook. He flipped through the pages, pausing every moment or so to read something he had written on that mission in '44. It took several minutes for him to reach the pages at the end. He knew what he was looking for, but so much had happened during that voyage, and he had written so much down. Someday, when he retired, maybe he'd write a book about the brave men on board that submarine and the misfortunes that happened to so many after they returned to civilian life.

Finally, Shipley reached the pages he was looking for and stopped. He pressed down the edges of the notebook to keep the sheets from flipping shut. Then he started reading. Only a few seconds passed before he reached over to the desk and pulled some sheets of paper to the edge of it. With pencil in hand, he started making notes on the paper from the lessons learned that he had written about twelve years ago.

He was still writing when a light knock drew him to the entranceway.

"Yes?"

"Skipper, here as ordered."

Shipley laid the notebook on the desk, reached over, and pulled the curtains apart. "Come on in, Arneau."

"Always feel as if we are in a telephone booth when we have these meetings."

Shipley chuckled. "Tight quarters make for a tight crew, as a former CO once told me."

"And what mental institution does he live in now?"

"Very funny. Here, sit down," Shipley said, patting the rack beside him.

Arneau seemed to debate sitting on the bed beside the skipper, but finally did.

Shipley patted the notebook on the desk. "XO, we are going into an area where to the best of my knowledge no American submarine has been since World War II: the Soviet backyard. They are not going to be happy if we are discovered."

"I imagine they are going to be furious within their xenophobic paranoia."

Shipley looked questioning at Arneau for a couple of seconds before he replied slowly, "Yeah, I guess so."

"So what are we going to do about it? We've got this Naval Intelligence Ivy Leaguer on board who seems to be name-dropping all over the place." Arneau leaned forward so he could look Shipley in the face. "You think he's telling us the truth?"

Shipley nodded. "He's got no reason to lie, XO." He raised his chin. "Officers do not lie. Our perception of truth may be skewed periodically, but Navy officers do not lie. Anyone who graduated from the Academy understands that."

Arneau leaned back. "No offense, Skipper. It's just too many cloak-and-dagger things here for me to take in." He glanced at Shipley. "But I guess you've done this sort of thing before?"

"If it weren't for Naval Intelligence and the 'top of the roof' gang in Pearl Harbor, the first year of the war in the Pacific could have been completely different." Shipley looked up at the overhead, his thoughts traveling back to those years. He nodded. "Funny thing about intelligence and this new field of cryptology the Navy is developing, we war fighters in the submarine forces, the surface Navy, and our beloved aviators—"

"Yeah, just ask those aviators, they'll tell you."

"—is we never truly appreciate intelligence until the bullets start flying. I heard Admiral Nimitz wrote a letter before he was relieved as CNO telling the Navy to never forget what intelligence did for us during World War II."

"Why would he write that?"

"I think he knew that as the years passed and congressional funding for the military started to be reduced, intelligence would be an easy target for reduction. As much as we might look down our noses somewhat on our intelligence and cryptologic officers, I would hate to see the Navy decide in its infinite wisdom that we should combine intelligence into operations."

"That would definitely screw up us operators."

"It also would screw up intelligence, which, we discovered in World War II, gave us a decided advantage over the Japanese."

"So I guess we are going into the Soviet backyard?"

"XO, we are not only going into their backyard, we are going to do this mission so the good Lieutenant Logan can take back the intelligence our Navy and our nation need. Just as important, we are going to come back with the boat and crew intact."

"An easy way to do that is to stay over the horizon, submerged, quiet, and out of sight."

Shipley shook his head. "A submarine afraid to sail into harm's way might as well stay in port tied up pierside."

"You seem to be looking forward to this, Skipper."

Shipley felt the blood working into his face. "Commanding officers never look forward to going where depth charges wait, XO, but we do what we are ordered to do."

Arneau knew he was close to stepping over the line. "My apologies, Skipper. I meant it as a joke, not a comment."

"I know." He nearly confided how close to bringing the missions of World War II to this task seemed to him, but then thought better of it. He doubted the XO would understand.

Shipley reached over for the paper from which he had been copying his lessons learned from 1944. "I've been making some notes for this mission, Arneau. We are going to have to be quiet if we want to get in undetected and leave the same way. We have too much loose gear about the boat, and the one thing we have not practiced well is silent running. Your job for the next forty-eight hours is to quiet the ship. Then, for the remainder of our journey to the OPAREA, I want the ship running on silent ops.

"Major areas of concern during World War II were the engine rooms, crew's quarters, and mess halls. The watches in the conning tower and control room are going to have to learn to whisper and watch their noise. We have a problem with the voice tube on the bridge. That means you and I have to lean down to the hatch to relay our orders. We've been shouting them. Voices can carry quite a ways over a quiet sea, and with the ice creeping closer to the northern shoreline along here, it means our voices will travel farther. We'll have to be careful." Shipley paused as his eyes scanned the paper. When he looked up, he saw Arneau staring at the black notebook Shipley had left opened on the small desk beside his rack.

"My notes from my missions during World War II."

"That would be interesting reading."

Shipley nodded. "It would, XO, but there are a lot of personal things in it also."

"Aye, sir, I understand." Arneau stood. "I'll get started on the quieten ship doctrine."

"Talk with Lieutenant Bleecker. He'll know how to make the engine room quiet and how to store the gear of his black gang so we don't have problems there. Another major area is the pump room. We can't have the pumps running most of the time while we are inside the Soviet Fleet operational area. Bleecker needs to be reminded about them. Can't have them kicking on automatically when we're running beneath a bunch of Soviet destroyers." He recalled when it happened during the war. It had not been a pleasant experience.

He handed the paper to Arneau. "Here is a quick list I made from my notes. You'll discover more as you make your inspections. Take the COB with you. Senior Chief Boohan may have some insights, and even if he doesn't, he needs to know what you're doing so it'll trickle down to the crew."

Arneau took the list. "Sir, are we going to tell the crew where we are going?"

Shipley shook his head. "The orders from Admiral Wright say that as few as possible know about this mission."

"Hard thing to keep from the crew. Think they haven't already figured it out?"

"I'd be disappointed if they haven't. I would like to keep it as secret as possible, but I don't intend to work hard on doing it. Everyone on board has a life invested in the success of the mission. Knowing where we are going and the danger in which we intend to sail will help us better avoid detection. The only ones near—"

A knock at the entranceway facing caused both officers to look up. Lieutenant Logan stood at the entrance.

"What is it, Lieutenant?" Shipley asked.

"Skipper, I wonder if my men and I can do some practice runs with rigging the equipment we brought on board."

"How hard is it to rig the camera to the periscope and the detector to the main induction valve? I thought you had already been practicing it."

Logan shrugged. "We have walked through it, sir, but I'm not comfortable they know how to do it expeditiously, nor am I sure the equipment will stay mounted once we put it on. Fact is, we haven't done it at all; just a walk-through. I figure—"

Shipley let out a deep sigh. "How much noise will this make?"

"More if we aren't allowed to practice doing it so we can rig it once we reach the OPAREA.

"You should have been doing this earlier, Lieutenant."

Logan looked at Arneau. Shipley followed the gaze and was surprised to find the XO looking angry.

Arneau cleared his throat. "My fault on that, Skipper," Arneau said curtly. "I refused them permission because of the disruption in the conning tower. As for the engine room, the main induction valves are closed. Hard to make sure something is going to stay mounted when the valves are closed. I told the lieutenant we would do it once we reach the OPAREA. Do it once and do it right."

Shipley looked back at Logan. "Get with the XO and he'll arrange some time today for your men to practice, Lieutenant. I guess I'm surprised to discover your men have never done this before this mission. Are you sure the systems will fit where they need to fit?"

Logan blushed. "No, sir; I was told they would, but the officer who was supposed to come on this trip was sick—"

"Sick? Lieutenant Logan, you continue to amaze me with these little tidbits about our mission that you seem to believe doesn't require you sharing with the skipper of the *Squallfish*. Is there anything else you haven't told me?"

"It was never my intention," Logan said quickly, then added, "No, sir; I don't think there is anything else I've forgotten." Logan scratched his head.

Shipley sighed. It was his fault. He had avoided the intelligence officer for the past few days as he continued drills and preparation for their adventure into the Soviet backyard.

"I'm not sure if they will fit, Captain," Logan continued. "This is the first time we've had an opportunity to take these systems on board a submarine. The Systems Command engineers say they will work, but none of us has worked with them. We've been studying the typed manual they sent with them."

Arneau shook his head. "I can see lots of planning has gone into this, Lieutenant."

"No, sir—I mean yes, sir; planning has gone into it. We just didn't know we were going to have to do it so soon."

"Neither did we," Shipley said, his thoughts on December 7, 1941. "XO, take care of the arrangements."

Thursday, November 29, 1956

"Listen here, my fine black gang," Bleecker said, a muscular arm gripping an overhead pipe and one foot braced on the knee knocker of the hatch separating the forward and aft engine rooms.

In front of the World War II mustang stood seven of his ten-man division. Behind him in the forward engine room were the other three. He saw the taller Potts in the rear with the man's shadow, Fromley, so close he was practically up Potts's ass. Someone said something.

"Keep your traps shut!" Gledhill shouted, turning to face the other six.

"Yeah," Bleecker added. "At least wait until I leave before you make any shitty remarks about your division officer." The sailors laughed. Bleecker smiled.

"I know we don't have these quarters often."

"Like in the middle of the afternoon," Petty Officer Max Brown ad-libbed.

"Brown, see me when this is over," Gledhill said softly. "Bring some grease so my foot doesn't hurt you too much."

"My fine friends," Bleecker continued, "there is a good chance that each of you may earn your Submarine Combat Patrol pin on this mission. And there is a good chance that none of us may ever be awarded it. And there is more than a good chance that most of you have no fucking idea what it is."

Bleecker stuck his head back inside the forward engine room. "You three able to hear me?"

When the three acknowledged that they could hear him, he turned back toward the aft engine room and continued.

"We at war, Lieutenant?"

Bleecker shook his head. "No, Otto, we aren't at war." Then after a slight pause he added, "Yet." He looked at the man's dungaree pants and pointed at the right pocket. "What is that, Petty Officer Lang?"

"What is what?" Otto Lang asked, his eyes wide.

"What is that in your pocket?"

Lang pushed his hand in his pocket and brought out bread squeezed together with a napkin into a moist mess. "It was a biscuit from breakfast," Lang replied, looking at the biscuit-napkin mess in his hand.

"Get rid of it," Bleecker said, shaking his head.

"How dangerous is this mission we're going on, Lieutenant?" Joey Anderson, the 3-M maintenance coordinator, asked.

"My fine gentlemen, we are going into harm's way." He poked himself in the chest. "There are only three of us on board who have survived combat patrols where the Japanese rained depth charges on us. That's the captain, Crocky—"

"The cook?" Potts asked with amazement.

"Yeah, the cook, Potts. And, me; I'm the third. But, then you all knew that."

"We should," Potts whispered to Fromley. "He's told us enough." Looking up, he saw Gledhill glaring at him from the aft engine room.

"I won't tell you where we are going, but I think most of you are smart enough to figure it out, and none of us is smart enough to speak Russian. What I will tell you is that we stand a damn fine chance of running into a former ally's destroyers, who would like nothing better than to relive their lack of experience from World War II and sink us. They can't sink us if they can't find us, and they can't find us if they can't hear us or we can outrun them."

Bleecker took his foot off the knee knocker and stepped fully inside the aft engine room. He motioned to the three sailors in the forward engine room. "Move closer."

The three stepped to the hatch and stuck their heads inside the aft engine room.

"We have to do everything we can to make the engine rooms and the pump room as quiet as possible. Most of the noise that comes from a submarine comes from auxiliary equipment such as the bilge pumps, toilets, evaporators, circulation pumps, and air exchange valves." He nodded at Gledhill. "Your LPO and I have prepared a list of things we think can bring the forces of evil raining on our Christian heads. The saints who are going to fight the battle of the noise are you." He swept his finger across the compartment, ending with it pointing at the three leaning through the hatch. "Nothing gets by you; you understand?"

"Yes, Lieutenant!" they said in unison.

"And do you think anything got by your LPO and me?"

"No, Lieutenant!"

He shook his head. "Well, think again. I have intentionally left at least one thing, maybe more, off the list. I expect you to find what it was and tell Petty Officer Gledhill or me, but one of you had better find it. Otherwise, if I have to tell you what it is, then I'll know we'll need to stay on board when we get back to Holy Loch for some remedial training."

A moan rose and fell within the compartment, drawing a smile from Bleecker. "I knew you would support me in this endeavor."

"That's not fair, Lieutenant," Brown said.

"Life's not fair—"

"—and then you die," the sailors finished in unison.

"What's an endeavor?" Fromley asked quietly, leaning toward Potts.

"It's a type of fish," Potts answered. "Now, keep your trap shut or—"

Gledhill turned and stared at Potts. He put his finger to his lips.

One day he was going to take the straggly little LPO's neck between his hands and twist it like he would kill a chicken. He looked down at the deck, ignoring the LPO's warning. Damn Fromley.

"Okay, now that we have that out of the way; Anderson!"

"Yes, sir, Lieutenant."

"You're the 3-M coordinator. I want the premaintenance scheduled for the next two weeks done in the next twenty-four hours." 3-M was the Navy shorthand for its Planned Maintenance System program. Each piece of equipment from a watertight hatch to a bullock to the helm to the pumps to the engine room had a 3-M card designed specifically for it. At set time periods, an assigned sailor would take the 3-M cards and do the checks and calibrations dictated on it. No varying. No skipping a step. And always on the mandatory hour-day-week-month time schedule.

"Lieutenant, I can't do two weeks of preventive maintenance in twenty-four hours. It's impossible."

"Nothing's impossible when you got a depth charge bouncing off your deck. You got nine other sailors to help you with your 3-M chores. Petty Officer Gledhill will make sure they're available."

A bare, muscular arm rose from the taller sailor filling the hatch. "How about us electrician mates, Lieutenant? Not much to do with batteries."

"Then, Petty Officer Tully, you don't know much about batteries." He turned to Anderson. "Joey, you got any 3-M cards for the pump room that Petty Officer Tully can have?"

"Yes, sir; you know I do. But we did most of the pumps and equipment in that compartment last week."

"I'll help you, Josephus," Otto said, raising his hand.

"Yeah, Otto and I'll do the pump room," Tully said.

"Not sure yet what is needed."

"Just give us the cards and we'll do them. If we see something that can wait, Otto and I will check with you."

"Sounds like a winner to me," Bleecker said. "Do them again if anything is due within the next two weeks. Same for the batteries. Look on the bright side, Petty Officer Anderson: you won't have to do them while we are on station." He looked at his sailors, letting his eyes travel from face to face. "Listen to me. What you've been used to since you came in the Navy is called peacetime operations. What you're about to experience is the next level of fun, which is some sort of intelligence reconnaissance in the Soviets' backyard. I met some Soviet sailors immediately after World War II. They are as young as you. They have families. They love their country. And they're paranoid as shit. They don't trust anything having to do with our country. They don't even believe in God.

"America to them is the antigod to their godless society. So if they think they have an American submarine in their backyard, they're going to try to blow the shit out of us. There ain't no other war going on, so they have been stacking up depth charges for such an opportunity." He poked himself in the chest. "We ain't going to allow that to happen. I didn't go through thirteen combat missions during World War II to get sunk in the North Atlantic because one of us failed to do our jobs. Understand?"

"Yes, Lieutenant."

"Then get busy. Petty Officer Gledhill, if you need me, I'll be in my office." The engineering office was Bleecker's bunk. He had been up most of the night with the skipper and the XO, going over the quieten ship policies. Submarines were supposed to be permanently in that condition. *Squallfish* was prepared for an emergent combat situation as much as Bleecker could make it. Even when you make an inspection for quieten ship operations, as soon as you're done, things start to move, sailors change something, or even someone flushes a toilet.

"Another thing: once we get on station, tell the crew there is no flushing the toilets until I say so."

"It's going to stink up the boat," Gledhill said.

Bleecker shook his head. "I doubt anyone will notice."

He stepped through the hatch into the forward engine room and kept moving forward, heading toward officers' country. It doesn't matter what does it, but quieten ship starts to come apart about as soon as the readiness is achieved.

Bleecker stepped through the forward engine room hatch, turning to secure it once past. This would be good training for Gledhill as well as the sailors. It would give them a sense of urgency knowing the probability of being depth-charged by the Soviets. He doubted the Soviets could hit the broadside of a barn with their meager knowledge of and experience in depth-charging submarines, but sometimes it's just plain bad luck that takes you down to the bottom.

During World War II, the threat of depth charges was something never far from the minds of a submariner. Perversely, Bleecker hoped they had some dropped while they were there. It would improve performance by the men in future missions. Of course, he wouldn't want them to explode too near the *Squallfish*. He chuckled to himself as he headed toward officers' country. Why in the hell did he feel this way, looking forward to this mission, a mission that might kill them all?

Depth charging really brought out the hidden reserves, and sometimes the hidden fears, of sailors. He had seen some great sailors, he thought, break down—reduced to emotional rubble in those moments. And he had seen some dirtbags rise to the occasion. You never truly know the character of a man until he faces the fear of losing his life.

He climbed the ladder in front of him to the second level. His black gang would be searching for that elusive thing he had said he had left off the list. He didn't think he had left anything off of it, but his first engineer used to do that. On his last day on board the *Wahoo* as a fresh young third-class petty officer, the elderly chief told him to always have confidence in himself, but never so much that he believed he knew everything.

He nodded to the greetings in the crew's mess as he stepped into it to grab a cup of coffee. Crocky shouted at him to quit taking his cups, they exchanged a few words, and then Bleecker continued his parade through the submarine.

He stuck his head through the curtain to the small radio compartment as he passed it, shouting, "Wake up!" at the radioman, Petty Officer Lamar Baron, sitting quietly at his position, reading a paperback book. He laughed when Baron jumped, spouting an obscenity at Bleecker before he recognized the officer, and then profusely apologizing amid Bleecker's laughter.

Then the mustang lieutenant quickly passed through the control room before reaching officers' country. Behind him, along his path, his presence had given a rise to crew morale, something he never recognized. If he had, he would never understand how.

When he stepped into officers' country, the skipper was sitting at the wardroom table, going over papers and drinking coffee. Bleecker set the nearly empty cup from the crew's mess on the rack beside the coffee urn.

He told Shipley what the black gang was doing and that he intended to catch a couple hours of sleep before lunch. Then, he'd make another inspection through his engineering domain to see how the troops were doing.

Bleecker gave Shipley a half salute as he left the mess. Bleecker loved the Navy. He loved the submarine service. And he loved the men who shared the cramped quarters of a submarine beneath the surface of the ocean. Everything was right with the world at that moment, that instant, and within his own being. Bleecker slipped off his shoes and slid into the bottom bunk of the small quarters he shared with Van Ness.

Bleecker put his hands beneath his head and wondered for a moment before sleep overtook him what he had missed in the quieten ship list. He looked forward to hearing what his sailors had discovered. He shut his eyes, and within seconds he was asleep. He never worried about oversleeping. Too many years of waking up on time.

"WHAT a load of shit," Potts said as he and Fromley stepped into the pump room. Tully and Lang were already inspecting the equipment. Otto Lang was holding a 3-M card in his hand. Several cards stuck out of his back pocket.

Potts flipped the cards from Lang's back pocket, sending them fluttering onto the deck.

"Hey, Potts, don't do that," Lang said, bending over to pick them up.

"Or, what, Otto? You gonna beat my butt?"

Tully, lying on the deck with his arm beneath the bilge pump, pulled the arm out and sat up. "Naw, but I might if you and your idjit friend don't get the hell out of here."

"Whoa!" Potts said, continuing to walk forward, waving his hands back and forth. "I'm really scared, Tully."

Potts and Fromley opened the hatch to the forward battery room.

"Ah, home, sweet home," Potts said. "Our own little kingdom. What a piece of shit."

"At least it is ours."

"From, they gave us the forward battery room because it was as far as they could send us without shooting us out of the forward torpedo tubes. Besides," he said as he secured the hatch to the forward battery room, "Gledhill or the asshole lieutenant will come check what we've done anyway. They don't trust us."

"Bleecker's gone to his rack. He's taking a sleep."

"How in the hell do you know that?"

"Because when he says he is going to be in his office, he means he is going to be in his rack."

"Why didn't I know that?"

Fromley shrugged. "I don't know." He picked up the logbook at the forward end of the battery compartment and laid the 3-M cards on top of it. "Which one you want to do first?"

Potts slapped the bottom of the logbook, sending the 3-M cards onto the deck. One of them landed sideways and slid through the narrow space between the narrow walkway and the battery rows.

"Ah, man; one of them fell beneath the batteries."

Potts turned and squatted. "From, why the fuck didn't you catch them?" He stuck his finger down but could barely touch the end of the card. After half a minute of trying, he quit and stood up. "Looks as if you may be in a world of shit if they realize we lost one of Anderson's precious cards."

Fromley squatted and started picking up the cards.

Potts reached down and jerked them from Fromley's hand. "Let me have them before you lose any more."

"I didn't lose that one," Fromley whined.

Potts slapped him upside the head, knocking the sailor against the batteries. "Don't argue with me. I don't like people who argue with me."

"I'm sorry," Fromley said, rubbing the side of his face. His eyes glistened.

"And, don't you start crying on me." Potts held the cards up. "What is this shit?" he asked, slapping the cards with the back of his hand, ignoring Fromley, who was still rubbing his cheek. He looked down and started through the cards. "Battery ventilation; check trickle discharge routine; airlift pump checks; battery inspection—"

"We can use the stuff we been putting in the battery record log," Fromley offered.

Potts smiled, his eyes widening. "Fromley, you just knocked off"—he raised the card—"three hours of work. Whoever said you ate shit and chased rabbits never saw you in the woods."

Fromley smiled, scratching his head, his face confused. "Tommy, I don't understand."

"You ain't supposed to. We got hundreds of cells, each cell producing about two volts of power. The way you write, it'll take more than three hours for us to do this one." He stuck the maintenance checklist for battery checks at the bottom of the stack. "Let's see what else we got here: water-cooling system; battery test discharge." Potts looked at Fromley. "This one sounds like part of battery checks to me; one hour." He put the card beneath the others.

"I've been thinking," Fromley said.

"Don't do that; it'll cause you to have a headache."

"No, listen to me, Tommy. If we don't do these checks, then we're going to finish ahead of Joe and Peter—"

"You mean Pedro, not Peter. He's not American, he's Mexican."

Fromley reached out and touched Potts, then bit his lower lip. "I didn't mean we gun-deck our 3-M, Tommy. I'm not serious. Gledhill will catch it if Anderson doesn't and Bleecker—well, nothing gets by the lieutenant," Fromley whined. "We have to do them." He nodded several times, his head going up and down. "They'll know we didn't do our checks."

Potts shook the hand away. "Oh, shut up, and let me worry about that." He swept his arm around the compartment. "These things don't move. They're filled with acid eating away at copper and shit, producing electricity until they run out of the stuff. Then they quit. Why the Navy thinks we need to keep a continuous check on them comes from a bunch of desk jockeys in Washington with nothing to do but print up these things." He held the cards up, pulled back as if to throw them, remembered the one stuck under the batteries, and brought them back down.

"Is that all?" Fromley asked.

Potts shuffled through the next few. "Naw, but the others seem easy to do and shouldn't require much time."

"Is the card for checking the electrolyte agitation system in there?" Fromley asked.

Potts opened his mouth to say something, but instead flipped through the cards. "Naw, I don't see it. But we have never checked it yet, From, so why start now?"

Fromley looked down at the spot where the 3-M card had slid through the narrow opening. "I bet the card down there is the one for the electrolyte agitation system."

"So what's the big deal, shipmate?"

"I remember at A-school our instructor said the greatest danger to batteries is an improper electrolyte agitation system. We should check that."

"From, your instructor lied to you. The greatest danger to the batteries is temperature greater than 130 degrees. They tend to blow up then."

Fromley looked back at the spot where the card fell through the crack.

"From, forget it," Potts said. Why in the hell did he put up with Fromley? Even the man's name pissed him off. He doubted that when the chips came down—and come down they would—Fromley would be there. No, whatever he had to do, he was going to have to do on his own. Fromley would just piss his pants if he told him.

"Just get me the electric meter." He shoved the cards into Fromley's hands. "You just check off the list while I do the work, make the right log entries, and I'll tell you if we should skip anything that doesn't make sense."

"What did I do wrong?" Fromley whined. "I ain't done nothing wrong."

"Did I say you did anything wrong, asshole? Did I? Did I?"

"No, but you sounded—"

"Sounded what? Pissed off?" Potts asked with a growl. "Damn straight, I'm pissed off."

"But I didn't do anything."

What a stupid person. "Listen, From, just because I'm pissed off doesn't mean it's you. Okay?"

Fromley smiled. "Good. You know, Tommy, I can do the checks, if you want."

"Yeah, and you can blow us to kingdom come. Just get me the voltmeter and let's get started. The sooner we start, the sooner we finish."

EIGHT

Friday, November 30, 1956

ARMS crossed, Shipley leaned against the starboard bulkhead of the conning tower, watching Logan and his two communications technicians trying to rig the camera to the search periscope for the third time.

The conning tower was the highest compartment in the *Squallfish.* It was in this eight-foot-diameter, fourteen-foot-long cylindrical compartment where the hatch above was the only thing keeping the ocean now covering the bridge area from drowning everyone in the boat. It was here skippers fought their submarines. Two periscopes protruded from the deck. The one Lieutenant Logan and his gang of two were working on was the search periscope.

"Skipper!" Arneau's head emerged from the hatch leading down to the control room. The XO's eyebrows wrinkled in puzzlement as he caught sight of the intelligence team around the search scope. Then he crawled into the conning tower.

"How's it going?" he asked quietly.

Shipley took a sip of his coffee. "Don't know. Lieutenant Logan had asked us for the attack periscope, but when we discussed what he was trying to do, I figured the search periscope was better. Wider optics than the attack periscope."

"Don't think it'll mess up the radar on it, will it?" Arneau asked softly.

Shipley's face creased for a moment as he considered the question. "I don't see how," he whispered, shaking his head. "The contraption they seem to be having problems getting secured to the eyepiece is down here. I think the controls beneath the eyepiece are complicating their effort."

Lieutenant Logan took a couple of steps to where Shipley and Arneau stood. "Yes, sir, Captain; you are right. We are having a challenge securing the camera to the eyepiece. According to Petty Officer Brooks, who worked with Naval Sea Systems Command in developing the connections, this is a different periscope."

"Well, *Squallfish* is a World War II–era submarine, Jeffrey," Arneau offered. "I think there are only a few subs left in service who use the—"

Logan interrupted, "Yes, sir; I know. We worked on the Kollmorgan attack periscope, which was similar to this one." He scratched his head.

"Then maybe the camera won't work on the search scope?"

"Aye, Captain," he answered. Logan reached up and zipped his foul-weather jacket up to his chin. "Cold down here," he said.

"When we're on battery power, we have limited spare power to provide a lot of heat to the boat." Shipley looked at the thermometer. "It's thirty-five degrees. This is a heat wave in comparison to what it'll be if we have to go farther north."

Logan nodded, as if he understood why diesel boats were perpetually cold. He pointed at the camera, now sitting on the deck. "There is the possibility we may have to go back to the attack periscope and see if we can mount it there."

"What if we have to fight our way out, Lieutenant?"

"It disconnects quickly, Captain."

Shipley looked at Arneau as he gave thought to the idea of taking away his attack periscope even if it could be returned quickly. But their mission wasn't to fight the Soviets, just find out what they were doing and sneak away with the current without them being aware the American dogs were anywhere in the vicinity. If he had to fire torpedoes, then he had better be willing to risk a wider war.

He let out a deep breath. "Then, give the attack periscope a try, Lieutenant Logan, but if I need the scope and it doesn't come off quickly, I will rip the contraption down and toss it in the corner. I am uncomfortable with tying up either of the scopes, but the attack scope is what makes this submarine a war-fighting boat."

Logan looked at the two sailors who had been watching, and he nodded.

"How do you know you are taking the photographs you need?" Arneau asked.

"Sir, we can focus the camera by looking through the lens. Might take some tweaking to coordinate the camera lens and the periscope lens, but we should be able to do it."

"About damn time," the one with the name "Cross" stenciled on his dungaree shirt mumbled. "Christly twits."

"What did he say?" Arneau asked Logan, uncrossing his arms and straightening.

Logan shook his head. "He's referring to the engineers at NAVSEA." The intelligence officer smiled. "Petty Officer Cross has been enlightening us to his experiences of working with government and contractor engineers." Logan spoke loud enough for the two sailors to hear. "He believes engineers never complete a project. They always find much, more, better things to improve, so unless you jerk it away from them, it'll never be done."

Shipley nodded with a smile. Quick on your feet, Lieutenant; but taking care of the troops can be a double-edged burden. "You're pretty quick, Lieutenant."

"That's why I'm in intelligence," Logan said with a twinkle in his eyes.

"And why do you think we're in submarines?" Arneau asked, crossing his arms.

A couple of seconds passed. "Because, XO, you are brave, selfless warriors willing to put personal comfort and families aside for the sake of our nation, or—"

Shipley grinned and looked at Arneau. "He *is* quick."

Arneau's face reddened slightly. "Too smooth, methinks," he replied, trying to make light of it. He motioned at Logan. "Go ahead, finish the sentence. 'Or' . . . what?"

"Or you love the cold."

The sound of hydraulics raising the attack periscope drew their attention.

Shipley pointed at the search periscope and nodded at Lieutenant Junior Grade Olsson. With a finger he made a downward motion.

"Lower the search periscope," Olsson said.

Chief Topnotch stepped over to the search periscope, shoved the handles up, and said, "Down search periscope."

The light noise of the hydraulics increased slightly, emanating from inside the periscopes where hydraulic cylinders above the conning tower worked to lower one periscope while raising the other.

Lieutenant Logan used the opportunity to move the few steps back to his men. The small size of the conning tower meant everyone rubbed against each other, as only inches separated them, but here was where the submarine was fought. You could still fire torpedoes without a conning tower, but you had no idea where they were going, much less if they hit anything unfriendly. Nope. No conning tower, no effective submarine, and most likely the boat would be heading down to the ocean depths—a tomb for all on board.

Shipley finished his coffee. From what he was seeing, the two sailors were having no more success with the other periscope than they had with the search one. Be something if the Navy sent the *Squallfish* all the way into the Soviet backyard to collect intelligence on them only to discover the intelligence shit didn't work. He smiled.

"You're happy about this?" Arneau asked.

"XO," Shipley said, his smile widening, "you get up on the wrong side of the rack this morning?"

A forced smile spread across the XO's face. "There's only one way to get out of the rack, and that is on the port side."

Shipley shook his fingers. "Touchy, touchy," he whispered.

Arneau's crossed arms tightened. "I just don't—well, you know," he said, nodding at Logan.

"Shall we go get some more of Crocky's afternoon coffee?"

"I think we received a message from the commander, Naval Surface Forces Atlantic, in Norfolk. They have run out of paint remover and want to know if they can borrow Crocky's coffee."

Shipley laughed. "Wouldn't surprise me."

Another head poked through the hatch. It was Petty Officer Baron, the leading radioman.

"Over here," Olsson said, seeing the sailor.

Baron crawled up into the already crowded conning tower. He was reaching into the left pocket of his dungaree shirt as he bumped and apologized his way toward the communications officer.

"Christly twit," Brooks said as Baron bumped him.

"Sorry."

"Shall we go, XO? It will lessen the number of bodies filling the tower."

Arneau acknowledged and waited for Shipley to ease his way to the hatch. Shipley turned with his back to everyone as he stepped on the ladder to head down.

"Captain, XO," Olsson said, holding up the message Baron had brought.

"What is it?" Shipley asked, not moving. Too much effort to fight his way to the aft section of the conning tower with this many bodies in it.

"Here, pass this to the captain," Olsson said.

Topnotch handed it to Logan, who passed it to Cross, who handed it to the XO.

Arneau scanned the message quickly. "Shit," he exclaimed as he handed the message to Shipley. "Makes me think of a great vacation planned, only to have the in-laws show up."

Shipley read the message quickly and then handed it back to Arneau. "Doesn't surprise me, XO. This is the North Atlantic, and when it isn't storming, it's whipping one up."

He started down the ladder, with Arneau following him.

Logan turned to Olsson. "What was in the message?"

"Bad weather headed our way. Off the Arctic and should hit us in the next twenty-four hours. Most likely we're going to be in it all the way to the OPAREA."

Logan scratched his head. "Shouldn't be much of a bother for a submarine, should it. You just do deep and ride it out."

Olsson nodded. "We'll do that as much as we can, but this is a diesel sub. We can stay down for two days, even three with a little conservation and scattering of CO_2 absorbent through the boat, but eventually we're going to have to surface for air. And from the message, it looks as if the storm will be going full blast by then."

"Will that change our mission?"

"I don't know what your mission is, but if it involves surfacing or being at periscope depth for the next few days, then at best it'll have to be delayed."

Logan shook his head. "Never mind." He glanced at Cross and Brooks struggling with the connection.

"You're gonna bite off that tongue one day," Brooks said to Cross.

"Bite me."

Logan looked at Olsson. "We could always sail away from the storm," Logan offered, more a question than a statement.

Olsson nodded. "We can if the storm is going in one direction very, very fast while we inch along submerged at the mind-numbing eight knots the captain has us doing now."

SHIPLEY finished his letter home, telling his wife about the voyage, leaving out the part about where they were. He and the others would slip the mail over to the *Stevens* when they rendezvoused in two weeks. Chances are he'd be back in Holy Loch before the letters arrived, but the act of writing June was important. It was sailors' way of keeping loved ones foremost in their minds as they sailed the seas, whether above or below the waves. Sailors had to feel they were doing this not only because they loved the sea and the Navy, but also because they were doing it for their families. Even Shipley believed what he was doing would bear fruit for his son and daughter.

He had this someday vision of him and his wife sitting on a front porch, watching their grandchildren play, and him knowing they played in an era of peace because he and others put themselves in harm's way today. Like most Navy officers he knew, it was only time before they had to fight the Soviet Union, and when they did, it would be superior firepower, technology, and tactics that would allow the U.S. Navy to control the seas. Control the seas and you contained the Soviet Union.

A knock on the passageway bulkhead caused him to turn to the closed curtains to his stateroom. "Yes," he said, raising the envelope and licking it.

Arneau stuck his head through the curtains. "Thought I would give you a status report before we had evening chow, Captain."

Shipley motioned the XO inside as he laid the letter on the small shelf that served as his desk. "Go ahead."

Arneau stepped into the small space at the entrance.

"Lieutenant Bleecker reports quieten ship is ongoing. Lots of maintenance checks to complete, but he foresees no problems finishing those in the next two days. Lieutenant Logan and his band of spooks finally figured out how to put the camera on the search periscope."

"Don't you mean the attack periscope?"

Arneau shook his head. "No, sir; seems they gave up after we left. Apparently the 'Christly twits' spook took the camera down, and sitting on the deck of the conning tower, took it apart and rebuilt it."

"I take it, it worked."

"First time. It slid on easily, and they were able to use some copper wire to secure it to the periscope."

"Good."

"Not too good."

Shipley lowered his head and looked questioningly at Arneau. "Well?"

"You can't lower the periscope with the camera attached."

"Well, we can't leave it up there with this weather coming, and once we arrive on station, having the periscope raised while we're submerged puts unnecessary noise in the water. Not to mention we run the risk of damaging it."

Arneau held up his hand. "Yes, sir, I know," he agreed, lowering the hand. "I have already told them to practice taking it down and putting it on until they have it down to a fine science. I told Logan there was no way they were going to leave that thing permanently attached." Arneau smiled. "Not only can't we take the periscope down, Skipper, but when it's attached, it takes up too much room in the conning tower. They are going to have to attach the camera when they are ready to use it and take it down when finished."

Shipley thought about that for a moment. "That may not be good either," he offered. "The only time they're going to have it attached is when we are near the Soviets. The only time we may find ourselves in a fighting situation is when they have the camera attached." He looked up. "I think I liked intelligence better when they stayed ashore and just sent us messages telling us what they had. This idea of putting them on subs . . ." Shipley paused. "Well, it just isn't done. Where are they?"

"They are in the forward engine room seeing how the radiation detector is going to connect," Arneau said, jerking his thumb over his shoulder. "Lieutenant Bleecker is with them."

Shipley laughed. "Better step down there, XO, and make sure Bleecker hasn't stuffed them in the aft torpedo tubes." His eyebrows furrowed. "Who was that sailor?"

"Which one?"

"Christly twits?"

"That was Brooks; the sailor from NAVSEASYSCOM."

"Well, I am sure that after an afternoon with Bleecker, he will learn new, more sailorlike socially accepted retorts to take back to the Navy Yard with him."

"I don't know if they'll be socially acceptable."

Shipley crossed his legs as he sat on his rack, resting his right arm on the shelf-desk. "How about the weather? Any change?"

"I swung by radio on the way here. Petty Officer Baron said no updates on or changes to the previous message."

Shipley uncrossed his legs, leaning forward with both hands on his knees. "Let's plan on surfacing after dark. We'll exchange our air and top off the batteries before the storm hits." He stood up, leaning forward over the small sink, turning on the water. "As long as the surface picture is clear, and weather permits, we'll keep doing that until the weather hits." He wet his hands, turned off the water, washed them, then turned on the water just long enough to rinse the soap off.

"I would think that they will cancel our mission," Arneau said.

"You could be right," he said as he dried his hands. "There is a chance they may cancel our mission. I can't see the Soviets coming out in this weather."

Arneau raised his right hand, two fingers touching his forehead. "Aye, sir. I will make plans and have the surface detail ready. Meanwhile, I am off on a rescue mission to engineering."

"I'll be in the control room, or the conning tower. Is the contraption still on the periscope?"

"I don't think so. I told them not to leave it on there."

"Let me know how it is going in engineering." Shipley smiled. "Let me know if you need medical help back there."

They laughed.

"Who's the officer of the deck, XO?"

"Lieutenant Weaver has the conn right now, Skipper."

"WHERE we goin'?" Washington asked Crocky as he slid a baking pan of hot bread from the oven.

"How the hell should I know, boy? Our job is to cook food. It don't make no never mind where we be going as long as the crew has their food."

"But I was talkin' with Marcos and he said we was headin' for the Arctic ice cap; that we was goin' to go under it and surface through the ice."

"That Marcos is full of shit." Crocky turned. Marcos was swapping the mess deck with a damp mop. "Marcos, come here."

The Filipino steward hurried to the end of the serving counter, staying on the serving side, his eyes huge. "Yes, boss?"

"What this you tellin' Washington?"

Marcos shrugged. Santos walked up beside him, wiping his hands on the towel he was holding. The crew swore the two were brothers or slightly mismatched twins.

"Santos, what the hell you doin'? Quit wiping yore hands on the towel. That thing is full of germs and shit. Marcos, I asked what is this shit yore hearing?"

"I heard we going underneath the ice, Petty Officer Crocky. We going to be first American diesel submarine to go under the ice."

"Yeah, and we would be the first one never to come out because no other diesel submarine would be that foolish." Crocky shook his head, pulling his apron up and wiping his hands on it. "Listen to me, you two." He swung his finger to Washington. "No, you three. No way this boat is going to go up under the ice shelf and then surface through centuries-old thick ice." He dropped his apron, the cloth draping back over the huge stomach years of eating his own cooking had grown. "We used to talk about that during the war. We'd run out of air before we could get through. Now, this *Nautilus* might be able to do it because this nuclear shit is supposed to run forever. But we diesel sailors ain't gonna do it."

"Where we goin', boss?"

"Marcos, why you care? Submariners don't need to know where they goin'. All they gotta do is make sure we stay evens."

"Evens?" Santos asked.

"Evens," Crocky replied. "Where the number of submergings and the number of surfacings come out even."

"Even?"

"Shit, man; you don't know arithmetic? Two, four, six, and so on and so on. That be evens, man. You can't have an odd number without sinkin'."

"We don't want an odd number."

"What's odd number?" Santos asked, looking at Marcos.

Marcos responded in Filipino, the words rolling out rapidly and sharply. Santos's mouth opened and he nodded. "Evens and odds." He smiled at Crocky.

Crocky looked at Washington. "What you smilin' about, boy?

Get that trash together and take it to the trash room. We got dinner coming up here and we still got the trash from lunch."

"Sure thing, boss."

"And quit that 'boss' shit. I'm Petty Officer Crocky to you and those stewards of ours." He looked at Marcos and Santos. "We done talkin'. You two get back to your duties. We got dinner comin'." Crocky walked over to the coffee urn and filled his cup. "Christ. My head hurts now from all this Navy trainin' I gotta do for you three. Someday it better count when I get to the those Pearly Gates."

"If we goin' under the ice, then you might get there faster."

"That might be more like hell, because I'd still have you three with me, Washington. How long it gonna take for you to get that trash out of here?"

"Santos!" Washington shouted. "Give me a hand with this trash!"

"Shit, man," Crocky interrupted. "There ain't enough trash for a workin' party. Santos gotta finish cleanin' the tables and gettin' the trays ready." Crocky set his cup down awkwardly. It turned and spilled, gray, growing-old coffee running down the stainless steel cabinet. He calmly picked up his cup and filled it again. "Plus, he gotta clean up this coffee area. It's a mess."

Washington pulled the bagged trash from the small cabinet where they stored it between runs. Three bags were stuffed into the storage area. He pulled them out on the deck.

"You make sure they're tight. I don't want you havin' to clean some passageway again because Senior Chief Boohan catches you spillin' trash."

Washington spent a few seconds making sure nothing was leaking. A leaking bag meant the sailor spent time cleaning up after it, wiping down the bulkheads, sweeping and swabbing the deck. It was better to be sure. If it was leaking, better to be cleaning it here than in the passageway, where everyone eventually passed you, including that cracker Potts. It had been days since the incident in the mess hall, but Washington had met bigots on the streets of Philly. They might go deep like a submarine and stay quiet, but they never changed their spots.

He lifted the trash bags and started toward the doorway.

"Be careful with them," Crocky said.

As Washington stepped into the passageway, Crocky went back into the small kitchen area, his attention focused on the beans simmering in the huge pot and the potatoes his three sailors had peeled after breakfast. Mashed potatoes were easy to make and leftovers turned into midrats, which turned into potato pancakes for breakfast.

WASHINGTON worked his way carefully along the passageway heading toward the forward torpedo area. Trash was stored in the torpedo rooms until it could be dumped overboard through the aft escape hatch. Crocky said that during World War II they sometimes shot it off the boat through the torpedo tubes.

At-sea trash eventually settled to the seabed, where sea life made short work of it. Those few instances when a trash bag surfaced, it quickly disintegrated and the trash would float for hundreds of miles, dragged by currents and winds.

Several times on this trip Washington had had to brace himself against the bulkhead, holding the trash out alongside him, to allow others to pass. A couple of times ahead of him, he heard someone warn of trash coming. He hoped they were not referring to him.

FROMLEY stepped into the forward battery room. Potts was still in there, smoking.

"You know you ain't supposed to be smoking here," Fromley warned. "It could blow us up."

"Screw them, From." Potts stuffed out the cigarette. "We ain't blown up yet, have we?"

"That boy from the mess decks is coming."

Potts's eyes lit up. "You mean that black son of a bitch that ratted on me to Bleecker?"

From smiled. He had made Potts happy. "You mean Crocky?"

"Naw, asshole; I mean the other one."

"Yeap, that's the one."

"Why is he coming?"

"He's carrying the trash."

Potts rubbed his hands together. "Means we have missed a lot of opportunities." He reached behind him and flipped the air exchange back on to allow the smell of smoke to be drawn from the battery room.

The smile left Fromley's face. "Lieutenant done told you to leave him alone."

"What he told me was that black nigra Crocky wanted me to leave him alone."

Fromley glanced at the rear hatch and then at the forward, as if trying to make up his mind which way to run. He licked his lips. "You ain't going to do anything, are you?"

"What's it to you? I'll do whatever I want."

The sound of the hatch being opened stopped their conversation. Potts shoved Fromley into the small space on the port side of where the aft hatch was located. He slid into the starboard side, smiling at the fear etched on Fromley's face. *What a coward*, he thought.

A bag of trash was set inside the forward battery room, followed quickly by Washington carrying the other two bags. The cook picked up the bags and started along the narrow passageway between the two rows of batteries, careful to keep the bags from touching them. Crocky told him not to worry because the batteries were nearly impervious—though "impervious" was not the word Crocky used—to anything but salt water.

Potts stepped into the passageway. "Well, if it ain't our asshole buddy, Fromley." He turned to glance at Fromley, who was shaking his head. Potts motioned him out, but Fromley shook his head.

Potts turned back to Washington. Washington held the three bags in his hands.

"You on my turf now, asshole. I guess you thought it was cute having your LPO talk to my lieutenant."

So that explained why he had had no trouble from the leader of the bigot club on board *Squallfish*. Washington bit his lower lip. Just he and Potts here in this compartment, the man's backup frozen somewhere behind the batteries. In the projects, they'd get rid of him. Maybe this was the time to settle it?

"Hey, who left this hatch open?" came an angry voice from behind Washington.

Washington looked over his shoulder. The LPO for these engineers stood there. "I did, Petty Officer Gledhill. I was going to come back once I got the trash through and then shut it."

"No, you aren't. You set those bags down, shut the hatch, and then continue out the other side. Don't be going through my spaces without doing it properly. You understand?" Gledhill looked past Washington. "Potts, what are you doing? Give the man a hand. Grab one of those trash bags and help him get this shit out of here."

"I was, uh, just going to tell him the same thing, LPO." Potts glared at Washington's back as he grabbed the trash bag.

"And where is your shadow, Fromley?"

A hand rose from the other end of the port battery array. "I'm here."

Potts opened the forward hatch and set the bag of trash on the other side. Then he pulled the hatch closed and secured it, smiling as he did so.

Gledhill turned, watching Washington secure the hatch. "Now take your trash and get out of here, sailor. This isn't the place to be lollygagging and scuttlebutting."

"Shore thing, boss," Washington said, putting on what he called his southern cotton-pickin' voice.

Potts stepped out of the way. As Washington edged by him, their eyes met. In this minute within the battery room, Washington realized Potts would kill him if the opportunity rose.

"Potts, open the hatch to the forward torpedo room for him so we can get this trash out of here. And who's been smoking in here?"

Potts opened the hatch, pushing it outward. As Washington passed, he whispered, "Your time is coming."

Washington kept quiet. Maybe Potts's time was coming.

Washington heard Potts tell Gledhill that the smell of smoke was probably from the trash. Minutes later Washington went back through the forward battery room, and the three sailors were gone. He was glad, but he did not breathe easier until he was back in the crew's mess.

"About time you got back," Crocky said when Washington walked in.

"Lots of traffic."

"I know." Then in a loud voice Crocky mimicked, "All hands fore lay aft; all hands aft lay fore; all hands amidships stand by to direct traffic!" Crocky laughed. Then he saw the questioning looks on the faces of Washington, Marcos, and Santos. Santos was leaning over to Marcos, looking at Crocky, and saying something in Filipino.

Crocky stopped laughing. "Don't tell me you three don't know what that means?"

"What does it mean?" Washington asked.

"It's what we used to say during the war whenever general quarters was sounded. Get it?"

Marcos and Washington shook their heads. Marcos asked Santos, who shook his head also.

"Never mind," Crocky said with a wave at them. "Christ, grant me the fortitude to survive this mission."

Washington eased into the cooking area. He looked at Crocky with new respect. The man had never said a word about talking to the mustang about the problems with Potts, but Potts knew. Now he knew. Any trouble he was going to have with Potts would come in the dark, without warning. If Gledhill had not shown up when he did, Washington knew Potts would have tried something. He had seen it too much in Philadelphia. He shivered involuntarily. He joined the Navy to get away from all that and to earn the GI Bill so he could go to college. But even here on board the *Squallfish*, wherever he turned they surrounded him.

The battery room was a dangerous place for a fight. Even a new sailor on board a submarine, such as he, knew that.

NINE

Friday, November 30, 1956

"DO we understand each other, Captain Zegouniov?" Zotkin asked.

Anton stood in front of the scientist's wooden desk feeling like he were some errant schoolboy being lectured by the headmaster.

"I understand, Doctor Zotkin," he said, putting his hands behind his back. "But the aft torpedo room should be repaired, not sealed. If we are to do a proper—"

Zotkin raised his hand as he stood. "Stop! I am the one who decides whether the *K-2* is ready for the test." The man put his hand on his chest.

Anton wondered for a moment if Zotkin was having a heart attack and was surprised to discover that he hoped it was the case.

A couple of breaths and Doctor Zotkin dropped his hand. "You are causing me distress, Captain. You come with all the best recommendations. If you are unable to accomplish what is best for the Soviet Union, then maybe we should discuss—"

Anton interrupted. "Sir, with all due respect, no one has ever questioned my loyalty. I have served—"

Zotkin straightened, his face turning a beet red. "I am not questioning your loyalty, Comrade Captain! I am asking if you are dedicated to the *K-2* project. I am asking if you are going to do as I ask."

Anton stopped. What had started with Zotkin ordering his work force to seal off the forward torpedo room without discussing it with Anton had caused this confrontation. He searched for a moment to figure out how something begun at the collegiate level could have spun out of control. He was still investigating the fire. He thought a sailor with a cigarette had caused it by trying to grind it out on the deck where oil and grease gathered.

Neither man had budged on his position until Anton announced he intended to reopen the torpedo room. Sealing it off did not necessarily make it watertight, and a submarine not watertight was soon a tomb on the bottom. He guessed he could have been a little more tactful.

Zotkin had thrown himself into his desk chair and ordered Anton to obey his decision as if Anton were some junior officer right out of the Academy.

Navy captains are not known for "Aye, aye, sir" acceptance of ignorant orders. But seldom did they confront those senior to them, as Anton did now. What was he thinking? They usually saluted, and then departed to do the right things, ensuring smarter people in the chain of command were aware. This time maybe it was fatigue, stress, or an unusual desire to step to the front of the formation and disagree. But disagree he did. It had worked once.

"I am still responsible for my boat and the crew, Doctor Zotkin. I do not want a confrontation with you. Maybe we should raise the issue to Admiral Katshora and others," Anton said, bluffing. Did Zotkin have the connections? Had Zotkin discovered that Anton had few if any? But coming from the Kremlin was many times all others needed to know to create a climate of deference.

Several awkward moments of silence grew between the two men.

Zotkin sighed. "Captain, I think we can resolve this between us. We both want the same thing. I am as concerned as you for the welfare of your crew." Zotkin touched his chest. "I am, even if it seems I may be putting the project ahead of this humanity. If so, you are probably right because the importance of *K-2* to the Soviet Union—the party—is so vital to our national security. That is why I push myself and I push all of you. It is for our nation." He stood, pointing at Anton, then poking himself in the chest. "You, I, and they are all expendable for the good of the Soviet Union." He leaned forward, his hands spread on the desk. "You love this great country of ours as much as I do. Forces of evil surround us who would love nothing more than to destroy us. They recognize that communism is inevitable. So they watch, wait, and will pounce when they believe they are powerful enough to destroy us. That is why we are racing every day to achieve parity and eventually military supremacy. For one reason only: to ensure our survival."

"I understand that, Doctor Zotkin," Anton said with a deep breath. He reached over, pulled a straight-back chair up, and sat down. He took off his gloves. He nearly grinned because he saw in Zotkin's expression that the good doctor thought the conversation was over.

"That is why I must do whatever is necessary to ensure *K-2* is a success," Zotkin finished, the last words trailing off.

"Doctor Zotkin, I am your loyal servant, but I am also the captain of the *K-2*. It is my responsibility to ensure that when the *K-2* goes out—"

"In one week."

"—that it is shipshape and capable of finishing the test. Failure to have a successful demonstration of your atomic engine—"

"Reactor."

"—reactor would be catastrophic for you, for me, and for the Soviet Union."

"The reactor will be a success," Zotkin protested.

"The reactor can be a success and no one will know if the *Whale* is on the bottom because the aft torpedo room was improperly prepared," Anton said in a cautious voice, hoping to resolve the argument to where he could reopen the aft torpedo room. "If the valves and switches within the room are improperly closed, then the *Whale*—"

"*K-2*, if you don't mind, Captain."

"—then the *K-2* could find itself in the muddy bottom of the Barents beneath thousands of tons of seawater." He was the captain, and he alone was responsible for the safety of the boat. Not someone who was going to be on a destroyer on the surface while the *Whale* was deep beneath the ocean.

Zotkin leaned back, shaking his head. "You are exasperating me, Comrade Captain. What would you have me do? Let you reopen the rear torpedo room? Then what?"

Anton crossed his arms. "I would reopen it to ensure we have sealed the valves, the switches, and the aft torpedo tubes so it is truly watertight. Then I will have my men close the watertight hatch so it is sealed off. But we need to put a watch in there—a sailor—to make sure we don't spring a leak. That way we'd be able to take actions to ensure the test is a success and the *K-2* doesn't run the risk of taking on water without us knowing it immediately."

"I don't understand. All I have done is take care of a problem that both of us faced. I have asked the machinists to weld the hatch shut."

"You also have told them to weld the aft escape hatch shut. That means if we have to evacuate the boat, we have only the main hatch above the conning tower and the hatch above the forward torpedo room."

Zotkin shook his head. "There is no danger, Captain. The *K-2* is the most expensive project in the Soviet Navy! We are sparing no expense to ensure its safety. We have the best minds in our nation working on this project. And you want to bring it to a stop because of a small fire on board caused by a careless sailor with a cigarette."

Anton uncrossed his arms. "I am not saying we stop the project, Doctor Zotkin. I am saying your way endangers the safety of the crew and might even cause the test to fail. I think neither of us wants that.

"If you would, call off the machinists. I will personally double-check the aft torpedo room myself. Then I will declare it inoperative and will station a watch inside it while we are under way." He touched his chest and nodded toward Zotkin. "This way both of us can achieve a successful test, which is what we both want."

"The test will be successful! There can be no doubt!"

Anton leaned back. "You are right, Doctor Zotkin. I agree."

HALF an hour later, Anton was climbing down the ladder into the conning tower. Gesny, Lebedev, and Tomich stood at the base of it. All three looked questioningly at him. Gesny looked as if he were surprised Anton had returned. Anton thought he detected a slight smile about to break out across his XO's face.

"And?" Lebedev asked, unable to wait for Anton to step off the ladder.

Anton let out a deep breath and smiled. "Get the machinists off my boat. Tell the quarterdeck watch not to allow anyone else on board who is lugging welding gear. XO, reopen the aft torpedo room." He looked at Lebedev. "Operations Officer, once the compartment is reopened, you are to strip it of everything not vital for its watertight integrity. Then you are to ensure the compartment is ready for submerged operations. I want to inspect it personally when you are ready." He pulled off his gloves and jammed them into his pocket. "We are going to take the *Whale*, as scheduled, on the sea trials.

"I want the *Whale* ready for operations; therefore I want to ensure the fire has not done anything that will cause a danger to the boat. You are to tell me immediately if you discover something." He glanced at the zampolit. "Doctor Zotkin and I are committed to having this be an historic success of the Soviet Navy moving into the atomic age. Lieutenant Tomich, may I suggest a party-political discussion on how the glory of technology is furthering communism?"

The smile left the zampolit's face as the young officer pondered for a second Anton's recommendation. Then a broad smile spread across his face. "I could use Doctor Zotkin as an example," he said, his enthusiasm growing. "We could talk about Soviet science and its importance to the party; to the Soviet Union; and to spreading the equality of the people under communism."

"I think it is a great idea, Josef. You have taken a poor suggestion of mine and turned it into a great party-political agenda."

Tomich nodded, his eyes wide. "If you will excuse me, I have to prepare."

The officers waited until the zampolit disappeared down the ladder to the control room.

Anton turned back to Gesny and Lebedev. "Well, Lieutenant Commander? What are you waiting for?"

Lebedev smiled and clapped his hands. "Thank you, Captain, thank you." He turned to leave.

Gesny reached out and touched his shoulder, stopping the operations officer from leaving. Then he looked up at Anton. "Comrade Captain, are we to man the aft torpedo room once under way?"

"We will put a fire and safety watch inside it. Otherwise we will consider it inoperative."

Gesny opened his mouth to say something. Anton raised an

eyebrow. "Aye, Comrade Captain. Lieutenant Commander Lebedev, reopen the hatches to the aft torpedo room."

"And, make sure they have not lost their watertight integrity, Comrade Ops," Anton added.

"Yes, sir—no, sir," Lebedev replied as he grabbed the ladder and started into the control room below them.

"Sir, did Doctor Zotkin say anything about changing the duration of the test or if the test would be modified in any way?" Gesny asked.

"No; we both agree that we cannot let such a small thing as a fire in a torpedo room stop the sea trials. We have a time schedule to meet."

"Aye, sir," Gesny said with a passion that matched the lack of expression on his face. "This is a great day for our Navy."

"Yes. Yes, it is."

"Doctor Zotkin was very passionate about the sea trials. His exuberance was contagious."

"Oh, yes. He will go down in history one day as the father of the atomic Navy."

"I am sure of that," Anton added.

Gesny looked down at his shoes as if admiring the shine.

"XO, I am going to my stateroom for a few minutes. I would like some of your time when you are available to go over the sea and anchor details for our sea trials."

ANTON took his coat off and hung it on a metal hanger screwed into the thin bulkhead that separated the passageway from his tiny stateroom. It was early afternoon. He had missed lunch, but he could always grab a sandwich.

When he turned, he knocked his dress coat from the hanger onto the deck. When he bent to pick up the coat, he saw the letter Admiral Katshora had sent by courier three days ago. He had never ignored an admiral's communiqué.

He slapped the envelope against his palm a couple of times before sitting down and quickly opening it. He read it as quickly as he opened it, then read it slowly, taking in what the short note said. He looked at his watch.

"Captain," Gesny said as he stuck his head through the curtain.

"Yes, XO?" Anton folded the letter calmly and stuck it back into the envelope. Gesny watched.

Gesny handed him a message. "This came in from Northern Fleet headquarters. Looks as if our friend the Norse god is going to shower us with his blessings for the next few days."

Anton read the message. "You're right. Good thing we are inside and well protected."

"This will interfere with Doctor Zotkin's sea trials of the atomic reactor."

Anton bobbed his head. "You could be right, XO. Unfortunately, as powerful as we all like to think we are, we cannot control the weather."

"Yet."

"Yet."

"Doctor Zotkin may want to go forward with it, Captain. He is tied to his timeline."

Anton nodded. "I understand, but until we see what your Norse god throws down on Severomorsk and the facility, we will have to wait. Either way, it does not look good for us going into the Barents."

He laid the message on top of Katshora's letter. "I have found our weathermen are more weather guessers than forecasters." He nodded at the message. "It says the winds will pick up at noon tomorrow and increase with intensity, bringing with them gale force winds by the day after tomorrow. By then we should be hit with snow and ice."

"Won't be the first I've gone through that."

Anton did not reply. The Arctic was fairly new to him. He had not spent sufficient time in it to find the operating environment common. He had heard of the terror the weather brought with it, slamming against humanity, daring you to come out and face it.

"What are your recommendations, XO?"

"We should prepare the boat for foul weather. I have already ordered the chief of the boat to remind everyone of the dress requirements. Last year we had one of these come through here. At that time I was in Severomorsk, across the bay. We had several sailors lose fingers and toes. Had two disappear forever. To this day we don't know what happened to them. And that was inside ice-free Kola Bay."

"I need to go to Severomorsk today, XO, for a meeting with the admiral. I would like to do it with as little fanfare as possible."

Gesny nodded. He understood easily why Anton would not want Doctor Zotkin to know.

"I will arrange it. Your driver is outside—"

"My driver?"

"Yes, sir. I saw him this morning when I arrived, and he said he was waiting for you."

Anton ran his hand through his hair. "Of course. I had forgotten I had asked him to wait today," he lied, wondering why Popov was waiting unless it was for this meeting. But then how was a car going to get him across the bay?

"Do you want me to send him home?"

"No," Anton said as he stood. He reached over and slipped both the message and letter into his coat pocket. "Let me step out and talk with my driver. I need to let him know what time to come back."

"Should I go ahead and plan your trip across the bay?"

Anton shook his head. "No; it looks as if arrangements have already been made. Unless asked, XO, I don't see any reason to share with anyone other than you my visit to the admiral." He pulled his foul-weather jacket off the hanger. "Let's keep this visit between us, XO?"

Gesny stepped back, half in the passageway, to give Anton room to slip on the jacket.

Gesny ran two fingers squeezed together across his lips. "I have no idea what the captain is talking about. Besides, the walls have ears, and those ears are linked to—"

Anton held up his hand. "Thanks."

ANTON opened the rear door of the ZIL; Popov called it a limousine. He told Anton the design had been copied from both European and American limousine designs. Of course, in the Soviet Union, anyone who merited a limousine could have it as long as he took it in black.

Popov folded the morning copy of *Pravda* and laid it on the seat beside him. "I thought you had forgotten."

"I nearly did."

"It is good you came when you did because I have been running the engine since this morning and the gas is below half now." Popov faced forward. "I will take you to where you need to be. And, I will be there when you return."

Anton knew that Popov and he had never discussed anything about today. He started to pull the letter out, but it was stuck beneath the straps and buttons of the foul-weather jacket he wore over his working uniform. "I need to be back for discussions later with the facility manager."

"Doctor Zotkin will not miss you for the remainder of the day. He is deep into his plans."

"I have no idea what you are talking about, driver."

"Driver, driver, driver. That is all I hear about the people's profession." Popov pulled the fingerless gloves tighter, put the car in reverse, and looked in the side mirrors as he squealed out of the parking space. "I hate it when the back window freezes."

At the end of the drive leading up to the parking area, Popov turned to the left, away from the normal direction taken in the evening when work allowed him to return home.

A few miles later, Popov turned between two warehouses. In the distance, Anton could see a small dock nestled alongside a smaller building. Popov slammed on the brakes, causing Anton to brace himself against the forward seat to keep from being tossed onto the floor. He thought in the icy haze of the front windshield that he could see something tied up alongside the pier, but with the tide out, the shore and the high pier mostly hid it.

"Have I offended you, Comrade Popov, or have you decided we both need to die?"

"Driver, driver, driver," Popov mumbled. He reached up and pulled the wool watch cap he wore down over his ears. He turned to Anton. "Your ride is down the ladder of the pier. It will take you to your meeting in Severomorsk. I should be here when you return, unless I run out of gas or the weather causes me to think of my warm home in Murmansk or you find me frozen. If you find me frozen, the keys will be in the ignition."

Anton opened the door, shutting it quickly behind him. The Arctic wind whipped between the side of the building and the ZIL, sending a slight burn along Anton's cheeks. When he stood, he could see the starboard outline of a boat with the bow pointed out to sea. He flipped up the flaps of the foul-weather jacket against the wind, then walked quickly to the wooden ladder leading down from the old rough-hewed pier. Tied up alongside the pylons was one of the Navy's new torpedo speedboats.

Two sailors helped him on board. A spry Navy officer, his head hidden beneath a heavy woolen watch cap but his foul-weather jacket open to reveal his rank, shook his hand. "Comrade Captain, welcome to the *Bolshevik*, sir. I am the skipper, Lieutenant

Commander Jasha. Admiral Katshora sends his regards, sir."

Anton acknowledged the greeting while taking in the torpedo boat. The *Bolshevik* was the first of her class. From what he recalled from the article in *Krasnaya Zvezda*, the military newspaper published by the Soviet Ministry of Defense, the *Bolshevik* was slightly more than twenty-five meters long, had a wooden hull, and was capable of speeds in excess of forty knots.

Jasha smiled. His cheeks were bright red from the weather, and Anton wondered how long they had been waiting. "I hope I haven't kept you waiting long, Captain," Anton said, bestowing on Jasha the honorific title every commanding officer of a ship was given. He pointed at the jacket. "I would recommend buttoning up before you freeze."

Jasha smiled.

They are so young today, Anton thought, but then maybe it was the years piling up on him.

"Cast off all lines!" Jasha shouted, his hands cupped to his mouth. He turned forward and did the same thing.

"Captain, if I may, belowdecks would be better for you."

Anton allowed a sailor to lead him below. Behind him he heard the engines revving up, and by the time he had slid into the lone table that made up the twenty-man mess, the *Bolshevik* was skipping across the choppy waves of Kola Bay, heading toward Severomorsk. He leaned back, his body adjusting to the penetrating cold trying to seek solace beneath his garments. He shut his eyes and wondered why the secrecy of this meeting with Admiral Katshora.

SHIPLEY stood on the bridge. Evening came early to the northern latitudes as winter approached. The sound of the diesel exhausts masked the air exchangers as they pumped in the cold, fresh air of the Arctic and shoved the carbon dioxide–rich internal air out. It would be a tough ride to do four days submerged in a diesel submarine. The wind was already picking up. Senior Chief Boohan had handed him a watch cap with eyeholes and lips cut into it. He had smiled at first, but after ten minutes topside, he had pulled the makeshift mask over his face.

Arneau appeared in the hatch, wearing a foul-weather jacket, his face covered in a Boohan-tailored watch cap. "Skipper, you've been up here thirty minutes," he said as he continued scrambling up. "I would like to relieve you."

Shipley started to protest, but realized that in this weather, thirty minutes could be a lifetime. Behind Arneau, reliefs for the two topside observers followed. They, too, wore the face masks.

"See you in thirty minutes, XO," Shipley said as he stood near the hatch, watching the sailors relieve each other. He did not see how the boat would be able to surface if the storm was going to be as bad as weather reports indicated.

"I recommend that you, I, and Alec take rotating turns. I didn't realize how cold it was up here, Skipper."

Shipley nodded. If it weren't so damn cold, he might have been tempted to start a series of humorous "And how cold is it, XO?," but right now the heat from Crocky's day-old gray, tannic-acid–filled coffee would feel great, even if it burned the tongue as it went down.

Breathing was terrible in the freezing air. Even breathing through the watch cap was painful, as air seemed to freeze his lungs with each breath. The off-going watch walked painfully to the hatch and disappeared down it. Shipley looked at Arneau and nodded before grabbing the ladder. The gloves were probably keeping his hands from freezing to the topside rungs. A fresh burst of wind whipped over the stanchion of the bridge, rippling through the mask and chilling his cheeks painfully. He did not turn to see how it affected Arneau.

Moments later, Shipley was in the conning tower. The belowdecks hatch was closed, while the hatch leading up to the bridge remained open. The watch standers within the conning tower were dressed in their foul-weather gear. Ice formed along the top of the hatch, and fog obscured the inside of the gauges aligning the bulkhead of the conning tower. He started pulling his gloves off.

"Skipper, if I may recommend, sir," Senior Chief Boohan said, "I'd wait until you were in the control room before taking anything off." The chief of the boat pointed to the thermometer on the bulkhead.

Shipley leaned forward, reaching up to rub the glass.

"Uh, sir!" Boohan shouted, causing Shipley to pull back. "I wouldn't touch anything breakable up here."

Shipley leaned close and saw that the mercury was completely in the reservoir at the bottom of the thermometer. It was below zero in the conning tower.

"We should shut the hatch to the bridge."

Lieutenant Van Ness spoke up. "Sir, if we do that we won't have any way to talk to the bridge."

"Cliff, you're the navigator and the admin officer, correct?"

"Yes, sir."

"Then let's get the sound-powered setup between the conning tower and the bridge repaired. It's one thing to shout back and forth during normal weather, but another . . ." He stopped. He wriggled his toes and could feel them wriggle, but was unsure if he truly felt them. He realized he still had Boohan's watch cap covering his face. Shipley reached up and pulled it off. He looked at Boohan. "Ought to patent this, COB.

"I'm going to the wardroom for a cup of coffee and then will be in the control room until my turn to relieve topside. Lieutenant Van Ness, keep an eye and be prepared to order a dive if necessary."

Van Ness saluted.

When Shipley turned, a sailor was opening the hatch. A moment later, Shipley was below the conning tower in what felt like a heat wave in the control room. He looked at the thermometer, which read twenty degrees. From the bridge to the conning tower, twenty degrees was a heat wave.

The operations officer, Lieutenant Weaver, was in the control room. Shipley told Weaver what he would find topside in terms of weather when the officer relieved Arneau. Shipley told him where he would be for a few minutes, then he would come back to the control room.

Petty Officer Baron opened and ducked through the aft hatch. He saw Shipley. "Captain, Mr. Olsson asked me to find you and ask you to come to the radio shack, sir."

Shipley pulled his gloves off and put them in his pocket. "Did he say why?"

"No, sir," Baron answered, starting to shiver.

"Let's get out of here, Petty Officer Baron. When you get back to radio, you put on your foul-weather gear before you head back this way again." He would have to put off the coffee for a few more minutes. The radio shack was near the control room, but when Shipley stepped through the hatch, the warmer submarine spaces hit him in the face, bringing pain to his cold face. He reached up and touched it, running his hand around his face. Everything seemed to be there. He wriggled his toes again when they reached the curtain of radio. He could feel them. He told himself to slip on an extra set of socks before he went topside again.

"Skipper," Olsson said when he saw him. "Christ, sir! What's wrong with your face?"

Shipley ran his hand across it again. "Feels all right to me, Mr. Olsson. Why? Is something missing?"

"No, sir; just it's so red."

"I've been topside. What is so important while we are surfaced that you need me here?" He was slightly irritated, but being irritated when someone needed you was a quick way for them to find ways to never need you.

"It's Lieutenant Logan. . . ."

Behind Olsson, the smaller Logan stuck his head out and raised his hand. "I'm here, Skipper."

"What is it?"

"Sir, we need a secure space to discuss the message that just came across."

"Lieutenant Logan, how many times have I told you that we don't have secure spaces on the diesel? Secure spaces, as you intelligence types think of it, don't exist here. This is the radio shack; this is the *Squallfish*; and this is as secure as it gets. Now, what do you have?" Before Logan could answer, he looked at Olsson. "You know anything?"

Olsson shook his head. "No, sir; Lieutenant Logan asked me to leave while he deciphered the message."

"Okay, Lieutenant Logan, what do you have?"

Logan looked at Olsson and then at Baron. "Maybe if we can talk with just you and me," he said, pointing at Shipley.

Shipley let out a deep sigh. "Okay. Mr. Olsson, would you and Petty Officer Baron give Mr. Logan and me a few minutes alone?"

"No, sir; I mean yes, sir."

"Don't go far, as we won't be here long."

"I thought I'd go get some coffee. It's getting cold in here."

It felt like a heat wave to Shipley. He glanced inside the radio shack but did not see a thermometer.

Shipley nodded. He told Olsson about the need for his foul weather gear through the control room and asked him to bring him a cup back. Petty Officer Baron headed aft, probably to the crew's quarters.

"Okay, Lieutenant Logan. We have cleared the immediate vicinity. What is so all-fired important that you have made me clear radio?"

He handed the message to Shipley, who read it, then reread it.

Then he looked up at Logan. "This is nuts. Is this something Naval Intelligence dreamed up?" he asked, shaking his head.

"I can't answer that, sir. It's from CINCNELM."

"CINCNELM is in London. He won't be here when this goes to shit." Shipley paused for a moment, reading the message again. What were they thinking in London and in the Pentagon? This wasn't Japan they were asking him to do, and they weren't at war with the Soviet Union. "There are right orders and there are dumb orders." He shoved the message into Logan's hand. "This is a dumb order, and all it's going to do is get us all killed."

"What do I tell CINCNELM?"

"You"—Shipley leaned forward until his face was inches from Logan's—"don't tell them anything. That's my responsibility," he said, enunciating each word.

"But Admiral Frost wants me to respond expeditiously to this order, sir."

Shipley leaned back. Surely Admiral "Thirty-one-Knot" Burke isn't listening to this. But then Admiral Laurence "Jack" Frost, the Director of Naval Intelligence, had been Admiral Burke's flag captain during the war. Probably why Frost was the DNI now. Shipley took a deep breath, reached over, and took the message from Logan. He would not be getting this message if Admiral Burke was not aware of what he was asking. "Let me have this. We'll draft a reply later. You go ahead and draft one for me to reply to this ludicrous mission that has gone from dangerous to deadly." He leaned down, his face hard. "And don't send it or anything else without my permission. Understand?"

"Yes, sir."

The forward hatch opened, and Lieutenant Junior Grade Olsson thanked the person holding the hatch as he stepped inside the passageway. He held two cups of coffee in his hands. "Here, sir."

Shipley thanked him. He looked at the clock on the bulkhead inside the small radio shack. He had ten minutes before he needed to relieve Weaver. He'd make a quick head call and then relieve the operations officer so the man could crawl topside to rescue the XO who by now was counting the seconds.

"We are going to be busy for the next couple of hours exchanging air. When we finish and are settled down for the night, we'll work on our response."

Shipley cradled the cup with the palms of his hands, enjoying the feel of the heat against his skin. He set the hot cup down just long enough to pull on his gloves for the journey back through the control room toward officers' country. Neither of the junior officers spoke. Shipley's mind whirled with the implications of what he was being ordered to do.

Picking up his cup, Shipley turned toward the forward hatch. As he grabbed the handle, he turned. "By the way, Lieutenant Logan, don't ever order any of my officers out of their assigned areas again without my permission." He looked up. "Understand?"

TEN

Sunday, December 2, 1956

ANTON stood in the hatchway to the forward torpedo room. The place stank of the fire from a week ago. Everything loose had been moved out since his return from visiting Admiral Katshora. The work party had tried haphazardly to scrub away the soot and stains of the fire, but it was impossible among the wires, cabling, and pipes that ringed the small compartment, most of which would have to be ripped out and replaced eventually. It was something the yards would have to do when the *Whale* went through her routine upkeep. He ran his hand through his hair. That was something he should know: when was the *Whale* next scheduled for her yard period?

"I think this is the best we can do," Gesny offered from inside the compartment, turning to face Anton. A smear of soot marked the XO's right cheek. "Everything that can burn that can be taken out has been taken out. Thankfully, torpedoes were not items we had to deal with," Gesny said, repeating the observation nearly every time the two of them talked of the fire. If torpedoes had been in the aft torpedo room, chances are none of them would be standing on the *Whale* now. Most would be dead.

The XO swept his hand around the compartment. Behind him a couple of sailors squatted near the controls to the torpedo tubes.

"We can maintain access to the compartment along the port passageway"—he pointed toward Anton—"since it circumvents the reactor room that should keep Doctor Zotkin happy." He slapped an overhead pipe. "As you ordered, Captain, I have instructed the operations officer to maintain a security and safety watch in this compartment all the time."

"Good," Anton said. It helps when you have competent people who do what needs to be done with you telling them only once. "Has Doctor Zotkin been briefed yet?"

With a pained expression, Gesny replied, "I am sure it will salve his sense of security, Comrade Captain. But if not, it at least makes me happy."

Anton turned to leave. "Good job, XO. Two days to go."

"Two days," Gesny replied as he followed Anton along the narrow passageway. "We are lucky you were able to convince him to delay the testing."

Anton grunted. "One day is not much of a delay. Besides, Commander Gesny, I think the weather may control the at-sea testing more than anything we do. Even our esteemed scientists are unable to control the giant of the North when it roars down on us."

"Captain, you are a poet and don't know it."

"I don't think I will give up this job yet."

To the right of the narrow passageway was the reactor room, a steady hum emanating constantly from behind the bulkhead, providing nonintrusive background noise in the area. Anton wondered how much of that steady hum emanated into the waters. Would it be something the Americans could track when the Soviets' atomic Navy sallied forth into the world's oceans?

The meeting two days ago with Admiral Katshora would have been routine except for how it had been accomplished, under an atmosphere of secrecy. It made Anton nervous. Katshora never asked him to keep a meeting secret between them, but Anton's political sense and survivor instinct told him that Zotkin would be furious to learn of the two Navy officers getting together without his knowledge. Anton had seen the political games at the Kremlin. The winners moved up. The losers tended to disappear.

Crashing sounds came from ahead, immediately followed by screams of someone in pain.

What now? Anton asked himself. He ducked his head, moving forward as fast as the narrow confines of a submarine allowed. Ahead, sailors were shouting at each other. Someone had fallen.

The watertight hatches were all open while the boat was tied to the pier, expediting his race. Behind him he heard the XO hurrying. Gesny would not have to watch his head as they moved like he did.

The radio shack was on his left. He nearly hit the radioman, who was leaning into the passageway looking toward the crowded control room. "Out of the way!" he shouted as he neared, pushing the sailor back into the small confines of radio.

Sailors were grouped around someone on the deck of the control room.

"Make a hole," Anton commanded as he entered.

Lebedev squatted, holding the hand of the man on the deck.

"What is it?"

Lebedev looked up and stood, dropping the hand.

On the deck was the man Anton had seen more than a week ago being carried away on a stretcher. A few tufts of hair dotted the top of the man's bright red face. Numerous open sores covered his lips.

"Who is this?"

"Chief Ekomov, Captain."

Ekomov! He was the first person Anton met when he reported on board the facility. He had been sitting at the end of the hallway, reading a newspaper. Anton looked closer, aware of how much the man had changed.

"One of our engineers until a month ago, when he came down . . ." Lebedev paused, looking over Anton's shoulder at Gesny.

Anton turned and saw Gesny shake his head so slightly it was barely discernible, then looked back at the operations officer. "And what?"

Lebedev looked down at Ekomov, whose eyes were closed. The man's chest barely moved. "He came down sick. Probably the Arctic weather." Lebedev touched his chest. "Lung disease most likely."

"Make way! Make way!" came a shout from the forward end of the control room. It was the new surgeon, Doctor Forov.

Forov pushed his way through the crowd, squatting quickly, his growling stomach resting slightly on his thighs. He reached out to touch the injured chief but quickly withdrew his hand. "*Blyad!*" the surgeon shouted, standing up. He took a step back. "Who has touched this man?"

Forov revolved in a circle, looking at each person. He was a couple of steps away when his gaze turned on Anton. "Comrade Captain, have you touched this man?"

Forov's breath hit Anton. The stale, dank odor of vodka caused his nose to wrinkle in disgust. So this was why Forov was in Kola Bay?

"I am the only one," Lebedev answered before Anton could reply. "He was one of our—"

"Quick," Forov interrupted, pushing Lebedev toward the forward part of the boat. "Get in the head, take your clothes off, and scrub every part of your body."

Lebedev raised his hand toward his head. Forov grabbed the hand roughly, pulling it down. "Do not touch your face until you have washed your hands." He shoved the hand away from him. "Do you understand me?" Forov asked, his face close to Lebedev's. The doctor's head turned from side to side as he looked into the operations officer's eyes.

Lebedev turned his head to the side, trying to avoid the man's breath.

"Don't touch your face," Forov said, his voice lower.

Forov looked at Anton. "Comrade Captain, I recommend everyone here—including you—do the same thing."

"Doctor, I have an injured man on the deck."

Forov looked down. "You have a dying man on your deck, Comrade Captain, and we do not want others to join him."

A few sailors started to ease out the forward hatch. Without turning, Forov shouted, "And that goes for you sailors also! You understand?"

"Yes, sir!" several cried, then bolted forward, where the crew had a smaller berthing area than the large crew quarters located just prior to the reactor room.

Forov looked at Lebedev. "I thought I told you to go scrub yourself. Scrub the skin red, young man."

Lebedev looked past him at Anton, who nodded. Lebedev turned and quickly left the control room.

"You need to help Chief Ekomov, Doctor," Anton said.

Forov looked down at the man. "Ekomov—is that his name?"

"Yes, he was one of our engineers—" Gesny started.

"Then, he worked in the reactor room," Forov finished.

"Yes."

"Then there is nothing I can do."

By now there were only Anton, Gesny, and Forov standing in the control room with the dying Ekomov. Forov's urgent orders to the crowd had sent them scurrying away quickly.

"You have to do something," Gesny said.

Forov shook his head. "The man is as good as dead." Forov ran his hand through his beard, then realized what he was doing and quickly removed it. "I must shower myself," he muttered.

"What is wrong with him?" Anton asked.

"Radiation poisoning," Forov answered.

"Radiation poisoning?"

Forov nodded. "Doctor Zotkin and his scientists are still experimenting with the lead shielding. Too much lead and the submarine becomes too heavy—its center of gravity shifting too much for the design controls to compensate." With his left hand raised and palm straight, Forov drove his hand downward like an arrow. "It would cause the submarine to sink like a stone."

"But too little?" Gesny asked.

"Too little is what we had when this chief was in the reactor room. Too little lead lets the radiation escape. That is what happened to this man. Too much radiation has penetrated his skin. This radiation is destroying his insides." Forov licked his lips. "It is a painful death."

Anton and Gesny exchanged quick glances.

Forov saw them and shook his head. "It is all right now. The current engineers have been working the reactors for more than a month. None of them has suffered the unexpected consequences of the first group. We can thank Doctor Zotkin for that."

"I saw this man when I arrived nearly two months ago," Anton said. "He was up, moving, talking, reading."

Forov shrugged. "Once captured, radiation goes on to do its deadly business. We don't know as much as we want to about it. We have been studying the effects and trying different methods to cure it. So far we have not been successful, but we are gathering lots of data from the few survivors of the first team."

Forov looked from Anton to Gesny and then back again. He pointed at them. "You did not know this?"

Anton shook his head.

Forov blanched. "I am sorry. I should not have told you. I thought Doctor Zotkin would have . . ." He stopped. "I am sorry. I have spoken too much." He turned to the ladder. "I have to call and get the attendants down here, Comrade Captain. They know how to remove the body—"

"It is not a body, Doctor Forov," Anton said, his voice crisp and sharp. "It is an injured sailor, and you will treat him."

Forov put a foot on the bottom rung. "There is nothing I can do. He is as dead now as he will be within the hour."

Anton stepped forward. Forov's breath caused his nostrils to widen. "If you go up that ladder without seeing to this man, I will have you arrested. Do you understand me?"

Forov took his foot off the rung. "Maybe I could give him a shot of morphine or something to ease his pain."

"You do what you are here to do, Doctor Forov."

Forov wiped his hands on his pants and squatted beside Ekomov.

Anton stared as Forov tentatively reached forward and unbuttoned Ekomov's sleeve. Forov looked up at Anton. He jerked his thumb over his shoulder. "I have to go to medical for my kit."

"You have two minutes, Doctor."

"Yes, Comrade Captain."

Anton watched the heavyset bear of a man disappear through the forward hatch. His first impression of the man had been much different. Crisis and fear provided the true metrics of a man, not appearances, and in this instance Forov had been found lacking. If radiation had caused Ekomov's condition, then how could it affect those around him?

"You think Chief Ekomov is radioactive?" Gesny asked.

"It does not matter right now, XO. What matters is that we do something for the man. Would you go topside and call the attendants or whoever it is Forov wants to come? Tell them to hurry. Maybe the facilities from where Ekomov came will have the medical care he needs."

Gesny's feet disappeared through the hatch overhead at the same time as Forov reappeared through the forward hatch. Without speaking to or looking at Anton, Forov knelt beside Ekomov, pulled a syringe from his small black bag, and quickly injected the contents into the man's upper arm. Then he stood. "That should take the pain away."

A white-smocked scientist climbed down the ladder. He stepped off the ladder, staring down at Ekomov.

"Well," Anton said, "are you here to help him?"

The man shook his head. "No, sir, Comrade. Doctor Zotkin asked me to bring you this." He handed a sealed envelope to Anton.

Above them the noise of several people climbing onto the bridge reached them.

SHIPLEY, Arneau, and Weaver bent over the navigational chart spread across the wardroom table.

"This will be most difficult, Captain," Weaver said.

Lieutenant Van Ness stepped into the wardroom. "Sorry, Captain. It must be something I ate."

"Don't let Crocky hear you say that," Arneau said.

"Yeah, he'll be most upset," Weaver added.

"Yes, I know it will be difficult, but our orders are to be prepared to do it *when so ordered*," Shipley said.

"You've done this stuff before, haven't you, Skipper?" Arneau asked.

Shipley nodded. "Once. Tokyo Bay. And we nearly lost our lives doing it."

"We were at war then. They were waiting and watching."

Shipley picked up his coffee from the next table and sipped the hot drink. "Yeah," he said as he set it back down. "We were at war and we were winning." He looked at the three officers. "No offense, but to continue to answer your question, I was with a crew of veterans who had numerous combat missions under their belt; knew what depth charging was like; and knew everything necessary to save the ship from sinking."

"Captain, we may not have fought in World War II, but we know the *Squallfish* and we know how to fight it," Arneau said sharply.

Shipley nodded. "I did not mean to indicate any lack of confidence, XO, so don't get your bowels in an uproar." He reached forward and tapped his finger on the chart. "If—no, *when*—we are ordered to do this, we are going to go into Soviet territorial waters. We are not at war with the Soviet Union, though there are those who believe we should do it now and get it over with. But the fact is, we are not at war. Therefore, if we are detected, we are expendable."

"Expendable?" Van Ness asked.

Shipley nodded. "Which is better for America? Admit they

had a submarine inside Soviet waters, or say we acted on our own or we were off course."

"Kind of hard to be off course inside Kola Bay," Weaver said with a nervous chuckle.

Shipley agreed. "Yes, it is." He lifted his cup again. "Unfortunately, I would like to keep this from the crew, but it will be all over the ship by nightfall." He sighed. "When we return to Holy Loch, Naval Intelligence and the Naval Investigative Service will be all over us debriefing the men, having us sign nondisclosure statements, and threatening everyone with jail if they so much as breathe a word of this."

"That will frighten them?" Arneau said with a short laugh. "How do you frighten men who risk their lives in a steel coffin?"

"You don't, but as long as those of us here keep our concern to ourselves, it will give the crew confidence. All they need to know is that we are on a surveillance mission. Every one of you, including me, needs to keep as much of the information concerning this mission among ourselves as possible. It is nigh impossible to keep our destination from the crew, but there is no reason to be broadcasting it. Everyone understand?"

They nodded in agreement.

Weaver leaned forward. "Skipper, if we are detected, it isn't as if we have a whole open ocean in which to hide. We only have one way in and one way out of Kola Bay."

"Then we better not be detected," Shipley said. He looked around the table. "Everyone understand?"

Van Ness put his finger on the entrance to Kola Bay, touching the small port city of Polyarnyy near the entrance. "Right here is where it is going to start getting scary."

"I'm scared already, and we haven't even gotten there," Arneau added.

"I feel better knowing that," Weaver added.

"Why right there?" Shipley asked.

"Kola Bay is littered with wrecks, Skipper. There are a couple, according to the Coast and Geodetic Survey charts I have on board. Lots of them sunk during World War II. If we venture outside the navigation lanes, we run the risk of running into them."

"Does your information tell you their depth?"

Van Ness shook his head. "The publications are made for surface ships. It tells them where they are and if the Coast and Geodetic Survey materials are accurate. The charts are accurate around the U.S. coast, but around here?" Van Ness shrugged. "I doubt they have the same degree of accuracy. Good chance most of these wrecks are based on word-of-mouth recordings."

"But ought it not tell you something?" Weaver asked.

"It does," Van Ness replied. "It tells me where they think a wreck exists. Then it warns navigators to stay within the navigational lanes—stay between the buoys when you're entering and leaving Kola Bay."

"How deep is Kola Bay at the navigational lanes?" Shipley asked.

"It doesn't say."

"Doesn't say! What kind of help is the Coast and Geodetic Survey giving us if they don't even tell us the depth?" Weaver said sharply.

Arneau touched Weaver on the arm and then looked at Van Ness. "Do we have an idea of how deep it should be?"

Van Ness shook his head. "I can't tell you, XO. I wish I knew. I looked through the books I had after our meeting yesterday to see what I could find on Kola Bay." He touched the chart on the table. "This is all we have on board. It's large-scale and doesn't identify where the wrecks and sandbars are."

"Sandbars?" Weaver asked.

"Kola Bay is ice-free year-round. Seems the currents and the ice outside of it cause the bottom terrain to shift during the winter. The Soviets have to remap it every year. Doesn't exactly say 'sandbars,' but does refer to a shifting bottom. Could be gravel."

"Things just keep getting better."

"I wouldn't worry too much, Alec," Shipley said to his operations officer. "We are going covert. They won't know we're there, and if we do this right, they won't know when we depart. It's a matter of good seamanship."

"And a shitload of good luck," Weaver added.

Van Ness leaned forward. "Once we enter Kola Bay, Skipper, I recommend we use the navigational lanes for the first leg. First leg will be from abeam Polyarnyy on a course of one-eighty." Van Ness picked up a pencil and lightly traced the route. "This will keep us in the center of the bay entrance. It also will keep us well away from known wrecks." He straightened for a moment before leaning forward again. "Then we turn slightly southwest for the second leg. This will take us into the area of the bay where we need to be. We will have Severomorsk to our southeast, and the facility that Lieutenant Logan wants to see will be directly opposite, on our northwest." He moved the pencil back to the second leg. "This is the most dangerous part of the navigational picture, Skipper. It's narrow. There are multiple wrecks on both sides of it. And according to what I had available, there is a portion of this leg just before we reach the wider-open area between Severomorsk and the target where shallow water forces surface ships into two narrow channels."

Shipley took a deep drink and let out a sigh. He looked at Van Ness and smiled. "Well, Lieutenant, can we get into where we need to be while completely submerged?"

Van Ness straightened. His face wrinkled in concentration as he bit his lower lip. "I don't know, sir. I know the Soviet cruisers and warships can go back and forth between them."

"How about their submarines?"

"I don't know."

Shipley looked at Weaver. "Go get Lieutenant Logan and have him come to the wardroom."

Weaver nodded.

"He's in the forward or aft diesel spaces," Arneau said. "I think he and his team are practicing putting the air testers on the main induction valves."

Ten minutes later, Weaver returned with Logan in tow.

Logan glanced down at the chart and then up at Shipley. "Sir, do you think it wise to be doing this in an open area?"

"Lieutenant Logan, an open area to a submariner is anything above the surface of the water. We're down at 150 feet, doing eight knots, heading south-southeast." Shipley touched the chart. "We have some questions about our mission."

Logan looked around the wardroom. "Sir, I'm not sure I can talk about it out here."

"Lieutenant Logan, while you are aboard my boat, I am all the authority you need. What I tell you to do, you do. Understand?"

"Yes, sir, but—"

"There are no 'buts' on my boat." He leaned forward. "Here is Kola Bay. We are doing the navigation picture for our transit into the bay and for our escape afterward." Shipley looked at Van Ness. "Show him."

Van Ness took his pencil and put it on the narrow portion of the transit between the entrance and the wider area between Severomorsk and the facility. "Right here are two narrow navigational channels: one for ships entering the main part of Kola Bay, and one for them exiting. The C&G surveys warn ships to be alert for shifting shallows caused by winter conditions and of wrecks scattered along the north and south sides of the bay."

Logan nodded, his attention on the chart. "You have a better chart than this one?"

"This is the only one we have. We had expected to be in the Iceland–U.K. gap patrolling seemingly calm waters, drinking our coffee, eating our pastries until relieved in thirty days," Arneau corrected. "We had not expected to be risking our lives in the middle of the Soviet Fleet."

"Not to mention the Soviet Northern Fleet headquarters," Weaver added. "It would be like having a Soviet submarine sail into the harbor of Norfolk Naval Base. We'd sink the son of a bitch."

Everyone looked at him.

"I'll have no more talk of sinkings," Shipley said. He looked at Logan. "The question we have, Lieutenant, is do the Soviet submarines egress from Kola Bay submerged, or do they have to exit on the surface here, where C&G warns ships to be alert."

Logan's eyes narrowed as he stared at the chart. Everyone waited for him to answer. Shipley was beginning to believe the intelligence officer did not know, when the young man finally relaxed and confirmed it. "I don't know, sir, but I can send a message to Naval Intelligence, asking them. They'll know, and we should get a reply within twenty-four hours."

Shipley turned to Van Ness. "What is our estimated arrival time off the entrance?"

"At current course and speed, we should be there tomorrow night—midnight, Greenwich Mean Time."

The U.S. Navy ran on GMT, as did the Royal Navy. Greenwich Mean Time was the common time used in the days of sail so captains could calculate their longitude from the Greenwich meridian. As navigation improved over the years into the twentieth century, the original purpose was clouded. Since their days and nights ran together beneath the ocean waves, submarines needed the common time element even more than the surface forces.

Shipley glanced at the Navy clock on the wall. The huge black hands showed a few minutes before 2100 hours. "That's cutting it close, Lieutenant. That means we may have to break radio silence if they require any additional information. It also means that we will not have an opportunity to ask for clarification from Naval Intelligence if their reply is ambiguous." Shipley looked at Arneau. "XO, you get with Lieutenant Logan and help him ask the right questions."

"Yes, sir."

"For all of you, regardless of the reply, we are going to go ahead with the orders if we are told to execute them."

"It'll be dangerous."

"If we weren't used to danger, we would not be in the silent service. We'd be skimmers, watching the sun rise and set as we bore holes through the ocean."

"Yes, sir, Skipper," they said in unison.

"Once again, even though the crew will eventually find out everything, I do not want us discussing it with them. The less they know, the better it is for them. There is enough speculation ongoing now. Better they speculate than we read about this in the newspapers once we return."

"There should not be anything in the newspapers, sir," Logan objected.

"Aye, sir," Arneau answered, speaking to Shipley but glaring at Logan. "Lieutenant Logan, if you will stay behind, we'll work on the message."

"Sir, shouldn't we do that in the radio shack?"

"Lieutenant, there isn't room for both of us in the radio shack," Arneau said sarcastically. "This is our classified briefing room, where we can talk secret shit, drink coffee, and eat a meal. Besides, you see this?" he asked as he reached behind him and tugged at the curtain. "This is our own soundproof curtain."

SHIPLEY was in the conning tower when Arneau crawled up the ladder.

"Up scope," Shipley said after a quick glance at his XO. Shipley squatted slightly, grabbing the handles as the periscope rose. He put his eyes to the scope as it continued to rise, watching the water slide away as the periscope broke surface. It was dark; his quick look revealed no navigation lights of ships and also revealed no sign of stars. Van Ness's eight-o'clock report a few minutes earlier spoke of a quarter moon, but if it was out there, the clouds hid it.

The submarine rocked slightly, and as Shipley watched, a wave broke over the periscope.

"Switch to diesel," he said without removing his eyes. "And prepare to surface." He listened as the conning tower watch echoed his orders into action.

Shipley stepped back from the periscope. "Periscope down. Surface the boat."

The two "oogles" of the submarine horn sounded throughout the *Squallfish*. Silent, he watched the crew respond to the officer of the deck's orders as Lieutenant Junior Grade Olsson surfaced the boat. Shipley knew the communications officer was nervous with the skipper standing behind him. He had been there; done that; and survived it. No other way to learn unless you were doing.

"Ballasts clear!"

"Ballasts clear," Senior Chief Boohan echoed.

"Very well!" Olsson replied in acknowledgment.

The real key to surfacing and taking a submarine down was the chief of the boat. If you had a good COB, there was no way a junior officer or even a senior one could screw up a command and endanger the submarine. The COB would never permit it. Tactfully the COB would say something such as "Say again, sir!" The second time you screwed up a command, the COB would let you know with a curse and a dance of annoyance. Shipley smiled. A dancing senior or master chief was a sight to behold. He had his share of their mentorship his first year in the service.

"What you got, XO?" he finally asked.

Arneau handed him a metal clipboard.

Shipley lifted the metal top of the clipboard and read the draft Arneau and Logan had worked. "Good message. Add a paragraph asking them for any information on the depth of Kola Bay, then go ahead and send it. Let's see if Naval Intelligence can reply in time. Be sure to tell Mr. Olsson when he gets off watch to keep any messages coming in from Naval Intelligence among him, you, and me."

"And Lieutenant Logan."

Shipley nodded. "And Lieutenant Logan."

Shipley lifted the draft message to read the message below it. The bright red ink of the TOP SECRET stamp drew his attention. He looked at Arneau, whose eyebrows rose when their eyes met. "Guess we get to do it," Shipley said, shutting the clipboard.

"Yes, sir. I thought I'd schedule a meeting for later."

Shipley looked at the clock. It was after midnight. "The sooner the better. I want to discuss rules of engagement. I want to be certain that we have touched every base to ensure a safe and successful return to Holy Loch."

Around the conning tower, the noise of the overhead hatch opening, ears popping at the change of pressure, and the scrambling of Mr. Olsson as he scurried up the ladder, quickly followed by two topside observers, obscured the words exchanged between Shipley and Arneau. The cold Arctic air whipped through the opening, quickly bringing the temperature below freezing.

Shipley looked at the open hatch leading down to the control room.

"Want me to shut it?"

"No, XO. We need fresh air more than comfort right now." He handed the clipboard to the XO. "As for the meeting, we'll do it after we have exchanged air, topped off the batteries, and settled down for the final leg of our transit," he said.

"Aye, sir."

A sailor emerged from below with a foul-weather jacket in his hand. He mumbled "Captain" as he handed it to Shipley, who quickly put on the garment.

Arneau disappeared down the ladder.

Shipley's thoughts went back to years ago during World War II when they had prepared for the mission into Tokyo Bay. Back then, not only did they have two weeks of transit time to prepare, but also they had known long before they left Pearl Harbor where they were headed. This time they were going in cold—he smiled at the double meaning—and he didn't even know if they had sufficient depth for the *Squallfish* to do it submerged.

ELEVEN

Tuesday, December 4, 1956

"CAPTAIN," Arneau said, knocking on the bulkhead near Shipley's stateroom.

Shipley's eyes opened. He looked at the small clock on his desk, a gift from June years ago. The hands showed five-fifteen. He pushed himself up on both elbows and looked at Arneau. "What is it, XO?"

"Sir, you wanted to be in the conning tower when we had to turn into Soviet waters."

"How long—"

"About thirty minutes until we turn." Arneau put one foot into the small stateroom and set a cup of steaming coffee on the small desk. "Compliments of Crocky. Got there as the light turned red."

"Thanks." Shipley spun his feet off the bed. "I feel like shit."

"Well, if it's any consolation, Skipper, you look it, too."

"Thanks, XO. What every skipper needs: a smart-ass exec."

"Some have to work at it. For me, my father said it was something inherited from a long line of Jewish activists."

"Activists? Is that some sort of sect within the Jew religion?"

Arneau smiled and shook his head. "Never mind, Skipper. Poor joke on my part. And, it's the Jewish religion, not the Jew religion."

Shipley took a sip of the coffee, enjoying the fresh taste and smell of what would grow into a bastion of tannic acid and gray sludge by the end of the workday.

He set the cup down and quickly put on his shoes.

"Torpedoes?"

"All tubes are loaded."

"Both forward and aft crews briefed?"

"Both briefed. No one is to even open an outer door on a tube without your express permission or order."

Shipley nodded. "Good." He tied the last shoe, stood, and grabbed his coffee. "One thing I have yet to learn is how to climb those ladders with a cup of hot coffee in my hand."

"But we do it."

"And we make a mess each time, but this is too good to waste."

Moments later the two stood in the conning tower. Van Ness was hunkered over the small navigation table, with the lead signalman petty officer shoulder to shoulder with him.

Shipley took the few steps to where the two men were working. "Report, officer of the deck."

"Sir, steering course one one zero at eight knots."

"Depth?"

"Oh, sorry, sir. Depth one hundred fifty feet."

"Time to turn?"

Van Ness straightened, twiddling his pencil with both his hands. "Sir, estimated time to turn is fifteen minutes. New course will have us crossing the twelve-nautical-mile territorial waters of the Soviet Union in thirty minutes."

Shipley quickly looked around the compartment, lowered his voice, and replied, "Cliff, I know it's hardly a secret with the crew where we are or even where we are going, but let's at least pretend they don't know. Okay?"

Van Ness blushed. "Sorry, sir. I said—"

"I know what you said, navigator. What's next?"

"Recommend we come to course one seven five degrees"—Van Ness glanced at the clock on the bulkhead, then back down at the chart—"in five minutes."

"Weren't you the OOD last night when I left, Mr. Van Ness?"

"Yes, sir; but four hours on watch; four hours off; and the next thing you know, you're right back up here."

Shipley smiled at Van Ness's attempt at humor. Van Ness was

not his best OOD. When he reviewed the man's personnel qualification standards, he had seen where his predecessor had the same impression. "Okay, make the turn as scheduled." He looked at the officer. "How long until we reach the entrance of the bay?"

"At this speed it will be twenty-one hundred hours, sir."

Shipley turned to the XO. "XO, I want a quiet ship, and I want sonar extra alert. Any sign of warships, I want to be notified. Make sure it's in the captain's night orders."

"Aye, sir."

Lieutenant Logan and his two communications technicians crawled up the ladder into the conning tower.

"Captain, XO," Logan acknowledged, "looks as if this is it," he said with excitement in his voice. "This is going to be great."

Shipley nodded, thinking, *I felt the same way on my first mission out of Pearl. It only took that one mission to change that excitement to mind-numbing fear*. He pointed to the far end of the compartment. "Let's step over here for a moment, Lieutenant."

Logan nodded at Brooks and Cross. "You two, wait here."

The two sailors from Naval Intelligence set their gear on the deck while Shipley, Arneau, and Logan stepped away.

Shipley said quietly, "Lieutenant, I wouldn't be too enthused over this. When we cross into the territorial waters of the Soviet Union, we are entering their territory. Anything that happens to us will be denied by our own Navy and our own government."

A look of disbelief crossed Logan's face as the smile faded. "But—"

Shipley held up his hand. "There are no 'buts' in the submarine service, Lieutenant. There are just 'ah, shits' and 'thank Gods.' The other thing is we have not heard from your Admiral Frost. We need to know how their submarines enter and leave the bay. It would be best if we are able to do the bulk of this mission submerged. Sailing into Kola Bay on the surface is not what I call conducive to a long life." He stopped. Shipley looked at the faces of the two men. He wanted to say he was going to abandon the mission, but he knew he wouldn't.

He had never failed to complete an assigned mission, and this late in his career he was not going to do it now. If the U.S. Navy thought it important enough to risk his life, the lives of his men, and the submarine in which they rode, then it was a mission he would complete. He took a deep breath. "If the Soviets do it surfaced, we will have to do it the same."

"I would think we would want to go through the narrows during the night," Logan offered.

"You're probably right, and since our navigation plan has us arriving off the mouth of the bay at twenty-one hundred GMT, we should be off Severomorsk by dawn." He looked at Arneau. "XO, have Cliff check the tides. It would be nice to pass through the narrows during high tide." He turned back to Logan. "It would also be nice to have Naval Intelligence come through on time." Then he said quietly, "And it would be nice to have some 'Notice to Mariners' charts of the area, but we don't."

"Notice to Mariners?" Logan asked.

Shipley nodded. "They're charts that give you the depths, location of undersea obstacles, and updated information derived from other mariners. Unfortunately, we don't. Your message to Naval Intelligence asked them for the soundings, so hopefully they'll include any updates on this area." He chuckled. "It's not as if we can go to the C&G and ask them for updates."

"If Suitland fails to answer before we reach Kola Bay, sir, will that mean we'll wait until Suitland replies before entering?"

"Suitland?" Arneau asked.

"Yes, sir; the Office of Naval Intelligence is located there."

"I thought it was in the Pentagon."

"No, sir. The DNI stays in the Pentagon most of the time, but the real nerve center of Naval Intelligence is in Suitland, Maryland, at ONI."

"Do you two mind?" Shipley asked, a slight smile turning the left side of his mouth up.

"Yes, sir; I mean no, sir. The message did go out, sir," Logan quickly replied. "I checked with Mr. Olsson earlier this morning when I was reading the daily intelligence report."

"We get a daily intelligence report?" Arneau asked, one hand coming to rest on his hip. "When did that start?"

Logan blushed. "Sir, I had it started when I knew I was coming on board," he stuttered.

"Why wasn't I aware of it?" Arneau looked at Shipley. "Did you know, Skipper?"

Shipley shook his head.

"Captain, XO, you are welcome to read them. I had originally proposed a daily intelligence briefing when I came aboard."

Shipley nodded. "I remember, XO. I told him to just keep me informed when something came up. I figured a daily briefing might give me more information than I need, plus there is a propensity for Naval Intelligence to spend an exponential amount of time debriefing you when they think you might know something they want to know." He paused for a moment, thinking back to the day-after-day debriefing the crew went through when they returned from Tokyo Bay. "Even you, or they, don't know what it is they want to know." It had been thrilling at first to be able to help Naval Intelligence, but the third and fourth trips back for the same set of questions made the process seem more confrontational than collegial. He already knew those strange fellows wearing Navy khakis would be waiting for them on the pier when they returned to Holy Loch. He dreaded it. The less the crew knew, the quicker they would be released. He had no illusions about how long the XO, operations officer, and he would be grilled—probably until the next mission of the *Squallfish.*

"I want to read them," Arneau said, poking himself in the chest with his thumb. "I want to read everything that comes into this boat and everything that goes out." He looked back at Shipley. "I will have a talk with Mr. Olsson."

Shipley looked up at the overhead. "Lieutenant Logan, you and your men are kind of early this morning. What are you doing in the conning tower?"

"I asked the OOD if we could practice setting up the camera one last time before we enter the surveillance area, Captain."

Shipley looked at Arneau. "XO, make sure when they raise the periscope for Lieutenant Logan and his men that the OOD slows the boat to four knots. I want no cavitations from the screws, and I don't want wave action noise from a raised periscope beneath the water."

"Aye, sir," Arneau answered. "Lieutenant Van Ness, you hear the skipper?"

"Yes, sir."

Shipley shook his head and thought, *There is no way on this submarine that we are going to keep this covert mission from the crew.* Arneau was grinning when he looked at him. "Knock off that shit-eating grin, XO. Tell the OOD to do whatever is needed to help them, but don't surface."

Shipley let out a deep sigh, the fog of his breath rolling up in front of his eyes. He zipped up his foul-weather jacket. Why did he have the feeling that Tokyo Bay was a breeze compared to what was being asked now? Maybe it was because with Tokyo

Bay the ocean was just outside the harbor entrance. Here he was going to be miles from the Barents if they were detected.

"Permission to come to new course, Skipper?" Van Ness asked.

"Very well."

Van Ness gave the order.

The helmsman reported, "Coming to course one seven five, speed eight knots."

Shipley turned when he heard the helmsman respond to Van Ness's command.

"XO, slow the boat to about six knots. Have Cliff do the navigational calculations for the slower speed. Additionally, I do not want to close the entrance to Kola Bay nearer than twenty nautical miles without my express permission."

"Roger, sir." Arneau stepped over to Van Ness, who gave the orders necessary to reduce speed to six knots.

"Let me know if sound detects any traffic in the area." He glanced at the sailor wedged against the far port bulkhead. The man's head was barely visible above the turned-up collar of the foul-weather jacket. A set of headphones pinned the wool watch cap down on the man's head.

"Aye, sir," Van Ness replied.

The slight feel of the turn caused everyone to shift their center of gravity slightly. Moments later the helmsman said, "Steady on course one seven five, speed six knots."

Five minutes later, Shipley turned to Arneau. "XO, I'm going down to the wardroom for breakfast. I'll be there for a while; then I'm going to do a walk-through of the boat from the forward torpedo room to the aft one."

Arneau acknowledged Shipley's orders and waited until the captain disappeared down the ladder. Then he turned, glared at Logan, and said, "My mind is still not made up about you, Lieutenant. I'm going to have a talk with my communications officer and then I may be back." Arneau turned, grabbed the sides of the ladder, and climbed down to the control room. He was heading toward the radio shack and an ass he was going to chew out before breakfast.

Van Ness walked over to Logan.

Logan met the blue eyes of the Dutch American. "Glad they're gone. I'm sure you guys are used to them, but they make me nervous. I'm sure they want me off the boat as fast as I want to get off it."

"They make me a little nervous when they're both in the conning tower."

"They make me nervous because I'm on your boat."

Van Ness smiled. "Now, how can they be off the boat?"

Logan's eyebrows rose. "They can't, but I am willing to make the sacrifice and leave the great and wonderful *Squallfish* as soon as possible."

"Well, looks as if you are stuck with us for a while. By the way, the XO told me he wanted no wave noise when we raised the periscope."

"What's wave noise?"

Van Ness's eyebrows wrinkled into a V. "I think he means when the water ripples around the periscope or the snorkel creates a modicum of cavitations in the water."

"A modicum?" Logan said with a grin.

"Lieutenant, you and I are the same rank, so don't make fun of my speech," Van Ness said with a smile, wanting to help Logan as he did everyone.

Logan nodded. "I get the feeling you submariners don't have a sense of humor, or if you do, you leave it ashore when you put to sea." Changing the subject, he added, "Does that mean we are going to be operating the periscope under the surface, or are we coming up to periscope depth?"

Van Ness's eyes shifted to the left for a moment as he thought. "They didn't tell me to stay at a hundred fifty feet."

"I think they're okay with us coming up to periscope depth. It'll give us an opportunity to see how the camera works in daylight. We haven't had a chance to practice it except at night."

Van Ness bit his upper lip, thinking about the idea of changing the depth without notifying the captain. The captain and the XO did say to help Logan. Van Ness relaxed and smiled as he realized he was following orders. "I understand. The XO did say to reduce any chance of wave noise, and there is less noise with a periscope breaking the surface than doing it at this depth. At this depth we run the risk of damaging the scope. Don't want to do that."

"Good. I'll let you know when we're ready."

Van Ness walked back to the navigation table and told the leading signalman to work out the calculations of a six-knot transit. He did a quick caliper check along a dead-reckoning line, which showed them eighty nautical miles north of the entrance to Kola Bay. Most of the transit would be within the territorial waters of the Soviet Union. When they reached the entrance, they would be ten nautical miles off the Soviet coast that bordered the western side of the entrance.

"Steady on course one seven five; speed six knots," the helmsman reported.

Van Ness smiled. This was a good time to show the skipper how well he conned the boat. "I would like to take us to periscope depth and do it at a five-feet-per-minute rise rate. Angle on the bow, five degrees."

Senior Chief Boohan crawled into the conning tower. He heard the command. "What ya doing, OOD?"

"Oh, hi, COB. Just bringing the boat to periscope depth slowly. Good training for the crew. Got Lieutenant Logan and his men up there," he said, pointing upward while shaking his head back and forth, "practicing their camera tactics again."

Boohan shook his bald head and chuckled. "I know what you mean. I'll be glad when they're off my boat. I'm going to get a quick bite; then I'll be back, Lieutenant."

Logan gave the chief of the boat a hard glare. Boohan turned and crawled back down the ladder, heading toward the crew's mess.

"Passing one four five feet," the helmsman announced.

"Very well," Van Ness acknowledged. He enjoyed the feel of the deck when he had the conn. No one ever fully understood the pride and pleasure of guiding a warship through the seas until they had done it themselves. If he was going to be at periscope depth, he might as well top off the batteries. So, following Shipley's standing orders of always charging the batteries when able to do so, Van Ness made a couple of mistakes compounding the one of bringing the boat to periscope depth. He called the maneuvering room and gave them a heads-up on reaching periscope and snorkel depth in twenty-five minutes.

WASHINGTON lifted the metal canister with the trash from the morning breakfast.

"Where you goin'?" Crocky asked.

Washington looked at the canister he was holding. "It's full. Thought I'd take it up to the forward torpedo room to store until we can dump it overboard."

"Why don't you wait until we finish breakfast?"

Washington set the canister down. "It's full, Petty Officer Crocky, and since we're surfacin', it'll be one less bag of trash to pitch overboard."

"I ain't heard no surfacin' horn, Petty Officer Washington, and what is this you doin' somethin' I ain't asked you to do?" Crocky wiped his hands on his apron, ignoring the sailors as they progressed along the chow line. "Usually I can't get you to wipe the tables down, much less carry the trash forward without a lot of wailin' and whinin' on your part. So why you wanna do it now?"

"Hey! Petty Officer Crocky, we goin' to get fed or what?" one of the sailors holding a metal tray near the instant eggs asked.

Crocky lifted a metal spoon and waved it. "You wait, you hear. I'll feed you when I'm good and ready." He looked the sailor up and down. "Besides, you look as if you could miss a meal or two."

The sailors laughed. "Ah, come on, Crocky."

"Hey, Jonesy! What you in a hurry for? Don't you know Crocky's chow can drop a moose at twenty paces?"

"Twenty paces ain't near enough what you need if you eat enough of that chow. Ain't ever goin' to make it to the head in time."

The sailors laughed.

Crocky scooped up a huge spoon of eggs and slapped the concoction on the metal tray. "There, now stop bothering me, boy."

"Yes, sir."

Washington lifted the canister and wormed his way from behind Crocky to the small entrance. Stepping into the chow hall portion of the mess, he worked his way across, and was soon in the passageway leading forward. He didn't know if they were surfacing, but he had seen the water in the glass tilt slightly with the forward side up, so they were at least changing depth upward. Heading up didn't necessarily mean surfacing, but if he had to carry the trash out after they surfaced, he'd run into Potts and his sycophant cracker, Fromley. Washington had worked hard the past week to avoid them. Once they switched to diesels, the electrician mates would be doing their routine maintenance on the batteries. This way, he could avoid them.

Washington lost his balance for a moment when he stepped into the passageway and bounced off the port bulkhead. The lid trapped his thumb for a moment. "Ouch! That hurt."

Shifting his feet apart, he set the canister down and grabbed the handles again. It'd be a real mess if he dropped this. And, he'd be the one having to clean it up.

He went through the control room listening to complaints about the smell, but this was fresh trash. Crocky never allowed old trash to crowd his mess.

He reached the battery room, set the canister down, and opened the hatch. No one was there, which was the way he planned it. There'd be more trash after chow, but he could put off bringing it forward until they dived again. Give Potts and Fromley time to finish their battery checks before he had to pass through their domain. Made him think of the gang turfs in Philadelphia. He'd no more pass beyond Walther Avenue than the man in the moon. But neither did the gangstas, as they call themselves, cross Walther into his domain.

He lifted the canister and stepped inside the forward battery compartment. Most times the compartment was empty, but he knew the electrician mates had a rotation to observe, though he had been lucky the past week, and with the exception of the chow hall had managed to avoid the "Laurel and Hardy" assholes. For a moment he wondered if the sailors even bothered to check the forward battery compartment. If they didn't and if something went wrong, then Potts and Fromley would be history.

He felt the vibration of the boat as it shifted from battery to diesel power. It also caused the contents to shift, and before Washington could recover, the lid fell off, striking the tops of the nearby batteries. A few sparks flew up as the metal lid rolled across negative and positive poles before bouncing onto the narrow deck between the battery banks.

Washington's eyes flew wide as his head twisted from side to side, watching the batteries, but other than the sparks, everything seemed back to normal. What Washington failed to realize was that at that moment the boat had shifted from electric power to diesel, so the batteries were in that small space of null time between powering the *Squallfish* and awaiting their top-off from the diesel

Washington quickly picked up the lid, put it back on the canister, and hurried into the forward torpedo room.

EACH of the *Squallfish* battery compartments was filled with two massive 126-cell batteries. Each cell had a smaller battery hooked up in sequence to power the electric motors that drove the two shafts of the *Squallfish*. The cells were what Potts and Fromley were responsible for inspecting to ensure that each cell was functioning properly. It was the cells, called batteries by the crew, that Washington's lid had serendipitously damaged, causing a cross circuit among four of the cells.

Submarine batteries were designed for high resistance to huge shocks, but those shocks were expected to come through the absorbers upon which the two batteries were mounted. Batteries produced hydrogen gas when they operated. The ventilation of the *Squallfish* dissipated this gas throughout the ship. It mattered little whether the batteries were charging or powering the electric motors; they were producing hydrogen discharge. As long as the discharge remained at less than 4 percent, there was no danger. Above 4 percent, there was a danger of fire, and when it reached 9 percent, the hydrogen concentration was such that any flame or spark would cause an explosion.

WITHIN a couple of minutes, Washington had sealed the garbage in the burlap bags designed to hold the trash. He set it on top of others near torpedo tube number six, to await when the forward escape hatch was opened. Then he, Santos, and Marcos would return to dump the trash overboard. He hurried, wanting to be back in the crew's mess before his twin nemeses arrived in the forward battery compartment.

Passing through the battery compartment the second time, he failed to notice the red readings growing on two of the batteries. But then Washington would not have known what he was seeing if he had looked. He was still working his way through the *Squallfish* qualification standards. He had yet to reach the battery section.

"WHAT the hell!" Shipley cried, sliding rapidly from his seat. He knocked over his coffee as he jumped up and started racing toward the control room. They were on diesel power! What the hell!

He reached the control room at about the same time as the XO, who was already scrambling up the ladder toward the conning tower.

"What the fuck are you doing? What are you thinking?" Arneau was screaming as Shipley climbed into the conning tower.

"What's going on?" Shipley asked.

Van Ness turned toward Shipley, whose eyes glistened. "I was—I was just helping out Lieutenant Logan. He was—"

"He was what?!" Arneau shouted. "Trying to get us sunk?"

"I haven't surfaced. You said not to surface."

"What is our depth?" Shipley asked. What in the hell was Van Ness thinking? It was daylight, and here they were . . .

"Fifty feet, sir," Senior Chief Boohan replied.

"What's above the waterline?"

"We have both snorkel and periscope, sir," Van Ness answered.

"Shit," Shipley said, shaking his head. Logan and his men stood quietly around the search periscope, where the camera had been secured. Shipley took one look and knew the periscope was above the waterline, cutting a wake behind it. "What's our speed?" he asked quietly.

"Six knots, sir," Chief Topnotch answered from near the torpedo firing controls. "Numbers one and two diesel are connected to the electric motor. Using numbers three and four to recharge the batteries, sir."

"Lieutenant Logan, how long to disconnect the camera?"

"We've been practicing, sir," he replied with a grin. "Cross and Brooks are able to disconnect it in thirty seconds," he said with pride.

"Then disconnect it."

Logan's eyebrows wrinkled. "Do you mind if we take a photograph of this merchant before we do it?"

Shipley looked at the chief. "We have a contact?"

"Yes, sir; two screws. Sound got it less than a minute ago."

Shipley looked at Arneau. "I take it, XO, you didn't know we were changing our depth?"

"No, sir."

"Get this camera off the periscope." Shipley turned to Van Ness. "Officer of the deck, how long has sound had the contact?"

"Sir," Van Ness answered, licking his lips, "we just got it before you entered—"

"Sound," Shipley interrupted, "what type of ship is it?"

The young sailor slipped his earphones off, letting them hang around his neck. "Not sure yet, Skipper. I have tentatively identified it as a merchant vessel."

"Lieutenant," Shipley said to Logan, pointing at the camera.

"Yes, sir."

The two communications technicians worked hurriedly, the camera coming off the search periscope quickly.

Shipley glanced at the clock on the bulkhead. It showed eight-thirty.

"XO, you have the conn. Prepare for emergency dive to one hundred fifty."

"This is the XO. I have the conn. Stay on red light. Report."

"Course one seven five, speed six knots," the helmsman replied.

"Depth fifty feet," Chief Topnotch, the chief of the watch, reported.

"Very well," Arneau replied.

"Camera's down, Captain," Logan said as he and the two sailors lugged the gear over to one side, away from the center of the conning tower.

Shipley grabbed the handles and spun the periscope in a 360-degree rotation. "What is the bearing of the contact?" he asked without moving away from the eyepiece.

"I have one niner zero, sir."

Shipley spun the periscope in that direction. He saw the vessel. Raised forward and aft superstructure with a bridge superstructure center. It was a merchant. White topside with rusty red main hull. An array of antennae, including direction-finding apparatuses, dotted the top of the bridge area. "Mark! Distance?"

"Ten thousand yards."

"Set."

"Set!"

Figures of a few merchant seamen moved across the deck of the merchant. He saw no fingers of congregating seamen along the safety rails pointing his way. He turned the periscope away from the merchant vessel to look at the snorkel. No black or white smoke coming from it. *Thank God for small favors. Maybe . . . just maybe*, Shipley thought. But then he realized he would not see any smoke coming from it. The cloud of gray-black smoke that would have coughed upward through the snorkel would have come in the first few seconds of the diesels cranking up.

"Down periscope."

"Tell the control room to take the boat down, Chief." His voice was calm, completely opposite to the empty-pit feeling around his midsection. If the vessel has seen them . . .

"Sorry, Skipper," Lieutenant Logan said. "I saw it was a merchant vessel and thought it would be a good training exercise for us to photograph it."

Shipley spun on the intelligence officer. In a seemingly calm voice he said, "Lieutenant Logan, you know what our merchant captains are instructed to do while at sea?"

Logan shook his head.

"You should. You're an intelligence officer. Even if you weren't an intelligence officer, I'd expect you to know. Our merchant captains report every contact they encounter; especially submarines." He pointed up. "You think they don't do that shit in the Soviet merchant fleet?"

Logan blanched. "No, sir; I mean yes, sir. I guess I didn't think."

"Who is the captain of this boat?"

"You are, sir," Logan replied, his voice shaken as he took a step back.

"Don't forget it. No one does anything on the *Squallfish* without my permission, especially having to do with anything that may put the boat onto the surface during daylight. You understand?"

"Yes, sir, but—"

"What did I tell you about 'buts' on board *Squallfish*?"

"Yes, sir."

Shipley turned. "Lieutenant Van Ness, would you go ask Lieutenant Commander Weaver to join you and me in the wardroom?"

"Yes, sir," Van Ness replied weakly. The officer quickly left the conning tower.

Relieving an officer of the deck was for a major infraction, but on board a warship examples had to be set to ensure that everyone understood what could and what could not be done.

"Tell engineering to switch back to battery," Arneau ordered. "Then prepare to make our depth one hundred feet."

Where had the XO been when Van Ness was off on cloud nine bringing this boat to the surface? Wasting time chewing out Olsson instead of making sure the boat was safe. He'd talk with the XO privately later. And what or who gave Van Ness the belief he had the authority to change depth without his permission? He still had training problems with this crew, and here he was about to take them into a hostile area where this sort of thing would mark their grave on the bottom of a Soviet bay.

Within a minute the *Squallfish* was heading deeper, at a

sharper angle than he would have liked, but well within the safety parameters of the boat. The whys he would find out. Ultimately he was the reason why anything happened on his boat.

He turned to Arneau. "I will send Mr. Weaver up to relieve you, XO, once I've had a little chat with him and Lieutenant Van Ness. By then you should have us settled on course, speed, and depth." He nodded at the signalman who was manning the navigation table. "Have SM2 Smuckers double-check our projected route to Kola Bay, if you would."

"Aye, sir."

"And XO, make appropriate changes to my standing orders that no change to course, speed, or depth—unless necessary for the safety of the boat—is to be done without my or your express permission."

Arneau raised his hand in a mock salute and acknowledged the order. "Aye, sir."

ON the merchant vessel, the captain lowered his binoculars, reached up, and pushed the collars of his foul-weather jacket up along his neck. He was sure it was a submarine periscope. He scratched his heavy beard. A few bits of ice fell from the tips of it.

His first mate had looked through the glasses and saw nothing. It could have been a whale, but whales at this time of the year were farther north. This didn't mean they weren't here, though it would be unusual for one to be this far south and to be alone.

"It would be January before the ice forced them this far south," he said aloud.

"Force what?"

The captain shook his head. "I was thinking maybe it was a whale I saw."

"Not time for them," the first mate replied crisply. "What are you going to do?"

If he reported it, he would have to sit through endless hours of interrogation by the Soviet Navy's GRU.

GRU stood for Glavnoe Razvedyvatel'noe Upravlenie, meaning Main Intelligence Directorate. The full name for the Soviet Navy's intelligence arm was Main Intelligence Directorate for the General Staff: GRU GSh. But everyone referred to it as the GRU.

He let out a heavy sigh. He did not want to report it. He was the only one who saw it. He would like to continue his trip to Murmansk without a nervous eye toward Severomorsk. He should have kept his mouth shut. It had been months since he had seen his family.

"Should I get the sighting forms for you, Comrade Captain?"

"Sighting forms?"

"Yes, sir. According to instructions, we are to report any sightings, whether we are sure or not."

That answered his question for him. His first mate could be KGB. Many citizens did their patriotic duty for the Komitet Gosudarstvennoy Bezopasnosti, which in English stood for Committee for State Security. He did his, and if he was standing in the shoes of the first mate and someone failed to do his patriotic duty, he would report him. Loyalty transcended all else when it came to protecting the motherland.

"Yes. I am not sure it was a submarine. Most likely if it was, it was one of ours." He let out a deep sigh. "If so, I fear the young captain of the submarine will have a heavy lesson to learn in letting a poor merchant seaman spot him, don't you think?" He forced a laugh.

The first mate grinned. "I am sure it is one of ours. Who else would be out here on such a day?"

"It looked as if it was heading in the same direction as us."

"Then maybe we will see it surface when we enter the channels. Maybe it is going to the Navy base."

Within thirty minutes, the merchant skipper had transmitted the sightings report to the Soviet Northern Fleet headquarters. Messages seldom instantaneously arrive at their destination. They pass through a series of buffers, bottlenecks, and handling until some radioman on the other end prints it off and routes it manually to whichever department he believes should receive it.

An hour later, the radio operator for the merchant vessel handed the captain a receipt. He showed it to the first mate, standing beside him. "There; that should alert our Navy."

"*Da.*"

At Severomorsk, the report was eventually delivered to the inbasket of the on-duty officer who had gone to an early lunch. Two hours later, when he returned, he read the report. Northern Fleet headquarters received many of these every week, so it was with a sense of the routine why the message of a possible submarine off the mouth of Kola Bay elicited no surprise or sense of urgency in the lieutenant commander.

An orderly put a fresh cup of coffee on the duty officer's desk as he called a messenger to him. Reaching for it, his hand brushed against one of the stacks of paper cluttering the top, scattering papers on the wood floor of the old building.

Ignoring the accident, he took a sip of the thick, hot coffee. A cluttered desk was a sign of an intellectual. He laughed. If that was so, then the duty officers must the smartest men in the Soviet Navy.

He motioned a messenger to his desk. While the messenger waited at the front of the desk, the duty officer stamped the message "SECRET," slipped it into a brown envelope, and licked the flap to seal it. He taped a receipt to the top of it before handing it to the messenger. The duty officer reminded the sailor to bring the receipt back to him.

Then he ordered the sailor on his way, the message heading for Admiral Katshora's office. If it was a submarine, then it would belong to the Northern Fleet Submarine Force. The duty officer was a destroyer sailor—an officer of the surface force. He smiled. If it was a submarine, which he doubted, he pitied the poor skipper when Katshora finished with him. Submarines were the silent service—the unobserved service—always below the surface and never detected.

He laughed. He hoped it was a submarine. Submariners were an arrogant lot, what with their bravado about the dangers of being beneath the waves. Well, they could have their bravado. He preferred being able to step off a sinking ship onto the surface of the ocean to having to swim up from the dark depths of the sea.

TWELVE

Wednesday, December 5, 1956

"CAST off lines one, three, and five!" Anton shouted.

Along the pier sailors lifted the lines off the bollards. On board the *Whale*, sailors pulled the lines on board, hand over hand. No matter how far into the future this atomic power took the Soviet Navy—or any Navy—no ship would ever find a way to replace the mariners who did the real nautical stuff of the centuries. Atomic power could not cast off the lines; sailors did. Atomic power could not remove the rust and replace the paint; sailors did. Atomic power could not sail the ocean by itself; sailors did.

"Lines one, three, and five on board!" shouted Chief Starshina Slavik, who was standing—feet spread—on the aft deck.

Lieutenant Tomich stood alongside the chief. As Anton watched, the zampolit spread his legs and put his arms behind him back.

Of course, Chief Slavik was the real leader down there. The chief was in charge of the boat's condition. He had sailors who were nothing more than labor, responsible for keeping the boat shipshape and the watertight integrity between compartments functioning properly. All of it labor. Work, work, work. If it required something only a man could do, then it was Chief Slavik and his band of nose-picking, butt-scratching sailors who received the dubious honors.

Without smiling, Anton congratulated himself on his idea of letting Tomich play the role of the "sea and anchor" officer, in charge of leading the men in casting off and tying up. Making Tomich a stakeholder in the fate of the *Whale* meant fewer opportunities for the zampolit to cause problems.

Where would the Soviet Navy be without its zampolits to show it the party-political correct way to run a fleet? His eyes widened at this thought of treason. He took a deep breath and tried to forget it. The Soviet Union was a new country building upon the bones and history of hundreds of years of capitalist enslavement. The only way to bring the ideals of communism quickly into today was constant political indoctrination. To understand the principles of communism meant a stronger, safer Soviet Union.

"Cast off lines two and four!"

"Aye, two and four!" Chief Slavik echoed.

Echoing commands was something every Navy did. He had heard the British and the Americans doing it during World War II. The Polish Navy vessels, smaller and older, that had managed to reach Soviet ports had been refitted after Germany attacked them and manned by Polish sailors. They had done it the same way.

He leaned down to the voice tube. "XO, ahead one knot, left full rudder." When the XO's voice replied, Anton pushed the brass covering closed on the tube. It was a habit of submariners to close everything after them, from moving from one compartment to the next to closing openings such as the sound-powered voice tube he was using. Nothing was ever left open.

Belowdecks, he heard the faint echo of his command. Anton looked forward, watching for the bow of the *Whale* to twist away from the dock. He glanced aft to ensure that the strain on the remaining number six line loosened instead of tightening.

Seconds passed before he saw a slight opening between the bow of the *Whale* and the pier.

His chest touched the cold railing of the bridge as he looked aft. Tomich was watching him. Slavik was kicking a pile of line on the deck and shouting something at a couple of sailors, who scrambled to wind the line properly. He looked forward. The numbers one and two lines had already disappeared into their storage areas beneath the deck.

"Cast off line six!"

"Aye, sir!" Tomich shouted.

Slavik glanced at the zampolit, opened his mouth to say something, but instead just shook his head and echoed the order to the working party near the stern. On the dock, a couple of sailors easily pushed the line off the bollard, while the two on board the *Whale* quickly reeled it on board.

Slavik, tall and lithe, suddenly took off toward the far aft section of the *Whale*. Tomich watched for a moment before dropping his hands to his sides and quickly following.

Anton turned forward. He lifted the cover to the voice tube. "Ahead two knots; rudder amidships."

The *Whale* inched forward, moving away from the pier toward the man-made channel leading to the open bay. The hatch opened on the side of the dry dock to Anton's right. Doctor Zotkin stepped through, with several of his scientists following him. Their eyes met, and Zotkin raised his hand and waved.

For that brief moment, Anton felt a wave of respect and gratitude toward the man who had made everyone's life a misery with his insistence of everything being done his way. A man who ultimately was responsible for the deaths suffered by sailors who were shoved unprotected into the atomic era of tomorrow. A tomorrow that would see the Soviet Union achieve an age-old Russian dream of an oceangoing Navy capable of going anywhere, fighting anywhere, and controlling the seas it entered. And he—Anton Zegouniov—would be one of the leaders of achieving that dream. Without thought, he raised his hand and saluted the Soviet scientist. Zotkin nodded.

"Two knots—rudder amidships!" came the familiar cry of his XO, Gesny, through the sound tube.

This sea trial was to test the repairs to the damaged aft torpedo room. The weather had created an opportunity for Anton to convince Doctor Zotkin of the necessity of ensuring that the repairs were effective. Better to do it inside Kola Bay. He had been surprised over the ease with which the good doctor had agreed. He had expected Zotkin to downplay the front heading their way and insist that they go into the Barents and conduct the sea trials. Instead, here he was in the early-morning hours of a Wednesday heading out again into Kola Bay to practice submerging and surfacing.

Looking forward, the sailors quickly entered the boat through the forward escape hatch. Lieutenant Tomich's head appeared at the edge of the railing as the zampolit climbed onto the bridge. Behind him came the chief. The chief quickly saluted, reported lines stowed, and the ship was ready topside for sea. Then just as quickly Slavik disappeared down the hatch belowdecks. But Tomich stayed, standing slightly to the left of Anton, one step back.

"Good job, Lieutenant," Anton said without turning.

"Thank you, Comrade Captain. I do not think other zampolits have had the opportunity you are giving me."

Anton guffawed. "I am sure other captains recognize the importance of your job and the caliber of officers who are assigned to your important duties. It would be a travesty for us not to expand those skills into helping the ship fight."

"Yes, sir. You are right, of course, and I will not forget this honor."

That is my intention, Anton thought. Tomich could have refused, which would have been the political officer's right. But the man had jumped at the offer, which, regardless of Anton's intention, had raised his confidence in the zampolit.

The bow of the *Whale* crossed from beneath the top of the covered dock into the open. Freezing rain started to work its way across the boat as more and more of it emerged into the open. Dark gray clouds covered the sky, and the bay appeared like whipped bits of cream on dark chocolate, changing with the wind from the north. The trapped cold beneath the covered pier seemed almost warm as the Arctic wind and rain strapped a cold, icy cloak around the bridge, bringing conversation to a stop. Each breath seemed to be of ice as Anton maneuvered the boat through the channel leading from the hidden facility into Kola Bay.

He looked at the small dock on the port side of the entrance to the covered area. Tied alongside in the falling rain was the torpedo boat *Bolshevik*. Lieutenant Jasha stood on the open bridge, saluting. Anton returned the honor. Jasha looked inside the covered dock area, drawing Anton's attention. He glanced aft and saw Doctor Zotkin and his group heading toward the torpedo boat. He wondered what was going on with them.

"It is cold up here, Comrade Captain."

Anton looked at Tomich. "You are welcome to keep me company for a few more minutes, Lieutenant. It is an opportunity few have to get a submarine under way. I will see it is entered in your record."

The zampolit beamed, his smile stretching from side to side. "Thank you, Comrade Captain."

Even the honor of getting the *Whale* under way failed to keep the zampolit topside much longer. As the rain picked up its attack, Tomich excused himself and disappeared down the hatch.

Anton smiled. He glanced back. The *Bolshevik* was still tied to the pier. This weather might be too much for the small boat to handle.

He tightened his gloves and raised the collar of his foul-weather jacket. Even water-resistant winter-issue coats would provide holes for the rain that turned to ice upon hitting. Maybe he would grow a beard, like some of the other officers. He reached up, untied the straps of the hat, and let the fur-covered flaps fall over his ears.

He opened the sound-powered voice tube and shouted down more commands, keeping the boat in the center of the channel. The two sailors standing watch topside—one on the starboard side and the other on the port side—hunkered down inside their heavy coats. The one facing forward with him caught the full force of the weather. The watch staring aft had his collar up, the rain beating against the back of the foul-weather coat.

There was nothing more to do but wait until they reached the deeper waters of Kola Bay. Then he could take them down.

The sound of a ship's horn drew his attention. Across the bay several dark shapes of Soviet destroyers became visible. The *Whale* never got under way without the inevitable escorts provided by Admiral Katshora. The Friday meeting crossed his mind.

Even here, where the weather could kill you in minutes, the battle for the hearts and minds of the fleet continued.

Zotkin was right. There are always lives lost in bringing new technology to the fleet. A successful sea trial would vindicate the loss of lives. *Stand aside, Britain and America; here comes the Soviet Union.*

Gesny appeared in the hatchway, no hat on his head. The icy drizzle pelted the small bald spot in the center, turning Gesny's hair around it into a patch of ice.

"Get a hat, XO," Anton said.

"Just a quick message from the commodore of the destroyers approaching. He sends his regards and best wishes."

"Tell him thanks."

"He also passed along the contact frequencies and their operations zone while we are submerged."

"They should be standing outside of our OPAREA," Anton said.

Gesny lifted a Navy message. "Seems we are going to do more than test the repairs of the aft torpedo room, Captain."

Anton raised his binoculars and scanned ahead of their intended path. "How's that, XO?"

"Seems this is going to be the sea trial we thought we had put off until better weather. Seems Doctor Zotkin, while we were arguing to delay the at-sea operational test, has convinced Admiral Katshora that we should go forward and do the tests inside Kola Bay."

Anton dropped his glasses. "Are you sure?"

Gesny nodded. "I'm sure. When you come below, we will have the message and test plan laid out, sir."

"But we did not come prepared—"

Gesny shrugged. "Seems that is not a consideration, comrade."

"I'll be below when I get below, XO. Have everything ready. Did they send us the operational order with the communication channels, order of events, officer in tactical charge, depths, courses, everything we need to do it?"

Gesny nodded. "We received a package just before we sailed. The message told us to open it. We did. It's there."

"Someone from the Soviet Submarine Force had to approve it."

"Sir, my head is freezing."

"Get below, XO. You could have passed all of this via the tube."

"I tried, sir, but the weather is making it hard for the whistle to be heard up here. Besides, I thought I might want to see your face when I told you this news."

"How far to deep water?" Anton asked, shivering.

"We are twenty minutes to shallow depth for diving."

"Then we dive in twenty minutes."

"Comrade Captain," Gesny shouted above the noise of wind and the rain, "give me five minutes and I will come relieve you?"

Anton shook his head. "No need for both of us to be frozen. Tell the cook I will want the hottest cup of chocolate he can brew when I get off the bridge."

He turned and glanced at the two watch sailors, then back to Gesny. "Send up watch reliefs in five minutes."

Gesny nodded and disappeared down the hatch.

Five minutes later two sailors appeared and relieved the two on deck.

Anton heard the periscope spinning again as the navigators took lines of bearing on the navigational aids aligned along the channel and up on the hills behind them. He glanced at the hills and withdrew the thought about using those navigational aids. The rain blocked them out. Visibility was dropping fast. Anton raised his binoculars and scanned ahead for the two destroyers heading toward them.

He flipped open the tube again. "You have radar contact on the destroyers?"

"That is a negative, sir," came the garbled reply. Anton leaned closer, careful not to touch his ear to the metal. "Too much land smear."

"Very well," he replied. He turned to the lookouts. "Keep a close lookout off our port bow!" he shouted above the noise. "We have two of our surface ships out there. Should be about ten to fifteen kilometers!"

"Aye, sir!" they shouted in unison, both turning in that direction.

He touched his cheeks, pushing them in with his gloved hands, seeing ice fall from them. He now understood better why beards seemed the norm for Arctic sailors.

Here he was not concerned about keeping a visual for 360 degrees. They were inside the protection of the bay, where no enemy warship could reach them. As for air, everyone knew the Americans were flying reconnaissance missions over Soviet territory. One day they would shoot one of them down and prove to the world the secret war America was fighting against the Soviet Union. If America would leave them alone, they could achieve their goal of a workers' paradise, but that would be a threat to capitalism.

Anton squinted, reaching up carefully to wipe his eyebrows. The Arctic was nothing anyone could imagine. It would freeze a wet face, killing the skin beneath it, causing it to fall from the face when it melted. He pulled the cape over his hat down tighter, trying to preserve what little body heat he had from escaping.

The bow of the *Whale* left the entrance channel and entered the bay proper. Water washed across the bow, and Anton felt the first yaw of the water as the stern cleared the channel. Yaw was a condition where wave and wind combined to cause the bow of the ship to move one way and the stern the other. He ordered a ten-degree port rudder to compensate for the wind, and was relieved when the *Whale* steadied up on a straight course.

He lifted the lid. "Officer of the deck, all ahead ten knots."

Atomic power meant having no concern about speed when you needed it. It also meant they had warmth beneath the hull. Battery power had no ability to provide much heat to the crew, as nearly every amp was needed to drive the shaft and light the boat. That would be one diesel boat experience Anton looked forward to never experiencing again.

He barely heard the whistle, but he flipped open the metal covering. It stuck briefly to his heavy gloves. "Go ahead!"

"Ten minutes to submerge depth!"

"Roger!"

Ten more minutes of this. He wiggled his toes. A strong wind hit him in the eyes, causing him to shut them briefly. When he tried to open them, eyelashes came off on his cheek, where they had frozen to his skin. He was on the verge of asking the XO to relieve him when Gesny again appeared in the hatch. This time he had a heavy wool cap on top of his head.

"Captain, we have radar contact on the two destroyers!" he shouted. "We are six to seven minutes from submerge depth! Recommend you come belowdecks and we navigate these last two miles!"

Anton nodded. "Brilliant idea, XO!" He turned to the watches. "Get below, you two *matrose*, before you freeze." Matrose was the rank of seaman in the Soviet Navy.

He watched the few seconds it took for the two men to reach the hatch and almost fall through it in their speed to escape the Arctic attack. Bits of ice decorated the decks around the hatch from their foul-weather coats. As cold as he was and as numb as his feet and hands felt, Anton forced himself to check the bridge to ensure that the caps were locked on the sound-powered pipe. He looked forward to check the deck, but the rain was coming down so hard only the nearest part was visible. Even the bow was hidden beneath the Arctic blast. Ice was beginning to cake the boat. Anton looked aft. Rain hit the deck but bounced up as pellets of ice, sticking to the rough walking area. He could see the stern plane towering several feet above the rudder. They would have to be careful when they returned that no sailor fell overboard from the ice.

Then he turned and hurried down the hatch to the comparative warmth below, stopping just inside to secure the hatch. When he dropped to the deck, he nodded at Chief Starshina Slavik. "Chief, have someone double-check the hatch," Anton said, his voice chattering from the cold.

Slavik scrambled up the ladder and double-checked the wheel of the hatch. "All secure," he announced as he hurried down, back to his position near the planesmen.

The conning tower was boiling in comparison to the bridge. He glanced at the thermometer. It was minus ten degrees Celsius in the conning tower, but probably another ten degrees colder on the bridge. His face tingled, turning slowly into pain as the blood rushed into the nearly frozen spots on his face.

"Captain," Gesny said, handing Anton a small cup of hot chocolate.

He nodded in thanks.

"Up periscope," Anton said, sitting the cup on a nearby shelf. A short circulation of warm air hit his face. He would have smiled if he had quit shivering.

He wondered briefly if the Americans had discovered this important change of heated conditions within their *Nautilus*, regardless of where they operated. He had heard that the *Nautilus* had kept its operations to the Eastern Seaboard of the United States and in the Caribbean. If so, then this was another first for the Soviet Union; the importance of a heated submarine in winter conditions would bring cheer to the crew.

The hydraulics of the periscope rising drew his attention. He squatted, lowered the periscope handles, and put his right eye to the eyepiece. This also meant that in the warmer climates of the world, they should be able to have air conditioning. He had heard the Americans were already experimenting with it on board the *Nautilus*.

He leaned back from the periscope. "XO, does the *Whale* have air conditioning?" he asked Gesny.

The XO's eyes widened. "Comrade Captain?"

Anton shook his head. "Never mind." He put his eye back to the periscope. It was pointed aft toward the facility, but other than the dark smudge of land, the rain obscured it. He spun the periscope forward, trying to see the two destroyers heading his way, but they, too, were hidden behind the curtain of rain. He knew that all across their decks the icy grip of the Arctic was taking its toll. Sailors would be out on the destroyers, chopping away the ice before it built up to a point where it was useless to try. Ice could capsize a warship as easily as a torpedo taken amidships.

Anton stepped back. "Down periscope." He stepped to the ladder. "I'm going down to the control room," he said, then disappeared down the ladder to the compartment below.

Gesny followed.

"Do we have the destroyers on sonar?" he asked the officer of the deck.

Lieutenant Vladimir Antipov stepped forward. Anton grinned. Antipov was what he referred to as his "catchall" officer. The young man from the Ukraine was the navigator, the administrative officer, and the communications officer. The only two officers junior to him were Lieutenant Kalugin and Ensign Rybin. Kalugin worked in the reactor room under the chief engineer, Lieutenant Commander Tumanov. Rybin was Antipov's assistant and always seemed to disappear whenever Anton appeared.

"Sonar! Status report, if you please," Antipov ordered.

"We have reached diving depth, Captain," Gesny said.

"Two contacts, Captain; ten and twelve degrees off our port bow," the starshina manning the sonar console reported.

"Let's go back up," Anton said, grabbing the ladder and hurrying back up to the conning tower. Gesny was right behind him.

"Sir, we are at diving depth," Lebedev said.

"Officer of the deck, dive the boat," Anton ordered.

"Depth, Comrade Captain?"

"Make our depth sixteen meters, Lieutenant Lebedev."

"Aye, sir. Make depth sixteen meters," Lebedev repeated to the chief of the watch.

Near the planesmen, Chief Ship Starshina Mamadov grabbed the hydraulics control handles of the ballasts and pulled them back. The sound of the vents opening and water rushing into the ballast tanks rushed through the skin of the boat.

Chief Arkanov acknowledged the order and echoed it to the planesmen. Mamadov leaned over their shoulders, watching the depth gauge as the submarine submerged. He leaned down and mumbled something to them. The two sailors eased up on the planes, and the submarine started to level out.

"Trim forward," Lebedev said.

"Approaching fifteen meters depth," Arkanov announced.

"Ease planes."

Then, as if the crew had worked together for years instead of weeks, the *Whale* leveled off. Anton glanced at the depth gauge. They were directly on sixteen meters.

"Final trim," Mamadov announced, reaching down and slapping the nearest planesman on the back.

"Status report," Anton said.

Unconsciously, he reached up and started to touch his face. Gesny reached out and touched his arm, stopping him. Anton looked at the hand on his arm, then at Gesny, and nodded thanks as he dropped his arm back alongside. Many had lost bits of flesh from touching it too soon after the Arctic had done its best to freeze it off.

"Boat steering course zero niner zero, speed ten knots, depth sixteen meters, sir!"

"Thank you, Lieutenant Lebedev."

Lebedev stepped to the navigation table where Lieutenant Nizovtsev sat.

"Captain," Nizovtsev said, "recommend fifteen minutes on heading zero eight five. That should take us off the shelf edge and over the deeper fathoms."

"Very well," Anton acknowledged. He looked around for the hot chocolate, saw the cup on the nearby shelf, but doubted it was still hot now.

Anton reached up and grabbed a handhold on an overhead pipe. His gloves protected any chance of flesh freezing to it, but then maybe this was a precaution that would be forgotten with atomic power? "XO, I thought the weather forecast said it was another few hours before the storm was to reach here."

"I am checking, Comrade Captain. It is possible that this is only a small storm and that it will pass through the area quite quickly. In which case, when we surface tomorrow, it could be gone."

Anton nodded. He opened and closed his hand holding the pipe but felt no pain. Then he clinched and unclenched the other hand, checking for frostbite. Terrible frostbite meant numbness, and numbness meant the loss of an extremity. Silently, he did the same thing to his toes, thankful of the slight pain he felt, but it would be later in his stateroom before he could inspect every inch of his body. He nearly grabbed his crotch, sure everyone would understand, but a captain must never open himself for ridicule.

Fifteen minutes later they were over the deep area of Kola Bay. He waited another ten minutes, asked for a depth reading, and satisfied, he ordered them to fifty meters depth. Put a little water between him and those surface warships boring holes in the bay. With their attention on the ice buildup on their decks, he wanted to reduce any opportunity of them taking off his conning tower.

The pain in his face was beginning to subside. He gave some standing orders to the officer of the deck. Lieutenant Lebedev acknowledged each order by repeating it. Behind the officer of the deck, the chief of the watch cuffed the sailor responsible for log entries, who leaped to the task of writing down Anton's orders.

"XO, Lieutenant Lebedev; once the underway watch is set, if you would find Lieutenant Commander Tumanov, let's meet in the wardroom in fifteen minutes to go over the at-sea trials we have been cast into."

"Yes, sir. Here is Doctor Zotkin's envelope for you, sir." Gesny pulled it out from inside his foul-weather jacket.

Anton took it. He wondered what the "good doctor" had to say this time. Whatever it was, it was thick. This explained why Zotkin agreed with Anton's argument about testing the aft torpedo room repairs. The doctor never intended to just send the *Whale* out for a few dunks. The timetable was everything to Zotkin, and if weather was unbeatable for the sea trial in the Barents, then they would do it in Kola Bay and declare success. Success was the barometer of leaders.

Govno. Shit. He hoped it was not a dissertation warning him of the consequences of failure. Failure for a submariner was to have an odd number of surfacings and submergings.

Anton nodded. "I will meet you three in the wardroom in ten minutes." He turned and headed down. Moments later he was in his stateroom, taking his gloves, coat, and shoes off. He looked in the mirror at the bright splotches on his face, touching them lightly. The pressure turned the area white, only to have it bounce back to red when he pulled his finger away. He smiled. Elena would not have a man missing a nose and cheeks from this trip. Fingers and toes were the same.

He changed his socks, slipped on a different pair of shoes, and grabbed different gloves from his locker. He placed the cast-off items near the ventilation shaft along the deck so any moisture could dry from the heat. He smiled as he held his hands in front of the vent, letting the warm air flow across them. He was going to love atomic power.

He picked up his other fur hat and put it on. Then, tucking the envelope beneath his arms, Anton headed toward the wardroom. Once there, he laid the papers from Doctor Zotkin on the table. The man never ceased to amaze him with his desire for power and his great paranoia.

Anton had his hands wrapped around the cup of hot chocolate when Gesny stuck his head through the wardroom curtains. "Lebedev is coming. He is checking the watch bill and making a change. We had one of the engineers come down sick—"

"That was Petty Officer Brest, right?"

"Yes, sir; one of the newcomers. Been on board only a couple of months, but unable to get out of his rack this morning."

"Maybe I should have allowed them to sleep in the berthing area instead of restricting the men to the boat."

"I don't think it was that, Comrade Captain. He had blood on his lips when they helped him off the boat."

"Radiation?"

Gesny nodded. "Most likely. Brest worked the water coolant system nearest the reactor." Gesny took his fur watch cap off and tossed it on a nearby seat. Then he scratched his head. "We can ask Tumanov when he comes."

Lebedev stuck his head between the curtains, gave a small salute to Anton, and went over to the serving line, pouring himself some hot chocolate. "I saw Anatole on the way down, Comrade Captain. He sends his apologies. He is changing his watches to compensate for the loss of Brest. He will be here in five minutes."

Gesny nodded at the papers lying facedown on the table. "Doctor Zotkin?"

Anton nodded. "Seems this is going to be more than just a trip into the bay to check out the aft torpedo room. Speaking of which, Lieutenant, how does it look?"

Lebedev slid into the vacant space alongside Anton, sipping his hot drink too fast. "Woo! That burned," Lebedev said.

Gesny placed his cup on the table and pulled a chair up to the table. "Sip, don't chug."

"Lieutenant: the aft torpedo room?"

"I swung by there from the conning tower, sir. We have a fire and safety watch in the space. I checked the valves and the tubes. There are no leaks."

"Just now?"

"Aye, sir. And we were at fifty meters when I checked. I believe the repairs will hold. There was nothing in the damage that penetrated the hull, sir. All the damage was confined to the internals of the aft torpedo room."

"That's good. Let's hope you're right. Fire has a way of doing unseen damage when valves, pipes, gears, et cetera are involved," Anton said. He picked up the papers from the table and handed them to Gesny. "It seems Doctor Zotkin views this trip as more than an opportunity to check out our repairs."

Tumanov whipped the curtains back and stomped into the wardroom. "Comrade Captain, Comrade XO," he said sharply as he grabbed a ceramic cup and poured some hot chocolate for himself. "My apologies for my tardiness, sirs. I had some problems to attend to concerning the engineering spaces."

"You mean Petty Officer Brest?"

"That, plus a couple of my sailors think it might be dangerous to perform their duties."

Anton's eyebrows arched. "They are refusing?"

Tumanov shook his head, setting the cup down on the table and pulling a chair from the next table. "That has been resolved, Comrade Captain. The men realize the great honor they are being given in helping the Soviet Navy achieve atomic power. Unfortunately, sometimes this honor of doing something so new and unfamiliar makes them antsy about performing in the confines with it."

"I know of the problems you have had with radiation," Anton said, his voice cold. Officers on board a warship should be under the command of the captain, but here sat the chief engineer of the *Whale*, and he reported to Zotkin.

Tumanov nodded as he sipped some of the hot drink. "Yes, sir; everyone knows, unfortunately, and many try to blame Doctor Zotkin for it." Tumanov's head moved from side to side a couple of times. "Granted, there were some small mistakes when we started this secret project, but there are always mistakes with new technology. We do not dwell on the mistakes; we just take the lessons learned, correct them, and move on." Tumanov waved his hand in the air, as if motioning away the recent past.

"We lost some men making those mistakes."

"Yes, sir, we did. But we have thicker protection between the reactor and the engineering spaces now, sir," Tumanov said.

"Show some respect," Gesny said.

Tumanov started to say something, thought better of it, and instead replied, "My apologies, Comrade Captain. I am concerned about the success of the sea trials we are about to begin. If my tone seems disrespectful, it is not meant to be so."

"You speak plainly, Commander."

Tumanov's eyebrows wrinkled. He looked at Anton. "I was told we were going to go from the test of the repairs directly to the Barents for the sea trials."

Lebedev and Gesny looked at Anton. Anton nodded at the papers in Gesny's hands. "Our chief engineer is partially right, isn't he, gentlemen. Doctor Zotkin is probably on his way to the destroyers, where he and Admiral Katshora will accompany the *Whale* inside Kola Bay, where we will do the operational tests." He nodded at Gesny and Lebedev. "It appears we will participate in an antisubmarine exercise while doing the operational maneuvering to test the limits of atomic power."

Gesny unfolded the papers. He scanned them as Tumanov continued.

"Comrade Captain, I have divided the watches into three sections for our week. There will be a chief of the watch present at all times. I will periodically inspect the spaces and take readings. I believe you have the test schedule?"

"Most of what Doctor Zotkin says in the paper is predicated on him having communications with the *Whale*. We have the first set of three tests we are to do." He looked at Lebedev. "Operations Officer, you are to rework the watch bill so we have our best in the control room and in maneuvering when we start each of these tests."

"Yes, sir."

"The tests are going to challenge the *Whale* in quickness of depth, quickness in changing courses, and depth; and the ability of the atomic power to give us, submerged, speeds similar to what we are able to achieve on the surface—"

"When we finish," Tumanov interrupted, "Doctor Zotkin wants to know if the only thing stopping atomic power from providing the *K-2* with everything we want in terms of speed and maneuverability is the mechanical nature of the submarine infrastructure."

Gesny's face reddened. He would leave it to the XO to talk to the engineering officer about proper protocol. Like him, he knew Gesny hated the idea of an officer on board his ship not being under his chain of command. What XO wouldn't?

Anton let out a deep sigh. "Lieutenant Lebedev, I will expect you to function as the officer of the deck within engineering during every test. XO, you will function as the overall test evaluator."

Tumanov raised his hand. "Comrade Captain, I believe Doctor Zotkin wanted me to be the overall test evaluator." Tumanov reached over and started pulling the papers toward him.

Anton reached over, smiled, and took the papers from Tumanov. "No need to look, Lieutenant Commander Tumanov. I found nothing in there that said that."

"But, if I may, sir," Tumanov replied, reaching forward.

Anton smiled. "As the captain of the *Whale*, Chief Engineer, I am capable of reading them. Besides," Anton continued without looking at the papers, "I am the commanding officer of the *Whale*, and as the commanding officer, I am responsible for the success of the tests. I will decide how we conduct the tests so we may provide the Soviet Navy with the best answers." He leaned forward. "We do understand who the skipper of this submarine is?"

"Yes, sir," he stuttered. "But if I could look at the papers, I might be able to show you where Doctor Zotkin—"

"Do you think I am wrong?" Anton asked, his voice tight.

"Sir, we all make mistakes."

"Lieutenant Commander Tumanov, I may be wrong sometimes, but on board the *Whale*, even when I am wrong, I am always right. Do you understand who the captain of the *Whale* is?"

"Yes, sir," Tumanov answered, his voice weaker.

"Good. You, Lieutenant Tumanov, will be in the engineering spaces at all times during the tests. You will be the engineering watch officer so you can ensure that we have the best test results."

It seemed to Anton that the man's face grew even whiter.

"But sir—"

"There are no 'buts' on board my ship when I speak."

Anton turned. Standing there watching was the zampolit, Lieutenant Tomich. Their eyes met for a fraction of second before Tomich turned and left the doorway to the wardroom.

No one spoke.

THIRTEEN

Wednesday, December 5, 1956

"DOESN'T tell us much, does it?" Arneau asked, passing the message back to Shipley.

"At least they did something," Shipley replied. He let out a sigh and leaned back against the bulkhead of the conning tower, putting his hands in his pockets. Across the compartment, small fogs of breath attested to the frigid condition of the submerged submarine.

Arneau looked at Logan. "How long do you think it will take them to track down one of these convoy skippers from World War II?"

Logan shook his head. "I don't know, sir. All I know is what is in the message. Admiral Frost has directed his staff to Leesburg, Virginia, where a couple of merchant captains have retired. Leesburg isn't the easiest place to get to. It's out in the boonies and miles from Washington."

"If anyone would know about navigating Kola Bay, it will be one of these skippers," Shipley said. He handed the message to Logan.

A few seconds of silence passed. Shipley looked at the depth. The clock read 2045 hours. "Officer of the deck, what time to the mouth?"

Lieutenant Weaver walked to the navigational table, ran his

finger along the dead-reckoning pencil line, and then glanced at the Navy clock. "About forty-five minutes, Skipper."

Shipley nodded.

"What are we going to do, Skipper?" Arneau asked.

Shipley pushed off the bulkhead. "We are going to execute our mission." He looked at Weaver. "OPSO, let's take her up to periscope depth. Have sound keep a three-hundred-sixty-degree lookout for any traffic in the area."

"Aye, sir. We still have the merchant vessel from earlier," Weaver said, wishing he had not mentioned it after the words were out. That the skipper was less than pleased with Van Ness would be an understatement.

"Course and speed?"

"Target course remained one eight zero at ten knots. Range fifteen nautical miles."

Then the merchant would be on the horizon. Little chance of anyone seeing the periscope, and if he was going into Kola Bay, he needed the batteries topped off. Surfacing or snorkeling inside the Soviet bay would be dangerous, but it was something he would have to do at least twice while there.

Behind him, he heard Arneau speak to Logan. "Guess Naval Intelligence hasn't been much help, Lieutenant. We are going to go in cold, and let's hope we come out the same way."

"Sir?"

"A hot time by the Soviets is not what we want."

Shipley turned to the two men. "Lieutenant Logan, are your men ready?" He turned. "Officer of deck, take us up to fifty feet—periscope depth."

"As ready as they'll ever be, sir. They are in the after engine room rigging up the air sampler." He bit his lower lip. "Skipper, are we going to be able to use the main induction values while inside the bay? I mean, we have to surface for our equipment to sample the air."

Shipley nodded. "I know, Lieutenant. Unless we find ourselves hiding from the Soviets, we will surface when the chances of them seeing us are reduced. I don't think they expect an American submarine inside their twelve-mile limit, much less this deep inside their national waters. I'll give you all the time I can for you to do your spook stuff, but when I say we dive, we dive." The deck tilted as the *Squallfish* started up.

"Yes, sir; I fully understand."

"What are these air samples supposed to tell us, Lieutenant?"

"They're supposed to tell us, XO, whether the Soviets are experimenting with atomic radiation at this facility."

Shipley nodded. "If they are and we can detect it, Lieutenant, it would seem that whatever they are doing is endangering their men."

Logan nodded. "I don't know that much about radiation or nuclear power, Captain, but I know it kills if you get too much of it. Ask those people at Hiroshima or Nagasaki."

"Passing one hundred feet," the planesman reported.

"One hundred feet—aye," Senior Chief Boohan repeated.

"One hundred feet," Weaver echoed. "Sound, any contacts?"

"Only the original one, sir. Still on course one eight zero at ten knots; range fifteen nautical miles."

"Make our depth fifty feet," Weaver repeated.

"Officer of the deck," Shipley called, "ready snorkel. Prepare to switch to diesel. Have Lieutenant Bleecker give me a call."

"Aye, sir."

A couple of minutes later, at seventy-five feet, the intercom buzzed. It was the chief engineer.

"Lieutenant Bleecker, this might be our last chance to top off the batteries before we start our entrance to the bay. Make the most of it. It most likely will be twenty-four to thirty-six hours before we have another opportunity," Shipley said into the handset. He had given up trying to keep their destination secret from the crew. Even the electrician mates and torpedomen knew they were heading toward the Soviet Northern Fleet headquarters. The primary purpose was clouded in the scuttlebutt of whispers.

He listened as Bleecker passed along his plan for keeping the ship making way while charging the batteries. Engines one and two would be directed to the electric motors, while engines three and four would be directed to the batteries. The estimated time to achieve full charge would be six hours.

He hung up the handset. Six hours on the surface at the mouth of Kola Bay was not his idea of an ideal location or time, but the night and the paucity of shipping traffic significantly reduced opportunities for the low profile of the *Squallfish* to be detected.

"XO, I want the topside watches changed every fifteen minutes instead of thirty. You and I will alternate."

"Maybe I should take the first watch, Captain. You did it last time."

Shipley liked the idea but decided against it. The captain's place was on the bridge when a submarine first surfaced.

Since the incident with Van Ness and Logan, with the exception of minutes, either Shipley or the XO had been in the conning tower. Shipley's intention was to keep it that way until they were safely out of Kola Bay and back in international waters.

"Up periscope," he said.

Another body crawled into the conning tower.

"Chief Belford," Shipley said to the man as he stepped off the ladder, "have they finally captured you for the watch bill?"

"Ah, Skipper, I've always been on the watch bill. You're just never here when I've been here."

The grind of the hydraulics filled the background noise inside the conning tower.

"What do you think of this trip so far, Chief?"

"I think me and my lads are going to have a lot of work to do once we tie up back at Holy Loch. You know how much damage Arctic seawater does to a good paint job?"

Shipley squinted his left eye shut as he pressed the right to the eyepiece as he rode the periscope up. "Can't say that I do, Chief. But a good boatswain mate such as you will make short work of it."

"Just a lot, sir; a hell of a lot. We're going to look like shit when we sail in."

"Get me a bearing on the contact, Chief."

Shipley spun the periscope around so it aligned dead-on with the bow of the *Squallfish*. Dark water spun across the scope. Then suddenly the scope broke the surface, a different darkness covering the scope.

"Fifty feet!" he heard from Boohan, who was looking over the shoulders of the planesmen while still within reaching distance of the control handles to the ballasts.

Shipley saw the white stern light of the merchant vessel they had been trailing during the evening hours.

"Set."

"Bearing one eight five, ten degrees off our starboard bow," Chief Belford said.

Shipley stepped to the left, spinning the search periscope ten degrees to the right. He waited for the water to clear the scope, but when it didn't . . . "Christ," he exclaimed, for he knew what it was. Eyes turned toward him, wondering if something was wrong. It was rain, and it was coming down hard.

He stepped away from the periscope. "Snorkel?" he shouted.

As if expecting his question, the hull vibrated as the diesel engines came online. He put his eye back on the scope and turned it aft, barely making out several bursts of gray-black smoke from the induction valve.

The XO climbed up into the conning tower. "Skipper, I wish you'd let me take the first watch topside."

Shipley stepped away from the periscope, looked at Arneau, and nodded. "Okay. You win, XO. You take the first thirty minutes, then I'll come topside to relieve you." Should he tell him about the weather? Then, as much as he would have enjoyed letting Arneau discover it himself, the dangers of the Arctic overcame the urge. "You will need your rain slick over your foul-weather jacket, XO. It's a rough one up there."

The XO acknowledged his comment.

"Officer of the deck, surface the boat," Shipley ordered. "Periscope down."

Three minutes later the *Squallfish* was on the surface. The waves rocked the boat a little. The safety ballast beneath the bottom of the boat remained filled with water, acting much like a keel to help steady the ungainly maneuverability of a surfaced submarine.

The quartermaster scurried up the ladder and undogged the hatch, throwing it back. The clang of it hitting the bridge deck echoed through the conning tower. Shipley smiled. "XO, I'm dressed for it. Go get your rain slick and relieve me as soon as possible." He tugged the foul-weather jacket. "This thing won't be of much use against the cold once it's soaked."

"Sir, I have some rain slicks up here," Senior Chief Boohan said before Arneau could hit the ladder.

The quartermaster leaped down the last few rungs.

"In the locker," Boohan said to Belford.

Chief Belford pulled a bunch of rain slicks from a nearby storage locker. "Sir, this one might fit you," he said, handing one to Shipley, who looked questioningly at him.

Belford shrugged, the scar on his right cheek seeming to glow in the red light of the conning tower. "I always keep three rain slicks in the locker here, sir, in the event of foul weather. That's not to say Arctic weather is never foul, but just when you think the Arctic has thrown everything it can at you, it always has another trick up its sleeve that needs one more garment on your shoulders."

"Thanks, Chief," Shipley said as he slipped the rain slick over his jacket. The rain slick was more like a poncho than a coat. It had a spot for your head to stick through in its center, but no sleeves or pockets to mark it as an article of clothing. Most sailors avoided using it because once on, it made movement hard, but for topside watches, it helped keep the sailor dry.

Cumbersome now with his head through the rain slick, Shipley pushed his hands from underneath it and climbed up to the bridge. "XO, I expect to see you in thirty minutes." So began one of the more routine jobs of the Navy: topside watch. Two sailors followed Shipley up and took positions on the port and starboard sides of the bridge.

Looking forward, ice was already beginning to cover the forward exposed section. Aft, it was the same thing. The main induction valves were open, spitting out the filthy air of twenty-four hours and bringing into the boat fresh, freezing Arctic air to replace it. It would be hours before the *Squallfish* would be able to return to a more moderate freezing temperature inside the boat. Belowdecks, out of sight of Shipley, sailors were layering up with T-shirts, shirts, sweaters, watch caps, and scarves. Diesels never had the spare power to be able to fight the cold of the depths, much less the cold of the Arctic.

"WHAT is the temperature?" Anton asked Gesny.

"Sir, it's thirteen degrees Celsius."

Anton shook his head. "It's below freezing topside."

"Minus fifteen degrees when you came belowdecks, sir," Gesny said.

"And we are basking in heat at thirteen degrees. A diesel would be lucky to reach freezing in this weather."

Gesny nodded, no smile breaking his face. "That is true, Comrade Captain, but then we are lucky—would you say—to be on the first atomic-powered submarine of the Soviet Navy."

"This will be a terrible secret to let the surface force know, Comrade XO," Anton said, his voice serious.

Gesny cocked his head to the side.

"If they found out how cozy it is going to be for submariners, then they would try to replace us." Anton smiled, a slight laugh following.

Gesny nodded, his lower lip pushing up the upper. "That is so, Captain."

Anton laughed. "XO, you have to learn to enjoy what the Navy gives you."

"Yes, sir."

Anton pointed up. "We're at fifty meters depth. Let's take the *Whale* to sixteen meters and check how our surface comrades are doing."

Moments later the *Whale*'s periscope broke the surface. The sun had set, but the freezing rain continued. He felt the slight vibration along the scope as the rain turned to ice on contact with the metal. He did not want to keep it above the surface for long. Spinning the scope, Anton spotted the faint running lights of the two destroyers. On board one of them would be Doctor Zotkin and his team of scientists. He wondered if the German scientist Doctor Danzinger would be with them or if the presence of a German scientist would be something Zotkin kept hidden from the bulk of the Soviet Navy.

"Target bearing zero four zero degrees!" the sonar operator shouted. "Second target bearing one one zero degrees!"

Without removing his eye from the scope piece, Anton asked, "Okay, sailor: what type of targets are they?"

"They are Soviet destroyers, Comrade Captain."

Anton grinned. "And you are able to tell me that from the sounds?"

A slight pause and then the sailor said, "No, Comrade Captain; I heard you tell the XO what the two ships were."

Anton stepped back and nodded. "I am glad you are listening to what is going on around you. Now tell me why, based on your own observations and sounds, you think they are destroyers. Can you do that?"

The sailor grinned. "Yes, sir; I can do that."

"Then do it, and then tell me why they are destroyers."

The sailor slipped his earphones on, lifted a pencil, and began to measure the sound intervals and screw rotations.

Anton watched for a few seconds and turned back to the periscope.

A good sonar operator could tell from the noise of the screws how fast a ship was traveling; whether the ship was approaching or separating; how many screws a ship had and even how many blades on each screw; and from just the noise of the screws, most ships could be identified to a specific class. Warships were what Soviet sonar operators were trained to detect and identify. All else were merchants, but even in war a submarine's primary targets were most times in the merchant fleet of the enemy. Deny an enemy its supplies and you choke him to death on depleted resources. He wondered for a moment if that was still true in today's modern world, where aircraft could lift so much. The Americans, the British, and the French had kept a continuous airlift going only seven years ago, to keep Berlin resupplied. Not much a submarine could do against an airlift.

Lieutenant Antipov climbed into the conning tower.

"Lieutenant, are you not the officer of the watch in the control room?" Gesny asked.

"Yes, sir, I am, but—"

"Then return to the control room. You are not to leave your post when you are the assigned watch. Do you understand?"

"Yes, sir, Comrade XO, but this message came in for the captain."

Gesny took it. "Now return to your post."

Antipov nodded sharply and disappeared quickly down the ladder.

Anton raised his head when he heard the exchange, but then returned to the periscope. XOs had their duties to do also.

Gesny unfolded and read the message, letting out a deep sigh.

"Captain," he said, touching Anton on the shoulder.

Anton stepped back and took the message from Gesny. Anton nodded at the periscope, and Gesny grabbed the handles and began his own search of the surface. "It is very terrible out there," he said.

Anton read the message. "But it looks as if Admiral Katshora has decided to continue onward with the sea trials."

"Yes, sir; I guess he believes the protective arms of the bay are sufficient against the weather."

"For us, the weather is something we can avoid for the most part as long as we stay submerged, but the destroyers are probably already heavy with ice."

Stepping gingerly, Gesny rotated the periscope, observing the surface conditions for 360 degrees.

After a couple of minutes, Gesny stepped back. "The periscope is getting covered with ice, Captain."

"Bring it down."

"Lower periscope," Gesny said to the chief of the watch.

The sound of hydraulics pierced the conning tower as the periscope slid downward into its sleeve.

"We will have to be careful raising it later, XO. If the water freezes around the periscope, we run the risk of breaking the lens. It would blind us."

Gesny nodded.

"Admiral Katshora sends word that we are to remain inside Kola Bay for the sea trials. I wonder why he felt he had to send this. We already decided to stay within Kola Bay and reschedule the at-sea trials in the Barents for a later date." He looked at Gesny. "I think that is the prudent action to take."

Gesny nodded and let out a deep breath. "Most likely Doctor Zotkin has been trying to change his mind. Maybe the admiral wanted to make sure we knew his position."

Anton nodded. "I think you are probably right."

"It means we will have to do everything over again, Captain. Someday we are going to have to conduct operations in the open ocean, and out there on the Barents Sea are some of the worst waters in the world. Someday we are going to have to prove to those who may have misgivings about bringing atomic power to the Soviet Navy that it is a good thing. That it is capable of taking us outside our waters."

"Just for the warmth, you would say?"

"The warmth of the sailors makes for a better environment. The ability of atomic power to take this ship anywhere is the reason we are here. Maybe we—"

Anton's smile left his face. "Are you lecturing me, Comrade XO?"

Gesny stopped in midsentence. Stuttering, he apologized. "I did not intend for my comments to seem counter to your wishes, sir. I was thinking of how great and wonderful it is going to be to see this power"—he clenched his fist—"in every submarine within our Navy. We will truly achieve the centuries-old desire of Russia to be a global sea power."

Anton's lips narrowed. "We are the Soviet Union now, Comrade

XO," he said, more for the benefit of those listening than truly believing his words. "Russia is but one of many within our socialist camp."

Gesny nodded. "I believe I am only digging my hole deeper, Comrade Captain. If I may start over: if we are able to perform in this weather in the Barents, then we can perform anywhere."

"That is true, XO, but we need to see what impact atomic power is going to have on the mechanical conditions of the boat. We need to know that the *Whale* will hold together as it picks up speed, makes emergency dives, emergency surfacings. We need to know every bit of data we can gain and how atomic power affects performance."

"Yes, sir, and we can do most of that in Kola Bay. But until we do it in the Barents, there will be questions about its utility."

Anton held Katshora's message up. He started to ask Gesny if the XO thought he should send a message back to the admiral telling him, *No, the XO was right. Admiral Katshora was ensuring he knew they were going to remain within Kola Bay and to ignore any message or order that directed the* Whale *to head toward the Barents.*

"We will, XO. Right now, let's lead our crew through this weather and back into the facility." He unfolded the message. "Looks as if we will be out here for a minimum of another twenty-four hours."

"XO!" Shipley shouted down the hatch. "Let's take the bow down a few feet, clear it of the ice buildup!" He looked aft. The main induction valves were open and easily visible through the rain because the ice along the warmer edges marked their openings.

He leaned over the hatch again. "I want to close the main induction valve and then immediately open them," he said. That should clear the ice from them. Too much ice and they may fail to close properly when they dived. That would start a series of events such as what happened to the *Squalus* in 1939.

He heard the snorkel pick up the burden of exchanging the diesel exhaust as the icy outline of the main induction valves disappeared. Several seconds passed, and he saw the aft section of the boat resurface. The exhaust noise of the snorkel eased as the main induction valves reopened. He squinted and thought he could hear the noise of the air being exchanged through them, feeding the four Fairchild diesel engines as they sped the *Squallfish* forward.

A moment later, the XO's head emerged from below the deck, his body covered by the rain slick. Behind him, two sailors emerged also, relieving the two topside. Shipley and Arneau waited until the watches were relieved before doing the same.

Shipley stopped in the conning tower on the way down for a moment to chat with the crew and take off the rain slick. Chief Belford hung it up in the narrowest portion of the conning tower, the aft bulkhead. Lieutenant Weaver was the officer of the deck. He enjoyed the relative warmth of being belowdecks, though everyone had gloves, foul-weather jackets, and watch caps pulled down against the Arctic wind and rain whipping through the open hatch.

"Any word from Naval Intelligence?"

Weaver shook his head. "Not yet, Skipper."

"I'm going to the wardroom and a fresh cup of old coffee; then I'll be back. Keep an eye on the topside watches."

Five minutes later he was back, taking his familiar position against the starboard bulkhead of the conning tower. The temperature showed ten degrees above zero, but it felt warmer after the thirty minutes topside. Shipley picked up the nearby handset and called engineering. Bleecker wasn't available, but minutes later the chief engineer called back. His men were checking the batteries, but he estimated a minimum of two more hours. Two more hours of thirty-minute rotations for him, the XO, and the sailors as the *Squallfish* continued its approach to the mouth of Kola Bay.

"You know, Skipper, we might be able to follow that merchant into the bay," Weaver offered after minutes of silence.

Shipley raised his eyebrows, looking at the operations officer. "How's that?" he asked.

"We do an end run to get aft of him, sir. It's dark. It's going to be dark most of the time this far north and this close to winter. We can stay on the surface for most of the trip."

Shipley bit his lower lip. "They'll have radar tracking the ships coming and going."

"We have a low profile. In this weather with rain, wave, and—there's the land smear effect, which clouds radar returns within confined areas such as Kola Bay. Just a thought, sir. We could still get incoming messages and charge the batteries."

Shipley nodded. "Let me think about it." And think about it, he did. Diesel submarines seldom had the opportunity to approach targets submerged. Battery power may be the key to submerged operations, but by their very nature they provided insufficient speed long enough for a submarine to catch its prey. A burst of max speed at depth in a diesel could find the boat powerless and having to surface. So positioning for attack was usually done under the guise of darkness. The diesel would surface and then race to get in position to await their prey. The unsuspecting target eventually came to them, growing larger in their crosshairs until torpedoes were spewed out seconds apart, separating as they ran for a time-distance spread.

Readings in the *U.S. Naval Institute Proceedings* talked of new tactics nuclear-powered submarines would bring to the fleet. A fleet of nuclear submarines with speed limited only by mechanical and human factors. A nuclear submarine could dash forward faster submerged than a diesel submarine could surfaced, so the dash and wait tactic—the "end around" he talked about earlier—would be taught only in the history classes of the Academy instead of the war-fighting tactics courses.

He leaned against the bulkhead, feeling the cold through the cork-covered bulkhead. It meant that men such as he and those who fought in World War II keeping the Japanese away while America geared up to fight a war they never wanted would be anachronisms—a chapter in American history—as nuclear energy changed at-sea warfare.

Shipley shivered as he drained his coffee, the liquid already cold. Would the *Squallfish* ever lose this cold seeping into its every rivet, bulkhead, and compartment, or would it become part of the ship forever?

He leaned away from the icy contact. They could do this. It would be a visual approach on a target that may have seen them earlier. But this was peacetime. Merchant vessels around the world were not keeping lookouts for danger. In this weather, he doubted the Soviet merchant vessel would even have watches topside; they'd be crowded in the bridge or belowdecks, warm. A burst of Arctic air whipped through the open hatch above, bringing icy rain with it. Everyone hunkered lower, trying to pull their heads inside their foul-weather jackets.

"Jesus Christ," Senior Chief Boohan said from near the helmsman, where he stood watching the young sailor.

Shipley would be unable to use radar because Soviet electronic surveillance units would pick them up by the time he had made three sweeps. But if they followed the stern of the merchant, it would be the merchant lighting their way—figuratively. They'd break off near their destination, do the mission, and thanks to the Soviet merchant, he would have the return plot ready for escape.

"LOOK here, Fromley," Potts said, squatting in the middle of the deck. "That nigger's been here." He picked up several shavings of potato peel.

"How you know it wasn't one of the Filipinos?"

"Eat shit, From. I know it was him. The son of a bitch has dumped trash all over my compartment." He stood and handed the wadded-up potato peels to Fromley. "See? What did I tell you? He's coming down here when we ain't here and making a mess with this crap they call food."

Fromley held the potato peels up to the light. Then he looked at the deck. "I don't see anything else," he said.

Potts grunted. "Shit, From; it's probably because he's scared and picked some of it up." He pointed at the batteries. "I bet most of the trash he shoved underneath the batteries."

The aft hatch opened, and Lieutenant Bleecker entered. "What's the problem here, Potts? You're supposed to be checking the charges, not standing around scuttlebutting."

Potts grabbed the potato peels from Fromley and held them up to Bleecker's face. "Look here, Lieutenant. Look what we found on our deck."

Bleecker's head turned from one side to the other as he looked at the potato peels. "Looks to me, Potts, as if you have a wad of trash. Did I guess right?"

"Yes, sir," Potts replied, pulling the potato peels back, holding them in front of his face, and grinning. "I found them, sir, right there when I started the second half of my checks. I wouldn't have seen them otherwise."

"That's good, Potts. If you'd keep your spaces clean, you wouldn't find trash that big. Now toss it in the shit can and get back to work."

Potts looked shocked. "But sir, don't you get it. That colored boy did this. He came in here and dumped this on our decks."

Bleecker's eyebrows wrinkled into a V shape. "Potts, is this the only thing you've found?"

"So far, sir, but we just found it." He pointed at Fromley. "From and I are going to give the compartment a thorough inspection and see where he's dumped the other trash."

"Potts, take my advice; better yet, take my order. Get your mind off Crocky and his stewards. Remember our conversation a week or so ago?"

Potts nodded. "Yes, sir."

"It still holds." Bleecker held out his hand. "Give me that trash."

Potts handed it to him.

"There." Bleecker closed his hand and crushed the potato peels closer together. The veins on the back of his huge hands looked like mountain ridges running haphazardly across a treeless plain. "The trash is gone." He kept his hand closed. "Now I'm going to take care of this." He walked to the forward end of the compartment, opened the hatch, and stuck his hand inside over the trash can in the forward torpedo room. "There; your compartment is once again shipshape." He looked at Fromley. "Give me the logbook."

Fromley, who had been carrying the logbook in his hand, handed it to Bleecker. While Bleecker flipped the pages looking for the latest entries, Fromley looked at Potts with a fearful expression.

Potts pursed his lips, his nose wrinkling, and shook his head very slightly. No way Bleecker could tell they had been gundecking the log. At least he wouldn't be able to if Fromley did what he had told him to do.

Bleecker quit flipping the log. Potts and Fromley stood quietly as the chief engineer scanned the entries with his finger. Every few seconds an "uh-uh" or an "umm" escaped from Bleecker's lips.

Sweat broke out on Fromley's forehead. The temperature was twenty degrees in the forward battery room. He shifted on his feet.

Without looking up, Bleecker asked, "You nervous or something, Fromley?"

"Yeah, Fromley," Potts said, before he could answer. "I've told you to quit that dancing." Potts looked at Bleecker, who continued to scan the log. "I've told him, Lieutenant, that the better way to keep warm is to layer up, put on more T-shirts, but From thinks moving keeps the blood circulating and keeps him warm."

Bleecker shrugged as he flipped a page backward. "To each his own, but Fromley, that shuffling bothers me, and I can see how it gets on your shipmate's nerves. Go stand over there with him if you can't stop it."

"Yes, sir," Fromley replied, his words shaking.

Bleecker looked up. His eyes narrowed. "If you're cold, then why are you sweating?"

"I'm not sweating, Lieutenant," he said, glancing wide-eyed at Potts.

Bleecker slammed the logbook shut. He looked at Fromley and then at Potts. He opened it again, and then moved to the batteries. "These readings you have from a moment ago. You guys do them accurately?"

"I gave them to Fromley," Potts said.

Fromley looked at him but said nothing.

"Fromley, according to the log, this cell should be half charged. Kind of impossible, considering we've only been charging for less than two hours now. The ampere reading you have in the log is higher than what I am looking at." He looked at Potts and Fromley.

When neither spoke, he tossed the logbook onto the deck. "I think if I check each one of these, I'll find every one of them different from what you have logged." He rubbed his chin, his face growing redder. "Why is that, you think?"

"Maybe From misunderstood me?"

" 'Maybe From misunderstood me?' " Bleecker mocked. "Do I look stupid, Potts? Do I?" He looked at Fromley. "How about you, Fromley? You think these years in the Navy have decayed my mind past the point where I can recognize gun-decking when I see it?"

"No, sir," Fromley said. "I have never thought that."

"Well, you must have. I think if I went cell by cell and compared the amperes with your half-hourly checks, I'll find enough discrepancies to court-martial your asses to Leavenworth, Kansas, for the rest of your lives—which considering how young you two are, wouldn't be worth much after a stint in that can." Bleecker moved toward the two men. "Potts, you think you're big and mean and everyone owes you respect for being big and mean. In Leavenworth, they'll have you for breakfast." He turned to Fromley. "And you, Fromley. You wouldn't live a week there before you discovered how much men would like to share you."

"Share me?" Fromley asked, not understanding what the lieutenant was talking about.

Bleecker leaned forward, his face a few inches above and from Potts. "Potts, I'm going to go aft and check the aft battery compartment and the two engine rooms. When I come back I want those log entries correct. You understand me?"

"Yes, sir," Potts answered meekly.

As Bleecker reached the aft hatch, he turned. "I'll be sending Gledhill up here to show you how to do it. He'd better come back with glowing reports on the two engineers in the forward battery compartment. You two understand me?"

"Yes, sir," they answered.

The hatch shut behind him, and they both watched quietly when the wheels turned as Bleecker sealed the hatch on the other side. After several seconds, Potts bent down and picked up the logbook.

"Let's start over, Froms," he said calmly. "And this time get it right."

"I only put down what you told me," Fromley whined.

Potts slapped him upside the back of the head, hard. "If you had put down what I said, asshole, he wouldn't have figured it out."

Fromley rubbed his head. His eyes watered. "But I did. I only put down what you said."

"What an asshole," Potts said, moving to the first cell. "He came up here just to give us a hard time. I bet he doesn't do that to the others. Just us two because we know what that nigger is doing, and that Bleecker is a nigger-lover. You know how I know? I'll tell you. Because he and Crocky were on other boats together. That's why he's the way he is, and when I confronted him with the evidence of that colored boy trashing our compartment, look what he did." Potts squatted down near the cell. "He took it away from me, crushed it out of existence, and tossed it away. He covered up for him, and now he's trying to railroad us into a court-martial."

"But there were only the potato peels."

Potts looked at Fromley. "You gonna stand there arguing with me, or are you gonna take the readings as I give them to you?"

Fromley opened the logbook. "Maybe we should do it right this time?" he asked meekly. "Then, when the lieutenant looks at it—"

"Froms, shut the fuck up." Potts leaned over and read the ampere readout on the meter, glanced up at the clock on the bulkhead, and then gave the accurate reading and time to Fromley. He turned and looked at Fromley, who wet the tip of the pencil and wrote something in the log. "You better get it right this time."

Fromley took a deep breath. "I will if you will give it to me right," he said, lifting his chin.

For the next several minutes Potts moved from one cell to the other. Then he stood and went over to where Fromley was writing down the information. He jerked the logbook from him and looked at it. "Jesus Christ, Froms. What the fuck are you doing? We don't want to start a new set of log entries. We want to go back to where we started this set and change the times and the entries to match what I'm giving you. What do you think this shows if you start a new set of entries?"

"The correct readings?"

Potts shoved the logbook at him. "Take this, Shit for Brains, and erase the entries I've given you"—he put his finger on the first entry made after the departure of Bleecker—"here. Then go back to this entry." He flipped a couple of pages forward. "Start here. Make sure the cell I give you matches the one here. Change the time to match the time I give you and change the ampere readings to match the new ones I give you."

"But—"

"Don't 'but' me, Froms. You've gotten in enough trouble with Bleecker without us leaving him enough evidence to send us to a court-martial. Just do as I tell you."

Fromley scratched his head with the hand holding the pencil. "Okay, but all this erasing and changing are going to show up when someone reads the log."

"People do it all the time."

Fromley shook his head. "No, they don't. When they make an erroneous entry, they line it out, and right below it, they make the corrected entry."

Potts sighed. "What you want to do? You want to start a new logbook, or you want to correct the entries?"

Fromley looked at him. "I don't want to go to Leavenworth, where I'll be shared."

Potts laughed. "Ain't no one going to share you, Fromley. You're too ugly." He touched the logbook. "Now do what I say." He looked at the clock. "Damn, we're over two hours behind now thanks to Danny 'the Greaser' Bleecker. I hate mustangs," he said, shaking his head. "They're a pain in the ass."

"Yeah," Fromley said with a chuckle. "A real pain in the ass."

"Yeah. They can't make up their minds if they want to be an officer or keep playing at being enlisted. Just like he did when he came down here covering up for Crocky."

SHIPLEY straightened from the navigation table. He glanced at the clock on the bulkhead and cocked his head to one side. It is amazing how much the Navy runs on its time. Time becomes more important when you never know which time zone or what part of the day you're working.

"I have to go up and relieve the XO, OPSO." He looked at Van Ness. "Cliff, work with Alec here to bring us an interception course to the merchant vessel. No closer than a thousand yards astern of her. Don't want a silhouette giving away our position."

"Aye, sir," Van Ness answered. In the back of his mind was the question of whether he was still on the skipper's shit list for his actions yesterday.

Shipley looked at the chart again. "Not much information." Logan stood quietly to the side. "Lieutenant Logan, just so I'm sure you understand, there are to be no more transmissions from the *Squallfish* without my express permission."

The intelligence officer nodded. "Yes, sir."

"We still haven't heard from Naval Intelligence."

"Yes, sir, I know, but they'll reply."

"I hope so." Shipley turned back to Weaver and Van Ness. "I want to do this quickly and quietly. Brief the XO and, Lieutenant Weaver, when you and the XO are ready to execute, do it." He buttoned up the top layer of his foul-weather jacket and grabbed his rain slick off the hook on the aft bulkhead. Bits of ice fell onto the deck.

Shipley was as excited as a submarine captain could be as he climbed up the ladder onto the bridge to relieve Arneau. The icy rain was still coming down, as thick as it was thirty minutes ago when the XO had relieved him. Neither man spoke as Shipley took the binoculars. Arneau pointed off the port bow about two points. Though he said nothing, Shipley knew the merchant vessel they were about to shadow lay in that direction. The sting of the Arctic air hurt his lungs as he breathed. He pulled the watch cap down with its cut eyeholes and mouth over his face.

Arneau stepped back from the hatch to let two sailors emerge. And he stood there until the two off-going watches dashed down the ladder to the relative warmth of the inside of *Squallfish*. Then he nodded at Shipley and disappeared.

Ten minutes later he felt the submarine change direction, and he knew Arneau and Weaver were maneuvering the boat toward the stern of the merchant vessel.

Shipley walked over to the nearest watch and shouted in the sailor's ear, "Keep a close watch off our bow, sailor! We are going to pass close to another ship!" He couldn't see the man's expression through Senior Chief Boohan's makeshift winter mask, but the man nodded his understanding. Shipley told the other lookout the same thing. Now three of them served as the eyes of the submarine, for belowdecks it was only sound, hunkered over the sonar position, who would be able to detect anything they might miss. He had secured the radar by having the fuse removed and placed in the OOD's box so they could quickly restore it, if needed. He did not want any more Van Ness incidents while they were inside Kola Bay.

FOURTEEN

Thursday, December 6, 1956

"WE'RE through, sir," said Arneau as he stood near the sound operator, the ping of the echo sounder audible from the earphones the operator had lying on the narrow shelf he called a desk.

"What depth are we showing beneath us?" Shipley asked from the bridge, squatting near the open hatch.

"Two hundred feet," Master Chief Boohan replied, his face appearing in the red light of the conning tower.

Shipley stood, the cold trousers touching his legs, and he looked forward. Two thousand yards ahead, which was one nautical mile, the stern light on the freighter led the path. The light was all that was visible in the thick fog that had appeared after the freezing rain had passed.

The narrow passage about which he had been concerned was discovered not to be as narrow as it was shallow. The constant echo soundings sonar did gave them depth readings. Deep enough to dive, but too shallow to evade any concerted ASW effort. He turned on his flashlight. The red lens across the light kept the glow red. Shining it on his watch, he saw it was nearly midnight Zulu time.

"Depth three hundred feet and dropping rapidly, Captain," Arneau added.

Shipley turned off the flashlight. He acknowledged the report, raised his binoculars, and searched right and left. The fog was too thick for him to see the shore, and he was in too precarious a situation to use the radar. At least the rain had slowed to a drizzle.

"Four hundred fifty feet!" Boohan announced.

"Not so loud," Arneau cautioned.

Shipley glanced one last time at the merchant freighter ahead of them. They had been quiet as possible with their voices while following the Soviet freighter into Kola Bay. In calm seas voices could carry quite a distance, though with the rain, wind, and seas they had had for the past three hours, it had been hard for them to hear each other as they maneuvered into position behind the freighter, using it to guide them into the bay. The passing of the storm and the fog that rolled up behind it changed everything but the waves, which continued to be pushed by the wind. Not gale force, but sufficient for a wave to crash over the stern every now and again. The wind was southerly and could carry their voices the nautical mile to the freighter.

"Let's take the boat down, XO," Shipley said, then added, "But pass the word: don't use the horn." Logan's head appeared in the hatch. "Lieutenant Logan, before I tell you to get the hell out of the hatch, what do the Soviets use for diving? A horn, beeping, or what?"

Logan shrugged. "I don't know, sir."

Shipley nodded. "Well, don't ask Naval Intelligence; we've gotten one message that failed to provide enough answers to justify the cost of sending it. And they have yet to reply to our questions on Soviet submarine tactics. We'll be in Holy Loch by the time they do. Now get the hell out of the hatch so we can submerge."

Behind Logan, he heard Arneau ordering the intelligence officer to get his butt off the ladder. Logan jumped down.

Logan looked up at Shipley and held up a sheet of paper, the familiar blocked diagram of a Navy message visible in the red light of the conning tower.

"XO, tell me when the 'Christmas Tree' is green with the exception of the topside hatch."

"Aye, sir."

He heard the diesels switching to battery, looking aft as the main induction valves closed. He looked up at the snorkel, surprised—though he shouldn't have been—to see ice caking both the snorkel and the periscope shafts. Once they submerged, the waters would deice the bridge, the decks, and the superstructure.

What should have taken less than a minute for a 2,000-ton, 350-foot submarine with 100 sailors to disappear beneath the waves stretched into nearly three before Shipley heard the cry "All green except main hatch!"

"You two, get below. Secure your positions and prepare to dive," Shipley said to the topside watches.

Within ten seconds the two topside watches disappeared through the hatch. Shipley did quick looks forward and aft. A wave washed over the stern, rolling up the deck to splash against the conning tower. Then he checked the bridge area, making sure everything was secured. They had been on the surface for several hours, changing watches and personnel throughout that time to protect against frostbite. Satisfied, he scurried down the hatch. Pausing on the topside rungs of the ladder, Shipley pulled the hatch shut and dogged it down, ensuring watertight integrity.

Before his feet touched the deck of the conning tower, the cry of "All green!" came from the control room below.

"Take her down to fifty feet, officer of the deck."

"Aye, sir," Lieutenant Weaver said.

Shipley shivered, then turned the makeshift face guard up, rolling it into the shape of a watch cap. "Seems so bloody warm inside here after thirty minutes topside." He patted his cheeks, the gloves keeping him from feeling them. Shipley glanced at the thermometer. It showed sixteen degrees. "Regular heat wave down here."

"Yes, sir; blazing summer weather," Arneau answered, hunching his shoulders inside the buttoned-down foul-weather jacket. The watch cap was pulled forward over the XO's forehead and across both ears.

Boohan ran out the bow planes on the *Squallfish*. "Bow planes out," he announced.

Topside, Shipley knew the water was rushing over the periscope support structure, clearing the ice.

"Passing thirty-five feet," Weaver announced. Then, the operations officer turned to the planesmen. "Ease the planes."

The diving angle started to change as the submarine angled toward fifty feet.

"Flood forward trim from the sea," Weaver added.

The boat began to level off as the planesmen eased up on the angle of the planes. A couple of minutes passed as the *Squallfish* eased its depth to fifty feet. The tilt of the deck disappeared, and Weaver looked at Shipley. "Final trim, sir."

"Up periscope." As the shiny metal column rose, Shipley squatted, slapped the handles down when they emerged, and pressed his eye to the scope. He could see nothing as he waited for the lens to emerge above the surface. Then suddenly it was up and above. He walked the scope around, taking in the dark, naked surface, which seemed to put the *Squallfish* in a bowl of water sealed off by fog. Waves washed over the periscope, and try as he might, he could not see the stern light of the merchant they had been following.

"Sound, you have anything?"

"Just the merchant, sir."

"Bearing, range?"

"Target bears one niner zero at one thousand yards."

Shipley stepped back. "Periscope down. Come to course two hundred, speed eight knots." He looked at Arneau. "Don't want to run up her butt. We've already lost a thousand yards of separation in the dive."

Arneau nodded.

A hand emerged from the ladder below, setting a cup of steaming coffee on the deck. The steam and aroma rose quickly through the cold, cramped conning tower. Another came through the hatch, then a third, followed by several more cups of coffee setting in a semicircle on the deck around the hatch. Crocky's head, a Navy watch cap pulled over his ears, followed, the blackness of the veteran's skin blending into the watch cap he wore.

"Thought you might need something hot and fresh," Crocky said, not coming any farther into the conning tower.

"Come on up," Shipley offered.

"Steadying on course two zero zero," the helmsman announced.

"Sir, if it is all right with you, ain't nothing outside those bulkheads but sea. I am fine right here."

Weaver squatted and passed the coffee around, handing the first cup to Shipley. The heat from the ceramic cup felt wonderful through the gloves Shipley wore. He turned to say thanks, but Crocky had disappeared belowdecks. Wasn't often you could get the head cook away from his kingdom of the mess.

Shipley sipped. It was fresh, which meant Crocky had specifically made the coffee for him and the others.

"Depth?" Shipley asked.

"Fifty feet, sir," Weaver answered with a puzzled expression.

"I meant below us," Shipley explained.

"Do a ping," Weaver told the sailor manning the sonar. He held up one finger. "Just one."

The ping of the echo sounder reverberated through the hull.

"Six hundred feet."

"Take her down to two hundred feet." Shipley turned to Van Ness at the plotting table. Lieutenant Logan stood beside him.

Shipley and Arneau joined them. Logan straightened and with a smile handed the message to Shipley. Shipley took it and looked at Logan. "Tell me what it says."

"Well, sir, it says Soviet submarines usually enter and exit Kola Bay on the surface."

Shipley looked at Arneau. "Seems we already have that figured out." He looked at Logan. "And did they say anything about the operating depths inside Kola Bay?"

"They are asking C&G Survey if they have any data."

Shipley handed the message back to Logan. "By the time we get that answer, we will be able to answer it ourselves." He looked down at the chart. "Okay, how far are we from our objective?"

Van Ness nodded at Logan. "I have done a dead-reckoning course from when we turned to where Lieutenant Logan's intelligence data show the facility to be. I recommend . . ."

For the next few minutes Lieutenant Van Ness recommended two course turns at specified times if they continued at eight knots. The last turn would bring them up at approximately five hundred yards from the facility that overhead reconnaissance flights had photographed.

Shipley looked at Logan. "Is this going to be close enough?"

"It should be, sir. We have to surface so the air samplers can operate."

Shipley looked at Arneau, then at Van Ness. "What time will we be arriving off the objective?" He knew that. The main induction valves could be opened only when the submarine was surfaced. *Let's hope this fog holds*, Shipley thought.

"We should be directly offshore of it by zero six hundred, Skipper."

"That'll give us about an hour of darkness before the faint Arctic dawn rises," Arneau said.

Shipley turned back to Logan. "How long will you need to take sufficient samples and get your photographs? I don't want to hang around here too long, and I would like to get out of the Soviets' backyard as soon as possible."

"Sir, we need only about thirty minutes, an hour at the most."

Shipley did a sharp shake of the head. "Lieutenant, we are going to be surfaced while you gather your air samples. I want to know as soon as you have sufficient samples so we can submerge and head for open water."

Shipley looked at Arneau, then back to Logan. "If we get there and the place is crawling with patrol craft or it looks as if we are going to be detected, we are going to submerge. As long as we can, we'll remain in the vicinity until we can accomplish the mission at hand."

"Hopefully the fog will hide us," Logan offered.

"Fog is like sex, Mister Logan; one moment it sends waves of anticipation and worried excitement all over you, and the next moment it's gone."

Behind Logan, Shipley saw Boohan turn and look. The master chief mouthed as a question the words "worried excitement" before the chief of the boat turned back to the planesmen.

"Sir, I have to do two things with the air samplers," Logan answered. "One is measure the radiation around this source. The other is to circulate the air from the outside through the sampler long enough for the filters to capture whatever is in the air. Additionally—"

" 'Additionallys' are like 'buts,' Mister Logan. There are none on my boat. Try to get everything you need within twenty minutes. While you're photographing and gathering, be prepared to disconnect immediately. Understand?"

"Yes, sir," Logan answered, then after a slight pause added, "Sir, if we are going to be surfaced, then can we take the photographs topside?"

"Why have you been practicing to use the periscope if you want to do it topside?"

"I didn't think we would have the opportunity, sir," Logan replied with a shrug.

"Sir, I recommend they use the periscope," Arneau interjected.

"Why?" Shipley asked.

"The periscope will give Lieutenant Logan's people a higher point of view on the facility. The periscope will allow them to magnify any points of interest, but most importantly, if we are detected, the fewer people and equipment topside, the quicker we can dive."

Shipley turned back to Logan. "I think the XO has answered your request."

"Depth beneath the hull is past eight hundred feet, sir. No ping returning," Boohan said from across the small conning tower compartment.

Shipley looked up, his eyes seeing the thermometer. It now read nearly twenty-five degrees. He lifted the coffee and took a drink, enjoying the taste. The initial warmth of the liquid was quickly dissipating in the below-freezing conditions of the conning tower.

"Skipper, it's going to be about five hours before we arrive at the objective," Arneau started.

"You're right, XO. Go below and catch some winks. I need you fresh when we arrive."

"Sir, I was thinking . . ." The XO went on to propose that Shipley take the first sleep, arguing that the skipper had the first and last watches topside. Shipley needed the rest, and the boat would need him once they arrived on station.

Shipley wanted to continue the argument, but realized that if he failed to take advantage of a few hours of sleep now, he would be exhausted if they had to do an escape and evasion. He bit his lip for a moment before nodding. "Wake me in three hours."

"Four," Arneau said, holding up four fingers.

Shipley nodded. "Not one minute past four, and call me to the bridge if anything happens. I don't want any surprises."

"Sorry, Skipper," Logan said.

Shipley looked at the young officer and raised one eyebrow. He sighed. "Not your fault, Lieutenant Logan. We are all victims of emergent circumstances. Maybe in our lessons learned report once we're back at Holy Loch we can recommend if they intend to do this again, they make it a regularly scheduled mission so crews—both yours and the submarine force—can work it up properly." He nearly added, *if we get back*. Hopefully the Navy would find a better way to do these intelligence-gathering missions than endangering a submarine in Soviet waters.

s through the hatch and in the control
l tes to check on things, then headed
f ather coat off and then lay down on
t coat over him. He was asleep within
s

A e periscope. "Periscope down."
lowering the submarine filled the
cc Gesny. "You think we will need a
conning tower once we have atomic-powered submarines, XO?"

Gesny shrugged. "They will have to make the periscopes longer."

"If we can have atomic power"—he lifted his hands, palms outstretched—"and this warmth. Can you believe with the Arctic only feet from us, we have this much warmth?"

"You may be right, Comrade Captain."

"Periscope down," Ensign Rybin, his voice low, said from near the planesmen.

"Speak up!" Gesny snapped. "Everyone must be able to hear your commands when you are the officer of the deck."

"Green board!" came the voice from the control room.

Anton nodded.

Gesny shouted, "Very well!"

Even though they had not surfaced because of the weather, they were simulating taking the boat down from a surface position.

"Make our depth fifteen meters, XO." Anton glanced at the clock on the bulkhead. It was nearly 0500. Daylight in another couple of hours would bring a slightly brighter day, but one that could confuse whether it was dawn, dusk, or midday because the light was the same. Darkness reigned for most of the winter months.

"Aye, sir." Gesny turned to Rybin. "Officer of the deck! Make depth fifteen meters!"

"Bow planes ten degrees!" Rybin shouted.

Anton smiled.

"That's more like it, Ensign!" Gesny shouted, glancing at Anton.

The XO's eyes twinkled, but the face remained as impassive now as it had since Anton met him. It was Gesny's eyes, Anton decided. The eyes betrayed the mood of the XO, but you had to be quick or you'd miss his humorous moments.

For the next few minutes, the planesmen and helm worked together while the chief of the boat, Chief Ship Starshina Mamadov, worked the hydraulics control handles controlling the water flow into the ballast tanks. The familiar rumbling of the hydraulics associated with the ballast tanks vibrated through the *Whale*. Anton's forehead wrinkled as he heard the noise and felt the slight vibration, wondering how far it carried in the water.

Noise in the water traveled faster than noise in the air, and it was noise that antisubmarine forces used to find, track, and destroy submarines. The ballast hydraulics were noisy during World War II, and they were noisy now. When the Soviet submarine fleet joined the global navies of the world, Anton surmised that noise would be the great equalizer. With atomic power as the common energy for submarines, it would be stealth and firepower that determined the difference. He wondered how the top-secret hydroacoustic coating being added to the submarine hulls in the Pacific Fleet was going. With atomic power along with this special coating designed to reduce noise in the water, the Soviet submarine force would be even more formidable. He imagined for a moment American submarines being forced to surface by a superior Soviet submarine force.

"Steady at fifteen meters."

Master Ship Starshina Mamadov's report brought his thoughts back to the exercise.

"Periscope up," Anton said, stepping to the instrument. As it rose from below, he squatted and put his eye to the eyepiece. The periscope broke the surface. Anton waited the few seconds for the water to drain off the lens. He leaned back. "It's quit raining."

"That's good news," Gesny said.

Anton leaned against the periscope, wondering if Gesny really believed it was good news or was just echoing his skipper's sentiment. For some reason, he had developed a fondness for the taciturn Gesny. How could a man go so long with so little expression of emotion? But the incident in the facility when Gesny had pulled him away from the scene with the stretchers had revealed the man's loyalty. Loyalty was a virtue highly prized within every Navy in the world.

Anton spun the periscope, searching for the escorts. The exercise now consisted of him targeting the destroyers, reporting when he had simulated torpedo firings, and then the destroyers were to commence an ASW attack against him. His job was to engage, evade, and escape.

"Do you see them?" Gesny finally asked after Anton had spun the periscope several times.

"I believe we now have fog," Anton replied. He stepped back, nodded at Gesny, and motioned to the periscope.

Gesny stepped to the periscope, draped his hands over the handles, and commenced searching, stepping around the conning tower as he spun the scope.

Anton looked aft at the sonar operator. "Sonar, you have them on sound?"

"Aye, Comrade Captain. First target bears zero two zero true and second target is behind us now bearing one nine zero."

"Range?"

"No range, Captain. I can commence target motion analysis to determine it, but it will take several minutes."

"Then do it." He looked at Rybin. "What is our course and speed, officer of the deck?"

Rybin looked past the helmsman at the gauges on the forward bulkhead. "Sir, we are on course zero nine zero at eight knots."

Gesny stepped away. "Fog," he agreed. Then he looked at Rybin. "Ensign Rybin, an officer of the deck always knows the course, speed, and depth of his boat. He doesn't have to look at the gauges."

Footsteps on the ladder drew the attention of Anton and Gesny. The dark hat of the zampolit filled the hatch for a second before the smiling face of Tomich looked up.

"Ah, Comrade Tomich, welcome to the conning tower," Anton said, wishing the man had stayed in the warmth of the officers' mess instead of crowding an already crowded compartment.

"What would the captain like to do?" Gesny asked, ignoring the zampolit.

Tomich smiled, climbed into the conning tower, and stepped aside near the forward bulkhead on the starboard side of the helmsman. Anton appreciated the political officer staying out of the way. He had little say as to where and when a zampolit could go. To refuse a zampolit access to men or compartments would be a strike against an officer's career, if not his life.

"Let's use sonar for a targeting solution. Then as soon as we report our simulated firing, I want to do a full right rudder, burst our speed to about fifteen knots, and create a knuckle in the water."

A knuckle was when water was churned behind a submarine, creating a swirling condition that could reflect sonar and put noise into the water. Many times a knuckle confused surface sonar into believing they had the submarine located.

"Then we'll take her deep at three knots, with another right full rudder. We'll coast away from our firing position. We'll want to steady up going in the opposite direction we are on now."

"Aye, sir."

"Down periscope," Anton said as Gesny stepped away.

Gesny slapped the handles into the upright stored position as the scope started down.

"If we do that maneuver," Anton continued, "it will expose our shaft to the destroyer bearing zero two zero. But the knuckle should shield the cavitation noise of our propellers from the sound heads on the target at one nine zero. The goal is to get behind the target bearing southwest of us. Then we'll do another complete one-eighty turn and come out as close behind him as possible. That way we'll ride his baffles while they search."

Anton stayed silent as the XO and Ensign Rybin put his orders into action. He waited while the sound team developed a profile of the surface. Thirty minutes of riding at periscope level should give the ASW teams on the destroyers sufficient training. He knew it should be easy to track a target that is maintaining the same course, speed, and depth. The noise from the pumps was the major source of sound on a submarine, so only a deaf sonar technician could miss hearing the *Whale* at this depth and distance.

"Sir," Rybin said from the plotting table, "we have solutions on the targets." A broad grin spread across the young officer's face.

"Well, Comrade Rybin, why don't you give them to me?"

"Comrade Captain, target Alpha now bears zero one zero, left-bearing drift, on course two seven zero, speed eight knots."

"Eight knots seem slow," Gesny said.

"That is because we have fog on the surface, and target Alpha is approaching the operational area of target Bravo," Rybin answered.

Gesny raised his eyebrows as he looked at Anton.

Anton ran his hand over his mouth to hide the smile. He knew where Rybin got that tidbit of information. The more he worked with Gesny, the more respect he grew to have for the officer.

"And target Bravo?"

"Comrade Captain, target Bravo bears one seven zero on course zero eight zero at eight knots, sir."

Anton looked at Gesny. "Looks as if they have us located, XO."

"Aye, sir. Looks as if Bravo is attempting to push us toward Alpha."

"Ensign Rybin, what do you recommend?"

Rybin licked his lips for a moment. "Sir, I would recommend putting your plan into action."

"How?"

The man's eyes widened, and the officer whirled back to the plotting table.

"What is the range to the two targets, Comrade Rybin?" Gesny asked.

"Sir, Alpha is one thousand meters and Bravo is at approximately two thousand meters," the young ensign answered without looking up from the chart. Then he sprang upright. "Sir, I recommend we come to course zero one zero—"

"Why?" Gesny asked.

"Sir, it will point our bow at Alpha. It will hide our screws from his sound heads."

"But Bravo will pick them up."

"XO, Bravo already has them," Rybin answered. "This will be a simulated torpedo firing on Alpha."

"Alpha has a left-bearing drift," Gesny said. "Doesn't that mean it will be forced to change course?"

"Yes, Comrade XO," Rybin said, his voice wavering for a moment. "But when it changes course, it will have to change toward us."

"But I may want a beam shot at him," Anton said.

"Sir, we are unable to see him because of the fog. If he turns, he will come into visual range. A visual torpedo firing is more accurate than sound."

Anton and Gesny glanced at each other, and both nodded simultaneously. Anton smiled. "Good work, Ensign."

A smile broke across Rybin's face. Anton thought he saw a few beads of sweat on the young officer's forehead, but in the red light of the conning tower, it was hard to be sure.

Gesny glanced down at the chart, placing his spread fingers on top of it.

"Up periscope," Anton said. "If Comrade Rybin recommends

a torpedo firing, then we should do so, XO. Set battle stations and bring the *Whale* to course zero one zero."

The beeps of general quarters sounded through the submarine. Soft, but constant. Sailors rushed from their bunks, the mess, and other areas of the submarine, hurrying to their assigned battle stations.

Lieutenant Antipov clambered up the ladder, his soft-soled shoes making little noise on it. The officer rushed to the torpedo panel.

"Report when the *Whale* is ready for battle."

"Coming to course zero one zero," the helmsman reported.

Rybin echoed the words. Nearby, the chief of the boat, Chief Ship Starshina Mamadov, lightly slapped a petty officer on the back of the head and nodded at the logbook.

Anton spun the periscope, searching once again for the two destroyers and having as little visual luck now as a minute before.

"Alpha is in a port turn, sir," the sonar operator reported.

"Very well," Anton replied without removing his eye from the scope.

"Steady on course zero one zero," came the cry from the helmsman.

Anton saw the white mast light and the port red light of the destroyer emerging from the thick fog. "I have Alpha," he said. "Mark!"

"Set!" Antipov announced. "Range six hundred meters."

"Battle stations set, Comrade Captain," Gesny said.

"This will be a forward firing exercise," Anton said. "This is where I would say, 'Make sure we don't actually fire a torpedo,' but we have no torpedoes on board."

"Yes, sir," Gesny answered drily.

"Log that," Mamadov ordered the sailor, tapping the logbook. "Log everything that is said when at battle stations. You understand?"

"Bearing—mark," Anton said crisply. "Bearing zero zero zero. Angle ten degrees port."

He heard the XO repeat the command. Anton stayed glued to the periscope, taking bearings and listening to the "marks" being repeated.

Antipov, the acting torpedo officer, shouted "set!" to the marks and reported the decreasing range to the target. Against the forward bulkhead near the planesmen, Mamadov watched the young sailor keeping the log even as he kept most of his attention on the planesmen. Once the captain gave the word for the evasive maneuvering, these two men would have to be spot-on with their execution.

Anton leaned away. Gesny was standing beside Antipov. Most were hovering over the firing key operator, who was manning the sound-powered telephone. "This will be a spread of four. Set shallow. Ten seconds separation."

Once the skipper had given the command to fire the first torpedo, the firing officer—Lieutenant Antipov—would take over and ensure that the other simulated torpedoes in the salvo were fired with sufficient separation so they did not interfere with each other and that they were fired with sufficient course-angle separation so that at least one of them would catch the target if the target decided to maneuver to port or starboard; speed up or slow down; or even attempt to back up.

He leaned into the periscope. "He's swinging toward us. This will be a firing solution," Anton said. "Bearing!"

"Three five seven!" Gesny sang out.

"Mark!" Anton said.

"Set!" Antipov announced. "Range three hundred meters."

"Angle on the port bow is five. Simulate firing. Fire one!"

"Fire one!" Antipov replied.

The firing key operator pressed the firing key—a huge brass knob fixed to the bulkhead beneath the ready light. "Fire one!" the operator shouted into the telephone. Then, the sailor reached up and turned "one" off and turned "two" on.

DOWN in the forward torpedo room, the tube captain, wearing his sound-powered telephones, heard the "Fire one!" command. His eyes were glued to the gauge board in front of him. His hand was positioned over the manual firing button in the event the solenoid firing mechanism failed to fire electrically. But this was an exercise, and there were never casualties in an exercise unless it was part of the exercise. Everyone on board the *Whale* knew they were out there to see what the atomic-powered engine could do. The exercise was to test the power in every circumstance.

Chief Igor Rashchupkina, the chief torpedoman in the forward torpedo room, had already pulled the lever that opened the torpedo tube doors. In a real firing, his job was to operate the opening and closing of the torpedo tubes.

On board the destroyers, the sonar operators had heard the opening of the torpedo tubes and reported it to their captain. Rashchupkina imagined the shouting going on in the combat center on board the surface ships and grinned. "Stupid skimmers."

"Number one fired electrically," the tube captain reported through his sound-powered telephone.

In the conning tower, the firing key operator echoed the report.

Anton kept the periscope up, watching Alpha target close his position. In a real-world scenario, he would want to watch to ensure that the torpedoes hit. He listened as the firing key operator simulated firing the other three torpedoes at the command of Lieutenant Antipov.

Anton grabbed the nearby microphone and pressed the transmit key. He reported his firing solution, time of firing, and spread of torpedoes. Quickly acknowledged by the referee on board target Bravo, he hung up the microphone.

"Okay, everyone. Time to play prey. Periscope down!" Anton shouted, stepping away from the scope and slapping the handles up. "Left full rudder, all ahead full!"

The *Whale* tilted to the left as the submarine twisted in response to Anton's commands. Anton reached out and touched the bulkhead for balance. The speed came almost automatically, unlike the ramp up to speed that came from batteries. He was growing to love atomic power with every passing minute.

"Take her down to sixty meters!" he continued. Behind the *Whale,* water churned upon itself, creating a knuckle that should help confuse the sonar operators on board the destroyers.

"Bearing to Bravo?" he asked, stepping to the center of the conning tower.

"Target Bravo bears two five zero degrees, sir."

"Then steady up on two five five at sixty meters."

Chief Ship Starshina Mamadov stood behind the planesmen, watching them turn the huge nickel-plated wheels, and glancing at the depth gauge as the *Whale* continued its twisting dive away from base course. This was what sailors were meant to do; not sleeping every night in a barracks, as if they were soldiers. Master chiefs were the same in every Navy. If it were easy, they would not need master chiefs.

"Passing thirty meters!" Lieutenant Antipov announced.

"All engines stop!" Anton ordered.

Almost instantly, the vibration of the shafts stopped. The *Whale* continued downward. Experience told him he had sufficient momentum to take him the remaining thirty meters.

FIFTEEN

Thursday, December 6, 1956

SHIPLEY yawned as he stood near the starboard bulkhead of the conning tower. "When did you detect them, sound?" he asked the sonar operator. He finished buttoning up his foul-weather jacket. Having slept under it, his body heat had kept the garment warm.

"About thirty minutes ago, sir. Twin screws, fast turns, and I classify them as possible destroyers."

"Have they detected us?" Shipley asked, knowing the answer. Destroyers would already have been raining depth charges over them if they had been detected.

"No, sir, but they are in a search mode. The sound of their screws rising and falling as they twist and turn. They seem to be searching for something."

"You think we might have stumbled into a Soviet exercise?" Arneau asked.

Shipley didn't answer. Why would the Soviets have warships out in the middle of Kola Bay searching the bay unless they thought someone was here who shouldn't be?

"Skipper?"

"Sorry, XO; I was thinking." He looked at the sonar operator. "Sound, have you heard any pings?" A ping would tell him if they were conducting ASW operations. Maybe they were new crews practicing maneuvering and sea operations. "Boring holes in the ocean" was the term the skimmers used for taking a warship out and letting the junior officers and sailors practice seamanship on it.

Lieutenant Logan stood off to one side, quiet and watching.

Shipley looked at him. "What are your thoughts, Lieutenant Logan?"

"Sir, Soviet commanding officers, like our own, get graded on their competence in seamanship and navigation. It could be they are conducting their own equivalent to our refresher training."

"I think I prefer Norfolk to Kola Bay," Arneau offered quietly.

Shipley nodded at Logan's answer. He looked at Van Ness standing near the plotting table. "How long until station?"

"We are within a mile of where we plotted, Skipper. By zero six fifteen we will be one mile off the coast of where we want to be." Van Ness straightened. "Of course, that is by dead reckoning, Captain. We need to take some sightings to derive our actual location."

Weaver spoke up. "We are on course one niner zero, speed six knots, depth one hundred fifty, sir."

Shipley nodded as he stifled another yawn. He looked at Arneau. "XO, lay below and get some sleep. I'll call you if we need you."

"But—"

Shipley held up his hand. "Same rationale you used on me, Arneau. I want you fresh if we have to run for it. I don't want you falling asleep on us."

"Never happen," Arneau protested.

"See you in a few hours."

"Aye, sir," Arneau said with the petulance of a Navy officer being forced away from the action. "I'll go try to sleep for a couple of hours."

Shipley held up three fingers. "Three hours minimum and then most likely you'll have to wake yourself."

Shaking his head, the XO grabbed the rungs of the ladder and slid down to the control room. Shipley turned back to Lieutenant Weaver. "Let's bring the boat up to fifty-five feet, officer of the deck. Let's do it slowly and without cavitating." He looked at Van Ness. "Tell me what we'll be looking for," Shipley said, referring to shore markings from which the navigator could take bearings. He saw Logan against the port bulkhead.

"Lieutenant Logan, where are your people?"

"They are standing by near the radio shack, sir."

"Very well. What do you want to do first? You have two crew members and two stations. We are going to have to surface for you to hook up the air samplers to one of the main induction valves."

Logan nodded. "I thought we would hook up the camera first, Captain, if that is okay with you. That way when we surface, we'll already be taking photographs. Then, when you give the word, we can hook up to the main induction valve."

Shipley nodded. "Okay. I'll use the attack scope for observation until we surface."

Logan nodded. "Aye, sir."

"There should be a water tower off our starboard side, sir," Van Ness said. "If we can locate that, then a couple of sightings as we move past it will give us our true location."

A few seconds passed as Shipley walked to the hooks in the aft portion of the conning tower and pulled the Boohan-modified watch cap off and put it on. When he turned, he glared at Logan. "Well, Mister Logan, are you going to get your sailors up here and hook up that Naval Intelligence piece of whatever, or are you going to stand there waiting for me to tell you to do it?"

Logan jumped. "Sorry, sir; no, sir," he stuttered, then quickly disappeared down the ladder. Behind him, Lieutenant Weaver smiled.

"Quit your smiling," Shipley said. He looked at the sonar operator. "Sound, you keep a close ear on those warships. I want to know every sound you hear. Our lives may well depend on you, son."

The sailor's eyes widened as he reached up and pressed the earphones tightly against his head. Shipley wanted everyone to understand how precarious their situation was. This wasn't an exercise where they could walk away and start over if they were discovered. At worse, they would all lie entombed or scattered across the bottom of Kola Bay or find themselves on the front page of the *Washington Post* and *Stars & Stripes*. Or maybe listed as missing somewhere in the North Atlantic, never to be heard from again. This was a different world they lived in from the clear-cut warfare of World War II.

"Passing one hundred," Weaver announced.

Shipley looked at the planesmen, not surprised to see Senior Chief Boohan standing above them. He had not heard the chief of the boat climb into the conning tower, but then senior chiefs, like master chiefs, were known for their stealth. Cunning also, he thought with a slight smile. A good submarine may be officially measured on the competence and performance of its skipper, but a good skipper reached those measurements by having great executive officers and heaven-sent chiefs of the boat such as Boohan.

Clanging on the ladder drew everyone's attention, and without even guessing, Shipley knew it was Logan and his two communications technicians, Brooks and Cross.

Cross was breathing heavily as the three men finally gathered in the conning tower. It was beginning to get crowded, but then Shipley recalled how ten of them used to crowd into the conning tower during World War II to conduct their attacks, bumping into each other, sweat pouring off their bodies from the heat of the Pacific, to puddle on the deck. Then they'd launch their torpedoes; cross their fingers; and then twist, maneuver, and change depth as they tried to evade and escape the Japanese depth charges.

Many submariners never returned, and most times you never knew how they died or disappeared. Just one day Pearl would announce that a boat was overdue, and as the days rolled up against each other and the submarine never answered its call, submariners would mourn in their own way.

"Skipper," Weaver said, his voice louder.

Shipley looked at him. "What is it, Alec?"

"Sorry, sir; I said we are at periscope depth."

Shipley nodded. "Raise the periscope." He squatted, slapping the handles down as the search scope emerged. He rose with the scope, and when it broke the surface, he did a quick scan of the area. "We still have fog, but I can see a faint light on the shore," he said. "The fog isn't as thick, but it's still out there." He bumped into someone, jarring him away from the scope. It was one of the communications technicians.

"Here," Weaver said quickly. "You two stand over near the aft bulkhead until the skipper finishes his surveillance."

Why so tense? Shipley thought. Maybe this mission was bringing back memories long thought buried. He had nearly screamed at the sailor. That wasn't him. He had deliberately fought against developing a reputation as a screamer.

"Thanks," he said softly.

He did not see Weaver nod in reply.

Another couple of rounds, and Shipley stepped away.

"Lieutenant Logan, it's all yours," he said.

Logan and his sailors quickly pounced on the periscope. Shipley worked his way through the crowd to the sonar operator, who reported no change in the sounds. The warships were still out there, and they were still boring holes through the water. When he turned back to his periscope, Brooks and Cross were stepping back from the contraption strapped to it.

"Do we know if this is going to work, Lieutenant?" Shipley asked.

Logan smiled and nodded. "Yes, sir; we've tested this several times on our trip here." He gestured to it. "Would the captain like to take a look?"

Shipley started to say no, but then stepped up to the camera. With Logan telling him how to operate the lens, Shipley leaned against it and peered through the camera, which allowed him to see through the periscope. Other than the handles being farther away, he could tell no difference. He leaned back. "How do you take a photograph?"

Logan told him. Shipley looked at the button for operating the shutter. "How many photographs can you take?"

Petty Officer Cross dragged a black briefcase over near the periscope. Logan squatted and opened it. "We have nearly a hundred frames capable of taking low-light photographs."

"So we'll know when you have enough photographs?"

"Yes, sir; unfortunately, we can't process them until we return. Naval Intelligence is going meet us with a photographer team."

"Why didn't you bring a team with you this time?" Shipley asked, thankful they didn't.

"They weren't available on such short notice, sir. Petty Officers Cross and Brooks are stationed at Edzell, Scotland, so it was easy to get them down here, and they had the proper security clearances needed to conduct this mission."

"Edzell, Scotland? Never heard of it. Where is it?"

"It's in Edzell, sir," Logan answered, touching his watch cap. "It was a World Wars I and II RAF base."

"Well, Lieutenant, I doubt we will ever see your photographs." He turned to include the two CTs. "Listen to me, for this is important. If you hear the 'oogle' go off and shouts of 'Dive! Dive!,' that means we are running from something that may have or has seen us. We can't let this periscope down with your camera on it. So if you want to save your camera"—he turned to Logan—"as well as the air sampler you're going to mount on the main induction valve, you're going to have to be quick in getting them disconnected. Otherwise one of my sailors is going to rip them off and throw them aside as we head for deep depths. Okay?" He looked at their faces as all three replied with loud "Ayes."

"Good," he said, turning back to Logan. "Now, how do you have your men dispersed?"

"Cross and Brooks will be in the aft engine room with the air sampler, sir, since it is the most cumbersome. They will operate that while I stay here and take the photographs."

Shipley agreed.

"Once I have used up the frames, I'll disconnect the camera even if we are still on the surface."

"Sir," Van Ness announced, "we have arrived."

"Up attack scope," Shipley said. He did one more sweep of the area, then ordered the *Squallfish* to surface. A chill ran up his back, and it was not because of the weather. The fog was still surrounding them, but it appeared to be less thick than when they submerged. He could make out faint lights on their starboard side. One light blinked steadily, most likely marking a large structure. Blinking lights along coastal structures served two purposes: it alerted aircraft of their height and, as far as he was concerned, it provided known geographical locations for mariners to take a bearing. Those bearings allowed a ship to refine its distance and location from shore.

"Okay, Lieutenant Weaver, let's take the boat up," he said, slapping the handles down. "Down periscope."

"Sir, recommend coming to course two two zero," Van Ness announced.

Shipley nodded. "Let's wait until we do a positioning once we've surfaced—that is, if we can get a couple of landmarks." His eyebrows arched. "We do have some landmarks to do a couple of fixes on, don't we?"

The beeps warning the crew of the boat surfacing echoed through the *Squallfish*. The boat tilted slightly as the American submarine finished rising the fifty-five feet to the surface. Throughout the conning tower and the control room beneath it, there were the routine sounds of the watches blowing the air from the ballasts, answering the nominal commands associated with bringing a boat sunk on purpose back to the surface of the sea.

Van Ness nodded. "Yes, sir; we have a few landmarks ready for fixing if we are within two or three miles of our dead reckoning."

"Well, I was able to see lights ashore. One of them could be on that water tower you mentioned earlier."

"Surfaced, sir," Weaver announced.

Van Ness and his signalman bent over the chart. The signalman put his finger on the chart and whispered something to the navigator.

"Yes, sir, Skipper," Van Ness said. "That should be the water tower on the chart."

One of the sailors from the control room rushed up the ladder through the conning tower to the main hatch above. He spun the wheel on the main hatch. Then he pushed it out and slid around to the side of the ladder.

"Switch to diesels," Shipley commanded.

"Sir?"

Shipley looked at Logan. "You're right, Lieutenant." He turned to Weaver. "Officer of the deck, we're going to have to secure one of the diesels so Lieutenant Logan and his team can take their air samplers. Put one diesel driving the shafts and the other two recharging the batteries. I want those batteries topped off if we need them. And tell the CHENG that I want to be able to switch three diesels to the electric motor if we need to sprint."

"Aye, sir."

Then Shipley climbed the ladder to the bridge as behind him he heard Weaver report the opening of the main induction valves. In the control room below, the Christmas Tree started changing from green to red across its board.

Two sailors followed from the control room where they had been waiting. Seconds after the *Squallfish* had surfaced, Shipley was once again in the Arctic elements freezing his butt off, and hoping they survived this perilous mission. Somewhere the Navy admirals who ordered this were sleeping warmly.

Three puffs of gray-black smoke coughed from the main induction valves along the aft portion of *Squallfish*. With the diesels driving the boat ahead at six knots, he was putting noise in the water. Hopefully, if the destroyers picked up the noise, they would think it was a merchant or fishing vessel. If not, the *Squallfish* was going to have a rough time making it back to international waters. He had little choice. Without a full battery charge they would have to make it back to the Barents Sea surfaced.

The signalman appeared through the hatch with a compass.

He quickly set the sighting compass on its stand, pointed it at the water tower, and wrote down the time and the bearing.

"What you got?" Shipley asked.

"Sir, the water tower bears two five five degrees; time zero five fifty-five."

Shipley raised his binoculars and did a sweep of the area. The freezing air caused him to cough once. He recalled the story of a person caught outside in the North Atlantic during World War II who froze his lungs, the air was so cold.

Something caught his attention, and he brought the binoculars back. He focused them on the dark area along the coastline. It took a few minutes of coming back to the object until he realized he was looking at a gigantic opening of a huge, covered docking area. It reminded him of the dirigible hangars he had visited after the war in Elizabeth City, North Carolina.

He dropped his binoculars, squatted, and stuck his head near the hatch. "Lieutenant Logan, look ahead of us—off our starboard bow." Shipley heard the hydraulics turning the periscope above him.

"Jesus Christ!" Logan exclaimed. "That's it, sir. That's it. Can we get off the front of it?"

"Lieutenant Weaver, come to course one nine zero. There's a slight bulge in the shoreline here."

"**SIXTY** meters!" Lieutenant Antipov announced.

The bow of the *Whale* eased up as the boat reached the depth. The only communications between them and the destroyers would be through underwater communications. Down in BCh-4, the radiomen would be monitoring for the results.

"Range to Bravo?"

The sonar operator looked at Anton. "Less than one thousand meters, Captain."

The sailor's voice did not sound sure. Anton looked over at him. The man licked his lips.

"If you are not sure, you need to tell me, Starshina."

The man dropped his head. "Sir, I have him bearing one seven five from us. The range is more a guess, Captain. Everything is being done passively."

"Good. Never hesitate to tell the skipper the facts, including when you are not sure."

Though the red lighting of the conning tower obscured the starshina's face, he knew the young man would consider it a rebuke. It was not lost on Anton that Mamadov would be chewing out the poor man's butt later. This was a good lesson for everyone.

"Final trim," Mamadov announced from the planesmen position, his eyes glued to the inclinometer above the two huge wheels.

"Final trim," Antipov echoed.

The deck was level and the boat was steady.

"Depth?"

"Captain, we make our depth sixty-three meters."

"Three meters is too much, Lieutenant. Three meters can mean the difference between slamming into the bottom of the sea or masking our movements beneath the sound layer."

"Aye, sir," Antipov answered.

Anton made a mental note to practice the maneuver again and again until the crew was able to come out with a final trim on the boat at the commanded depth. Submarines were not surface ships. They moved through a medium comprised of four directions: up, down, right, and left. A surface ship could handle only two. The only other direction was down. There was never an up direction for a surface ship.

Lieutenant Nizovtsev straightened from his plotting table. Soviet warships had two navigators assigned, and that was all they did: navigate. The *Whale* had only one, but then it was classified a research submarine until this testing was done with the atomic power. Anton could tell that Nizovtsev was going through nicotine withdrawal. Nizovtsev pushed his dark-rimmed glasses back off his nose and leaned back over the charts.

If Admiral Katshora was correct, then he would continue as the skipper of the *Whale* once Doctor Zotkin's research was finished. The *Whale* would shift its berth from the facility to the Northern Fleet's submarine headquarters, and the flag of the Soviet Navy would fly proudly from the stern while tied up. The *Whale* would be more than a test platform. It would be the Soviet *Nautilus*.

"Skipper, target Bravo passing down our port side, sir," Antipov reported.

Anton nodded. "Sonar, bearing?"

"Bearing one six zero, sir."

"Officer of the deck, bring us up to six knots." Anton looked at the sonar operator. "BCh-3, keep the bearings coming."

"Target Bravo bearing one five nine."

"Lieutenant Antipov," Anton said, "prepare to start our turn. Here is how we are going to do it." He nodded at the sonar operator. Sonar on Boyevaya Chart three is going to keep announcing the bearing of Bravo. I want a slow turn to the left that keeps those bearings drifting to the left until our course is the same as the true bearing."

"Left-bearing drift."

"Correct," Anton said with a sharp nod. He heard the OOD repeating sonar bearings from BCh-3.

"Aye, sir."

"Okay, left one-third rudder," Anton said, and then he looked at the sonar operator. "Keep the bearings coming, Starshina. And shout if you think I failed to hear you." He pointed at the young petty officer. "You understand?"

"Yes, sir."

"Then start."

"Bravo bearing one five three."

Then for the next few minutes Anton listened to the sonar operator reporting the bearings while he kept an eye on the *Whale*'s course. If the operator reported the sound of Bravo increasing, then he'd steady up, put on some speed, and separate them from the destroyer.

He also watched the compass as the *Whale* swung from course two five zero toward Bravo. The *Whale* was on course one eight zero when the sonar operator interrupted.

"Sir, I have another target in the area, bearing two five zero."

Anton's eyebrows arched, and he looked at Antipov. "I thought the operational area was supposed to be clear."

The communications officer shook his head. "No one is allowed in the area except us and the two destroyers. With the fog topside, it is possible a merchant or fishing vessel from Murmansk has wandered into the area."

Lieutenant Nizovtsev straightened from the plotting table. "The bearing cuts through the facility."

"It might be the torpedo boat that carried Zotkin and his team out to the destroyer."

"No, sir," the sonar starshina said. "Contact has two shafts, four blades on each propeller. I estimate revolutions for about six knots, and I have a right-to-left bearing drift."

Anton visualized the information. It would mean they had a

target between them and the facility on a southerly heading, probably following the coast, considering they were only about twenty kilometers out to sea.

"I've lost it."

"What do you mean, you lost it?"

"The noise is gone." The sonar operator looked at Antipov and Anton. He pressed his earpieces against his head; then, holding them firmly, he shook his head. "One moment it was there and the next gone."

"Could it have turned away from us?"

"No," Anton said, "it would have to turn toward us for us to lose the sound of its screws."

"But we should hear their screws regardless of which direction they're going," Nizovtsev offered, his hands patting the cigarette packet in his shirt pocket.

"It's the gradient," the sonar petty officer offered. "The waters are cold, so the sound is playing weird things."

"Where is Bravo?" Anton asked. The intrusion by the unauthorized vessel was the worry of the destroyers. The last thing they needed was to run into the stern of the destroyer he wanted to use to mask their presence. Knowing the waters were masking the intruder's noise meant it also would mask theirs.

"Bravo bearing one zero zero?"

"Our course?"

"Passing one five seven," Antipov answered.

"Let's swing her around quickly," Anton said, "and steady up on course one zero zero. Increase speed to ten knots." He felt the vibration of the shafts as the submarine picked up speed in its turn. Knowing that the water and the destroyer were masking his noise from the other destroyer, he felt confident they would not hear the *Whale* sliding into position behind Bravo's baffles. Eventually he would have to break away. Anton started thinking of his next moves. Heading westward would be his next maneuver, once he had the other destroyer's screws behind him.

THEY had been there an hour and were on their southerly heading again.

"We're directly off the entrance to the covered docking area again," Shipley announced. He scanned the inside of the area, still unable to make out much in the dark. He was sure there was one huge docking area and that it was empty. Whatever had been there was no longer. If the Soviets were developing a nuclear-powered submarine, where was it? He quickly spun to the seaward side, searching for the Soviet warships picked up earlier. Maybe it was out there in the fog with the other warships?

"Where are the warships?" he asked through the hatch.

A couple of seconds passed before Weaver relayed sound's bearings to the two warships.

He had barely raised his binoculars again when Weaver shouted from below, "Captain, we have a problem!"

Shipley squatted beside the hatch. "Say again."

"Skipper, sonar has picked up a submarine—a Soviet submarine. Sound has screw turns and pump noises in the water. Both together equate to a Soviet diesel class."

That answered his question. "Bearing and range?" He saw Logan at the periscope, bent over, and taking photographs.

"Bearing zero seven zero, sir. Noise constant. Slight left-bearing drift."

Shipley sighed. "Lieutenant Logan, how much longer?"

"Sir, I am about halfway through the frames," Logan answered, leaning back to look up at Shipley.

Logan's face was red—too red. "Pull your watch cap down, Lieutenant, before you lose that pretty face."

"Aye, sir."

"And the air sampler?"

There was a moment of awkward silence that Shipley filled. "Lieutenant, are you talking with your men in the engine room?"

"Yes, sir. They are still circulating the air through the samplers, sir. According to the specs for the system, we need a minimum of another thirty minutes."

"We may not have thirty minutes. Lieutenant Weaver! You listening?"

"Aye, sir."

"Be prepared for an emergency hard to port turn and a dive to one hundred feet." Then he thought about it. "We do have a hundred feet under us, don't we?"

A couple of seconds passed. "Sir, we would need to do a depth ping."

"No!" Shipley snapped. "No pinging of any kind." One ping would alert Soviet warships, and they'd pounce all over the *Squallfish* before they could reach deep water. He started to stand up again, but instead an idea came to him. "Lieutenant Weaver, have the damage control assistant break out the Geiger counter and bring it up here."

"Aye, sir," Weaver answered.

"And have it brought up to the bridge." He stood and looked to starboard. They were around the piece of land that jutted out into Kola Bay. It looked to him as if the Soviet engineers who built this covert docking area had dumped the rocks, soil, and debris along the edges of the channel leading into it.

"Come to course one seven zero, slow to three knots."

He saw the wake behind them bend to the right as the bow turned toward the covered facility and felt the vibration of the hull ease as the speed slowed. He waited a few minutes before telling the officer of the deck that his intention was to turn the *Squallfish* as soon as they made one pass by their objective.

Shipley took a deep breath, his lungs now used to the below-zero temperature. While it might mean little, if he could have the bow pointed north toward the exit of Kola Bay, he would feel better.

"I have the intruder's screw noise again, sir."

Anton nodded. "Guess he changed direction again."

"And he has slowed his speed."

Nizovtsev stood. "Captain, he is nearly directly in front of the facility."

Anton nodded again. "Guess it is the *Bolshevik* after all. Maybe the good doctor is returning to the facility."

A few seconds passed before the sonar operator spoke up. "Sir, with all due respect, it is not a torpedo boat. It has passed back and forth in front of the entrance to the facility at least three times."

"Then if it is not a torpedo boat, what is it?"

The operator scratched his head. "I don't know, sir. I just lost them again."

"How did we lose them?" Antipov asked the starshina.

"Sir, they are in our baffles."

"Then it is either an intruder, or it is the torpedo boat, or it is another participant they did not tell us about. Either way, if the unknown participant is a lost merchant vessel, then Northern Fleet headquarters will take care of it."

Anton listened to the argument. He did not want the *Whale* to lose this exercise. A diesel boat in the Great Patriotic War against three surface ships had little chance of survival. This was an opportunity for him to show the advantage of atomic power. He raised his hand, grabbed a pipe running by overhead as a handhold, and smiled. *No gloves, no coat, and most of all, warmth*, he thought. This alone was enough to convince him.

"I can't have him in our baffles," Anton said matter-of-factly, thinking the surface Navy may have added an unidentified participant to the game. Maybe they thought he would sneak back into the facility and leave them searching an empty ocean. Submariners never trusted those who moved in only two dimensions. "Come slowly to course two one zero and let's clear our baffles."

"Sir, that will expose our screws to Bravo."

"And it will put our bow toward Alpha," Anton offered. "And Bravo should mask us for a few minutes. Steady up on a course that will take us toward Alpha." What's a little hopscotch between baffles for an atomic submarine?

On board a diesel he would be running for deep water, attempting to evade the destroyers. Was he experiencing the future tactics of the Soviet submarine force, where submarines would be the ones toying with the surface ships instead of the reverse? Atomic power meant tossing away the tactics of the Great Patriotic War. "Keep us along the edge of the drop so we still have depth beneath us."

Around him he listened to the command as Antipov changed the course of the *Whale* without the depth changing. He was impressed.

"I have the intruder again. He is making revolutions for three knots."

"Bearing?"

"Target bears two four five degrees."

Nizovtsev put both hands on the chart. "Captain!" he said in a loud voice. "I am telling you that this intruder is off the entrance to the facility. It has been there for at least twenty minutes."

"I think it might be the torpedo boat going in to drop off or pick up people."

"Sir," Lieutenant Nizovtsev said, his voice tight, "BCh-3 has said it is not a torpedo boat. Sir, it is an intruder." He shrugged. "You are probably right in that it is a wandering merchant. It cannot be a fishing vessel, because BCh-3 says it has two shafts;

therefore it has to be a big merchant vessel." Then, with a mutter, the navigator added, "Either way, it is in forbidden waters."

Anton shook his head. Navigators had too much arrogance for the duties they were assigned. They were the only crew members who had no assigned duties except navigation. They did not even have to do party-political work. Plus Nizovtsev wanted his cigarette, so anything that caused the *Whale* to surface meant he could have one.

"Thank you, Lieutenant. I will consider your words."

He looked over at the starshina who was handling the log and saw the sailor writing in it. He knew the navigator's warning had just become official. Mamadov slapped the starshina upside the head, leaned down, and said something. The sailor turned the pencil around to erase.

"Leave it," Anton said. Logs should never be erased. Line out errors, but never erase them. The Navy was not about covering up things.

"I've lost the intruder."

"Let me know if you hear him again," Anton said. Most likely it was some type of transport, even if it was not the *Bolshevik*. They probably lost it because the intruder was now going into the facility. In his mind, he saw the two fingers of land that jutted out on either side of the channel leading into the facility. If the unidentified contact was following the coast—most likely because of the fog—then its screws would be masked when it turned out to sea the first time as it maneuvered around the northernmost finger. This most recent loss of contact probably meant that the intruder was either maneuvering around the second finger or, as he surmised, was turning into the facility.

"LET'S bring her around, Lieutenant Weaver. Lieutenant Van Ness!" Shipley shouted. "Give me a course to get us out of here!"

He looked aft and saw the faint wake starting to stretch to the right as the boat turned. "Bring her up to five knots, check with the CHENG, and tell me what our battery status is."

"Aye, sir!" Weaver shouted from below.

Chief Topnotch scrambled up the ladder, tugging the Geiger counter with him. Right behind him was Lieutenant Logan.

"It's getting crowded up here," Shipley said, looking at Logan.

"Just want to see what, if any, readings you get, Captain."

"Lieutenant Logan, you are supposed to be taking photographs."

The intelligence officer nodded. "I know, sir, but they are photographs of the same thing."

Shipley raised his gloved hand. "Both of you pull your watch caps down over your faces before you get frostbitten."

Logan's watch cap had holes cut. Topnotch's did not. The chief stood there with his entire face covered. "Okay, Chief," Shipley said.

Chief Topnotch rolled the watch cap back up. Shipley looked at the Geiger counter, unlatching the top cover. He flipped the switch to on.

"It'll take at least a minute for it to have a correct reading, Skipper," Topnotch said, reaching over and tapping the meter.

"How's that?" Logan asked.

"Geiger counters detect particles of radiation measured over time. The more particles, the more radiation. Counts per minute is the metric. We call it CPMs."

"Which radiation does it measure?" Logan asked. "Alpha, beta, or gamma rays?"

Topnotch looked at the lieutenant. "All three, I think."

"Gamma is the worst. Alpha can be stopped by the skin of the *Squallfish*. Beta has some penetrating power, but gamma can penetrate almost anything, especially the human body."

"Thanks, Lieutenant Logan," Shipley said, watching the needle on the meter creep upward. "It's moving."

The other two men leaned over and watched the needle.

"Definitely got radiation in the area," Logan said.

"Doesn't your air sampler tell us the same thing?" Shipley asked.

"No, sir. It only collects samples of the air while simultaneously filtering it through a special Naval Research Lab collector. We won't know until we return what the radiation readout is."

The needle kept moving, touching the red warning area and continuing onward. The three remained quiet as they watched the needle reach as far as it could go to the right, pegged at the end of the danger zone.

"Jesus Christ!" Shipley said, almost dropping the heavy boxed system. He looked at Logan. "What does this mean?" He held the Geiger counter to the side so both Logan and Topnotch could read it.

"Sir, I think it means we have enough." Logan shook his head. "If it is reading this high this far out"—everyone looked at the cavernous opening that was now coming up on their port side as the submarine finished its turn—"then the air samplers should have more than enough proof of what we came to find out. We can state emphatically that the Soviets are conducting a nuclear project here."

Shipley handed the Geiger counter back to Topnotch. "They are developing a nuclear-powered submarine is what they are doing. You two take this to the engine room and see what the reading is on the air sampler."

As the two men turned to go, he added, "And check my boat." He said each word clipped. "If we've filled the *Squallfish* with contaminated air, I want to know."

SIXTEEN

Thursday, December 6, 1956

"I have the contact again, sir," BCh-3 reported. "It has changed course with a right-bearing drift. It is heading in the opposite direction, Captain, and increased speed to eight knots."

"Bearing?" Anton asked. This intruder was beginning to bother him.

"Bearing two niner zero, sir."

Lieutenant Nizovtsev straightened again, his hand patting the cigarette pack in his shirt pocket. "The intruder is passing again in front of the facility. I have lost count of the number of times the 'merchant ship' has passed back and forth in front of the facility."

Anton bit his lower lip and dropped his hand from the hand hold. If they can hear the screws, then the contact has to have its starboard beam to them.

"How far away are we from the facility?" he asked Nizovtsev.

"We are sixteen kilometers now, Captain."

"Give me the bearings to Alpha and Bravo," Anton asked.

"Alpha bears zero one zero, speed twelve knots. Bravo bears one seven zero, speed ten knots."

"Do we have a course on them?"

"Alpha is on a due west heading, and Bravo continues on a projected course of zero six zero, northeasterly heading."

Anton sighed. He did not want to surface to report the intruder. Why couldn't the destroyers pick him up? Maybe because the intruder was no intruder, but an unidentified participant designed to lure the *Whale* into making the wrong move. Was Katshora bent on showing that regardless of the power plant on a submarine, it was still as vulnerable as a diesel? Why would he do that?

"Repeat our course, speed, and depth," he ordered.

"Sir, we are heading north on course zero one zero at speed six knots, at sixty meters depth," Antipov reported.

Anton sighed. He looked forward and saw Nizovtsev bent over the chart with his right hand clasping a pencil, but the man's head was turned, so the navigator glared directly at him. If he kept command of the *Whale* when this was over, Nizovtsev could pack his seabag.

"Sonar, could this be another one of our warships?" Anton asked.

The sailor acknowledged the question with a nod, his head bent over in concentration. "It has two screws, sir. It is maneuvering in front of the facility. Maybe it is there in the event we try to hide—"

"It should not be there," Nizovtsev interrupted. "It is not part of the exercise." He grabbed his clipboard from a paper-clip hanger above the plotting table. "According to the exercise message, we have our two destroyers and us out here. No one else, Captain." He hung the clipboard back up. "No one else," he mumbled.

"Okay, perhaps you are right, Lieutenant. Officer of the deck, take the boat up to fifteen meters."

"SIR!" Lieutenant Logan shouted from the conning tower up to the bridge.

Shipley appeared in the opening.

"They are disconnecting the air sampler, sir. We have enough data to answer Admiral Frost's questions."

Shipley nodded, unsure if Logan saw it. "Lieutenant Weaver!" Shipley shouted down.

"Aye, sir."

"What is our battery status?"

"Sir, I am waiting for Lieutenant Bleecker to respond."

"Give him another call and increase our speed to ten knots. Where are the contacts?"

"Sir, the two surface warships bear one one zero and one five zero. The submarine we hold at one one zero."

"Any signs of detection?"

"No, sir. They're probably just outside the range of the fogbank."

"If we have them, then they probably have us. I want to stay on the surface until we lose their cavitations. Assume they know we're here, but think we're some lost surface ship."

Weaver acknowledged as Shipley stood, raised his binoculars, and swept the seaward side off their starboard beam. He had this tight, sinking feeling in his stomach. He thought he had lost this friend of combat after World War II, but here it was back—*tight as ever*—reminding him of the danger they were in.

"Sir!" Weaver shouted. "The air sampler is off. Forward battery compartment is reporting six eight percent capacity. Aft battery compartment is at full capacity and ready."

"What's wrong with forward battery?" Shipley asked.

"Bleecker is on his way forward to check it out."

"THAT was Lieutenant Bleecker on the sound-powered," Fromley said. "He says they are showing less than seventy percent battery capacity in here."

Potts did not answer.

Fromley walked over to the feet sticking out from between the end of the aft side battery and the bulkhead. He tapped the end of the shoes with one of his. "Potts, you awake?" The foul-weather jacket was pulled over Potts's head.

The shoes rolled over, pointing up, and the jacket came down. "What's the problem, From? Can't a sailor take a nap without his shipmates waking him?"

"I just had Lieutenant Bleecker on the sound-powered. I think he is on his way here."

Potts pushed himself to a sitting position, then grabbed a steel beam running along the bulkhead to pull him out of the cramped area and onto his feet. "How long ago?"

"Just now. He says our compartment is showing less than

seventy percent charge while the aft compartment is registering one hundred percent. He wants to know what the problem is up here."

"What did you tell him?"

"I told him you did the cell checks and I logged them."

Potts grabbed Fromley by the collar. "When you gonna learn to keep your mouth shut?"

"But that is what we did."

"What we did was what we usually do, and that is making up readings so we can sneak in a nap while they keep boring holes on the surface. When was the last time either of us got a good night's sleep? You think out there in the Barents with the wind, waves, and currents, rocking and rolling this thing like it was a fair ride?" Potts hitched up his pants. He stroked his chin. "Christ, it's cold," he said, blowing air to see the white breath cloud that came out.

"We better get to checking the cells," Fromley offered.

"Yeah, we better. This time *you* check them and *I'll* write them down."

Fromley shuffled from one leg to the other. "But you're better at the batteries than I am."

"I'm better at anything than you are, From." Potts reached forward and poked the sailor in the chest a couple of times. "And don't you forget it."

Potts grabbed the logbook. "Start at the nearest cells and work your way aft. Read the first meter, which shows the charge status, and then the second meter will show the condition of the cell to discharge. The first one you want pegged to the right. Anything less than that should show you how charged it is. The second meter will show you the ability of the cell to pass along its charge with the other cells to the electrical motor. You got that?"

"Yeah, I got it. I know all that."

Potts took a position near the forward hatch, which was latched down tight because of the general quarters the skipper had ordered when they surfaced. You'd think the battery compartment would be warm with this much charging going on, but no—*like the rest of the Squallfish*—the cold Arctic weather turned the metal-encased warship into a refrigerator.

Fromley began to work his way down the line of cells, reading the two meters and reporting them to Potts.

At the logbook, Potts wrote the readouts down along a data column, recording each cell.

"Hey, we got a problem here," Fromley said.

Potts laid the logbook on the small shelf. "What is it?" he said with a snarl. "You got a hangnail or something?"

"It's these three," Fromley said, pointing but not touching the three cells. "Come here," he motioned.

Potts walked down the narrow walkway to where Fromley squatted. He squatted beside him.

"Look at the meters. They show no charge, but this meter shows them in the danger zone."

"What the fuck!" Potts said. He leaned down and tapped the meters. Neither moved. "That can't be right. We been charging for nearly two hours. We should be nearly one hundred percent charged."

Fromley whimpered. "You know what this means, don't you?"

"Yeah," Potts said. "It means we have a few bad cells."

Fromley shook his head. "No, it don't. It means none of these cells on this side are going to work. If one fails, they all fail. They're connected in series. With these three out of whack, it means none of these will work."

The after hatch opened and Lieutenant Bleecker walked in, securing the watertight hatch behind him.

Fromley let out a deep whimper. He knew if they had checked the cells as they should, they would have caught this casualty.

It took less than three minutes for Bleecker to figure out what happened. He walked over to the sound-powered phone and ordered Gledhill to send the engineers from the after battery compartment to the forward one. It would take at least an hour to repair these three cells. When he hung up the telephone, he turned to Potts and Fromley.

"You two lay to your berthing areas and remain there. You are not to leave it except to go to the head or to the mess decks. If I see either of you outside of your berthing area, I will personally throw you overboard."

Tears streamed down Fromley's cheeks. Potts's face blanched white.

"But Lieutenant—" Potts began.

"Fuck you, Potts; and you, too, Fromley. You two may have killed us. We are miles away from international waters and because you two didn't do your jobs you have put us in a position where if we have to run for it submerged, we might as well surrender because we will only have the aft battery compartment to power the electric motor. All because you two gun-decked your duties." Bleecker was angry. He never should have given these two a second chance. He thought Potts worth saving and that Potts had the potential to turn himself into a good sailor. Fromley! Fromley was a sycophant who could go back to being a civilian. He would never make a sailor. Why Bleecker thought Fromley was harmless was unforgivable. He knew he was responsible for this, even as he knew both of them were going to be court-martialed if they got out of here alive.

He looked around the battery compartment, then back at the two sailors standing in front of him. "Get out of my sight. I never want to see you two again until the court-martial."

"Court-martial," Fromley wailed. "I only did what Potts told me to."

Potts spun and with the full weight of his hefty body behind the blow, he hit Fromley upside the head. "Keep your mouth shut!"

The blow knocked Fromley off balance, sending the sailor, his arms outstretched, onto the cells charging on the port side. Sparks flew and Fromley's body shook as the powerful electric current charged through him. Smoke erupted from his coat. The lights flickered on and off.

Bleecker whirled around to the forward bulkhead and hit the emergency shut-down switch, stopping the flow of electricity from the diesel engines to the forward battery compartment. He turned and shoved Potts backward against the aft hatch. Potts's head hit the handle, cutting his head open and knocking him out. Blood started to puddle on the deck. Potts slid to the deck in a seated position, his head resting on the hatch.

Bleecker grabbed Fromley and jerked him off the open cells, lying him on the deck. The man was still breathing. He grabbed the sound-powered phone from its handset and called the control room.

"Medical to forward battery compartment on the double. We have a man down—electric shock." Then as an afterthought added, "And send me four stout sailors with handcuffs."

"WHAT'S going on down there?" Shipley asked from topside.

"Don't know, sir; the lights flickered for a moment."

"Call Lieutenant Bleecker and ask him what the hell is going on."

Weaver turned away from the opening and was heading toward the sound-powered handset when the grinding noise of someone calling reached him.

He lifted the handset, and on the other side was Bleecker. He listened, taking in everything, snapping his fingers for the logbook. When Bleecker hung up, Weaver shoved the logbook into the hands of the signalman. "Write this down: man down in forward battery room; electric shock."

Weaver grabbed the microphone to the speaker system. "Medical to forward battery room on the double," he broadcast.

Weaver turned. "Handcuffs?" He turned to Boohan. "Senior Chief, you hear that?"

"No, sir," the COB said from near the helmsman. "Something wrong."

"Someone hurt?" Boohan asked.

"Someone got electrocuted. Lieutenant Bleecker wants a working party of four men in the forward battery compartment. He wants them to bring handcuffs."

"You want the damage control party away?"

Weaver shook his head. "The CHENG didn't ask for a damage control party." He looked at Boohan. "He just asked they bring handcuffs."

Boohan turned back to the helmsman. "Sounds like a party."

"Take care of the working party, if you would."

Weaver stepped over to the hatch. "Skipper!"

"Handcuffs?" Boohan said, shaking his head. "What have those sailors done?" he muttered to himself.

Boohan slid down the ladder to the control room, opened the hatch, ducked, and hurried aft. Reaching the mess decks, he stuck his head in the door.

Crocky looked up. "Hi there, COB, you come for—"

"Crocky, grab your crew and come with me."

"Senior Chief, I got lunch to cook and potatoes on." Crocky pointed with the metal spoon at a nearby huge pot, water boiling, and steam floating up from it.

"Then turn them off. We got a medical emergency in the forward battery compartment."

"What's that got to do with us cooks? Somebody want us to feed them?"

"Ah, Crocky, don't give me a rough time. Just get your crew together."

"Let me secure the heat to everythin' but the oven. You think we're goin' to be gone for a while? I have biscuits cookin'."

Boohan let out a deep breath. "This could be life or death and you're worried about biscuits?"

Crocky wiped his hands on his apron, reached over, and turned off the heat for the pot. Crocky had Washington grab the two Filipino stewards, and within three minutes the four of them were following the COB, who shouted for them to put on their coats. The mess was warm, but once outside of the cooking area, the rest of the boat was below freezing.

"Can't you tell us what's goin' on?" Crocky asked Boohan as they hurried down the passageway, passing through the control room en route to the forward battery compartment.

"I don't know myself. I just know they want handcuffs."

"It's livin' too long in Scotland if they want handcuffs. They want whips, too?"

Boohan opened the hatch leading into the forward battery compartment. Potts's head fell into the opening. A moan escaped his lips, and the man's eyes fluttered.

"Jesus Christ!" Crocky said, stepping forward, grabbing Potts by the shoulders, and pulling him out of the battery compartment. He laid him onto the passageway deck leading toward the control room. "Washington, take care of this sailor."

Washington saw the face of his nemesis through the blood running from the gash on Potts's head. Taking care of Potts was the last thing he wanted to do.

"Do it," Crocky said again, his finger pointing at the man. "Make sure he ain't bleedin' anymore."

Boohan stepped inside. Fromley lay on the deck. First Class Pharmacist Mate Story leaned over the man, his stethoscope on Fromley's chest.

"He's breathing."

Bleecker was breaking out tools from the locker on the side of the forward bulkhead.

"Lieutenant, what you need?" Boohan asked.

"Get both of them out of here is what I need. And when they come to, handcuff them to their racks."

Blood was everywhere, and the smell of burning cloth and an

odor that Bleecker and Crocky had smelled before filled the compartment.

"I don't think this youngun is going to need handcuffs," Crocky offered softly, speaking directly to Bleecker.

Bleecker nodded. "Just handcuff Potts to his rack."

Without saying it, both World War II veterans knew the smell of burned human flesh. Beneath those clothes the doctor was peeling off Fromley, he was going to find fried skin. How much would determine whether Fromley lived or died.

Doc Story looked up from where he squatted. "Sorry, Lieutenant, but both of these men need to go to medical." Doc slid the coat away from the chest. The dungaree shirt was wet beneath it.

"Doc, I wouldn't try to undress him here." Crocky reached out and touched the pharmacist mate on the shoulder. "Let us take him to medical before you do anythin' else. You undress him here, what you gonna do then?"

Boohan looked at them and then said to Crocky, "You're right. Have your men take them to medical and stand guard. I'll bring the handcuffs along shortly."

Potts moaned. "What happened?" he muttered, opening his eyes. Washington's face was the first thing he saw. Potts's eyes widened. "What the hell . . ." Then he shut his eyes. "My head hurts."

Washington leaned down, his mouth beside the sailor's ear. "God hates you, Potts. You goin' down, man. They gonna love that little butt of yours where you're goin'."

Potts reached up to push Washington away, but Washington grabbed the hand and looked at Santos. "Take the other hand." The two men pulled Potts upright. Washington had never stood next to Potts until now. There wasn't much difference in height, but Potts did have him on weight. "Stand up," Washington said.

"Take him to medical," Story said as he stood. "We're going to need a stretcher for Fromley."

Bleecker turned back to the toolbox, grabbing hand tools. Pliers, two screwdrivers, and wire cutters came out. "You think you can move him into the passageway? I've got to start repairing the damage here."

Crocky, with the help of Marcos and Story, lifted Fromley from the deck. Fromley let out a horrid scream that filled the compartment. Story and Marcos jumped. Bleecker never batted an eye over the pain-filled scream. There was time for sympathy and punishment later. Right now, the boat needed these batteries.

Bleecker squatted in front of the cells where Fromley had landed. Neither he nor Crocky was surprised.

SHIPLEY stood and lifted his binoculars. This was not good news. He had one fully charged set of two batteries in the aft compartment. Looking around, he saw the faint light of what would not only be dawn but also would be the lightest it would be all day at this time in the Arctic.

"Captain!" Weaver shouted.

"I hear you, Lieutenant."

"Sir, sound is reporting the submarine is blowing ballasts, sir."

Shipley squatted beside the hatch. "Any change in its course, speed, location?"

"Ballast tanks blowing. Rapid left-bearing drift along our starboard beam toward our bow. I would say the submarine seems to be closing, sir. Not much of a drift. It's off our starboard bow, and if it keeps on this drift, the sound will pass down our starboard side. What's that?" Weaver asked someone inside the conning tower.

Shipley waited.

"Sir, sound seems to think the submarine is heading back toward the shore. He can't hear the sub's screws right now. He doesn't think it's that far from us."

Shipley bit his lower lip. Most likely they had sailed into the middle of an antisubmarine warfare exercise. Probably meant the exercise was over and the Soviets were preparing to head back into port for breakfast.

If the Soviet submarine was blowing ballasts and close to the *Squallfish*, that meant he had sufficient depth beneath the boat to dive. Except that the *Squallfish* had only one bank of charged batteries; four knots would be their speed submerged if he had to evade the Soviets in their own backyard.

"Lieutenant, increase speed to ten knots. Get us some maneuvering room away from the shoreline. Tell Van Ness to start giving us some headings back to the narrows. And tell me what that does to the drift on the sub contact."

He would use the diesels as long as he could.

Weaver acknowledged the order. Below, Shipley heard the officer of the deck giving orders to the helmsman. Shipley glanced aft and saw the faint wake start to curve to the right as the *Squallfish* started away from the shore and headed toward the narrows. They should be far enough way to avoid the destroyers.

"Sound says we now have a slight left-bearing drift, Skipper!"

Shipley raised his binoculars, scanning the visible area of the fog-enshrouded bay. He looked at the topside watches. "We got a contact ahead of us somewhere, off our starboard bow with a left-bearing drift," he said to the two men, who nodded. "Keep your eyes open and watch for any motion out there between our bow and along our starboard side."

The two sailors replied "Aye, aye, sir" in unison. Both looked to starboard.

"But also keep alert around us. I don't want all three of us watching right for the contact on our starboard side and us run aground on the port side."

One of the sailors pushed the other, pointed to the left side of the *Squallfish*, and so the watches divided their duties.

Shipley squatted beside the open hatch again. "Lieutenant Weaver," he said, "wake up the XO."

"Contact's bearing drift has slowed, Skipper."

"Very well," Shipley replied. This meant that their speed was changing along with the range, but which way and at what range? He was still too close to shore, but even as he watched, the shoreline crept behind the surrounding fog. He gave the Soviet submarine's closest range as a couple of nautical miles—four thousand yards—but neglected to take into consideration how enclosed bodies of water such as Kola Bay played games with underwater noises.

"WE are approaching twenty meters depth, Captain," Gesny said.

"Level off at fifteen meters," Anton ordered.

Across the conning tower, the planesmen spun their brass wheels. The tilt of the surfacing submarine eased as the *Whale* leveled off at periscope depth.

"Up periscope," Anton said, squatting so his eye could ride the scope up. Never surface a submarine in the middle of a bunch of skimmers, make sure you know the surface situation before you ever surface, as a former commander taught him.

He spun the scope around. "We still got a lot of fog out here," he said without moving away from the eyepiece.

"We could signal them," Antipov offered.

"I doubt either of us can see the other through the fog. Sonar, where are Alpha and Bravo?"

He listened as station BCh-3 reported the bearings of the two destroyers. Alpha remained northeast of them on a westward heading, or drift. Bravo was louder. Sonar thought the *Whale* was somewhere off the port stern of Bravo; therefore Bravo was heading northeasterly.

"Sir, we could use underwater comms," Gesny offered.

"Okay. Tell them we're surfacing and tell them where we hold them."

"Aye, sir."

"And while you're at it, tell them about the intruder near the facility."

"It appears the intruder has decided he shouldn't be there," Gesny added. "Sonar says his screw rotation has picked up."

Anton leaned away from the periscope. "Sonar, you still think it is a warship?"

"Its bearing drift has increased, sir."

"And?"

"I think we are closer than we think to it," the sonar technician said hesitantly.

Anton put his eye back on the periscope. "Bearing to intruder?"

"Intruder bears two eight zero degrees, Captain."

Anton watched the built-in compass on the scope as he aligned the lens on the bearing. "I see nothing. The fog is still lifting."

"Noise is increasing," sonar said.

Double shaft, left-bearing drift. He moved the scope, looking for the telltale profile of a merchant towering over the water somewhere out there. He saw nothing. "I don't see—" he said as he leaned away just as a bit of motion caught his eye and caused him to stop talking.

Anton quickly leaned back into the scope, squinting. "I thought I saw something," he mumbled.

"Contact is steady on bearing two six three degrees."

Anton shifted the alignment slightly. The fog looked darker here, but then, on the other side of this fog, was the shoreline.

"What is our range from shore?" he asked, leaning away from the periscope.

"Ten kilometers," Nizovtsev muttered.

"Lieutenant Antipov, do we have contact with the officer in tactical command?" he asked, referring to Admiral Katshora.

"I have told the skimmers we are surfacing. They are turning away to clear the area."

Anton nodded. "Then let's take the boat up."

Chief Ship Starshina Mamadov pulled the handles of the hydraulic main vent manifolds. The sound of compressed air pushing out the last of the seawater echoed through the boat. The boat began to rise.

"SIR," Weaver shouted through the open hatch, "sound reports no bearing drift on the contact! I repeat: no bearing drift!"

No bearing drift meant one of two things. Either the contact was on a collision course with the *Squallfish*, or the contact was separating from her. Since sound could not hear the screws, then that meant . . .

"All ahead full!" Shipley shouted.

"Sir, submarine is blowing ballasts again! It's coming up!"

The diesels kicked in. Shipley grabbed the railing as the *Squallfish* picked up speed.

ANTON leaned forward, putting his eye against the periscope, rocking slightly to adjust his vision. A dark shape filled the lens for a moment; then a violent blow rocked across the *Whale* and the submarine rolled to the right as the bow of the *Squallfish* rode over the periscope mount rising out of the sea.

SHIPLEY picked himself off the deck, grabbing one of the watches who had fallen on top of him. "You okay?"

"Yes, sir."

"All stop!" he shouted.

Lieutenant Weaver scrambled up the ladder. "You okay, Skipper?"

"I'm fine; get back below."

"DIVE! Dive!" Anton shouted. Water rushed into the conning tower. Mamadov grabbed the main vent manifold handles and pulled them all the way back. The sound of seawater filling the ballast tanks echoed through the compartment.

"Right full rudder. Level off at twenty-five meters."

The sound of metal scraping metal came from above for a few seconds before it stopped. The *Whale* and the *Squallfish* had separated.

"What the hell was that?" Nizovtsev asked.

"We just got run over," Anton said.

He looked at Antipov. "Send a Mayday message to the OTC. Tell him we have collided with an unauthorized vessel in the area."

Around him, sailors and officers rushed, turning valves and rerouting electric and water lines. Water was roaring in from a warped main hatch.

"Sir, recommend we go no lower. We should surface immediately," Gesny said.

Anton nodded. This was peacetime. The Great Patriotic War was more than twelve years ago. He had for a moment, without thinking, reverted to the tactics of that war: go deep and evade.

"You are right, XO. Sonar, where is the contact?"

"Sir, his screws have stopped."

"We have contact with the OTC. He is closing our area."

"Then let's get on the surface before they show up." Anton looked at the sonar operator. "You still have the intruder?"

"Sir, he is all stop. Last bearing was two eight five."

"We need to know where he is before we surface. Turn on the sonar and ping him," Anton said.

"DAMAGE report?" Shipley shouted through the hatch.

A full minute passed before Weaver spoke up.

"We are showing no damage forward, sir."

The XO's head poked up through the hatch. He looked up at Shipley and climbed the rest of the way out. "I'm here to relieve you."

"XO, I need you below. I still have the conn. Get me a course to get us the hell out of here."

The sound of a sonar pinging reverberated through the hull of the *Squallfish*.

"Sir!" Weaver shouted. "I think they have us."

"Have us. We ran across them," Shipley said quietly.

“I have a submarine surfacing!” sonar shouted.

Shipley and Arneau exchanged glances. Shipley squatted. Give me all ahead full, Lieutenant Weaver.” He looked up at Arneau. “Get down there with Van Ness and get us the hell out of here. We are going to have the entire Soviet Navy raining down on us inside of an hour. If they’re going to catch us, they’re going to have to do it in international waters.”

SEVENTEEN

THE diesels kicked in. Slowly at first, then the *Squallfish* knifed through the water away from the point of collision.

"Tell CHENG I need those batteries ASAP!"

"He's working them, sir!" Weaver shouted from below.

Shipley lifted his binoculars.

"I have a submarine surfacing off our starboard beam!" one of the watches shouted.

Spinning his binoculars in that direction, Shipley saw the forward section of a submarine rising at a forty-five–degree angle out of the water, splashing down as the tower surfaced. Must have been at depth, he thought at first, seeing the angle of the rise. Then he realized that they could never have collided if the other submarine—*Damn!* He had hit a Soviet submarine in their waters.

The periscope was pushed to one side. Before the *Squallfish* merged into the fog, the one thing he noticed was that the damaged submarine had no snorkel. He spun the glasses to the stern. In that quick instant before the fog closed around them, he saw that the Soviet submarine had no main induction valves.

As the *Squallfish* sped off hidden in the fog, Shipley heard the clang of a hatch hitting a deck.

"Logan, you get a photograph of that submarine?" Shipley shouted down the hatch.

"I got it, sir; I got it. Did you see . . ."

The rest of Logan's sentence was lost in the wind as Shipley stood. He wrinkled his face, feeling the burn of blood forcing its way into his cheeks.

"Twelve knots, Skipper, heading to fifteen!" Arneau shouted from below. "On course zero two zero. Distance to narrows is ten miles!"

Shipley acknowledged. Would they cover ten nautical miles before the Soviet Navy closed the narrows?

The cold from the past hour on the bridge seemed to evaporate as the *Squallfish* ran from Soviet Navy units somewhere off their starboard side. How quick the Soviets reacted would determine their margin of survival.

THE main hatch flew open, slamming onto the deck. Anton scrambled up the ladder and onto the bridge. His first looks were on the damaged periscope and bridge stanchions. Whatever hit them had done this, but overall it was minimum damage. It could not have been a large merchant. Motion caught his attention off his port bow. His eyes widened as the stern half of a submarine disappeared into the fog.

"Damn!" He turned to the sound tube and lifted the brass protective cover. "XO! Call the OTC and tell them we have collided with the other submarine in the exercise."

"There is another submarine?"

"I just saw one disappear into the fogbank on a northerly direction."

"But—"

"I know. They should have told us. They didn't. Now we have this." He was furious. Admiral Katshora should never have allowed the second submarine into the exercise without telling him. Submarines had been lost by collisions at sea and under the sea.

ON board the lead destroyer, the merchant captain's report had finally been read ashore and included in the consolidated daily sighting message sent to Admiral Katshora. He had read it while eating an early breakfast of bread, cheese, kasha, and two cups of tea. He also had discounted all the sightings except the one near Iceland and the one off the northern coast of Norway. Those two were probably American or British, who kept a continuous patrol trying to catch his submarines when they ventured forth.

He found both amusement and frustration whenever he read of the American and British patrols. They searched for something seldom sent forth. He had the finest submariners in the world, who only lacked modern submarines to sail. Atomic power would change that.

He grunted when he read the short message on the sighting near the mouth of Kola Bay. He looked at the time of the sighting: late yesterday afternoon. No one would be foolish enough to be in Soviet waters. He would find and sink them just as he did the Germans. Once again his sightings report was filled with sea life erroneously identified as submarines.

The telephone rang in his cabin. As he picked up the receiver, his door burst open and Doctor Zotkin rushed into the cabin, shouting something about his *K-2* project being rammed by a merchant vessel. And what was Katshora going to do about it? The doctor's reputation and tests were at stake. Katshora calmly hung up the receiver.

He wondered for a moment what the expression would look like on Zotkin's face if he picked the good doctor up by the seat of the pants, tossed him into the passageway, and kicked his ass all the way to the bridge. No one came into an admiral's cabin without first being invited, much less burst into it shouting at one.

Katshora stood without interrupting the nonstop tirade vomiting forth from Zotkin. He grabbed his heavy fur winter cap. The flaps were tied up along the sides, and on the front of the cap was the emblem of a vice admiral.

"Come with me," he finally got to say when Zotkin paused for a second to take a breath. "Let's go to the bridge and find out what the situation is."

"The situation is dire! Dire, I tell you! Everything I have worked for has—"

Behind Katshora, the telephone started to ring again. When he opened the door and motioned Zotkin ahead of him, the slight wind inside the ship blew the consolidated daily sighting report off the table, the papers scattering across the deck.

Katshora shook his head as Zotkin rushed by him and he shut the door. Minor irritants. Ankle-biters. Things that matter little sometimes build up. Zotkin kept his monologue going as they walked along the passageway. Zotkin's pace would separate him from Katshora by a few steps; then the scientist would slow down long enough for him to catch up. Listening to Zotkin, Katshora nearly smiled as he realized how unusual this must seem to a man who had never seen combat or spent a deployment on board a warship.

Zotkin obliquely criticized Katshora about how things had been going, specifically pointing out that it had been Katshora who had forbidden the scheduled tests in the Barents. Zotkin stopped for a moment to allow an oncoming sailor to pass, but when the sailor saw Katshora, he snapped to attention and pressed himself against the bulkhead.

The vice admiral stepped around Zotkin, by the sailor, and continued toward the bridge. Testing in the Barents in the dead of winter was a bad idea. It was an idea no sailor would have thought of. He never tried to tell the politically connected Communist scientist that weather is not subject to the whims of the Kremlin. You never truly knew what you said or did that earned you the free one-way trip to Siberia, though he doubted the dreaded Siberia could be much different from the long winters of Severomorsk.

At the hatch entering the bridge he turned to Zotkin. "Here you will have to keep quiet while we check on the condition of my submarine."

"But I am the test director."

"You are right. You are the test director. But I am the vice admiral who is going to make sure you have your submarine back so you can continue your tests."

Without waiting for a reply, Katshora opened the hatch and stepped onto the bridge to a chorus of "admiral on the bridge" announcements. He saw the motion of the starshina writing his presence on the log. Ironic how close the Soviet and American Navies were in their traditions and how they did their operations.

"What is going on, Captain?" Katshora asked the skipper of the destroyer.

Captain Second Rank Kuvashin saluted. "The *Whale*—"

"It is the *K-2*, not the *Whale*," Zotkin interrupted, irritated.

Katshora glared at the scientist, who quieted. Zotkin reached up and buttoned the neck of his knee-length winter coat.

"Go ahead," Katshora said to Kuvashin.

"The *K-2* was surfacing near an unauthorized vessel that had entered the operational area. It appears it surfaced beneath it."

"How does a submarine surface beneath a vessel? Did he have contact on it?"

"Apparently so, Admiral."

"Then they collided. Who is this intruder?"

"We had been tracking him. We put him down to either one of our patrol boats or a lost merchant vessel." Kuvashin glanced out the front windows of the bridge. "Fog is still hampering our tests."

"I think the tests are over with. Did you try to contact the intruder over bridge-to-bridge and warn him away?"

"Yes, sir. We have been trying since the collision, but he has yet to reply."

Zotkin opened his mouth to speak. Katshora looked at him. "One moment, please, Doctor." He looked at Captain Second Rank Kuvashin. "What is the damage?"

"Captain First Rank Zegouniov reports his periscope is damaged and unusable. He has sustained integrity damage to the conning tower. The main hatch has been warped. He is already working to correct it, sir."

"And the forward torpedo room that was damaged last week? Is it still secure? No problems?"

Kuvashin turned to the officer of the deck. "Lieutenant, ask the *Whale* the damage status for the rest of the submarine, specifically the forward torpedo room."

Katshora glared at Zotkin before the scientist could correct Kuvashin. Katshora turned back to the captain of the *Soznatelnyy*. "And the other vessel?" he asked.

"No report, sir."

"I want to know about the other vessel."

The bridge-to-bridge radio bleeped, and the sound of static interrupted the two men. Kuvashin motioned at the OOD, who handed him the microphone. "*Whale*, this is the commanding officer, *Soznatelnyy*; report, please. Admiral Katshora is listening."

"Admiral, Captain First Rank Zegouniov reporting, sir. The other submarine seems to be okay. It is heading northeasterly toward what we were calling contact Alpha. That would either be the destroyer *Soznatelnyy* you are on, or the *Byvalvyy*."

Katshora grabbed the microphone from Kuvashin. "What other submarine? There is no other submarine out here."

A moment of silence passed before radio static announced the pressing of the talk button on the other end. "But sir: we collided with another submarine. It has to be one of ours."

Katshora glanced around the bridge. Everyone was looking at him. Some openly, but most flickered a look from the corners of their eyes. *What submarine?* he thought. Then he recalled the sighting report he had read from the merchant captain only a few minutes ago. The British would not be so stupid as to send one of their submarines into Kola Bay. The Americans would never do something like this; they were too concerned with the safety of their superiority.

Katshora looked at the helm and saw a chief starshina standing near the helmsman. "Chief, go to my stateroom and bring me the consolidated daily sighting report. It is on the table beside my chair."

The chief saluted.

"Do it quickly."

Katshora raised the microphone and pressed the talk button. "Can you describe the submarine?"

"No, sir; I only caught a glimpse of the stern as it disappeared into the fog."

"Do you have a course, other than northeasterly?"

"That is a negative, Vice Admiral."

Katshora looked at Kuvashin. "Do you have the contact on radar?"

"No, sir. We have had it on contact, but land smear masks the contact. We have problems detecting the *Byvalvyy*, and she is only a few kilometers from us."

"Bring the ship to general quarters. Order the *Byvalvyy* at best speed to the restricted passage. Tell them to conduct active antisubmarine efforts. Tell them I believe we may have an unidentified submarine in the operational area." He paused, then added, "Tell him he has authorization to sink any unidentified ship between him and the entrance to Kola Bay."

Kuvashin hurried to the other side of the bridge, where the communications officer manned a bank of secure radios.

ANTON heard the orders Katshora was giving over the open speaker. The admiral must still be pressing the talk button.

Gesny's head appeared in the hatch. "Captain, we have a

problem! Forward torpedo room is flooding. I have a damage control party en route. The chief engineer is attempting to use the bilge pumps to maintain the flood. I have a damage control party en route to rig portable pumps."

"What is our depth?"

"We have more than one hundred meters beneath us, sir."

"Distance to shallow water?"

"Ten, possibly eleven kilometers to shore, sir. Another five to six to fifty meters depth."

"Turn the *Whale* toward shore." He'd beach the *Whale* before he would allow this to set back the Soviet Navy in achieving atomic power.

Shouting came from below the XO. Gesny bent below the hatch. Anton caught some of the words, and a chill went up his spine.

"Captain, the damage control team is unable to reach the forward torpedo room. They are running hose from where the waters are reaching to here. The forward torpedo room is flooded. The watertight hatch leading from the torpedo room to the passageway running alongside the reactor was never closed." Gesny paused, then said again, "It was never closed."

Looking aft, Anton saw the stern of the *Whale* dip beneath the calm waters of the bay. Water was slowly covering the aft portion of the *Whale*.

"Blow the safety ballast!" Anton ordered. The safety ballast was filled with seawater along the bottom of the submarine. The safety ballast tank worked much like a keel on a surface ship. It helped to offset the clumsiness of a surfaced submarine against the wind, wave, and current actions of the sea. It also provided immediate weight for submerging.

Blowing the safety ballast may compensate for a time against the flooding, but it would make the *Whale* less maneuverable.

The sound of hydraulics and pressurized air blowing out the seawater vibrated through the boat.

"Turn to course zero niner zero; all ahead full!" he shouted. Would they make it?

"XO, use the low-pressure air blower and make sure we have every bit of water emptied from our ballast tanks."

"Aye, sir."

Seconds later, Anton heard the whine of the air blower pumping freezing air from the Arctic into the ballasts, blasting out the last of the water from the tanks. For a moment he worried that the air might actually freeze the water, but he quickly pushed it from his thoughts. The decision was too late to reverse.

The *Whale* started to turn. Atomic power providing the push needed to overcome the pull of the freezing water filling the forward end of the submarine. Would they make it? What would happen when the water reached the reactor? He imagined a mushroom cloud over Severomorsk. What would Elena say to that?

"Speed? What is our speed?"

Gesny's head disappeared below. "We are making twelve knots, Captain!"

"I want all ahead full!" *Surely atomic power can provide more than twelve knots*, he thought.

"We are all ahead full, Captain. We are angled down by the stern. The atomic power is also fighting to keep us above the water, sir."

"The safety ballast?"

"Nearly empty, but not much difference in angle, sir."

Anton grabbed the microphone and passed along the bad news to Katshora. Katshora ordered the *Soznatelnyy* all ahead flank, intending to tow the *Whale* if needed.

BLEECKER held the end of a copper wire in one hand while he stripped the insulation from it with his knife. He needed sixty copper lines to bypass the bad cells. Standing above him, Gledhill watched.

Two electrician mates, Morgan and Garcia, worked their way opposite Bleecker, checking each cell along the starboard battery, reading the charge and pass-through before going to the next one methodically and professionally, as they had done so many times during their short careers.

Finished with this wire, Bleecker laid it on the deck alongside the others. He pulled another strip of wire off the roll, doing a rough measurement with his arms, and then cut it. He quickly shaved away the insulation on each end of the wire, did a quick look to ensure he was satisfied, then laid it alongside the others.

As he worked, Bleecker listened, but his concentration was on the wires and the next necessary steps to bypass the four damaged cells. If Fromley didn't die, he may kill him himself.

One of the cells might be all right, but it held 25 percent less charge than the cells ahead of it. From the damaged cells to the aft bulkhead, every cell was barely charged. The electric shock to Fromley had discharged all the cells connected along this series. A dead cell took longer to recharge than one with some charge. Bleecker did not understand the physics of the matter, but any type of charge seemed to jump-start the process.

"Anything I can do, Lieutenant?" Gledhill asked.

"You're already doing it, Petty Officer Gledhill. Keep answering the questions from the bridge. I hope to have the wires needed ready in the next ten minutes."

"Will it work?"

"If it doesn't, then let's hope Russian is an easy language to learn." He snapped the knife shut. "Check the air. What is the hydrogen level?"

He was bypassing the bad cells. If this worked, they should be able to reach a 90 to 95 percent charge quickly. That was as long as he could keep two of the diesels dedicated to charging. No way would they achieve 100 percent.

Gledhill checked the gauge. "Still high, Lieutenant. A little bit below four percent."

"That's a little better." Bleecker looked at the hatch leading to the forward torpedo room.

He laid this latest wire along with the others on the deck. He stood and hurried toward the intercom, bumping Morgan on the way. Hitting the button, Bleecker called the control room.

When he finished explaining what he wanted to do, he returned to the wires lying on the deck. He picked up one and began connecting it to the plus terminal on the charged side of the damaged cells. The other end he connected to the negative terminal of a good cell. He glanced at the master safety switch. It was still off.

He could not start recharging until the hydrogen level was lower, even if the safety manual said anything below 4 percent was acceptable. Too many times those safety manuals were written by ass-sitting sailors whose sea time could be counted in days instead of years.

No, there was nothing he could do until the hydrogen level was down to about 1 percent. Nothing, that is, unless the skipper wanted to take a chance on an explosion. His head snapped up. There was one thing, but it was up to the skipper, and it wasn't something submarines usually did in hostile waters. Especially when they were bolting for open ocean.

"SKIPPER!" Arneau shouted from the conning tower. "Bleecker wants to open the forward main hatch, sir. He has a reading of slightly under four percent hydrogen in the forward battery compartment and has to clear it."

"Four percent!" *Jesus Christ, the good news just keeps rolling in*, Shipley thought.

Shipley looked at the forward main hatch. With this speed on, he had wakes coming up nearly level with the deck. He needed those batteries, but he needed to get through the narrows before the Soviets blocked the egress points. If water hit the batteries, he ran a risk of not only ruining the batteries but also filling the *Squallfish* with sulfur dioxide, which could kill everyone.

ANTON shouted down the sound tube, "What is our depth reading?"

"Depth now showing eighty meters."

That was twenty meters less, but still too deep. If the *Whale* was going to sink, he had to be in shallow water, where it could be recovered.

"Damage report?"

"Sir, we have rigged deflooding for the aft portion of the *Whale*, but it does not seem to be working. They are still rigging the hose toward us. They are going to have to run them up through the conning tower to the bridge and over the side."

"Tell them to quicken the pace. They are taking too long." He looked at the stern of the *Whale*. The aft escape hatch above the torpedo room was hidden beneath the surface. Forward, the bow was riding higher.

He could have told them that. The forward escape hatch was well above the waterline. That was another egress point for the hoses. "Condition of the reactor room?"

"We don't know, sir. Lieutenant Tumanov just reported that he has ordered the reactor room abandoned. He says it is taking on water."

"Who gave him the order to abandon his post?" Anton shouted, anger flushing through him.

"Tumanov says it is on automatic. Nothing they can do with water seeping through the hatch between the engine room and the forward torpedo room."

"Seeping is not flooding," Anton said. He raised his binoculars and scanned the dark shadows of the coastline.

"Distance to shallow water?" he asked.

"Sir, if I may suggest, we are less than ten kilometers to the facility. We are not going to get much shallower here," Gesny said, finishing his sentence as his head appeared in the hatch. "We might be able to make it to the facility."

It was an idea. It was better than searching for a shallow place to sink.

"Make it so, XO. Take charge, change course as you need, and get us heading toward it."

"I will relieve you shortly," Gesny said.

"No!" he snapped. "We are in our right places until this is decided. Present speed?"

"We are still making twelve knots, Captain. The electricians are reporting a strain on the shaft, and the electric motor is nearing the red zone, but we are making way."

"Very well."

Gesny's head started to disappear belowdecks.

"Wait!" Anton said, bending down to the hatch. Their faces were less than a foot apart. "Keep us afloat for another forty-five minutes, XO. If the men can do that, we will be inside and at the dock."

Gesny nodded and disappeared down the deck.

Anton stood and looked at the aft portion of the submarine. If the water reached the reactor before they reached the facility, then everything would disappear in the explosion. Regardless of the power source, water hitting superheated temperatures created explosions. The reactor would be scattered over the hillside, surrounded by the body parts and metal of the *Whale*.

"Open the forward hatch, XO, but be prepared to shut it. I cannot slow down. Tell Bleecker and the torpedomen to expect some water, since it is breaking across the bow. I'll keep it open ten minutes, no longer."

Moments later, the forward main hatch opened and clanged on the deck. A sailor crawled out, wearing his heavy foul-weather jacket and a life jacket over it.

Shipley lifted the megaphone. "Hey, you!"

The sailor looked up.

"Get below, and when you get the word, then secure the hatch. Understand?"

The sailor nodded and gratefully went back belowdecks.

The last thing he needed was a man washed overboard. He shivered from the decision he would make if that happened.

THE bagpipes of a secure communications synching up caught Katshora's attention. The communications officer grabbed the handset. He could not hear what they were saying, but he was focused on the report coming from the *Whale* through the bridge-to-bridge radio.

Zotkin had finally run out of steam and was sitting in Katshora's chair near the starboard bridge wing. Someone had given the scientist a hot cup of tea. Hopefully it would keep the man quiet.

"What do you think, Captain Kuvashin?"

"I do not know, Admiral. If the submarine makes it back to its berth, then it would make it much easier to raise if it sinks—I think. I don't know enough about the test to understand its importance, but it seems to be important to our scientists."

Katshora nodded. Not everyone was aware of the atomic engineering plant on board the *Whale*. Most thought it was testing new submerging and weaponry technology. Only those with security clearances such as his understood the true purpose of the tests.

"Go ahead, Captain Zegouniov, and try to make the facility. We are closing your position."

After Anton had acknowledged Katshora, the aged admiral turned to Kuvashin. "Are we ready to tow if necessary?"

"Yes, sir, Admiral. I have two hawsers laid out aft. My chief starshina boatswain mate has his crew standing by."

"If we have to tow the *Whale*, Captain Kuvashin, I want to execute taking the submarine in tow the first time. We cannot afford to have any hiccups on doing this. Understand?"

"Yes, sir." Kuvashin went to the *Soznatelnyy*'s intercom and called the officer in charge of the tow party. He relayed not only the importance, but also ensured that the young lieutenant understood who would be held responsible if it failed.

Meanwhile, Katshora passed along the fallback plan to Anton so the submarine would be ready for towing. After they discussed it, Katshora and Anton realized that if the *Whale* was to be towed it would be bow first because the water over the aft portion of the submarine was approaching the conning tower. The bow seemed to be rising rapidly. He leaned against the railing, compensating for the tilt of the deck.

"HYDROGEN is down to three percent," Gledhill reported.

The intercom rang. Gledhill answered it. It was the control room asking how long.

"How long what?" Bleecker asked, a little miffed. "How long until we can finish the repairs? How long until we can start charging? How long until we have a full charge?" The knife slipped, nicking his finger. He sucked it for a second. "Tell them when I know they'll know," he said with a snarl. Then he mumbled, "Unless that's the captain asking."

Gledhill looked at Bleecker and then at the toggle switch, as if trying to decide how to respond to Lieutenant Weaver.

Bleecker rose from his squatting position and went to the intercom, wiping his bleeding finger on his pants.

"Alec, Greaser here. Here is what we have to do, and here is a projected timeline. Right now we are down to about three percent hydrogen in the forward compartment room. At this rate it's going to be another ten minutes until we reach two percent, when I'll feel safe about throwing the safety switch back to charge. Repairs are going to take another ten to fifteen minutes. Then, it's going to take about an hour to charge the batteries. I think that sums up the timeline."

"Wait one," Weaver acknowledged, as if knowing Bleecker was already heading back to his repair work.

"Jesus," Bleecker said, returning to the intercom. Alec was most likely relaying his words to Shipley. Bleecker watched the hydrogen reading as he waited. It was below 3 percent. Four percent was the critical point.

"Greaser, Alec here. Skipper says go ahead and finish repairs. Hold off on cranking up the recharge until he gives the go-ahead. He is also closing the forward main hatch. Too much water."

"He understands we run the risk of having a spark light off this hydrogen, if we don't lower it?"

"He understands. He also understands that we're at three percent, so there is little chance of that happening."

"Not little chance; less chance."

"He said go ahead and finish the repairs, but hold off on reconnecting the forward batteries to the diesel."

Bleecker started to argue about this book learning the skipper was throwing at him, but Shipley was the skipper, and they were running toward the narrows. He sighed. At least the skipper was a veteran and understood what combat required.

He looked at the wires on the deck and then at the battery. "Should take about another forty minutes to finish," he said.

"Want me to pass that along?" Gledhill asked.

Bleecker shook his head. He had told them an hour. If he finished in forty minutes, then everyone would be happy. He squatted back down alongside the damaged cells. They would be outside Kola Bay on the surface with another twenty to thirty minutes to go before the forward battery room would be fully charged. The skipper was going to want to submerge as soon as they passed the narrows. Damn, he wanted to submerge now. What's the purpose of a submarine if you couldn't submerge?

"Okay, everyone out of here but me."

"I'm staying," Gledhill said.

"You heard me, LPO; get your butt out of here."

"Lieutenant, you are going to have to throw me out."

"Me, too," Morgan said.

"And me," Garcia added with a Spanish accent.

"You're nuts if you don't."

"We're dead if we don't get this back online. Right, Lieutenant?"

"Not necessarily," Bleecker said, squatting back down on the deck. He lifted the first of the wires. "The Soviets could send us somewhere where it is really cold."

"That's argument enough to convince me I ain't leaving," Gledhill said.

"Us either," Morgan said, slapping Garcia on the chest. "If this is as warm as it gets up here, I don't want to see something colder."

"Okay, then it's your funeral."

"All of ours," Garcia answered, laughing. "Where's the tequila when I need it?"

"Gledhill," Bleecker said, "this is what we are going to do." Bleecker outlined the checks they would do. He would connect a wire to a positive or negative terminal on the good cell, then he would trail the wire over the bad cells, handing the wire to Gledhill. Gledhill would take the wire to the opposite positive or negative terminal and hold it. Then Bleecker would announce the terminal of the wire he had connected, and Gledhill would announce the terminal to which he intended to connect.

The terminals had to be of opposite polarity, or when the charge was restoring, the damage would be even worse than it was now. The wrong terminal would cause a short circuit, which could spark a fire, which would set off any hydrogen content in the atmosphere. The *Squallfish* could find itself on fire while running from the Soviets.

"Morgan, Garcia: you two finish up the checks on that side."

The two electrician mates acknowledged the order. They were starting down the last line of cells and would have to work around Bleecker and Gledhill.

Bleecker picked up the first wire and connected it. "Positive," he said, handing the end to Gledhill.

Gledhill held the wire above a terminal. He leaned down, looked at it, and then said, "Negative."

"Connect."

Bleecker watched for a spark. He held a rag draped across his wrist in one hand, and the tail wrapped around the cut on his finger. If a spark happened, maybe he could cover it before the hydrogen blew.

When nothing happened, Bleecker started with the second wire, and as they progressed with no explosion or spark, their pace quickened. But it was tedious. A careful job, but in the race to restore the cells to a configuration that would work, careful was as important as speed.

Behind him, Garcia and Morgan continued their cell checks. Bleecker glanced at the fuse box and the down handle. He was almost fanatical about watching it, as if it would flip up on its own. Once that handle was pushed forward, DC power would rush into the forward battery room and start charging the batteries. The sooner he and Gledhill finished, the sooner Shipley would have the battery power to submerge and disappear to the battlefield that belonged to the submarines.

"Lieutenant, we got two cells here that are below charge," Morgan said.

Holding a wire in his hand and without standing, Bleecker turned to look at the cells Morgan was indicating. The meter showed less than 50 percent charge. *What is wrong with those cells?* Bleecker thought.

Bleecker turned back to the repair work, connected the wire, and then trailed it across the damaged cells to the hands of Gledhill. "Take a quick look and tell me what the next cell reads," he said over his shoulder to Garcia.

"Negative," Bleecker said.

"Positive," Gledhill answered.

Bleecker watched Gledhill connect the wire to the correct terminal.

"Fifty percent," Garcia said.

"And the next one?"

"Forty-five percent."

"And—"

"Sixty percent."

"Good. Do the others show about sixty percent, or better?"

"The next one shows nearly seventy percent."

"Okay, the fifty percent cells are low as well as those past those cells, but they have some charge. So just log them, then move on down the line and keep checking them. A partial charge is better than no charge." He looked at the Navy clock on the wall. It read 0830 hours.

"Done," Gledhill said, leaning back.

Bleecker started on the next one.

EIGHTEEN

Thursday, December 6, 1956

AHEAD, the outline of the dark, cavernous opening to the facility shaded the heavier fog caused by colliding temperatures off the sea and shore. At the same time, the entrance to the short channel leading into it appeared ahead of the *Whale*.

"Time?" Anton shouted into the sound-powered tube.

"It is zero eight three two, sir!" someone in the control room replied.

"Speed?"

"Ten knots."

They had lost two knots of forward motion in the past thirty minutes. Noise from the hatch drew his attention.

Chief Ship Starshina Bersi Mamadov emerged, tugging a dingy yellow hose behind him. Anton stepped aside as the chief of the boat pulled himself onto the bridge. Mamadov looked at Anton and said, "Hose."

Behind the chief of the boat came Lieutenant Kalugin, helping pull the hose up from two decks below.

Anton was surprised to see the deputy chief engineer up here.

Mamadov looked at Anton. "The bilge pumps are shit, sir." He nodded at the hose. "We have the portable pumps ready to start, and this is the nearest opening to pump water out."

"Very well." He kept staring at Kalugin, who was bending over the hatch, pulling the hose up onto the small bridge area.

"We are attempting to run a third hose to the forward main hatch," Mamadov continued.

"Keep me appraised, Chief Ship Starshina."

Mamadov lifted a leg over the railing, found footing on the small ladder, and then hoisted himself over the side. Kalugin handed the end of the hose to Mamadov. Standing on the ladder, the chief of the boat kept playing out the hose until it hit the deck; then he scrambled as fast as a heavy foul-weather jacket allowed back onto the bridge.

"That should do it," the chief ship starshina said with a shiver. "There is wind whipping around the tower," he explained.

Mamadov reached into a side pocket and pulled some line out. He quickly tied the hose to the railing. "That should hold it."

Anton glanced over the side. The Arctic wind was pushing the hose forward and against the tower.

The two men turned to leave. Anton put his hand out and touched Kalugin on the shoulder. "Is there anyone in the reactor compartment, Lieutenant?"

Kalugin shook his head. "No, sir. I am helping out the damage control team."

"Where is the chief engineer, Lieutenant Commander Tumanov?"

Kalugin glanced at Mamadov, then back at Anton. "I do not know, sir. He may be . . ." Kalugin started to say. Instead he shrugged, and added, "Sorry, Captain; I do not know."

"Send a starshina to find him and have him come up here, if you would," Anton said to Mamadov.

The two men scrambled down the ladder into the conning tower. A minute later, water rushed through the hose, the pressure of the water pushing the sides of the canvas taut. Over the side of the bridge the rushing sound of water gushing onto the deck could be heard.

"Sir, I have a Spokoinyy-class destroyer starboard aft," one of the watches said, pointing behind Anton.

Anton turned and lifted his glasses. The bow of the *Soznatelnyy* emerged from the fog, the bow pointed dead on toward the *Whale*.

A burst of static on the bridge-to-bridge radio was followed by Admiral Katshora's distinct, raspy voice. "We have a visual on you, Captain Zegouniov. What is your situation?"

Anton pressed the talk button. "Admiral, we are nearly at the channel leading into the docking area."

"I can see that, Captain. What are your intentions, and what is your situation?"

"My intentions are to moor where we set sail from. I have internal and portable pumps working on the flooding situation—"

"And the flooding?" Katshora interrupted.

"And my speed is diminishing," Anton finished. "The flooding continues to gain, but we have just got the portable pumps online."

"And the atomic engine?" Katshora asked on the unsecured comms.

Over the bridge-to-bridge, Anton heard the voice of Zotkin telling the admiral not to mention atomic power. Anton would have smiled if the situation he faced had been different. He knew the words "atomic power" would be circulating through Severomorsk by nightfall, after the destroyer docked. It would be through the fleet within a week. It had been no accident that Katshora had compromised the purpose of the tests over the open radio waves. Maybe he wanted the Americans to know? Maybe he wanted the Soviet Navy to know? Maybe it was a good thing for morale? And just maybe the admiral was tired of Zotkin's arrogance and attitude and wanted to show who was the flag officer in charge of this activity?

Katshora continued, "You look as if only the forward portion of the *Whale* is above the waterline. You have a steep angle, Captain. Your bow is quite high. From the bridge to the stern, you are submerged. We will stand off at one hundred meters in the event you need us. I am prepared to take you under tow."

For the next few minutes the two veterans of the Great Patriotic War discussed how they would effect the towing if or when it was needed. Anton did not like the idea of the *Soznatelnyy* taking them under tow, but the exigencies of the situation overrode the tradition of the skipper to resolve his own problems. Towing would be a quick way to gain control. He raised his binoculars and scanned the entrance channel. The problem was that he did not believe he had time to put the *Whale* under tow before it would sink. The only salvation lay in getting pierside. Ashore, the quick-reaction team would be rigging deflooding stations along the pier. Between pumping water out and blowing high-strength pressurized air into the boat, he might be able to keep it afloat long enough to seal the hull around the aft torpedo room.

* * *

BLEECKER stood. He used the back of his hand to wipe the sweat from his forehead, though the temperature in the forward battery compartment was below thirty degrees. "That should do it," he said to Gledhill.

Bleecker turned to Morgan and Garcia. "Good job." The two electrician mates had finished minutes earlier. He walked over to the intercom and pressed the switch down, checking to make sure he was connected to both the conning tower and the control room.

"Go ahead," Weaver said when Bleecker called.

"We're ready to turn on the power in the forward battery compartment."

"Wait one," Weaver said.

Almost immediately, Weaver replied. "XO says go ahead, Greaser."

Bleecker grabbed the handle to the fuse box and shoved it upward. The buzz of power filled the compartment as the diesel engines diverted to the batteries started charging them.

"No sign yet," Gledhill said.

Bleecker nodded, his lips pursing outward. "We won't know for a few minutes. Those hands won't move fast as the cells charge." He looked at the three sailors. "Now we wait."

Five minutes later, Bleecker exhaled a deep breath. "Petty Officer Gledhill, I'm going to make a quick trip through the aft battery compartment and the two engine rooms; then I'll be back. Morgan, you and Garcia keep an eye on those low-charged cells and make sure they're taking a charge."

They acknowledged his order as the World War II veteran walked toward the aft watertight hatch. "I will swing by the conning tower and report to the skipper along the way." As he stepped out of the compartment, he turned to Gledhill. "If anything happens, you shut down the power and shout for me. Keep an eye on the hydrogen density. We don't want to waste all this repair effort, now, do we?" he asked with a grin as he shut the hatch and secured it.

"CAPTAIN," Arneau said from the hatch, "we are three nautical miles from the narrows, making twelve knots."

"Lieutenant Van Ness got us on track?" Shipley asked.

"Steady on zero three zero, sir. We should be entering the shallow waters within the next fifteen minutes."

From the fog off the starboard stern side the sound of a naval gun firing reached the *Squallfish*. The chill of recognition rippled through him, his mind back to World War II as he listened intently for the whistle. The whistling sound of a shell passed overhead, to explode about half a mile off the port beam.

"What the hell was that?" Arneau said.

"We've been located, XO. Double-check the Christmas Tree, our general quarters conditions, and tell Greaser I need those batteries ASAP." He added quietly, more to remind himself than to tell Arneau, "As long as we hear the whistling, we're okay."

"Aye, sir," the XO said, sliding down the ladder into the red-lighted conning tower.

Shipley raised his binoculars and scanned the fogbank, trying to locate the ship firing at them, when the second shell was fired. He doubted they could see him in this mess, so the naval gunfire was being targeted by radar. Turning forward, he searched the waters in front of the *Squallfish* as the sound of the third shell being fired reached his ears. The second shell landed off the port stern side at about five hundred feet, and then almost immediately the third shell hit two hundred feet off his starboard bow. They had him bracketed.

Where were rough waters when he needed them? Submarines had a low profile, but in rough seas they were nearly invisible when surfaced.

Bleecker's head appeared in the hatch. "Sounds to me like we have a destroyer on our tail, Skipper," the CHENG said with a tight smile.

Shipley nodded. "Does seem that, Greaser." The fourth shell was in the air. "What's the status?"

"We're charging now."

"I'm going to need them once we're through the narrows."

The fourth shell hit on the starboard side about three hundred feet out. "They seem to have our range," Shipley said.

"Hard to hit a submarine, Skipper."

"Takes only one, though."

"I'm on my way aft, Captain. The aft battery compartment is fully charged. We can run on snorkel if you want. I have two diesels charging, but can always bring one of them online if you need the speed."

Shipley nodded. "That would slow our charging of the forward battery, Lieutenant. What's the status on the forward battery compartment?"

Bleecker bit his lip as the sound of the next gunfire reached the boat. "I'd say about between fifty to seventy percent. Got some dead cells and damaged cells, but we gerry-rigged a fix around the dead one."

"What happened?"

The sound of a shell whizzing overhead drowned any response. "I'll have a full report, Skipper," Bleecker answered as he dropped down the ladder.

"We're in the narrows, sir!" Weaver shouted from the conning tower.

Shipley squatted. "Give me one ping for depth."

A few seconds later, Weaver shouted up, "We have one hundred forty feet beneath the hull."

Not much, Shipley thought, but it was enough to take the *Squallfish* off the surface. "Stand by to dive!" he shouted. He motioned the watches belowdecks, quickly following them, securing the hatch before dropping to the conning tower deck.

"Take her down to fifty feet."

He watched and listened as Weaver gave the necessary orders. Chief of the Boat Boohan pulled open the hydraulic control handles. The sound of water rushing into the ballast tanks filled the compartment.

"Vents open," Boohan said.

The planesmen spun the brass-nickel wheels. The chief of the boat watched the gauges above the planesmen from his position as the bow of the *Squallfish* slid beneath the waves.

"Bow planes rigged," Weaver added.

"Trim forty," Boohan said.

The planesmen turned the wheels slightly, easing the diving angle. Boohan pushed the control handles closed.

"I make our depth at fifty feet, Skipper," Weaver said.

"Very well. Up periscope." Shipley squatted and rode the periscope up, flipping the handles out and putting his eye against the eyepiece. It broke surface, taking a few seconds for the water to cascade off the lens. He spun the scope, catching a splash of a shell a couple of hundred feet off his port stern.

"They still shooting?" Arneau asked from the ladder as he emerged from the control room.

"Yep. They're still firing, but I don't have a visual on them yet," Shipley answered. Why would they stop firing? By now they had a course and speed on the *Squallfish*. If he had to start evasive maneuvering in the narrows, he had no idea of the depth on either side of them. The clock read 0845 hours.

ANTON fell forward against the bridge railing as the *Whale* shuddered. "What the hell was that?" he shouted.

"We don't know!" Gesny shouted back.

The *Whale* picked up speed for a moment. It was in the channel leading into the facility. Another ten to fifteen minutes and Anton would have the *Whale* tied up alongside the pier.

"Give me time, XO. Ten minutes, that's all we need," Anton said.

"Yes, sir," Gesny replied as an explosion shook the *Whale* and the normal sounds of an alive warship suddenly ceased.

Anton felt the drift of the *Whale* from its forward momentum. He bent over the mouthpiece. "Right full rudder." Glancing down the hatch, it was dark in the conning tower. Then the emergency lighting system lit up. The noise of the water being pumped over the side ceased.

"What happened?" Anton shouted into the mouthpiece.

"Right full rudder," Lieutenant Antipov replied.

"We are checking, Captain," Gesny answered.

When a minute passed without an answer, Anton made a decision that haunts commanding officers who have made it for the rest of their lives. "Officer of the deck, prepare to evacuate the boat." He could not use the words "abandon ship"; not yet. His throat would not let those words pass.

"Prepare to evacuate the boat," Antipov repeated, more a question than a statement.

"Have the men not involved with damage control wrap up against the cold and prepare to come topside when so ordered." It was only a hundred meters to the rocky sides of the channel. If the men had to swim for it, they had a chance. Most would not make it. Even this close to shore, the Arctic waters could suck the heat from your body in seconds.

"Aye, sir." A second passed, then Antipov added, "Sir, without power, we are no longer able to pump water."

He lifted the bridge-to-bridge radio and pressed the talk button, but no sound emerged. There was no power.

"Starshina!" he shouted to the sailor on the aft portion of the bridge. "Send a signal to the *Soznatelnyy*. Tell them we have lost power. Am grounding the *Whale* on the starboard side of the channel."

The starshina grabbed the portable signal light and quickly sent the message to the destroyer trailing the *Whale* a hundred meters astern.

If that explosion was the water reaching the atomic reactor, then he was surprised. It should have been catastrophic.

Gesny's head showed in the hatch. "Seems our electric motor has decided not to play with us, Captain. It is barely working."

"The reactor?"

Gesny shrugged. "Apparently it is still okay inside the sealed engine room. But waters are quickly reaching the forward hatch to it."

"Where is Tumanov? I sent for him nearly thirty minutes ago."

Gesny shook his head. "Who knows where Zotkin's chief engineer is, sir? I can send someone to find him."

Anton shook his head. "Should see him soon, XO. Let's get the men up above the waterline and prepare them to"—he paused for a moment—"to evacuate the ship, if need be."

"We have less than eighty meters of water beneath the keel, sir. Even if we settle her on the bottom, the bridge will be below the waterline."

"We need to prepare for them to leave the boat."

"I believe we still have some time, sir. I recommend we leave the men belowdecks, where we still have some warmth."

Anton nodded.

"Is the skipper ready for me to relieve him?"

"Too close to the goal to do it now, Commander Gesny."

"Sir," the starshina said, "the *Soznatelnyy* asks what they can do. And they are closing us. They want to take us under tow."

"Maybe we should flood the forward ballast tanks, Captain?" Gesny offered, his head emerging once again through the main hatch.

Anton looked at the XO for a few seconds, then shook his head. "I am thinking that if we shove the bow onto the rocks, the stern will settle on the bottom."

"Are we sure it will settle on the bottom, or pull us off the rocks and onto the bottom with it?"

Anton shook his head. "Do you have another suggestion, XO?"

Gesny pursed his lips for a moment. "I do not, Captain."

"Then let's put the bow to rest on the rocks. As soon as I give the word, flood the stern tanks. That should settle it onto the bottom as the bow comes to rest on the rocks."

When a few seconds paused between them, Gesny asked, "And then evacuate the boat?"

"If we are still above the waterline, we will evacuate the boat with the exception of minimum crew. The flooding should stop if we have a steep enough angle."

"We could refloat it when repairs are done."

"It will cover the aft escape hatch."

"Skipper, we would have to do it through the main hatch here and possibly the forward hatch."

Anton looked toward the bow of the *Whale*. Ice covered the deck. The approaching rocks lining the channel were less than fifty meters away. "We'll have to do it through the bridge."

"Speed?" Anton asked in the mouthpiece.

"Five knots and slowing," Antipov replied.

Anton nodded and looked down at Gesny. "Make it so, XO." He started to tell him to use the low-pressure air blower to pump air into the forward ballast tanks to complete the emptying of the ballasts. Without electricity, it would be hard to do. The normal engine room apparatuses limited atomic power to their limitations.

"Flood the aft ballast tanks, Commander Gesny."

Anton turned to the signalman. "Pass the following to the *Soznatelnyy*."

"TELL the engine room to bring three diesels online," Shipley said, his hands gripping the handles of the periscope. "Report when ready."

Weaver acknowledged the order, quickly hitting the intercom and passing the instructions to the maneuvering room.

Shipley looked aft, expecting to see the warship emerge from the fogbank at any time. He didn't understand why they had yet to catch up with them. Maybe the skipper of the warship had more restrictions in the narrows than imagined. If a surface ship had restrictions, then there had to be such shallow water around the channeled area that if he tried to take evasive action, he could find himself running aground. Or worse, sunk.

He saw two back-to-back splashes aft of the *Squallfish*'s position to indicate that the warship was still firing at them. The rapid succession showed that the warship was picking up tempo. If more than one warship was out there, the firing would be constant.

"Three online," Weaver reported.

It would slow the charging of the batteries in the forward battery compartment, but escape was more important now.

"Speed?"

"Twelve knots."

"Give me eighteen knots."

"We'll have cavitation, sir. The enemy will know where we are."

He leaned away from the periscope. "I think we can agree that the enemy already knows where we are." He leaned toward the eyepiece, then pulled back. "We have to get out of the narrows. XO," he continued, his voice calm. He leaned away from the periscope and looked at Arneau. "XO, ensure aft tubes are all loaded."

He saw the shocked expression, as if the idea of firing torpedoes brought home the precariousness of their situation.

"Sir, we were ordered not to engage," Lieutenant Logan said.

Shipley's head snapped around, his eyes angry with the intelligence officer. "What would you suggest, Lieutenant? We surrender, or we die?"

Logan said nothing. The intelligence officer looked down at the canvas bag at his feet that held the camera from the periscope.

Arneau turned to the intelligence officer and in a soft voice added, "Lieutenant Logan, you should go below and make sure you and your men are prepared to destroy any classified material you may have with you."

Logan nodded, grabbing the bag from the deck, thankful for a reason to leave the conning tower.

Shipley leaned forward to take another look just as a shell hit near the periscope and the snorkel. The boat shook, knocking Shipley and Weaver off their feet. For a split instance Shipley was back in World War II, undergoing depth charges.

Boohan grabbed an overhead pipe, his knees buckling, but he

remained upright. Arneau fell across the plotting table, knocking Van Ness to the deck. Freezing Arctic water burst along the seams of the periscope, soaking Shipley to his senses. This was 1956, and that was naval gunfire.

A voice shouted from the intercom. It was Lieutenant Bleecker. "We got flooding around the snorkel!" he shouted.

"Take her up to twenty-five feet!" Shipley shouted as he pushed himself up from the deck.

The planesmen spun the wheels, and the deck tilted as the boat moved upward. The water stopped coming in around the periscope. Shipley buttoned his wet coat. At this depth the conning tower was above the waterline. The bulk of the boat remained submerged.

"Eighteen knots, Skipper," Weaver said.

"Ask CHENG if the snorkel is still leaking and if it is functional."

A few seconds passed before Shipley heard Bleecker answer that the leaking had stopped and he could still use the snorkel.

"Keep her at eighteen knots." He turned to Arneau. "XO, get the damage control teams on these leaks. We're going to have to submerge again in fifteen minutes." Shipley estimated fifteen minutes. It could be sooner, but fifteen was the most he figured they could afford.

Shipley grabbed the periscope. The scope turned, but with a strain on the hydraulics. Water dripped on him with every turn of the scope. The lens had a crack in it. He hoped it was an inner lens. He aligned the periscope so he could see aft.

"Time to go topside again."

"You're soaked, Skipper. I can do it."

"After the damage control teams are set, get a dry set of foul-weather gear on, XO, and then come relieve me."

Without another word, Shipley climbed the ladder and spun the wheel, opening the main hatch.

"Topside watches, man your stations on the double," Weaver said from behind him.

Once topside, Shipley lifted his binoculars and spun them aft, expecting to see who was firing at them. Wherever the warship was in this fog, if its radar suddenly reflected the *Squallfish*, it would know one of its shells had hit the sub.

Shipley leaned down to the hatch. Arneau was nowhere to be seen. "Lieutenant Weaver, prepare to fire aft tubes one and two."

"Roger, sir; aft tubes one and two."

He would only fire them if necessary. Survival was important. Regardless of his orders, bringing the *Squallfish* out of Soviet national waters was more important than holding fire and being sunk.

"Bearing, sir?" Weaver asked.

"Use sound bearing, Lieutenant. I have no visual on him yet."

"Aye, sir."

Belowdecks he heard the sonar technician passing bearings to the warship. He had not ordered the outer doors opened to the torpedo tubes yet. When he did, a good sound operator on the opposing warship would hear the noise. At eighteen knots, he knew the skipper of the ship firing on them would realize the *Squallfish* was running.

"Sir, bearing two zero zero; no range."

"Make range at three thousand yards, officer of the deck." Regardless of the lucky hit on *Squallfish* by the warship, these shells were small in comparison to his memory of some battles in the Pacific. Small shells meant smaller main armament, which most likely meant, as Boohan surmised, that they had a destroyer on their tail.

"Set shallow," he ordered through the hatch, envisioning the sailors in the aft torpedo room using their mechanical key to change the default setting to ten feet. A long run at that shallow depth might throw the torpedo off, but if he had to fire, he doubted the target would be at long range. It would be a down-the-throat shot.

"Bearing two zero zero; angle on the stern twenty starboard!" came Weaver's cry through the hatch. "Noise signature increasing. Skipper, sound says the enemy has increased his propeller revolutions."

Shipley trained his binoculars along the bearing provided by sonar. *So, the warship has decided to close and finish the job*, he thought.

Two sailors scrambled up the ladder and took their positions as surface watches.

"One of you keep watch forward. Don't want to run into a vessel coming toward us. You," he said, pointing at the sailor on his left. "You watch the other directions. Our opponent is off our starboard stern area and approaching."

The whistling sound of another shell passed overhead, to explode a couple of hundred feet off the port beam of the

Squallfish. Another ten minutes. *Give me another ten minutes and in this fog I may be able to lose him. That's all I ask, Lord.*

"Sound increasing, same bearing, two zero zero. He's closing us, sir!"

"I know, Lieutenant. Tell aft torpedo room to open outer tubes one and two."

Belowdecks in the aft torpedo room, Petty Officer Darnell, the tube captain wearing the bulky sound-powered telephone, stood with legs spread between the two banks of torpedo tubes.

"Open outer tubes one and two," Petty Officer Darnell said aloud. He pushed the sound-powered speaker on the headset and acknowledged the order. The conversation moments earlier abruptly ceased.

Chief Torpedoman Kester acknowledged Darnell, "Opening outer doors tubes one and two." Not only was Kester the senior person in the torpedo room, but also his job was to work the manifold of valves and levers to open and close the outer torpedo tube doors.

Darnell's eyes narrowed as he fixed on the gauge board between the torpedo banks. He pulled his gloves off and jammed them into a small crevice between the torpedo tubes. Darnell rubbed the fingers on his right hand together a few times before raising the hand, poised to fire the torpedoes manually if the solenoid firing mechanism in the conning tower failed.

"Outer doors tubes one and two opened."

Darnell passed the word to the conning tower and the control room.

THE *Whale* was settling hard by the stern. The tilt of the deck caused Anton to hold on to the bridge stanchion to keep from sliding backward. He braced for when the boat hit the rocky bottom, though in the back of his mind he knew—*he just knew*—that he would get his bow on the rocks before that happened. The speed was slowing, but they were still moving forward.

"The bow is out of the water," Anton said.

The *Whale* was less than fifty meters from the rocks and debris that made up the man-made channel. Motion to his left caught his attention. He looked. It was the *Soznatelnyy*. The destroyer had sped past the stern of the *Whale*, putting its stern to the submarine port beam. *Ten minutes. Give me ten minutes and I will have the stern of the* Whale *beached and in position for refloating. That's all I ask. Ten minutes.*

A voice filled a megaphone from the *Soznatelnyy*. "Captain Zegouniov! We are prepared to take you under tow, sir!"

He had no megaphone to answer. The cold waters churned as the *Soznatelnyy* put on reverse engines. Anton estimated that the destroyer was fifty meters from him.

Anton turned to the signalman. "Tell them we are about to beach the *Whale* with bow on shore."

The signalman nodded and flashed the message.

"Captain," Antipov shouted from the conning tower, "we have slowed to three knots, sir! Making way another minute; maybe two; no more!"

It wasn't enough. He needed another five to six minutes to make the shore.

On board the *Soznatelnyy*, sailors were rushing around the stern of the destroyer. Two of the boatswain mates on board had the line-firing guns loaded and aimed at the *Whale*. Without waiting for direction, the two sailors on the destroyer fired.

"Watch out!" the starshina on the starboard side shouted.

Anton looked up. The monkey fists on the end of the lines were in midair, arching toward the *Whale*. Why in the hell did they fire? He had no one on deck to grab them, and monkey fists have been known to kill a man. Both lines angled down and splashed in the water on the other side of the stern portion of the *Whale*.

"What's our depth?" Anton asked the officer of the deck.

"We have twenty meters beneath us, sir. And our speed is barely making way now. What are your orders?"

Anton nodded. On board the *Soznatelnyy*, the sailors were hand over fist pulling the lines back on board for another firing.

By now, with the stern settling downward and the bow well above the waterline, it would be impossible for the *Soznatelnyy* to take the *Whale* under tow. It would be like pulling an anchor. It would endanger the destroyer.

"Tell them to fire those lines again only with my permission!" a voice shouted across the open water.

The raspy voice on the megaphone told him that was Katshora. The admiral must be thinking the same thing. How can you tow a ship already half sunk?

"Captain Zegouniov, this is the admiral. Good luck. We are standing by to evacuate the ship."

Anton pulled himself around to the side of the bridge where he was more visible to the destroyer. He raised a hand and saluted.

"Depth beneath us?" he asked through the voice tube. Slight waves moved away from the bow area. The *Whale* was still making way forward.

"We have sixty meters beneath us, sir," came the reply.

Taking a deep breath, he opened the sound-powered mouthpiece. "Flood the aft ballasts, Lieutenant." *Let's hope I haven't taken us to the bottom.*

The bow rose above the waterline nearly four feet.

The *Whale* shook as its stern hit the graveled bottom of the man-made channel. What little forward motion remained came to a slow all stop. He looked at the nearby rocks where he had hoped to beach the bow.

"Lieutenant, tell the men to evacuate the *Whale*! Open forward main hatch and use the main hatch."

"Sir?"

"Abandon ship!"

Anton turned to the signalman. "Tell the *Soznatelnyy* that we are abandoning ship." Now that he had used the words and made the decision, it became easier to say.

The groan of a ship in distress drew his attention to the bow. What had been several feet above the waterline was beginning to settle down. Even with the forward ballasts empty, the weight of the water in the AFT torpedo room was pulling the boat under.

"The inclinometer shows a two-degree forward change to our trim, Captain!" Gesny cried as he climbed the ladder to the bridge. "Sir, you are wet."

"It is the Arctic, XO. What should one expect?" He nodded at the bow. "We may not have saved the *Whale*," he said.

"But we tried, sir. This is not your responsibility. The intruder did this. When we catch him, he will not live long enough to tell his family of—" Gesny said, his words short and angry.

"No! Not yet. We are not done yet!" Anton shouted. "Quick! Pressurize the aft ballast tanks! Refloat them!"

"Sir, the men."

"Tell the crew to continue. They have three minutes to abandon ship." Anton turned to the signalman. "Tell the destroyer to get his boats over here *now*."

"Aye, sir," Gesny said, a slight smile breaking his face. The XO dropped through the hatch.

Anton heard the pressurized air pushing the water from the aft ballast that moments earlier he had flooded. He reached over and flipped the light switch. The light came on. He still had power coming from the reactor in the flooded part of the boat.

Shouts and the sound of hydraulic gears on board the *Soznatelnyy* told him the motorboats of the destroyer were being put into the sea. Anton looked at the stern of the destroyer, and standing there, holding on to the safety lines, was Doctor Zotkin. A moment of sadness for the man's plans filled his thoughts, but the here and now was of more importance. He had a crew and a boat to save.

"Give me speed!"

"We are showing two knots, sir," Antipov shouted back through the tube.

The forward hatch flew open, and men started pouring out.

The rocks were inching closer. Only a few more minutes. Anton lifted the megaphone. When the *Whale* beached, the boat would stop abruptly. He did not want his men tossed into the water. He warned them to hold.

Two minutes later the bow of the *Whale* crashed onto the rocks, knocking the crewmen forward to the deck and tossing Anton against the bridge railing.

"Flood the aft ballast tanks!" he shouted into the tube.

He turned and looked aft. The deck tilted as the stern went down again. This time when it hit the bottom, the shock was less. Anton turned back to the forward portion of the half-sunken submarine. He watched, waited the seconds out, while mentally crossing his fingers that the *Whale* would hold position. The bow shifted backward. The crew members forward spread their legs but stayed upright. Anton gritted his teeth as he watch the bow slide backward.

ANOTHER shell passed over the *Squallfish*, exploding forward off the bow. If the submarine had been going a knot faster, the shell would have hit the bow. This destroyer was getting too accurate.

"Sir!" Weaver shouted up through the hatch. "Sound reports enemy target shifting port, now bearing one eight five."

Shipley smiled. "Amazing what the sound of torpedo tube doors opening can do for a warship bearing down on you," he said.

"Sir?" one of the topside watches asked.
"What?"
"Did you say something, sir?"
Shipley shook his head. "Just thinking out loud."
Arneau's head appeared. "My turn, Skipper."
"We're nearly through the narrows; then you can take it."
Arneau shook his head. "Sir, we *are* through the narrows." He reached over, and before Shipley could stop him, the XO lifted the ends of his face mask. "You are getting frostbitten, Captain. If you want cheeks for your wife to kiss, then you need to let me have the bridge."
Shipley pulled the mask back down, aware that he felt neither the motion of the cloth when Arneau lifted it nor the brush of the cloth as he pulled it down. He sighed. He did not want to leave the bridge. This was where the captain should be.
"Sir, you are needed in the conning tower. There is hot chocolate there."
Shipley nodded. Crocky was at it again. "We are on course—"
"Zero three five at eighteen knots."
"Zero three five at eighteen knots."
"Please go, sir."
Shipley nodded and climbed down the ladder into the conning tower. He lifted the mask and hung it on an aft hook. Around the periscope, members of Bleecker's repair party were finishing repairs of the leaks.
"Is the destroyer closing?"
"Destroyer?" Weaver asked.
Shipley explained his reasoning as to the class of the ship.
"No, sir," sound answered. "It seems to have slowed, and it is zigzagging."
Through the hatch the sound of another shell hitting near the *Squallfish* caught his attention. "Quick: give me a single depth ping."
The sonar technician hit the depth measurer, and the sound of a single ping filled the boat. "Two hundred feet, sir."
"We are through the narrows. What is the status of our repairs?"
"Lieutenant Bleecker reports the snorkel will have to be sealed once we decide to submerge. We will be without the snorkel until we return to Holy Loch." Shipley nodded at the periscope. "And the scope?"

"We may have to sail submerged with it extended, sir. Otherwise, we will run the risk of breaking the damage control repairs to the seals."

"Depth restrictions?"

Weaver shook his head. "Don't know, sir."

Another shell whistled by overhead.

"Lieutenant, once we switch to battery power, our speed is going to come down from the eighteen knots to about five knots maximum. Five minutes at five knots, that Soviet destroyer is going to have us for cake."

"Orders, sir?"

"Tell Lieutenant Bleecker I want the maximum speed he can give me on diesel."

A minute later, the *Squallfish* increased speed to twenty-two knots.

Sound took off his headset. "Sir, I can't hear the enemy at this speed."

"Then we will pretend he has stopped chasing us."

"Without sonar, Skipper, we won't know his bearing."

"He's behind us, Lieutenant. And behind us he'll stay. He knows we have our torpedo tubes open, and most likely he's never been in combat. Most likely he would like for us to disappear before we shoot at him."

Weaver opened his mouth to offer counteradvice but then stopped. "Aye, sir." After all, here was a skipper who wore the submarine combat pin. Only the skipper, Bleecker, and Crocky wore the devices awarded to submariners who had been in combat. Many who earned them rested forever on the bottom of Earth's oceans.

THE boats from the *Soznatelnyy* tossed their lines to the sailors on the forward deck of the *Whale*. Someone stepped from the boat onto the deck of the *Whale* and looked up at Anton. It was Zotkin. Anton felt a sinking feeling in his stomach. The last thing he needed right now was a civilian.

Zotkin raised his hand and waved.

"What's wrong with him?" he asked Gesny.

"He's smiling, so someone close to him has died."

Zotkin spoke to one of the sailors, who guided the scientist to the rungs leading up to the bridge. A moment later the scientist crawled over the railing of the bridge.

"Congratulations, Captain."

"Congratulations?"

"Oh, yes; I was not sure at first, but then Admiral Katshora told me how this proved the success of atomic power." Zotkin reached over and put his gloved hand over the small light mounted on the conning tower railing. He looked at Anton and Gesny. "The reactor is still working?"

Zotkin laughed. "Flooded and it is still putting out power."

"The reactor room is not flooded, but the compartments around it are."

Zotkin shook his head as he stood. "It doesn't matter. What matters is we have shown that atomic power not only gives us extreme maneuverability, but also without atomic power the *K-2—nyet*, the *Whale*—would be sitting on the bottom of Kola Bay and every one of you would be dead."

Anton nodded. His eyes widened. Doctor Zotkin was right. The *Whale* had proven the value of atomic power. It also had sounded the death knell of diesel engines.

"But we are sunk," Gesny said.

Zotkin looked forward and aft; he laughed. Then he clapped his hands together and looked at both men. "No, we are not sunk. This is minor. Admiral Katshora says he can have it refloated within a week. And with atomic power still operating on board the *Whale*, we will have the ship—"

"Boat," Gesny corrected.

"The boat afloat and ready to continue. We have been successful. The Kremlin will be ecstatic."

"Ecstatic" is not the word I would use when Admiral Gorshkov hears how we were sunk, thought Anton.

"No, gentlemen. We are witnessing the emergence of the atomic-powered Soviet Navy. And, you helped me to do it."

Friday, December 7, 1956

ARNEAU stuck his head into the wardroom. "Can't get enough of that hot chocolate, can you, Skipper?"

"I believe I am beginning to dethaw," Shipley replied, reaching up and touching the two bits of gauze Doc had slapped on his cheeks. "Doc says they should be all right."

"Got a message for you here from CINCNELM." Arneau slid onto the bench beside Shipley.

"Hope it's good news."

"Read it."

Shipley read it to himself. When he finished he looked at Arneau. "Never thought I would get a 'well done' for nearly getting sunk and bringing home a damaged boat."

"Lieutenant Logan will be by later."

"I think he's been avoiding me."

"I can't imagine why you would think that. You only bite his head off every time you see him."

"I do?"

"You do."

"You sure?"

"Skipper, if Lieutenant Logan could have rowed away from the *Squallfish* his second day on board, I think he would have."

Shipley shrugged. "He must have a thin skin. So, why will he be by later?"

"He got a similar message from Admiral Frost. I suspect we will be receiving another from Admiral Burke." Arneau nodded at the message. "What do you think? It's a secret message."

Shipley smiled weakly and held the message up. "Secret means we can never tell anyone."

"But we proved the Soviets have a nuclear-powered submarine."

Shipley took a deep drink of hot chocolate and nodded. "Yes, we did."

"They don't know we know."

Shipley grunted. "Oh, they know we know. They know it was an American submarine that ran into their prototype."

"Good message, though, Skipper. I thought you'd be happier."

"I am, XO. I am happy that we did our mission. I am ecstatic, as you say, that we are alive and in international waters heading back to the Iceland–U.K. gap, where we will offload the evidence. And I'll be over the moon once we are tied up pierside at Holy Loch."

"There's a 'but' in there somewhere."

In unison both officers said, "There are no 'buts' on my boat." Then they both laughed.

"Something bothering you, Skipper?"

"I was just thinking that nuclear power means different tactics, different men to man the boats, and different warfare in the future."

"I guess—"

"No." He motioned. "You and I just saw the face of the enemy we are going to face in the years to come. That face is nuclear-powered. Missions such as this will be the norm in the years to come as we try to keep abreast of each other's technology. I would be seriously surprised if the Soviets don't do something similar to what we have. This is a time to look ahead."

Shipley turned the hot mug in his palms, enjoying the warmth against his skin. "What we learned will be used by such admirals as Rickover to convince Congress to build more *Nautilus*-type nukes."

The two men sat silent for a few seconds; then Shipley slid out on his side. "I'm going to have coffee now. Enough of this hot chocolate bullshit. You want one, XO?"

Arneau nodded. When Shipley filled both cups, he handed the XO his and then leaned back against the metal serving table. "For Lieutenant Bleecker, Petty Officer Crocky, and me, our time has now come and gone. The death knell of the diesel boats that helped win World War II is being struck." He gave a weak laugh. "We are going to have one almighty powerful submarine force when we finish."

"By the way, Skipper, it's Pearl Harbor Day."

"I know."